QUICKSILVER

Sam Osman was born in London to an English mother and Sudanese father. She read modern languages at Clare College Cambridge before joining the BBC. She lives in London with her husband, three children, a dog, four hamsters and a goldfish. *Quicksilver* is her first book for children.

www.samosmanbooks.com

QUICKSILVER

SAM OSMAN

MARION LLOYD BOOKS

First published in the UK in 2010 by Marion Lloyd Books
An imprint of Scholastic Children's Books
Euston House, 24 Eversholt Street
London, NW1 1DB, UK
A division of Scholastic Ltd
Registered office: Westfield Road, Southam, Warwickshire, CV47 0RA
SCHOLASTIC and associated logos are trademarks and/or registered
trademarks of Scholastic Inc.

ISBN 9781407105734

Printed by CPI Bookmarque Ltd, Croydon, Surrey
Papers used by Scholastic Children's Books are
made from wood grown in sustainable forests.

1 3 5 7 9 10 8 6 4 2

www.scholastic.co.uk/zone

For James
with love

"I feel that the ley-man, astronomer-priest, druid, bard, wizard, witch, palmer and hermit were all more or less linked by one thread of ancient knowledge and power, however degenerate it became in the end."

Alfred Watkins, *The Old Straight Track*, 1925

When wasted lie the pathways of the wise,
Two bloods will bond to fight a common foe,
As righteous heart with evil intrigue vies,
A greater deed from this dark quest will flow.

Accursèd hands, which from the shadows creep,
To thwart the noble aims of beast and man,
Shall find a purpose ancient, proud and deep,
Has lain within the leys since time began.

For evil is reborn in every age,
And fits the times by shifting shape and guise,
Forever tempting shaman, seer and sage,
To use for ill the power of the wise.

And so the force of light must weave and twine
The sacred threads that bind the worlds of men,
And set new champions 'gainst that dark design,
Until the scales are balanced once again.

Three born to wage that battle, side by side,
Bearing broken stars of hammered gold,
Must face the dark with sorrow as their guide,
Their blood's own truth, but to itself untold.

THE BOOK OF LIGHT Authors unknown

CONTENTS

Part Three: Meroe

Part Four: Shasta

PART ONE
The Progeny

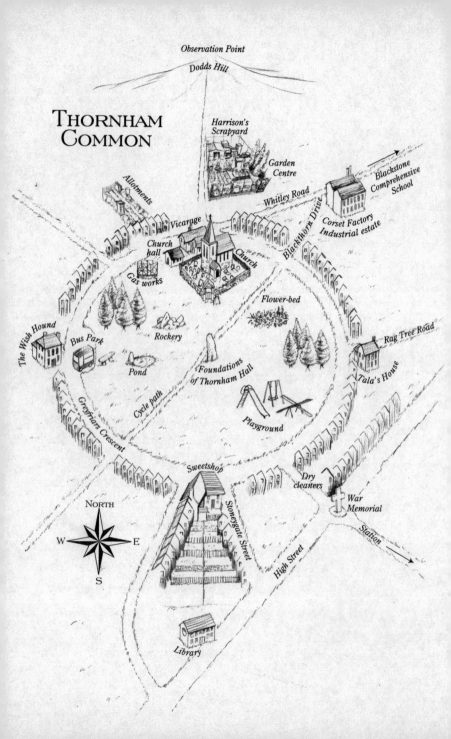

Observation Point

Dodds Hill

THORNHAM
COMMON

Harrison's
Scrapyard

Garden
Centre

Whitley Road

Blackstone
Comprehensive
School

Corset Factory
Industrial estate

Allotments

Vicarage

Church
hall

Church

Gas works

Blackthorn Drive

Flower-bed

The Wish Hound

Bus Park

Rockery

Pond

Foundations
of Thornham Hall

Rag Tree Road

Tala's House

Cycle path

Playground

Greyfriars Crescent

Sweetshop

Dry
cleaners

NORTH

Stoneygate Street

War
Memorial

Station

W   E

High Street

S

Library

1

Wolfie

When wasted lie the pathways of the wise
The Book of Light

Wolfie Brown awoke to the familiar smell of burnt toast and the grim prospect of delivering papers in the rain. No lightning flashed, no strange shadows played across his bedroom walls and no ghostly voices drifted through the floorboards. In fact, there was nothing to give him the slightest hint that this drizzly October Thursday had been awaited for a thousand years.

Ducking under the blankets, he pulled on the clothes he had been warming all night with his feet and ran downstairs. In the poky storeroom wedged between the kitchen and the sweet shop he found his mother bent over her easel, dabbing delicate white curls on to a portrait of a giant poodle.

"It's Mrs Poskitt's Monty. What do you think?"

Sarah Brown had a knack of making the pets she painted look just like their owners without the owners ever noticing. Wolfie stepped over a jar of brushes and a squashed tube of purple paint to get a proper look. He grinned. She had captured Monty's likeness to perfection – the doleful expression, the glint in his little black eyes and the dome of puffy fuzz perched on his head. With a few more whiskers and a headscarf it would have been the double of Mrs Poskitt.

"It's great," he told her, glancing at the clock. "Have you sorted the papers yet?"

"I've done my best, but that idiot at the warehouse sent all the wrong ones again." Sarah scooped her thick dark hair into a hasty knot and pinned it with a paintbrush. "I've burnt the last of the bread. Can you get yourself some cereal?"

"Don't worry, I've got to go. But, Mum . . . I need some dinner money. Yesterday they wouldn't give me any lunch. And I still owe three pounds for the school trip."

Sarah looked at him guiltily and felt in the pocket of her pyjamas. She pulled out a crumpled tissue, a rubber and stub of pencil.

"Can you see if there's any cash in the till? I'm a bit short this week."

This week and every week, thought Wolfie. He thrust aside the worn velvet curtain slung across the low doorway to the shop and banged open the heavy brass till. It was almost empty. As he scraped together a handful of

4

coins he sneaked a look at the dog-eared accounts book lying on the counter. He knew things were bad, but not this bad. She was behind with the payments for the gas and electricity and hadn't paid the cash and carry for months.

Leaning against the sagging, half-empty shelves, he gazed around the shabby old shop where he had lived all his life. Maybe they could tempt some customers back with a themed week or a special promotion. One look at the jars of melted humbugs, the faded packets of tobacco and the greying slabs of coconut ice told him it would take more than Sarah dressing up as a liquorice allsort, or a two-for-one offer on bubble gum, to turn their fortunes around.

Sarah poked her head through the doorway. "Do you think the vicar will mind *Woman's Weekly* instead of the *Church Times*?"

"No problem," said Wolfie. "He could do with a makeover."

He was always saying things to cheer her up, though he knew it was Sarah who had messed up the newspaper order – she often did. Unlike her father and grandfather, she just wasn't cut out to be a shopkeeper.

Wolfie wheeled his bike through the back yard and round the corner of Stoneygate Street to the front of the shop. So much for *Thornham's Oldest Family Business*. The outside of the building was even more dilapidated than the inside. The gold letters spelling out the words *Stanley*

Brown & Son, Tobacconist & Confectioner were so faded you could hardly read them. Sarah had talked about repainting the sign for years but somehow she never got round to it. She said it reminded her of the days when Wolfie's grandparents, Stanley and Merle, were alive and the sweet shop was the pride of Thornham, filled with the smell of home-made fudge and the buzz of gossiping customers. He supposed he should be grateful. At least his mother's hankering for the past hadn't prompted her to call him Stanley. He rode away, fed up with everything: with the cold drizzle stinging his face, with his battered bike and with being the only kid in his class without a mobile phone and a computer.

They couldn't go on like this. He had tried telling Sarah to sell up, buy a flat on one of the new estates, and paint full-time. But she refused even to talk about leaving. It wasn't just that the shop had been in their family for generations or that she and Wolfie had been born there: it was as if there was something else that kept her tied to the dusty jars of peppermint creams, the dawn scramble with the papers and the growing mountain of debt.

He was speeding along Greyfriars Crescent, head down, pedalling hard, when a man in tweed plus fours carrying a stout walking stick stepped out into the road followed by a huge grizzled dog. They disappeared into the misty gloom of the common, hardly noticing as Wolfie slammed on his brakes and swerved into the gutter.

*

The clock of St Michael's Church struck seven. Beyond the far reaches of the now-known worlds something shimmered in the twilight: a fragment of a long dead star, a glowing sphere of gas and dust. Its inner flame began to flicker and flare and when it was blazing brighter than a tiny sun, a glistening wave of sparks erupted from its core, reawakening the age-old arteries of power that circled the earth.

Like a silent river bursting a dam, a quicksilver flow of primal energy trickled, then streamed, then surged across space and time and earth and sky, through oceans and forests, caverns and car parks, boulevards and bus stops, until it reached the ancient place of power once known as Thornham Magna, on the outskirts of London. With a tremor that rocked the gasworks, the deluge branched into three streams. Two flowed down the high street, past the dry cleaner's, and on through Norwood, Penge and Bromley in search of pyramids and deserts, cataracts and mountains. The third cascaded down Blackthorn Drive and swept across the common to the sweet shop, pouring up the drainpipes and through the plugholes in search of Wolfie Brown.

2

Mr Forester

For centuries the Wish Hound Inn on Thornham Common had provided a last stopping place for weary travellers on their way to the capital. Now it was an Irish-themed pub, and Thornham was a sprawling suburb on the fringes of South London, whose hotchpotch of terraced houses, chain stores, small factories and allotments vied for space between a criss-cross of congested roads and rail tracks. King Henry VIII had destroyed the Benedictine abbey in the 1500s and soon after that the great manor house and part of the church had mysteriously burnt down, leaving the medieval core of St Michael's to be buttressed and turreted by succeeding generations. The rugged grassland of the common itself, however, had survived the years more or less unscathed. The wide curve of stony ground opposite the pub, where the village stocks once stood, was now used as a bus lay-by. The drovers with their flocks of sheep and geese had been replaced by dog walkers and skateboarders; children sailed toy boats on the dew pond and the ancient trackways were now a series of tarmac cycle paths that provided handy short cuts to the furthermost reaches of Wolfie's paper round.

He stuffed a crumpled copy of the *Thornham Gazette* through the last letter box on Blackthorn Drive, sped home past a gang of workmen scratching their heads over a burst water main and pushed open the back door. Sarah hastily pocketed a letter, her face pale.

"What's up, Mum?"

There was no use pretending.

"It's a final demand from the cash and carry. We've got to pay them by today or. . ." Her voice faltered. "I tried ringing all day yesterday but Mr Pullen won't take my calls – his secretary says he just wants his money."

"I'll make you a cup of tea," offered Wolfie, not knowing what else to say. He held the kettle under the tap and waited for the ancient plumbing to wheeze into action. Instead of the usual hissing and rattling in the pipes there was a violent gurgle and a pounding stream of water hit the bottom of the kettle and bounced onto his jumper. He snatched up a dishcloth. Underneath it lay his maths book and a history worksheet. He groaned loudly. He'd forgotten to do his homework. Just his luck that the strictest teacher in the school took him for both subjects.

He didn't know which he dreaded more, a mob of angry bailiffs or the wrath of Mr Grimes. A splinter of sunlight pierced the clouds, slanting straight into his eyes. He blinked and the perfect solution to both his problems popped into his head.

"I know," he said, with what he hoped was a tone of martyrdom, "I'll look after the shop while you go down to the cash and carry. If you see this Pullen bloke face to face, maybe he'll let you off till you get paid for Monty's portrait."

Sarah looked up into her son's wide green eyes, gold-flecked and glittering in the sunlight. She blew her nose.

"Well . . . I hate to ask you to miss school, but this *is* an emergency."

"If you want I could look after the shop all day," he offered nobly, but Sarah had already grabbed her coat and was rushing out of the back door.

Gloomily Wolfie opened his maths book. He had been set a series of geometry problems involving circles, squares and something unfathomable called pi. Although he carefully measured out lines with his ruler and swung the compass around the paper, the result was nothing like the neat diagram Mr Grimes had drawn on the board. Wolfie's looked more like a spiralling spider's web. He gave up and began to draw a cartoon of Mr Grimes impaled on the point of a compass.

Art was the only thing Wolfie was good at and, just like

Sarah, images had flowed from his fingers from the moment he had been able to grasp a crayon. The walls of his room were covered with his inventive fantasies: strange landscapes peopled with bizarre characters; comic-strip adventures starring heroes of his own devising; and terrifying monsters, whose leering faces sometimes startled him when he woke up in the night.

The doorbell jangled. He hurried into the shop and recognized the tweed plus fours, buckled, mid-calf, over red and purple chequered socks. The thickset elderly man inside them was struggling to free himself from a woolly hat, caught in the strap of his satchel. In a flurry of flailing arms, a bush of white hair finally burst free and shook itself like a small damp dog.

"Can I help you?" asked Wolfie.

Burrowing in his bag, the man pulled out a roll of yellowing parchment and, using the brass weights from the scales to anchor the curling edges, he spread it across the counter.

"Yes, lad, possibly you can." A pair of bright blue eyes stared eagerly at Wolfie from beneath jutting white eyebrows tinged with ginger. "Where might I find St Michael's Church?"

Reading upside down, Wolfie made out the words *Thornham Magna* written in old-fashioned script and some funny little drawings of buildings, fields and trees overlaid with a criss-cross of faded ink marks. It was some kind of map.

"St Michael's is across the common, next to the gasworks," he said helpfully.

"I see. And is it true that the ancient rite of raising the giants is still practised here?"

Wolfie shrugged. "Yeah, they do it every year."

His visitor trembled with excitement. "I do hope I get a chance to see it for myself."

Wolfie looked at him suspiciously. Why would anyone want to watch a bunch of pensioners with twigs in their hats doing the conga round the graveyard?

"And what do you know of the ghostly hound said to haunt the common?"

"The what?"

"The wish hound. . ."

"It's a pub . . . the Wish Hound is a pub," said Wolfie.

The man shook his head absently. "And where exactly is Dodds Hill?"

Wolfie pointed across the common. "Over there." In the corner of the map he made out the words *In the year of our blessed Lord fourteen hundred and fifty-seven*. "Er – you might do better with an *A-Z*. This map looks a bit . . . out of date."

The man jabbed a triumphant finger at a pencilled cross. "So! Just as I thought, your shop would be here."

"Maybe, but I'm pretty sure we've got some new street maps in the back. . ."

"No need, no need." The stranger stuck out a beefy hand. "How rude of me! Let me introduce myself. The name is Forester, Remus Forester."

12

Wolfie shook his hand doubtfully. It was a bit early in the morning for fending off lunatics. "Wolfie Brown."

Mr Forester looked around the shop approvingly. "I think this will do very nicely."

"What will?" snapped Wolfie, panicking that this weirdo was a debt collector from the cash and carry.

"You do take paying guests, don't you?"

Relieved, Wolfie shook his head. "It's Mrs Baxter at number 29 who does bed and breakfast."

"Number 29?" The eyebrows bristled. "That wouldn't do at all."

"I've heard it's great. They've got central heating, satellite telly. . ."

"No, it's got to be here. Any other number is quite out of the question."

"But we don't take lodgers."

"Are you sure?"

"Course I'm sure." Wolfie was beginning to lose patience.

Remus Forester leaned across the counter, sweeping a pile of paper bags to the floor. "Perhaps you should consider the advantages – a regular rent, almost no effort on your part. I'm not the demanding type. I wouldn't expect hot meals – I am a fruitarian, of course."

Fruitcake, more like, thought Wolfie, gathering up the bags.

"My needs are few. I wouldn't use up your hot water. A

bracing cold shower is more than sufficient to set me up for the day."

"Look, I'm sorry, Mr Forester. I don't care how often you wash or how hot you have the water," said Wolfie irritably. "We haven't got room for a lodger!"

"I have references," said Mr Forester, waving a couple of battered envelopes.

Wolfie was beginning to wonder if he was on one of those hidden-camera TV programmes. Just in case, he gritted his teeth into something that might pass for a smile and took the envelopes. One letter was typewritten and headed *The Society for the Investigation of Lost Knowledge*. It said that Remus Forester had been a member of SILK for many years and was best known for his seminal monograph entitled *Evidence for an Electric Universe*. The other, handwritten by a Mrs Stokes of "Moor View", Bodmin, advised that Mr Forester was a lovely gentleman, who hadn't been no trouble and always paid his rent on time, not like some others she could mention.

Mr Forester produced a large, leather-bound tape measure and, seizing Wolfie's hand, looped the ring at the end of the tape over his thumb.

"Stay there, lad," he ordered and began to walk backwards towards the door, unwinding the tape as he went. As he reached the magazine rack a sharp-faced man in a leather jacket hurried in from the rain.

"Good heavens!" exclaimed Mr Forester. "You are that reporter from the television news. Rex Slinfold, is it not?

I find your despatches from the far-flung corners of our planet most informative."

"Oh . . . thanks," said the new customer. "Look, sorry to jump the queue, I've got a plane to catch." He turned to Wolfie. "Can you cancel my papers for the next two weeks?"

Wolfie let go of the tape measure. It sprang back into its case with a satisfying ping, making Mr Forester leap in surprise.

"Going somewhere nice, Mr Slinfold?" asked Wolfie, hunting for the order book.

"India. I'm covering the election. Got to rush, I'll let you know when I'm back." Sidestepping Mr Forester, Rex Slinfold hurried away.

Wolfie gasped. Mr Forester was chipping at a crack in the wall with a small metal pick.

"Extraordinary," he declared as the pick bit into something solid, sending a shower of tiny sparks into the air. "Has your family lived here long?"

Wolfie was just wondering if he should phone the police when Sarah came running in, her hair tumbling out of its knot.

"It's going to be all right," she panted, unbuttoning her coat. "I saw Mr Pullen and he said if I do a painting of his son's stick insect he'll give us till Friday to pay the first instalment. Thanks, Wolfie. You can get off to school now. I'll finish serving this customer." She beamed at Mr Forester. "What can I get you, sir?"

Mr Forester beamed back. "I need a room that faces east."

Wolfie rolled his eyes at his mother. Then he noticed that she was still wearing her pyjamas. For the first time in his life he felt a desperate urge to get to school and experience the soothing sanity of being shouted at by Mr Grimes.

Remus Forester shook Sarah's hand warmly. "Perhaps we could discuss this over a cup of tea? I make my own tea bags, you know."

Wolfie backed away. As he wheeled his bike across the yard he could still hear a booming voice recommending an infusion made from the bark of the weeping birch.

3

Tala

Two bloods will bond to fight a common foe
The Book of Light

The second stream of energy rolled across the Atlantic Ocean, through the hills and plains of America to the foothills of California's Cascade Mountains, ruffling the undergrowth, sending small creatures scurrying from their burrows and fish darting from the strange currents rising through the creeks. Hot springs gushed and steamed, trickling loosened cinders down the steep volcanic slopes. Reaching the ancient forests of Mount Shasta, the energy rippled towards a small run-down cabin, pooling like syrup around the porch and lapping at the door frame.

Tala Bean ladled stew on to her plate. Her father handed her a hunk of thickly buttered bread, his face crinkling with pleasure as she dipped it in the gravy. Savouring the mouth-watering smell, she leaned forward to sink her teeth into the warm crust. There was a loud rumble. Her father's smiling face faded away and she woke from her dream to find herself staring down at a patch of scrubbed wood and her own thin arms. Had that noise been her father's stuttery old truck swinging into the yard? Crossing her fingers, she willed him to burst through the door with some exciting story about a freak storm cutting off the mountain roads.

The only sound in the silence was the gurgle of her empty stomach.

Where was he? She'd called his cell phone endlessly but the battery must be dead. Licking her finger, she thrust it into the empty box of cornflakes, searching for crumbs. It had been three days since her father had disappeared and two since she had eaten a proper meal. She stepped on to the porch and gazed at the dying sunset glowing luminous pink, smeared with a strange purple colour. She turned back to the house, pretending the ache in her stomach was hunger, but she knew it was fear. Raw gut-wrenching fear that something terrible had happened, that her dad was lying trapped beneath his truck, that he was. . .

She pulled open the fridge, rattling the empty shelves. He'd be back any minute, course he would, *and* he'd be hungry, so she'd better stop moping and get some food. She left a scribbled note, grabbed a torch and set off for their nearest neighbours, the Holts, who lived three kilometres away. There was no wind, yet the pine trees quivered as if touched by a breeze. In the distance the twin peaks of Mount Shasta sloped, white and glistening, towards the first stars glittering in the gloom. They looked brighter than usual. Perhaps she wouldn't need the torch after all.

The Holts ran a neat little poultry farm near the highway and Tala usually kept well away from them. Mrs Holt disapproved of Jack Bean bringing his daughter up on his own, and made it clear that she didn't think he was making a very good job of it. To her mind Tala was far too sassy for her own good and should brush her hair more often.

Tala hovered behind their barn, bracing herself for a lecture on grooming. She had just decided she would rather starve than ask the Holts for help when she jumped at the sound of a muffled bark and a shrill voice calling, "Come on out or I'll set the dog on you."

Tala was on excellent terms with the Holts' mangy mongrel but she stepped from the shadows and walked slowly towards the house.

"It's only me, Mrs Holt."

"Tala? What are you doing running wild this time of night, disturbing my hens?"

"Could you maybe let me have some eggs and bread?"

"Eggs and bread? Hasn't your father been to the store?"

"He went tree-felling near Klamath Falls and forgot to leave me money. He'll pay you back, soon as he gets home."

"You come right in here and tell me what's going on."

"It's OK, Mrs Holt. Forget the eggs, just the bread will do."

"You come in here," repeated the farmer's wife, pointing a bony finger at the floor. Reluctantly Tala climbed the steps.

"If your father isn't home, you're not going anywhere."

Mrs Holt pulled her into the kitchen. She looked Tala up and down. When she saw how pale and pinched she was, she stopped herself from commenting on the state of her tangled hair.

"What you need, child, is something to eat."

Tala was too tired and hungry to resist.

The following morning Bill Holt drove over to the cabin. When he found no sign of Tala's father, he rang the sheriff and, within an hour, two deputies were sitting in the Holts' kitchen, drinking coffee. Tala hunkered in a corner with her arms folded, glaring at them all as they whispered about emergency foster care and a protective custody order. When they saw she was listening, Mrs Holt turned away to clank cups in the sink and the officers walked outside, murmuring into their radios.

Tala hated the Holts with their pitying looks. She hated the sickening lurches from hope to despair every time the phone rang and she hated the sheriff's people and their dumb questions. Sure her dad had money troubles, sure he got depressed sometimes. What did that have to do with anything? One of them, a thin woman with cropped black hair, sat her down, explaining that a check of the local hospitals and a search of the mountain roads by the Highway Patrol helicopter had drawn a blank, so Jack Bean was now officially classified as "overdue". The officer reached to take her hand. Tala flung herself away, refusing to listen.

As soon as the deputies had left, she slipped out the back door and took off towards town, hoping to find someone who had passed her father's truck on the road or spoken to him at a gas station. As she passed the store, she heard Mrs Ryan's sing-song, la-di-da, holier-than-thou voice drifting through the shutters.

"What Jack Bean thinks he's up to running off like that I just can't fathom. You know he's part Modoc or Cherokee or some such and part heaven-knows-what-else. Of course, I have nothing against these people – there's not a prejudiced bone in my body – but they aren't like you and me, are they?"

Grunts of agreement seemed to encourage her. "We had him round once to sort out a tree that got hit by lightning and my Jeb always says he can't make nothing grow in our yard since that Indian's taken up the roots." Her voice dropped to a confidential whisper. "And then there was all that business when his wife upped and left . . . she was a strange one, that's for sure; didn't even take the baby with her . . . and the Lord alone knows where she came from or where she went."

Tala stomped through the door and fixed Mrs Ryan with a cold stare. The store went quiet. Two customers started to take a deep interest in a display of tin buckets.

Mrs Ryan smiled uneasily.

"What can I get you, Tala, dear?"

"My dad's people were living in America long before any rat-faced Ryans showed up. And the only reason nothing grows in your yard is your fat husband's too drunk to water it. *And*," she spat, as Mrs Ryan clutched the counter for support, "if you want to bad-mouth my mom, you'd best do it to my face!"

Tala turned and fled. Mrs Ryan clicked her false teeth and shook her head. "That just proves what I was saying – there's bad blood there and let's hope the good Lord finds it in his heart to forgive her those evil words."

Tala kept running until she reached the winding track leading to her home. Panting hard, she leaned against the prickly trunk of a pine tree and prayed that when she turned the corner, the big old truck would be standing outside the cabin. Please. Please, *please*. . .

But the yard was empty.

When the fierce disappointment had subsided into the dull ache she had been living with for days, she went inside. Tacked above her bed was a snapshot of her father, taken on a fishing trip they'd made last spring. Proud and laughing, he held a freshly caught catfish towards the camera, his battered hat tipped back over his straight dark hair, his eyes scrunched against the sunlight. A wave of misery passed over her. Quickly she slipped the photo into her diary, stuffed some clothes into a rucksack and from beneath her pillow pulled out her most precious possession: a little square box made from polished black stone that had belonged to her mother. Gently she lifted the lid. For a split second she thought the box was glowing. Puzzled, she stared at it. It must have been the light catching the glittery specks in the smoky stone. She zipped it into her rucksack and, feeling a little stronger, set off back to the Holts' farm, eager for the good news that would surely be waiting when she got there.

She saw the Holts sitting on the front porch and ran towards them. With a shake of her head, Mrs Holt said, "Don't fret. We'll surely hear something tomorrow."

Grief smashed the strength from Tala's limbs. Limp and shivery, she staggered to the bathroom and retched in the sink. Slumping on to the cold, tiled floor, she cried until she was too drained to move and lay there, refusing to answer when Mrs Holt rattled the door handle. Eventually Bill Holt unscrewed the lock and found her dozing fretfully. Gently, he slipped a cushion under her head, covered her with a blanket and tiptoed away.

That night the Holts sat up late, discussing what to do about the parentless wild child curled on their bathroom floor.

*

Tala woke late and shuffled into the kitchen, stiff and miserable. Mrs Holt, setting out her best teacups, looked up, her eyes bright with relief.

"I was just going to call you. Your Uncle Matthias is here. He's going to take you to England and look after you till . . . we know what's happening."

Tala frowned. "I haven't got an Uncle Matthias."

"It's on your mother's side, maybe more of a second cousin, but he'll tell you all about it himself and he's got the documents to prove it." Mrs Holt nodded at some papers on the table.

Tala snatched up a letter embossed with a notary seal. It stated that, in the event of their death or incapacity, Kara and Jack Bean appointed Matthias Threlfall legal guardian of their daughter, Tala.

"How did he know I was here?"

"Sheriff's office must have contacted him."

"They only found out Dad was missing yesterday morning. How come this Uncle Matthias took less than a day to get here from England?"

Mrs Holt waved Tala's questions away. You just had to take one look at the man to see they were related.

"Where is he?"

"Right here," came a low, powerful voice.

She spun round to see a tall, lean man in a well-cut suit standing in the doorway. He had thick dark hair and clear suntanned skin and as he came towards her, hand held out, she smelled the tang of expensive aftershave.

"Hello, Tala. I haven't seen you since you were a baby." He spoke with a faint mid-Atlantic accent and his manner was easy and assured.

Tala stayed where she was. Matthias pulled up a chair and helped himself to a freshly baked biscuit. "I don't know much about kids, but I'm sure we'll rub along just fine till they find Jack."

"Dad said Mom lost touch with her family. How come he never mentioned you?"

"You know how it is. Your dad and I kept in touch for a while after Kara . . . left." He pressed a stray crumb into the table. "But I was travelling all the time and when I moved to England we kind of drifted apart."

"So how come you got here so fast?" she asked fiercely.

"I was already in the States, at a conference. Your dad's attorney heard the news, contacted my London office; they called me and I came straight over."

"What conference?"

He handed her a folder. It contained a glossy programme, listing *Dr M Threlfall* as one of the keynote speakers, and a group photo of the delegates, Matthias standing tall and imposing in the centre. She jerked her chin at the table.

"Right, and when you went to this conference you just happened to take those custody papers with you."

"Tala, mind your manners," said Mrs Holt sharply.

"It's OK. She's got a right to ask." Matthias turned to Tala and said evenly, "My copy of the custody order is in England. I got this one from your dad's attorney." He rubbed the bridge of his nose. "Look, Tala. To tell you the truth, I'd forgotten all about that bit of paper. But since your mother insisted on making me your legal guardian, there's not much either of us can do about it. So if you give me my space, I'll give you yours, and we'll make the best of it."

Tala met his gaze. She didn't like the look of Uncle Matthias and he certainly didn't feel like family. But his eyes were a strange shade of green flecked with gold. And the only face she had ever seen with eyes like that was the one that stared back at her whenever she looked in a mirror.

4

Zi'ib

As righteous heart with evil intrigue vies
The Book of Light

T he sun sank low over the Sahara desert, turning the waters of the Nile into a rippling mirror of purple, gold and pink. From every mud-brick house in the small Sudanese village of Dar el Maarifa came the rhythmic *swish, swish* of stiff brooms brushing away the sand blown in by a dust storm. The storm had ridden the swell of the third stream of energy, appearing from nowhere to roll across the desert plains like a wave of brown mist. By dusk the dust had settled, enveloping everything in a layer of fine grit.

The village teacher, Sayeeda Shadia, lived with her son next to the school. Her house was as small and simple as all the others, but she had painted the front door blue and planted a purple bougainvillea beside it. The door opened and Zi'ib, a gangly boy of eleven, came out carrying a bucket of water. He had a delicate face, thick crinkly curls and startling green eyes. His mother would explain to curious strangers that he had inherited them from his father, who must have had some foreign blood in him, Syrian or Turkish perhaps. To silence further gossip, she also said she was a widow, although she still prayed that one day her missing husband would return to her alive and well.

Zi'ib sluiced down the window shutters and stared up at the emerging stars, wondering how much longer they would stay in Dar el Maarifa. He and his mother had moved house so many times; it was almost as if she were afraid of staying in one place for too long. While neighbours, schools and homes had come and gone, the night sky remained one of the few constants in Zi'ib's life.

He knew the constellations had names, but he had always liked to trace his own pictures in the mass of shimmering dots. He stood in the gloom, gazing at his favourite image of a sword. Tonight it looked different, clearer somehow and speckled with bright stars he'd never noticed before. Below it something glowed on the horizon. It couldn't be the last glimmer of the sunset because it was moving towards him. The blob of light grew and separated into the beam of headlights, bumping fast over the rutted track. Squinting hard, he made out the shape of a truck full of men. He heard shouting. Then the sudden sickening judder of gunshots. Shadia gripped his shoulders and pulled him into the house. Clumsy with fear, she slammed the door and turned the lock.

The truck swerved to a halt and the men leapt out. In a swirl of dust they jumped over walls, kicking at the shuttered doors. Zi'ib heard the frenzied bark of old Mama Fatma's dog, then another burst of gunfire. The dog fell silent but the screams began. Shadia pulled Zi'ib through the thin curtain dividing his bedroom from the living area.

"*Yumma*," he whispered.

"Be quiet. Get down."

A khaki cap flashed past the window. Crouching low, they groped across the room. Shadia put her lips to her son's ear.

"I will find you. You must stay strong."

Quickly, she pushed him down behind the bed. A booted foot thudded against the front door.

"Hide, *Yumma*," gasped Zi'ib, but there was nowhere for her to hide.

With a shuddering crack the door split from its hinges, a hand ripped back the curtain and a man burst into the bedroom, his eyes glittering above a sweat-soaked scarf. He swung his rifle, jabbing at the air. From the kitchen came the sound of smashing pots and splintering furniture. Zi'ib cowered beneath the bed, watching the raider's ugly black boots thunder across the floor, wishing he were a man. The rifle butt smashed into the framed photograph hanging on the wall. Zi'ib's fear shattered with the glass, releasing a surge of anger that flung him from his hiding place. As he lurched forward his ears filtered out the terrible sounds and his eyes saw everything unfold in slow motion. He saw Shadia turn and cry out a warning, saw the gun barrel jerk towards him; then he tumbled into darkness.

An irresistible flow of energy was now sweeping across the curve of the earth from the lost cities of Sudan and the mountains of Shasta to the vanished forests of Thornham, coursing through the ruined remnants of a once-powerful grid, churning the fates of three green-eyed children in its pitiless wake.

5

The Attic

Hunched against the driving rain, Wolfie threw down his bike and dashed into the kitchen. He hung up his dripping parka and breathed the smell of shepherd's pie and warm washing. The dishes were stacked neatly on the draining board and the table was covered with a brightly checked cloth and laid for supper. He knew the signs – his mother was in one of her "positive" moods.

Ducking beneath the curtain of sheets hanging from the airer, he tripped over a heap of bulging bin liners.

"What's in the bags?" he asked.

Sarah poked something in the oven. "Stuff for the jumble."

"What stuff?"

"I'm giving your room a good clear-out."

"Why?" asked Wolfie, bemused.

She handed him a bundle of papers. "More final demands. If I can't pay up, they're going to send in the bailiffs." She took a little breath. "So Mr Forester is going to be our lodger."

Wolfie stared at her, horrified.

"Mum – he's a maniac. And he wears stupid trousers that make him look like Tintin."

"It won't be for long – it's just to tide us over until. . ."

"Until what? Until he strangles us both with his tape measure?"

"Until things . . . sort themselves out."

"What do you mean, 'sort themselves out'?" He didn't know which he hated more – his mum at the end of her tether, or his mum fired up by some crazy idea that would only make things worse. She'd never remember to ask for the rent, and they'd end up homeless when Mr Forester demolished the whole building with his pick.

"What sort of weirdo comes knocking on doors asking for a room?"

"Don't be silly. He's not a weirdo – he's. . ." Sarah hesitated. "Eccentric."

"Anyway," said Wolfie, sealing his argument, "there's nowhere to put a lodger."

"Yes there is," mumbled Sarah. "He can have your room."

"Where am I supposed to sleep?" exploded Wolfie.

"You can have the attic."

"The attic?" Wolfie choked, scarlet with outrage. "Oh great! Thanks, Mum."

"Come on, we'll make it really cosy. I thought we could paint it a nice Mediterranean blue . . . and it's got a lovely view of the common."

"If it's so blimmin' great, give him the attic."

"Mr Forester needs a room that faces east so the vibrations don't upset his work."

Wolfie shook his head. Sarah Brown, the answer to every nutter's prayer.

"What vibrations?"

Sarah bit her lip. It had all sounded quite sensible when Mr Forester had explained it, but in the cold light of Wolfie's startling green stare, she began to have doubts.

"Well, he showed me that old map . . . and he wants a room here because the shop is on a direct line that goes from the church to Dodds Hill . . . It's what they call . . . a . . . ley line."

"Mum – the only thing that goes in a direct line from the church to Dodds Hill is what they call the 717 bus."

"I'm not going to argue. I've made up my mind and that's it."

Wolfie scowled. Sarah took the shepherd's pie from the oven.

"I've packed all your things. We can move them after supper."

"I'm not hungry!"

Wolfie stormed upstairs and flung himself on his bed.

Why couldn't freako Forester decide the chip shop was the gateway to some parallel universe and move in there? Reluctantly he sat up again. He might as well see how bad his new room was going to be.

The living space above the shop was narrow and cramped. Sarah's room and the bathroom were on the first floor, Wolfie's bedroom was up another winding flight of stairs and the trapdoor to the attic was down the landing, next to the airing cupboard. To get to it you had to pull a rope that let down a set of hinged wooden steps. One night when he was very small Wolfie had seen Sarah heaving bags of old clothes through the hatch. Convinced he'd caught her feeding bales of hay to a secret attic monster, he'd never gone near the steps again. Even now his hand trembled as he climbed the narrow treads. Fumbling in the darkness, he flicked the cracked Bakelite switch. The naked bulb spread a feeble glow over a wedge-shaped room with a steeply sloped ceiling, painted a nauseous shade of mustard and draped with cobwebs. Behind the piles of junk he saw a small iron fireplace, a narrow brass bed and little bay window with a built-in seat.

Hurling aside bundles of hand-knitted baby clothes, broken toys and dusty cardboard boxes, he spotted a large black artists' portfolio with Sarah's initials tooled into the leather. He leafed through the drawings. Squashed between a sketch of St Paul's Cathedral and a self-portrait of a young and carefree Sarah lay a letter. It was from the vice chancellor of her art school, congratulating her on her outstanding grades, granting her request to take time out to nurse her sick father and predicting a glittering future for her after graduation. Wolfie stuffed the letter back. Sarah had made no secret of the fact that she had left art school to nurse her dying father and never gone back. Only now did he realize how hard it must have been to relinquish her dreams. He dug through a box of canvases and found a painting of his grandfather, tired and hollow-eyed, leaning back on his pillows, and a view of the inside of the shop from the counter. She must have worked on these the year she came home. He pulled out a third canvas. Coldness swept his skin. It was a portrait of his father.

Wolfie knew it was his father, partly because the note on the back read *Happy Christmas, Ron, all my love, Sarah,* and partly because the face triggered faded memories of the photos in Sarah's album. When he was little she used to go through the snapshots, explaining which park or beach or fairground they had been taken at, and what fun they'd have going back there when his father came home. But as soon as he started school, he began to pester her with questions. Why didn't he see his dad at weekends? Why didn't he phone? Sarah would reply that she did not know, and grow so quiet and sad that he felt bad. After that, whenever he asked to see the album she would suggest a game or an ice cream, and then one day he saw that she had even put away the framed photo of the three of them taken the day he was born.

It was then that Wolfie started sketching his own versions of what might have happened to his father – he was a secret agent imprisoned by an enemy state or a fearless explorer trapped in the jungle. Over the years these heroic scenes became so vivid that even Wolfie found it hard to believe they had sprung from his imagination.

The steps creaked and Sarah appeared, balancing two mugs of tea and a plate of shepherd's pie on a tray.

"Peace offering," she said.

Wolfie quickly tried to ram his father's portrait back into the box.

"I'd forgotten I'd left that up here," she said, taking the canvas from his hands. "You know, you look just like him." Her eyes flicked between Wolfie and the portrait, a faint smile on her lips. "Same wonderful green eyes, same shaggy fair hair."

Wolfie's heartbeat quickened.

"What did happen to him, Mum?" he ventured softly.

Sarah slumped on the window seat, with the picture on her knees. "Like I've always told you, I honestly don't know. One minute he was here and the next . . . he'd vanished."

Wolfie held his breath. Maybe his dad really had been captured by enemy agents.

Sarah stared at the portrait. "Nobody believed me. The

neighbours, the vicar, they all thought I'd gone a bit crazy."

Wolfie frowned, not daring to speak.

"You were nearly two, just beginning to say a few proper sentences. We were so happy, planning our wedding, then suddenly your dad started getting depressed and spending more and more time up here."

"Doing what?"

"Just sitting on this seat staring at the common or fiddling with your grandpa's old radio. And when I spoke he'd turn and look right through me as though his thoughts were somewhere I could never reach." She took a sip of tea.

"Then one night he came up here after supper. I heard the trapdoor slam and I went into the storeroom to finish a painting of a young Dalmatian – I still see it around sometimes," she sighed, "though it's fat and arthritic now."

Wolfie bit back his impatience.

"At about ten o'clock I decided to go to bed so I locked the back door and took Grandpa his cocoa and medicine. Then I went up to the attic to see if your dad wanted anything and. . ." She swallowed hard. "He'd gone."

"He must have sneaked out when you were with Grandpa."

"No. I checked straight away. The shop door was still bolted on the inside and I had the back door key in my pocket."

"So he got a new one cut without telling you."

Sarah pulled out the heavy old-fashioned key made of hammered iron and weighed it in her hand. "It's hardly the sort they can copy at the station kiosk."

"So maybe he climbed through the window."

"All the windows were locked."

Wolfie was beginning to understand why everyone had thought she was crazy. She drew her fingers across the portrait.

"It was this time of year, wet and cold, but he didn't even take his coat."

"If he didn't walk out or climb out, what do you think happened?"

"I honestly don't know. And the police were useless. When I explained about the doors and windows being locked they said I should stop kidding myself because perfectly nice, perfectly normal people run away all the time. Usually they say they're just popping down the road for a packet of cigarettes."

"Great excuse if you live in a tobacconist's," muttered Wolfie, angry that his dad had run away and sad that Sarah just couldn't accept the truth.

She looked up and read the misery in his face.

"Believe me, the police were wrong. Your dad would never have run away."

"Did you search for him?"

"I put ads in all the papers and contacted the Salvation Army, but Grandpa was really ill by then and you were only tiny. I couldn't just up and leave the shop."

"What about his family — didn't they have any idea where he'd gone?"

"He didn't have any." Her eyes turned dreamy. "He always said we were all he had in the world."

How convenient, thought Wolfie.

"What about his work?"

She shook her head. "He'd been leading some environmental science project, but he gave it up to help run the shop."

Wolfie's anger gave way to helplessness. A scientist, ending up selling gobstoppers in a corner shop? How likely was that?

"What project?" he asked dully.

"Something to do with renewable energy, but you know me; even if he'd explained, I wouldn't have understood a word."

Couldn't she see it was all a lie? Wolfie forced himself to stay calm. This might be his only chance to hear the whole depressing truth.

"So, how did you meet him?"

Sarah stared silently at the painting.

"Please, Mum."

"He just walked into the shop one day for a paper. He was tall and weather-beaten and looked, I don't know, different from anyone I'd ever seen before — restless, with fiery green eyes and a way of making you want to listen when he spoke. We got talking and he started dropping round every couple of days for a chat. Then one evening he turned up and out of the blue he said, 'I think I love you, Sarah Brown.' Just like that. . ." She smiled, lost in the memory. "He always said it was destiny that brought us together. And when you were born he told me it was the most wonderful day of his life."

"So wonderful he couldn't wait to run off," burst out Wolfie bitterly.

"Don't, please. I *know* he didn't run off. And I know that one day he'll come back."

"It's been ten years, Mum. If he was coming back, he'd be here by now."

Tears welled in Sarah's eyes. "One day you'll realize that things aren't always the way they seem," she said softly, and propping the portrait on the mantelpiece, she hurried downstairs.

Wolfie felt wretched. After ten years the mystery was solved. His dad was a conman who probably couldn't believe his luck when he found a sick old man with a business and a daughter daft enough to swallow his stupid stories. When he realized the shop wasn't making money he must have legged it – probably taking the contents of the till with him.

He reached for the shepherd's pie, unable to tear his gaze from the powerful, troubled face in the portrait. Funny, his dad didn't look like a conman. He stabbed angrily at a lump of cold mashed potato. Idiot! Conmen spent their whole lives pretending to look trustworthy, and if this picture was anything to go by, that was something his dad was brilliant at. No wonder his mum had been taken in.

6

The Window Seat

Sarah came back, grim-faced, and thrust a broom into Wolfie's hand, plainly unwilling to answer the questions buzzing in his brain. They spent a cheerless evening cleaning out the attic and ferrying his things upstairs.

"So, shall we paint it Mediterranean blue?" she asked, arranging his drawing things on the window seat.

"Let's not bother," said Wolfie. "It's not like I'll have hundreds of mates swarming up here to try out my new computer."

Sarah flinched. It had always saddened her that Wolfie had trouble finding friends, but it wasn't like him to mention his loneliness *or* to complain about being hard up.

"What about your homework? Do you want some help before you go to bed?"

"It's French. Last time *you* helped, Madame Dubois gave me a D."

Sarah's face crumpled. Wolfie felt mean. He knew he couldn't go on sulking for ever. He smiled and put his arm around her.

"Vulfee," he trilled in a pantomime imitation of Madame Dubois, "you are eezer verree stupid or verree lazy – but your 'omework is an insult to zee language I lurve."

Laughing, she hugged him hard. "Sleep well," she said, and gathering up the brooms and buckets, she backed down the steps.

Wolfie climbed on to the window seat and peered morosely at the dim outline of the gasworks, Sid and Vera Poskitt taking Monty for a late-night walk on the common, and a glimmer of moonlight reflected in the pond. Why on earth had his dad been so interested in this dreary view over Thornham? Opening his sketchbook, he escaped into the world of his imagination, drawing for nearly an hour before his mind stopped racing.

Drained, he propped the pad against the glass and leaned back. The seat gave an ominous creak. He jumped up and saw that the top was hinged like a lid, and so riddled with woodworm it was giving way beneath his weight. Perhaps his dad had been in some kind of trouble; perhaps on that last fateful night he had hidden a message in there explaining everything. With trembling hands Wolfie lifted it open. The shallow compartment contained nothing but a dead woodlouse and a broken screwdriver.

Furious, he slammed down the lid. Releasing his pent-up frustration felt good, and he stormed round the attic, kicking everything within reach; even his precious sketchpad went skittering under the bed. Panting, he knelt to retrieve it. In the shadows, untouched by his half-hearted attempts to sweep the floor, lay an old leather suitcase. With a flutter of fresh hope he dragged it out, pressed the catch and pulled out a brown paper parcel. An acrid smell of mothballs stung his nostrils as he ripped it open. Inside lay a neatly folded suit.

Wolfie rummaged in the pockets. Nothing. He ran his hand over the lining. Something pricked his skin. Slowly his fingers curled around a scrap of paper pinned to the seam. Sick with excitement, he smoothed out a yellowing ticket printed with the number 317. Scrawled in biro on the back were the words *Stan Brown, collection Tuesday*. It was his grandpa's suit, still in its wrapping from the dry cleaner's. It must have been there for years.

He curled on the bed, biting back his tears. Why couldn't he turn the clock back to yesterday, when he still believed his dad was a hero and he didn't have to sleep in this crummy attic? A gust of wind parted the clouds and a shaft of moonlight fell across the window seat, sharpening the contours of his drawings, seeming to bring the images alive. He shuddered. One was of a forbidding, broad-shouldered man whose hawkish features rose from the folds of a lowered cowl. The other was of a man so haggard he looked more like a wizened puppet than

43

a human being. Matted hair sprouted from his scrawny skull and his wasted flesh clung to his cheekbones. And yet, in the bright moonlight it seemed to Wolfie that the sunken eyes burned with the same fiery spirit as the eyes in the portrait of his father.

7

The Desert Road

The energy rippling down the Nile erupted in a foaming torrent, sending clumps of purple water hyacinth bobbing in the dusk. Below the sixth cataract the flow began to seep into a web of thinner trails, fanning out across the endless rock-strewn scrubland. At a crossroads marked by a withered thorn tree, a single trickle broke free to meet a white Range Rover speeding down the desert road. The jeep hit a gnarled thorn root jutting through the tarmac and swerved into the sand, where the blade of an ancient, half-buried axe-head sank deep into its front tyre.

The driver jumped out, prodded the puncture and walked round to unload the spare. The back doors opened and two men got out. One was the British television reporter Rex Slinfold. The other, tall and rugged with a lived-in face and sharp grey eyes, was his cameraman, Christie Johnson.

Rex called to the driver. "For heaven's sake, Musa, get a move on."

Christie shot Rex an angry look and bent to help Musa jack up the jeep. Rex kicked the sand. "First they pull me off the India story because they want someone 'fresher', then they send me to this godforsaken hole and now we've got a damn puncture. This oil story is big and if we screw up our one-chance interview with the minister, my job's on the line."

Musa felt the tread of the spare tyre sink beneath his thumb. "This one's no good either," he said dejectedly.

Rex threw up his hands. "Great! Who was s'posed to check the jeep?"

"You were," said Christie. "You hired it."

In silence, Rex jabbed his mobile.

"Dammit. There's no signal. How far's the nearest town?"

"Fifteen, maybe twenty miles," said Musa.

Rex scrambled up a rocky ridge and glared angrily into the gloom. Nestling in the dip below he saw a dimly lit cluster of tents. "What's that down there?"

Musa shrugged nervously. "Maybe army, maybe engineers. . ."

"Well, I'm not staying here all night," said Rex. "Come on."

Christie and Musa slithered down the slope after him.

As they neared the encampment a harassed man in a dust-smeared white coat appeared, dragging a rusty gas cylinder. Surprised to see foreign faces, he called out, "Who are you? What do you want?"

"Great, you speak English," said Rex, pulling out his ID. "Rex Slinfold, British Press, this is my cameraman and driver. It's a bit of an emergency. We've got a problem with our jeep."

The man laid down the cylinder. "An emergency?"

"Yes," said Rex. "Flat tyre and a busted spare. And we've got to get to Atbara in two hours for an important interview."

The man gazed unsmilingly at Rex before proffering his hand. "Doctor Adil Margani. I cannot help with your vehicle and we have had no phone signal all day. However, you are welcome to stay here overnight."

Rex ground his fist into his palm. "That's it, then. No jeep, no phone, no story."

"There are many stories in Sudan, Mr Slinfold," said Dr Margani.

"What is this place, doctor?" asked Christie, frowning at the lines of worn blankets strung between the tent poles and the battered metal boxes stacked beneath the trees.

"A mobile hospital. Please, let me show you." The doctor gestured towards the nearest tent.

Christie and Musa ducked through the canvas flap, followed reluctantly by Rex. In the misty light of an oil lamp, rows of women and children lay huddled on mattresses, some barely conscious, others whispering and groaning. The smell of sweat and soiled sheets was overpowering. Fevered faces turned to stare at the new arrivals while two women in white muslin moved among the beds, sponging brows and swatting insects. Dr Margani glowered at Rex. "This is what *I* consider to be an emergency, Mr Slinfold. My hospital serves a vast area of scattered villages, treating the forgotten whose lives have been torn apart by disease, poverty and now, banditry. We have only a handful of volunteer staff and we are running out of antibiotics and anaesthetics, but people still walk miles to get here. Occasionally, if they are lucky, providence steps in." He pointed to a frail boy whose leg was wrapped in a blood-soaked bandage. The boy's eyes fluttered open. Christie saw to his surprise that this dark-haired, dark-skinned child had bright green eyes.

"His village was attacked by bandits who shot him when he tried to protect his widowed mother."

"What kind of bandits?" asked Rex, stepping forward to look at the boy.

"There's a rumour they were part of an intimidation campaign organized by one of the foreign oil companies trying to clear the area for drilling."

Rex reached for his notebook. The doctor went on, "Some village women carried him to the road and flagged down a truck driver who brought him here. But I am not equipped to treat injuries like his. If he doesn't get immediate surgery, he will lose his leg, if not his life. They call him Zi'ib."

"Chris, get your camera," said Rex.

8

The Book of the Dead

"All right, all right," croaked Wolfie as Sarah pushed open the trapdoor. It was the day of the school trip and he had meant to get up extra early.

"You've got a new delivery," said Sarah.

"Where?"

"Greyfriars Crescent, number 45. I've had to get all sorts of magazines in specially."

"45's a dump. Who'd want to live there?"

Sarah kicked the clothes strewn across the floor. "Since when have you been a connoisseur of gracious living?"

"Since I moved into the penthouse," retorted Wolfie, scrambling into his uniform.

"Mr Forester is moving in today, so please try to be nice

to him. And be careful, there's another burst water main on the crescent."

Number 45 stood at the corner of Greyfriars Crescent and Rag Tree Road. Set back down a long drive, it was one of the largest houses in the street, but over the years its grandeur had faded. Apart from an occasional tramp, it had been empty for as long as Wolfie could remember. The garden was a forest of weeds and thorn bushes and a mass of ivy clung to the brickwork. Sarah must have got the address wrong. The place looked deserted. He was about to cycle back to the road when he noticed a sleek, bottle-green Alfa Romeo parked round the side of the house. You'd think anyone with a car like that could afford to live somewhere decent. He shoved a thick wodge of magazines into the letter box. The pages ripped and buckled. Who cared? He was in a hurry, and no one could read that many papers anyway. The door swung open. He looked up into the face of a tall man with slicked-back hair, wearing dark glasses.

"Have you got this week's *Geoscience*?" asked the man irritably.

"Don't think so."

"What about my *Journal of Crystalline Structures*?"

Wolfie scrabbled in his bag. "Sorry . . . there's a spare copy of *Hello*!"

The man snorted and pulled the rumpled papers from his letter box. "Next time just leave them on the step. And find out what's happened to the rest of my order." The door clicked shut.

Wolfie stuck out his tongue. Out of the corner of his eye he thought he glimpsed a face at the downstairs window. He spun round and locked eyes with his own reflection, framed by trailing tendrils of ivy. He stared at it hard, as if seeing himself for the first time. The image suddenly shimmered and split in two. He stepped back. There *was* someone in the room. He had been staring through his own reflection, straight into an identical pair of emerald-green eyes. They belonged to a dark-haired, stubborn-faced girl who glared back at him. She must think he was spying on her. Blushing, he leapt on his bike and sped down the drive, haunted by that strange fusion of faces.

He finished his round as quickly as he could, threw the delivery bag into the outhouse behind the shop and, still smarting with embarrassment, pedalled hard up the hill, belted through the industrial estate and just made it to the school gates as a big red coach swung into view.

A huddle of children clustered around Marcus Harrison, admiring his new trainers. Marcus was tall for his age and would have looked less like a weasel if his cold blue eyes had been set a little further apart. He had a floppy dark fringe and the air of a boy who always got what he wanted.

For generations, the Harrisons had made an uncertain living running the scrapyard on Dodds Hill until Marcus's father, Reg, turned the firm into an architectural salvage business. A steady supply of fireplaces, cornicing and stonework – supplemented by the odd marble statue "salvaged" from its absent owners – now funded Marcus's extravagant taste in footwear.

Wolfie cycled into the playground, too preoccupied to notice the drawing pins scattered across the tarmac. His bike juddered as air hissed from the front tyre. He got off and pushed, ignoring the taunts of Harrison's cronies.

"Nice bike, Paper Boy!"

"Nice an-or-ak!"

Dumping his bike, he pushed to the front of the queue. He knew he'd be sitting on his own so he might as well get a window seat. The rest of the class scrambled on to the coach, chatting about their plans for the weekend. Jessica Lewis and Lucy Albright pulled out zipper make-up bags and started to preen themselves. Wolfie hunched down in his seat and opened a packet of crisps.

"All right, settle down," shouted Mr Grimes. He was stocky, with thinning mouse-grey hair swept back from his forehead and frameless glasses that magnified his shrewd brown eyes. He turned to a new girl standing by the driver.

"This is Tala. Tala Bean."

Snickers of laughter bubbled up from the coach.

"Beans, beans, that musical fruit," chanted a muffled voice. "The more you. . ."

"Stop that," barked Mr Grimes. "It's very difficult

joining a new school halfway through term and I want you to make her welcome."

Jessica and Lucy looked the new girl up and down, giggling as they took in her high-cheeked olive face, her thick straight brows, the tangle of dark hair that looked as if it had been cut with a pair of blunt scissors and the new blazer hanging stiffly from her bony frame.

"Seen her shoes?" sniggered Marcus.

Wolfie didn't look up.

"There's a seat at the back next to Wolfie Brown," said Mr Grimes, pointing down the coach.

"Nice one," mocked Wayne Snaith, a square-faced boy with blond hair shaven at the sides.

Wolfie groaned. Why did *he* have to get landed with some lame new girl?

The coach set off. The girl wobbled down the aisle. Falling into the seat beside him, she shoved her hands between her knees and bent her head. Wolfie was relieved. At least she wasn't going to try and talk to him. The coach swerved through the rush-hour traffic and they sat in silence, pretending not to hear the jibes and titters from the other seats. And then, to Wolfie's horror, the girl started to cry, her shoulders jerking as she sobbed. Marcus rose in his seat, signalling to Wayne across the aisle. Those two could sniff out tears like sharks smelling blood.

Desperate to keep the girl quiet, Wolfie dropped his packet of crisps in her lap. At first she didn't move. When she slid a glance at him through her tangled hair, he felt a shiver of panic. It was the green-eyed girl from number 45.

"Why were you staring at me this morning?" she demanded.

Flustered by her question and confused by her accent, Wolfie stammered, "I wasn't. . . I was . . . looking at myself."

A half-eaten cheese roll smacked into the back of Tala's head, followed by an empty Coke can.

Marcus Harrison's leering face appeared in the gap between the seats in front. Wayne thrust out his phone, eager to capture Tala's humiliation.

"Who's your girlfriend, Paper Boy?" sneered Marcus, his gaze flicking from one pair of green, gold-flecked eyes to the other.

"She your sister, Paper Boy? Some dirty little secret your dad forgot to mention before he ran off?"

Anger welled in Wolfie's throat but he knew better than to respond. He willed Tala not to start crying again. Slowly, deliberately she picked up the crisp packet, rolled it into a tight ball and shoved it into Marcus's gaping mouth. The chatter stopped. Tension sucked the breath from every onlooker. Marcus spat out the crisp packet, and as he did so, Tala emptied the dregs from the Coke can on his head. A gasp of fear and fascination rose from the surrounding seats. Marcus flicked his sticky fringe.

"You shouldn't have done that," he said icily.

Tala dusted the crisp crumbs from her skirt. Marcus

snarled at Wolfie. "You'd better tell that little psycho she's had it, Paper Boy."

"Yeah, Beanpole's had it," echoed Wayne, staring incredulously at the image on his phone.

"Gimme that," said Marcus snatching the handset, and jabbing furiously at the buttons.

Wolfie searched Tala's face. She was gazing through the window, riveted by the red double-decker buses and the crowds pouring out of the tube station. Did she have any idea what she'd just done?

The coach drew up outside the British Museum. Everyone leapt to their feet and tried to push to the front.

"Hold it!" yelled Mr Grimes, brandishing a clutch of papers. "This is an educational experience, not an excuse for larking about. Homework this week is an essay on Egyptian funeral rites. While you are in the Egyptian galleries, you will fill out one of these worksheets, which will give you all the information you'll need. Detention for anyone who fails to complete a worksheet." He surveyed the rows of bored faces, pained by his pupils' indifference. "History is about *you*," he said. "Don't you see that unless we try to unlock the secrets of the past, we'll never truly understand the present or the future?"

The coach driver rolled his eyes and, eager for his tea break, buzzed open the doors. Class 7G burst on to the pavement.

Wolfie watched Tala warily as they filed into the museum. Marcus was right, she *was* a psycho, and he'd better keep out of her way. In the Egyptian galleries he took a solitary route towards the mummies and gazed blankly at the shrivelled remains of a pharaoh. When he looked up Tala was standing next to him.

"I've read lots about the Egyptians," she said. "They used to hook people's brains out through their noses before they embalmed them."

Wayne and Marcus stole up behind her. She swivelled round. "And if they were morons they'd do it while they were still alive, 'cos no one would notice the difference. Then they'd stuff the hole with packs of chips."

"She's a Yank," said Wayne.

Marcus poked Tala hard in the shoulder. "Yeah. And I'll yank *her* brains out if she doesn't watch it." He grinned nastily. "You should be grateful, Beanpole. Me and Wayne are gonna do you a favour and teach you how we do things round here. . . You too, Paper Boy, 'cos it looks like you've forgotten the rules."

"Marcus!" Mr Grimes was heading across the gallery, waving a roll of crumpled paper. "You dropped your worksheet."

Marcus and Wayne slouched off.

Wolfie turned on Tala. "Just shut up. What's the matter with you?"

"They don't scare me."

"Well, they should. They get their kicks torturing kids like us. . ."

"Like us?"

57

Wolfie reddened. They both knew what he meant – outsiders, loners, kids who didn't fit.

Tala shrugged. It had been the same at her old school. She was used to it.

"If you're so tough, why were you snivelling on the coach?"

"I was . . . upset." Her green eyes met his. "'Cos my dad's . . . not around."

"So who was that bloke moaning about his papers?"

"My uncle . . . well, he says my uncle, but. . ."

"So where's your mum?"

"Dunno."

Wolfie frowned and softened his tone. "Where are you from?"

"California."

"Yeah, well, maybe it's different over there, but if you want to survive round here, you'd better keep your head down." Wolfie walked away, trying to control the spinning in his head. As he circled a statue of the dog-headed god Anubis, Mr Grimes plucked the worksheet from his hand.

"Wolfie, you haven't even tried to fill in the answers," he said wearily.

"Sorry."

"Come on, read the information on the exhibits and you might just glimpse the true glories of the past. Look: *Why were mummies buried with a personalized Book of the Dead?*"

Wolfie dutifully scanned the wallchart. "Er . . . to show them what to do in the afterlife."

"Exactly."

"And question two: *What form of alphabet did they use*?"

"Um. . ."

"Find out, boy! Where's your spirit of enquiry?"

Wolfie sloped off towards the display about Egyptian writing.

Oh yeah, he thought. Hieroglyphs – everybody knows that.

He stared at the ancient symbols – squiggly-looking birds, disembodied eyes and endless rows of people doing the hokey-cokey.

Write your own name using hieroglyphs.

He made a feeble effort to transcribe his name: two birds with big feet, a lion, a snake with ears and a load of feathery things. That couldn't be right. A detention loomed. He couldn't concentrate. He sensed Tala's unnerving gaze and hid behind a tall granite obelisk. Why should he care about hieroglyphs and books on the next life? He couldn't even work out what was going on in this one.

9

Stargazing

Anxious to avoid Mr Forester, Wolfie went straight to the outhouse after school to mend his puncture. He stayed there as long as he could but it was cold and he was hungry. He pushed open the back door and with a stab of annoyance saw a brown woolly hat hanging from the coat pegs and a stout wooden walking stick propped against the wall, its shaft a deep chestnut brown darkened with age, its gnarled handgrip polished smooth by use.

He slammed the door. A towering mass of brindled fur shot across the room, seeming to hover in the air before knocking him to the ground. He squirmed beneath a pair of massive forepaws, trying to dodge a dangling loop of drool.

"Mum!" he yelled.

Sarah came running from the shop.

"Elvis! Stop that," she ordered.

With an affectionate lick, the great dog let him go.

"Elvis?" grinned Wolfie, rearranging its absurdly large ears.

"That's what it says on his collar," sighed Sarah. "He belongs to Mr Forester."

Wolfie nodded, remembering how the two of them had nearly caused him to crash his bike.

"I'd no idea he had any pets till I caught that thing raiding the larder. But he's paying so much rent, I don't want to make a fuss – not unless having a dog around really bothers you."

Elvis swept the floor with his tail and gazed imploringly at Wolfie, his amber eyes gleaming in the firelight.

"It's fine by me," he said, smiling for the first time that day. He was more than happy to share his home with Elvis. It was his owner he objected to.

Sarah handed him a huge fruit salad and a pot of herbal tea on a tray. "Here, take this up to Mr Forester and take Elvis with you. He'll have to sleep in Mr Forester's room till he settles down. Tell him I'll leave the key out so he can let him out last thing. Oh, and ask what dog food I should get. He can't live on leftovers."

"Here, boy," said Wolfie. Elvis lumbered to his feet and followed him upstairs.

"Come," called a voice in answer to Wolfie's knock.

"In you go, Elvis," said Wolfie, pushing open the door.

His old room was unrecognizable. Books littered the floor, window sill and chest of drawers, and strange metal contraptions poked from the wardrobe. There were maps all over the walls, bundles of withered foliage hanging from the lampshade, postcards, photographs and lumps of crystal crowding the mantelpiece and a coal fire blazing in the grate. Wolfie was so used to being cold in bed it had never occurred to him that the fireplace might actually work. Mr Forester turned from the window, where he had been gazing at the night through an enormous telescope.

"Ah, Wolfie," he said. "I feel as if we are old friends. That's the joy of the less-travelled road; you never know what wonderful new companions you'll meet around the next bend."

I know one person who's round the bend, thought Wolfie.

Elvis padded towards the old man and nudged his hand. Mr Forester stroked his head. "What a fine fellow you are." He smiled at Wolfie. "I suppose you know that Elvis is a derivative of Alvis, meaning 'all wise'."

"Here's your supper." Wolfie had seen tastier meals served to the monkeys at London Zoo, but Mr Forester seemed delighted.

"Is this all you eat?" asked Wolfie.

Mr Forester nodded. "I've been a fruitarian for years. Of course I'm allowed the savoury fruits like avocados and tomatoes, but I have a rather sweet tooth."

Elvis sniffed the bowl.

"Not for dogs," said Mr Forester, gently pushing his muzzle away. "It's amazing how the human body can extract all it needs from fruits, but an animal like Elvis couldn't last a week without meat."

"Tinned or fresh?"

"Sorry?"

"*Dog meat* – which is better?"

"Well, as an advocate of nature's way, I'd always avoid anything processed."

Elvis stretched in front of the fire, resting his head on an old typewriter and his feet on the coal bucket.

"How long are you thinking of staying?" demanded Wolfie.

"A few months at least. Since my wife died I've lived all over the place, taking lodgings wherever my ley-hunting leads me. It's an odd existence, but I'm so pleased my research has brought me here."

Wolfie grunted.

"Would you like to look through my telescope? The view of the stars is breathtaking tonight," said Mr Forester, spooning up a chunk of banana.

Wolfie had planned to treat their lodger with cold contempt, but the offer was tempting. The telescope stood like the skeleton of a great three-legged beast and he approached it with awe, running a tentative finger along the polished brass barrel and tracing the inlaid twirls of mother-of-pearl.

"Look through the eyepiece and adjust that knob to focus," instructed Mr Forester.

At first it was a blur, and then a magnificent light show leapt into view. Shooting stars sped before Wolfie's eyes and bone-white galaxies and wispy clusters of planets glowed against an infinite darkness. He stood transfixed.

"Wonderful, isn't it?" said Mr Forester.

Wolfie nodded dumbly. It was as if the telescope had brought a thousand different worlds into the drab confusion of his life.

Mr Forester chewed thoughtfully. "It is humbling to think that the ancients had a far deeper understanding of the cosmos than we have today. I'm certain there are planets out there inhabited by beings still steeped in the knowledge we have so arrogantly tossed away."

"What? Little green men?"

"Unlikely. Since all life has sprung from the same primal stardust, there's no reason why, given the right environment, the peoples of other worlds should not have distinctly human form. Only a couple of years ago some German scientists discovered a tiny planet, potentially very similar to our own, orbiting the star GQ Lupi in a star zone called Gould's Belt. Just think. One of its inhabitants might be staring at us right now!"

"Mmm," said Wolfie, suppressing a smile.

"There are movements tonight I've been waiting years to witness," went on Mr Forester. "I'll be staying awake to chart them."

"Is that what you are then, an astronomer?"

"Not really. I was a civil servant before I retired. If I had to be labelled now, I suppose you might call me a prehistorian, but archeoastronomy and sciatherical study obviously play important roles in my work."

"Obviously," said Wolfie.

Mr Forester handed him the tray. "Tell Sarah the supper was delicious."

"OK. And ... um ... thanks for letting me look through your telescope. Oh yeah, she says Elvis has got to sleep with you."

Mr Forester looked startled. "Really?"

"She thinks it'll settle him."

"Well ... if she insists. I'll ... er ... clear some space."

Wolfie went downstairs, wondering if he could sneak another look through the telescope next time Mr Forester went out.

His mother was in the storeroom, humming to herself as she worked on a portrait of Mr B, the mean-eyed Rottweiler from number 52. She waited for him to make a rude comment about their lodger.

"He *is* a weirdo," said Wolfie, "but he's got some pretty cool stuff."

"He's also extremely generous. He's insisting on paying a ridiculously high rent *and* he says I'm to bill him on top for food. It's the first bit of luck we've had in a long time, and all because the shop happens to stand on that ley thingy."

65

She handed Wolfie a ten-pound note. "Here, you deserve it."

"Wow, thanks Mum," said Wolfie. "He said Elvis has fresh meat, not tinned."

"Fine. I'll see if we can get a discount for buying in bulk."

As a treat, Sarah went out and bought fish and chips. Afterwards Wolfie went up to the attic and looked up *sciatherical* in his dictionary. It took him a while since he was a bit hazy about the spelling but it turned out to be something to do with sundials. He grinned. Freako Forester was probably a world expert on garden gnomes as well. He was lying back on the bed staring into the shadowy slope of the ceiling, wondering how to spend his ten pounds, when he noticed a sheet of newspaper patching the space between the rafters. Squinting hard, he made out the faded headline: "*Mystery of Missing Archaeologist*". Intrigued, he jumped up and pulled at the soggy newsprint. It fell apart in his fingers, dislodging a layer of plastic sheeting that had been covering a small skylight. One corner of the cracked glass was missing, but through the grime he could see the watery gleam of the moon and a spattering of stars. He fell back on the pillow. It was strangely mesmerizing to be able to lie on his bed with the glittering night sky directly above him. He drifted into a dream where his father was calling to him through the darkness. He opened his lips to answer and a gobbet of icy rain plopped into his mouth. Then another and another. Leaping up, he stuffed a sock into the broken pane. The moon glow from the skylight seemed brighter, and a beam of light pierced the gloom. Probably the searchlights of a police helicopter looking for a criminal. He strained his ears for the whirr of blades, imagining his dad running down the street, desperate to reach the sweet shop one last time before they hauled him away. But the only sounds were the hum of traffic and the barking of faraway dogs.

He lay down, slitting his eyes to block out the glare. The room grew brighter. He tried holding the pillow over his face but he couldn't breathe and the light burned through the feathers, forcing its way into the deepest corners of his brain. He sat up. A narrow shaft of star-shine slanted through the skylight, tracing a silver path to the bay window. Shielding his eyes against the brightness, he saw a tiny gash – no bigger than a thumbnail – appear in the glimmering smoothness. Suddenly it whorled open on to an endless landscape so bleak, so menacing, so utterly desolate he instinctively clamped his eyes tight shut in horror. When he dared to look again, the landscape had gone, and the star-shine was pulling at him with fiery threads of light that throbbed with the rhythm of his own mounting heartbeat. His feet barely touched the floor as he followed the beam to the window seat and watched it pour like molten metal through the woodworm-riddled lid. Wrenching it open, he saw the light drain through the bottom of the compartment into a hidden space beneath.

He grabbed the broken screwdriver and hacked at the wooden surround until the seat came away with a splintering crack. Groping in the shadowy recess, he pulled out an old Bakelite radio, the size of a shoebox. The squat brown body had two fan-shaped openings in the front: one fitted with a tuning dial, the other overlaid with a fretwork sunburst.

Would it work? He uncurled the frayed, cloth-covered lead, plugged it in and twiddled the sturdy black knobs. Nothing happened. He shook the radio hard. It rattled like a can of stones. He unscrewed the back plate. A jagged piece of gilded metal poked through the wiring. Thin as a CD and about eight centimetres wide it had four sharp points, one drilled with a small hole, sticking up from a broken-edged base. He prised it out. One side was engraved with a pattern of spirals, the other with an intricate web of lines that reminded him of the diagram he had drawn for his geometry homework, the one that had earned him *D minus – see me* from Mr Grimes.

The object seemed to quiver beneath his touch, although it might just have been the tingle of his own excitement vibrating through his fingertips. He slipped the piece of metal back into place, set the radio down and, returning to the dusty debris, withdrew two thin boards of wood. They bore traces of a leather covering and were bound together by a much newer leather thong that allowed them to be opened like a book. Inside lay a few ragged leaves of fine pale parchment, singed at the edges and written in a language unlike any he had seen before. It was a strange, fluid alphabet of peaks and troughs that rippled across the pages like waves on windswept water, stopping every now and then to eddy around islands of upright strokes and slashes or crash against dark formations of dots and circles. He blinked. Each line seemed suddenly a landscape, each character a tree, a knoll, a desert oasis. He blinked and saw fish darting through rivers, birds circling the skies and dawn breaking over a mountain. Tantalized, as if the once-known meaning lay just beyond his memory, he turned through the pages. With a wild fluttering in his stomach he saw a set of symbols pencilled on the flyleaf. Maybe this was his father's writing . . . maybe it was a message written in code.

The green eyes in his father's portrait stared across the room. Wolfie knew it was stupid, but it felt almost as if his dad had wanted him to find this stuff. But how could his dad have known he would end up sleeping in the attic? Or finding the skylight? Or smashing open the window seat. . .? Angrily, he shoved the book and the radio in his grandpa's old suitcase. Why couldn't he just accept that his dad had run off because he didn't care? If he'd wanted to leave Wolfie a message, he'd have written a note or sent a postcard like any normal person.

It seemed as if he had barely closed his eyes when he heard Sarah come running upstairs shouting, "It's gone six!"

He jumped out of bed and tried to drape himself casually over the wreckage beneath the window.

His mother's head appeared through the trapdoor.

"What are you doing?"

"Tai chi. I do it most mornings." He waved his arms and tried to look as though he was getting in touch with his inner self.

"What have you done to the window seat?"

"Oh, that." He adopted a pose he'd seen in a kung fu movie. "I, er. . . Mice. Whole nest of 'em. I had to rip the seat out to get rid of it."

Sarah shuddered. "I'll get someone in to sort it out."

"No need," said Wolfie quickly. "I'll mend it tonight."

"This from a boy who got an F in woodwork. Come and have breakfast. I've paid the electricity bill, so there's bacon and eggs to celebrate."

In the bathroom, Wolfie caught sight of his reflection in the mirror. There were dark rings under his eyes and the clothes he'd slept in were creased and grubby. He splashed his face with cold water but nothing could wash away the haunting memories of the night.

Mr Forester was already at the kitchen table, toying with a slice of grilled papaya. Wolfie muttered a greeting and sat down to his bacon and eggs.

"You don't seem to be enjoying your breakfast, Mr Forester," said Sarah. "Would you prefer a grapefruit?"

"No, thank you," replied Mr Forester dejectedly. "I'm just a little tired and disappointed."

"Oh dear," said Sarah. "What's the matter?"

"Well, to be honest, I'm being plagued by trouble with azimuths."

Sarah looked horrified. Mice, moths; the house was infested. "Mr Forester – what can I say? I'm so sorry. If they've eaten holes in your clothes, I'll mend them straight away and I'll go out this afternoon and get a spray."

Mr Forester looked at her, bewildered. "A spray?"

"Or mothballs would probably do the trick."

"I'm not sure I'm quite conversant with the techniques you describe. You see, by my calculations, there should have been a most interesting planetary alignment last night. I stayed glued to my telescope for hours but saw nothing. I just don't understand it."

"That's a shame," said Sarah, relieved. "Can you catch it another time?"

"No – it happens only once a decade and somehow I was in the wrong place. But I was so sure. . ."

"What about?" said Wolfie.

"That a beam of starlight would point right into this house and lead me to something I've longed to see for years."

Wolfie choked on his bacon.

"What thing?"

"An opening into the Wilderness Between the Worlds."

Fear flooded Wolfie's brain. "The what?" He stared down at his fried egg. Instead of a glistening golden yolk he saw the menacing landscape he had glimpsed in the starlight.

"Wolfie, there's no time to chat. You can talk to Mr Forester later."

"But, Mum—"

"Hurry, it's nearly half-past six."

Wolfie set off on his paper round, dizzied by a whirl of questions. The Wilderness Between the Worlds? What was it? Where was it? Is that what he had seen in the starlight, or was his tired brain just overreacting to another of Mr Forester's crackpot theories?

10

The Village

"This won't take long," said Rex, fanning himself with his notebook as Musa sped towards Dar el Maarifa. "All we need is a bit of background: a few shots of Zi'ib's house, and anything we can get on these mysterious bandits."

The phone lines had started working at dawn and the hire company had sent out a mechanic from Shendi with two new tyres.

"That's it, up ahead," said Musa, turning off on to a dirt track. Rex squinted at the cluster of mud-brick dwellings rising from the scrubby sand. A pair of buzzards fluttered from the carcass of a dead sheep, their yellow claws the only flash of colour in the dun-coloured landscape. As they stepped from the truck, an old woman emerged from one of the houses, hastily pulling a muslin shawl over her head. On hearing they were from the press, she began pointing to Zi'ib's house and speaking angrily in Arabic, barely pausing for Musa to translate.

"That's the house. Zi'ib's mother was the teacher, a widow, quite new to the village. She was the only person they took but no one knows why she was singled out. People are afraid. She says she'll see if the women who found Zi'ib will talk to us."

Rex went off with Musa and the woman. Christie entered Zi'ib's silent house and stood for a moment blinking at the smashed crockery and overturned chairs. Swinging the camera on to his shoulder, he searched for shots that would tell the story of Zi'ib's ordeal. On the bedroom floor he found a patch of dried blood and beside it, in a pool of shattered glass, a framed black and white photograph of a young family. The slim, pretty woman, draped in the silky folds of a flower-patterned *tobe,* held a baby boy on her lap. The man wore a pale suit and stood with his arm around her, proud and protective. Christie picked away the slithers of glass and focused his camera on the three smiling faces. What would happen to that poor kid now both his parents were gone? He felt an urge to salvage anything he could to remind Zi'ib of home. There wasn't much. He collected a leather-handled penknife, a chipped enamel bowl and a sheaf of papers stuffed under the mattress. Dropping them all on to a rumpled sheet, he slid the contents of his wallet and one of his business cards into the photo frame, added it to the pile and knotted the bundle tightly. Rex was watching him from the doorway.

"I'm taking this back for Zi'ib," said Christie. "It's the least we can do."

Rex shrugged. "Come on, the women who found him have agreed to talk. They're waiting by the jeep."

Relieved to be back in the comfort of the Khartoum Hilton, Rex turned up the air conditioning. As he reached for the phone to order the largest burger and fries that room service could supply, it began to ring.

"Hey, Rex, how're you doing?" The familiar voice of Steve Goodrich, Head of News, didn't pause for a reply. "Great piece. The phones have been going crazy since it went out."

"You're kidding."

"It's the boy. Funny how some stories catch the public imagination. There's a doctor in London who specializes in gunshot injuries. He's says he'll operate on him if he can be flown to England, and some kids' charity is offering to raise the money. But he needs a sponsor, someone who'll be legally responsible for him on the flight over and while he's in London."

"Hang on, Steve."

"It's just a formality."

"I don't know anything about kids."

"Come on, Rex. Soon as he gets here, this charity INFASIC – Interfaith something-or-other for Sick

Children – will take over. Your local vicar's been on to us, he's on their board, says they do this kind of thing all the time. Think of the headlines: *'The Caring Correspondent, The Injured Boy He Couldn't Bear To Leave Behind'*."

"Well, I suppose. . ."

"We're emailing you a form. Just sign it, we'll do the rest."

"All right. I guess."

"Good man. By the way, how'd it go with that cameraman? Interesting showreel, but he usually works alone."

"That explains why he's such a po-faced know-all."

"What do you mean?"

"Seemed to think he had a better grip on the story than I did. Spent most of his time sliming up to the locals – you know the type."

Ten minutes later the phone rang in Room 15 of the Hotel Saladin.

"Hi, Christie. Steve Goodrich – great job on the wounded kid."

"Thanks."

"Some charity's going to fly him to London for treatment."

Christie broke into a broad smile. "That's great! When's he going?"

"Soon as we get the paperwork through."

"Let me know if there's anything I can do."

76

"Will do."

"Cheers, then."

"Hang on. I hear you've got a feel for the place, good rapport with the locals. . ."

Christie frowned.

"So why don't you stay on to do another piece. It's a bit of a mystery, might be just your kind of thing."

"Sorry, mate. I'm not doing any more stories with Rex Slinfold."

"No worries. You'd do the interviews yourself – a couple in Sudan, one in London and a few shots of some old ruins in the desert. What do you think. . .?"

"OK," said Christie. "Tell me more."

11

St James's Hospital

Through a drugged haze of unfamiliar smells and sensations, Zi'ib saw a woman standing by his bed and heard snatches of Arabic that made him feel sick.

". . . bullets shattered your leg . . . badly infected . . . inserted a metal pin. . . It's going to take a while . . . but the surgeon, Mr Andrews . . . he's bit of a genius with injuries like yours."

She didn't tell him that he had nearly died, that the infection was so bad the doctor had struggled to save his leg, or that he might never walk properly again.

"Where . . . am I?"

"St James's Hospital in London, England, and I'm Mrs Atif, one of the social workers here."

Zi'ib focused on her gleaming red lipstick. "London?"

"You were on television and a charity raised money to bring you here so Mr Andrews could operate. You're a very lucky boy, Zi'ib."

"My mother. . .?"

"No news yet, dear. I know it's hard, but try not to worry."

Zi'ib's eyes burned. How could he stop worrying about the only person he had ever loved?

Outside, the London landscape grew vivid in the glow of the setting sun as the people of the city went about their business. Most of them felt nothing but the deadening rumble of the passing traffic. But some grew twitchy and glanced up to see the pigeons rise suddenly from the pavements, unsettled by a flow of energy rippling down an ancient pathway from Thornham. Unseen, unheard, it swirled through the blackened labyrinth of chutes and spillways in the boiler rooms beneath St James's Hospital. Drifting up through the echoing ducts of the central heating system, it licked at the gaudy murals decorating the children's wards, bathing the whole wing in a healing swathe of celestial fire. There it stayed, silent, invisible, twisting time like thread on a spindle, until the moment came to retrace its course and rejoin the brimming currents surging through the sacred grasslands now known as Thornham Common.

12

Cosmic Muesli

After three weeks in his new lodgings, Mr Forester had settled in to a busy routine and now spent most of his mornings ghost-hunting. He was not searching for spooks and ghouls, but for ethereal traces of the megalithic stone circle that he believed had once stood on Thornham Common.

Squinting through the eyepiece of his theodolite, he rotated the head in a wide arc, looking for the points marked on his hand-drawn map. A large lumpy rockery, scabbed with lichen, a few swings and the sweet shop flitted past. He tried again: a little boy launching a paper boat on the pond, a queue at the bus stop, and the sign of the Wish Hound pub swinging in the wind.

The sky darkened and fat splashes of rain blurred the lens. Mr Forester sighed and rolled up his map. Elvis picked up the equipment bag in his powerful jaws and together they plodded across the common, weaving through a criss-cross of ruined stonework poking through the mud. Saddened to think that this was all that remained of the medieval splendours of Thornham Hall, Remus Forester had been writing a short monograph about its history.

The Hall had been built by Sir Guy de Monteneuf, a wealthy Templar Knight who fought in the crusades. According to legend, he had been taken captive by Saladin in 1187 during the siege of Jerusalem. An old man had appeared in his cell by moonlight, offering to negotiate his release on condition that he swore to tunnel a secret vault beneath the manor house he was building on his lands at Thornham Magna. Sir Guy agreed and the old man gave him the plan for the mysterious vault, drawn in blood on a piece of silk. The next day Sir Guy was released and, since he was reputed to be an honourable man, there was no reason to doubt that he had kept his half of the bargain.

In the 1980s the council had tried to level the remains of the Hall to make way for a skateboard park. Thankfully, the doughty members of the Thornham Preservation Society had lain down before the bulldozers and forced the council to declare the foundations a site of historical interest. They had even erected a plaque on the tallest stone, engraved with the de Monteneuf family crest – a riven star encircled by a ring of thorns.

Some people still complained that the foundations were an eyesore. But there were others, like Mr Forester, who liked to linger by the plaque and imagine what Thornham must have looked like when the great stone hall, with its sturdy walls, arched doorways, towered battlements and hidden vault, was still standing.

Wolfie was spending his Saturday morning looking after the shop so his mother could finish a painting of an elderly gerbil belonging to Mrs Baxter's niece. There had hardly been any customers and he had spent most of the time doodling on the paper bags and watching Mr Forester through the window.

He still wasn't sure what to make of their lodger *or* his wacky theories. A whole lunch hour spent searching the school library and the internet for references to the Wilderness Between the Worlds had drawn a blank. Since then he'd been purposely avoiding Mr Forester – that way it was easier to convince himself that the whole weird business with the starlight and the window seat had been some kind of sleepwalking episode, induced by a surfeit of cod and chips.

Helping himself to a Mars bar, he glanced down at his doodle. His stomach gave a nervous leap. He had sketched the bleak, menacing landscape he had struggled so hard to forget. He felt an overwhelming urge to weave it into a story of his own making, and he was carefully adding a hunched, ragged figure stumbling across the craggy darkness when he saw the vicar approaching the door. Eager to avoid a discussion about the missing issues of the *Church Times*, he ducked under the counter.

"Ah, Wolfie," said Reverend Peasemarsh addressing the empty space above Wolfie's head. "Just the chap I was hoping to see."

Wolfie stood up, feeling foolish.

"Hello, vicar."

The vicar folded his dripping umbrella and leaned conspiratorially across the counter. "Would you like to help with a little fund-raiser I'm organizing?"

"Um, dunno. What with my homework and my paper round and . . . helping in the shop and . . . everything."

"There's always time for a good cause, Wolfie. Did you catch the recent news coverage of a field hospital in Sudan that's desperate for medical supplies?"

"Er, not sure," said Wolfie, who had no idea what the vicar was talking about.

Mr Forester came in, clanking his tripod and a fold-up fishing stool. The vicar raised his voice above the noise.

"The plight of this hospital was highlighted by our local celebrity, Rex Slinfold, and as chair of *Interfaith Action for Sick Children*, I thought it only right that our community should do what it can to help. We flew one of the injured children to London for treatment and he'll be staying here in Thornham while he convalesces. Sadly, those left behind aren't so lucky, so I'm raising more funds to send them much-needed medicines." He dropped a sheaf of photocopied fliers on the counter. "If you could deliver these on your paper round, I would be most grateful. I'm looking for speakers to give a talk in the church hall, so we can charge a small entrance fee and donate the proceeds. I'd booked Rex Slinfold to kick things off this Wednesday with a talk about his experiences in Sudan. Unfortunately he's been called away on a story, so I'm rather desperate for a replacement."

Mr Forester thrust his equipment through the gap in the counter. "I may be able to help you there, vicar."

"Marvellous," replied Reverend Peasemarsh with a gappy smile. He put out a hand to pat Elvis and seemed genuinely hurt when the dog trotted past without even a sniff in his direction.

"Yes. I'd prepared an illustrated lecture for the Preservation Society," went on Mr Forester, "but when I explained my subject matter, they said all their slots were full. Most strange. Their newsletter said they were crying out for speakers. Anyway, it might be just what you are looking for."

"Splendid – and you are?"

"Remus Forester. I lodge with the Browns."

"And what is the title of your talk, Mr Forester?"

"I'm calling it 'Thornham Magna – A Raisin in the Cosmic Muesli'."

"I see," said the vicar. "Well, cookery is always very popular. Pop round to the vicarage this afternoon and we'll set it up for Wednesday night." He hurried through the door and bumped into Tala hovering in the rain.

Wolfie grimaced. Not *her* again. Dodging her fierce green-eyed stare all day at school was getting on his nerves.

"Come inside, my dear. You're getting drenched," called Mr Forester. Elvis barked loudly and bounded forward to greet her, howling piteously when Mr Forester dragged him into the kitchen.

Tala pushed a cheque across the counter. "For my uncle's paper bill."

"Thanks." Wolfie stuffed it in the till.

"Can you get American papers?"

"Dunno. Why?"

"Not that it's any of your business. I want to check out some ads I put in." She handed him a list of dates and titles.

Wolfie caught a whiff of turpentine. Sarah had come through from the storeroom in her paint-spattered overalls, and was staring at Tala. She jerked the list from his hand. "I'm sure we can get hold of the *Los Angeles Times* and the *San Francisco Chronicle*. I'll talk to the wholesaler about the others." There was something about this skinny, bedraggled girl that drew Sarah's attention. It wasn't just her sad green eyes, which were so like Wolfie's, the droop of her shoulders or her tight scowl. It was as if she were a fragile vase falling slowly to the floor, and if someone didn't reach out to catch her, she would break.

As Tala turned to leave, she said kindly, "You shouldn't be out in this weather without a coat."

"I haven't got one. I left in a hurry and forgot to pack it."

Wolfie watched, amazed, as Tala burst into tears. You could never tell with girls. One minute they were acting all tough and ready to dump you in it with Marcus Harrison and Wayne Snaith, the next they were getting hysterical over some stupid coat. Sarah gathered Tala in to her arms.

"Can't you get a new one?" she asked.

"My uncle gave me some money," sniffed Tala, "but I used it to pay for those ads. They're about my dad. He's . . . gone missing."

Sarah pulled Tala into the kitchen, called to Mr Forester to put the kettle on and started rubbing her hair with a tea towel.

By the time Wolfie had served a couple of customers and plucked up the courage to peek into the kitchen, Tala and Sarah were sitting at the table, laughing and sipping one of Mr Forester's revolting herbal teas. It felt weird having a kid from school in the house, but it was nothing compared to everything else that had happened lately.

"I'd better get back," said Tala. She pushed Elvis's head gently from her knees. He licked her hand. "He's a great dog. Have you had him long?"

"He's not ours – he belongs to Mr Forester," said Sarah, gathering up the mugs.

Mr Forester shook his head, smiling. "Sarah's teasing, my dear. Elvis and I are great friends – roommates, in fact – but he's her dog."

Sarah frowned. "He arrived the day you did," she stammered. "Naturally I thought . . . I mean—"

"I assure you I haven't owned a dog since I was a boy," said Mr Forester.

"But I saw you with him," said Wolfie. "That day you came in asking about a room."

"That was the first time I'd ever set eyes on him. He started following me as soon as I got off the bus but disappeared while I was exploring the common. When I got to the shop he was sitting outside. Naturally I assumed he lived here."

"But you said he needs fresh dog meat," said Wolfie.

"I was merely remarking on the peculiarities of canine digestion."

Elvis slunk into the storeroom.

Mr Forester burst out laughing. "I thought it rather strange that you wanted him to sleep in my room."

Sarah clamped her hand to her mouth. "Why on earth didn't you say something?"

"I didn't want to make a fuss so soon after moving in."

"And I didn't want to make a fuss about you having a pet."

Everybody was laughing now.

"Looks like Elvis had it all planned out," Tala giggled.

Sarah grew serious. "His real owners must be frantic. I'll

put some notices up and tell the police." She looked at Wolfie. "But he's going to have to go to the dogs' home."

"You can't!" cried Wolfie.

"Love, he costs a fortune to feed." Sarah flushed and glanced at Mr Forester. "I'm really sorry. I've been putting the money on your bill."

Mr Forester gave a little cough. "He's been such a staunch companion on my field trips, I'm not sure I can do without him." His blue eyes twinkled. "So as long as we can make some alternative sleeping arrangements, I'd be very happy to continue paying for his rations until he's claimed."

"Please, Mum," begged Wolfie. "He can sleep in my room."

"Don't be silly – how would he manage the ladder?"

"He did fine the other day; two bounds and he was up."

Sarah sighed heavily. "All right, just until he's claimed."

Still chortling, Mr Forester went upstairs.

"At least this will keep off the rain," said Sarah, helping Tala into an oversized green mackintosh. "She's coming round for supper on Wednesday and going with us to Mr Forester's talk," she told Wolfie.

"What do you mean *us*? I'm not going to any boring. . ." He broke off, looking thoughtful. If "cosmic muesli" had anything to do with astronomy, Mr Forester's talk might turn out to be very interesting indeed.

13

The Vicarage

The Reverend Godfrey Peasemarsh rubbed his hands together and spoke very slowly and clearly. "It's steak – and – kid – ney pud – ding. I found – the re – ci – pe in *Wo – man's Week – ly*."

Zi'ib stared disgusted at the mess on his plate, picked politely at the slimy dough floating in a pool of brown sludge and shifted his plastered leg, pretending the pain was affecting his appetite. In fact it didn't hurt much at all, and although he would be on crutches for quite a while, the swiftness of his recovery from the complicated surgery had astounded everyone at the hospital.

As soon as Mr Andrews announced that Zi'ib was well enough to be discharged, Mrs Atif had tried to contact Rex Slinfold. When he didn't return her calls, she spent a whole day trying to find Zi'ib an emergency foster placement and had been at her wit's end when Reverend Peasemarsh, the chair of INFASIC, phoned her to offer Zi'ib a temporary home.

Leaving St James's had been a wrench. After the initial shock of waking up in a foreign hospital, Zi'ib had grown used to the bright bustle of the ward and the sight and sound of other children. But here, in this big draughty vicarage, with nothing to distract him, he felt lonely and panicky. The vicar was kind enough, but he didn't seem to realize that however loudly he spoke, or however slowly he moved his lips, Zi'ib could not understand a word he said.

They finished their "jam − ro − ly − po − ly − and − cus − tard", which looked exactly like the first course, except the sludge was red and yellow, and the vicar helped him to the sofa. To Zi'ib's astonishment, Godfrey Peasemarsh suddenly clamped his hand over one eye, dropped to his knees, and began to rock backwards and forwards, patting the carpet. Zi'ib lowered his eyes respectfully. This prayer ritual seemed a bit strange, but Mrs Atif had explained that he might find some traditional English customs a bit odd at first, and he should do his best to be tolerant. When the vicar began to intone a mournful chant that sounded a bit like "maa lenz . . . maa lenz", Zi'ib joined in as best he could.

The vicar suddenly scooped up some tiny object, licked it and jammed it in his eye. He looked sharply at Zi'ib, who was still murmuring "maa lenz" and rocking to and fro.

Maybe you weren't supposed to join in, thought Zi'ib. How was he supposed to know? How was he supposed to know anything? The vicar squinted and blinked a few times to settle his contact lens, shot Zi'ib another suspicious glance and bustled off to the kitchen with the plates. He returned with a brown paper parcel and a carrier bag full of clothes. Together they picked through the tattered oddments left over from the last jumble sale, trying to find anything that would fit a tall, skinny eleven-year-old. Zi'ib chose a couple of jumpers, an old green parka and some sweatpants baggy enough to stretch over his plaster. They were itchy and musty but at least they would keep him warm. Godfrey Peasemarsh helped him to change and handed him the parcel.

"It – came – this – mor – ning."

Zi'ib ripped off the wrapping, gasping when he saw the bed sheet from home. He loosened the knot and pulled out some old papers, the pocket knife that had belonged to his dad, an enamel bowl and the photograph of his family. Tears blurred his eyes. He held the frame close, fingering the chips in the thick black paint and the brass catches that held the rough wooden backing in place, but couldn't bear to look at the faces, not yet. A bundle of dollar bills and a business card dropped into his lap. He stared at the money, bewildered. The vicar, looking equally surprised, leaned forward to read out the name on the card. "Chris – tie John – son, cam – e – ra – man." He glanced inquiringly at Zi'ib. Zi'ib shrugged.

"We'll – have – to – o – pen – you – a – bank – account."

Zi'ib buried his face in the familiar folds of the sheet. The smell of home turned his misery to anger. He should be there now, looking for his mother. He had no idea who this Chris – tie John – son was or why he had sent him the dollars, but they had to be enough to buy a ticket home.

The vicar gave him an encouraging smile and pointed to the door. "Come on. It's time for 'Thorn – ham Mag – na – A Rais – in in the Cos – mic Mues – li'."

Wrinkling his nose, Zi'ib leaned on his crutches in the doorway of the long, low building squeezed between the churchyard wall and the gasworks. This place had the same damp fusty smell as his clothes and made him ache for the brittle scents of the desert. Although it was crowded with people sitting in grey plastic chairs, he knew it wasn't the church – the vicar had already shown him that.

Reverend Peasemarsh pointed to a seat next to Sid and Vera Poskitt, but Zi'ib hobbled towards a space at the front, beside the only two children in the room – a girl in a green mackintosh, and a boy with shaggy fair hair. He sank down shyly and the vicar brought him a plastic milk crate to rest his leg on.

"Zi'ib, this – is – Woool – feee – Brrrrr – oww – nnn – and – er. . ." He lifted his eyebrows questioningly at Tala.

"Tal – aa Beee – an."

Zi'ib's lips twitched. He kept his eyes fixed on the floor. A pretty woman with wayward brown hair sat down next to him. She smelled nice, a mixture of chocolate, warm dog and – oddly – paint. She regarded him curiously for a moment, as if wanting to ask him a question, then patted her chest and said, "I'm Sarah Brown. Welcome to Thornham."

Zi'ib shook his head. "*Ana ma b'atakalam ingelezi.*"

She smiled and offered him a sweet from a paper bag. He helped himself hungrily. "*Shukran gazeelan.*"

Wolfie and Tala stared at Zi'ib's hunched shoulders and crisp dark curls. So this was the boy there'd been all the fuss about; he'd been all over the *Thornham Gazette*. Zi'ib slowly raised his head. He met one pair of startled green eyes and then another. Eyes just like his. He felt a flash of recognition, a deep unnerving connection. He was sure they felt it too but immediately they looked away. Zi'ib frowned. Maybe he was wrong; maybe all he'd seen in their faces was pity. Maybe in England loads of people had eyes like his.

The lights dimmed. The vicar climbed onstage, draped a white sheet over a pole suspended between two stepladders and turned to address the audience. Zi'ib made out his own name and the words "Sudan" and "Dr Margani"; then people started pointing and nodding at him. He hated all this attention.

The vicar sat down at the side of the stage and to a patter of applause a ruddy-faced old man with white hair

93

made his way on to the stage. Zi'ib's spirits lifted when he began to fiddle with an old slide projector; at least there'd be something interesting to look at. The man clicked a remote control. After a moment of whirring and creaking, a picture flashed up on the sheet. Zi'ib's heart sank. It was a photo of a lump of rock.

14

Mr Forester's Lecture

"**T**onight, ladies and gentlemen, I want to take you on a journey through time and myth to a vanished landscape," began Mr Forester, breathy with excitement. "And share with you some startling discoveries concerning the lost wisdom of the ancients. Discoveries which, to my amazement, have been dismissed by those who call themselves *professional historians.*"

Wolfie's shoulders sagged. It didn't look as though Mr Forester was going to be saying anything about astronomy after all. Lulled by the whirr of the projector and the warmth of the airless hall, his eyes drooped. Tala jabbed him awake with her elbow. "Don't look round. My uncle's just come in."

"So?"

"I never told him I was coming."

"This is a megalith," Mr Forester was saying, pointing with his walking stick. "It weighs four tons and stands on a site one hundred and fifty miles from the place where it was quarried. I have calculated that, using tree-trunk rollers, it would have taken a thousand men seven weeks to move that stone to its final resting place." He flashed up some slides of what looked like giant benches and tables made of granite slabs. "So imagine the manpower and expertise necessary to construct these dolmens, whose capstones alone can weigh over ten tons."

A slide of Stonehenge appeared, its towering circlet of rough-hewn stones rising majestically from a misty plain.

"To quarry, transport and erect a stone circle of this magnitude would have taken generations of struggle and sacrifice and many of the megalithic masons would have been injured, even killed, in the process." His magnificent eyebrows shot up his forehead. "So why did they do it?"

"The truth is, the henge builders were not primitive hunter-gatherers struggling to survive their hostile environment. They were sophisticated scientists who developed natural technologies that we, with our tinny computers and tawdry gadgetry, can only dream of today. They understood that the cosmos is a living entity sustained by powerful energies that flow through the veins of our planet like the blood through our bodies. What is more, they knew how to use – and crucially, how to *replenish* – those energies.

"In their wisdom they sought out stone with strong energy-conducting properties – like the bluestone of the Preseli Hills of Wales – and transported it hundreds of miles to places where the most powerful of these energy paths converge.

"And why? Because the stone circles and megaliths they erected were not mere temples and totems but power stations and pylons, designed to husband, harness and direct this precious energy to fertilize the land, to heal the sick, and even, yes, even to transport people and thoughts across vast distances."

Gasps of amazement as well as murmurs of "tosh" and "ridiculous" rippled around the hall. Wolfie and Tala had been giggling at the vicar, whose head was tipping forward and jerking up again whenever Mr Forester raised his voice, but now they were listening hard, trying to work out if Mr Forester was inspired or just bonkers. Even Zi'ib was moved by the passion of the old man's delivery.

"This mercurial earth energy, this life force, has been called many things. To the ancient Greeks it was celestial fire, to the religions of the East, *chi* or *prana*. In the West it is sometimes described as ley energy because the paths through which it flows are known as leys, or ley lines.

"*Ley* is a Saxon word meaning meadow, but it also echoes the Sanskrit *lelay*, meaning to flame or sparkle. For, like a web of glowing threads, these power lines link our earth to the wider cosmos, creating a single self-regulating system that we neglect or disturb at our peril."

A hillside popped up on the sheet, with the stark outline of a figure holding two long poles etched into the chalky grassland.

"This is the Wilmington Giant, an ancient drawing of a prehistoric surveyor, or *dodman*. *Dodman* is the Old English word for snail, used to describe the men who marked the leys because their trademark sighting staves resembled a snail's horns."

Mr Forester suddenly thumped his chest. "I too am a dodman, a surveyor of the leys." In the beam of the projector, his eyes were ablaze and his ruddy face took on an arresting quality that surprised and impressed his audience. "By following in the footsteps of our noble forebears, I, and many like me, seek to retread and reclaim the forgotten grid. This is not a quaint hobby but a necessity!

"Man has been ignoring the old pieties and destroying the natural balance of the cosmos for too long. The leys are withering. To replenish them we must look to our ancestors for guidance. We must use our minds to reclaim the wisdom enshrined in their temples of earth and stone, and our feet to renew the lost energy paths they once revered. For unless we learn how to re-engage both mentally and physically with the earth's energy grid, we face catastrophe.

"I am convinced that our forefathers wove the secrets of their technologies into the fabric of their sacred structures. To our shame, we no longer understand those complex messages. Our very ability to interpret them has atrophied with neglect."

The image switched to a shadowy, stone-lined corridor lit by a single beam of light pouring through a slot above the entrance. Something about the laser-like ray held Wolfie transfixed. The whirr of the projector grew insistent in his ears.

"This ancient passage tomb, built in the fourth millennium BC, was designed so that on each of the solstices the rising sun would shine straight through the roof box and point a finger of light at the spirals carved into the walls of the inner chamber."

Mr Forester's voice grew faint and the plastic chairs and scuffed parquet faded away as Wolfie was drawn into that ancient darkness. He could feel the slant of sunlight on his cheek, smell the cool damp earth and hear the hum of human throats singing out a primal song of welcome.

The slide changed to a close-up of the spirals slashed by a dagger of sunlight. Kindled by the beam, the spirals were detaching themselves from the stone and coiling towards Wolfie as if searching for his soul.

"Thus, the ancient sages call to us across the centuries," boomed Mr Forester's faraway voice. "Crying out their secrets in a language that we are now too primitive to understand."

The spirals snaked closer. Struggling for breath, Wolfie raised his hands to ward them off but they struck at him, again and again, jolting through his body, electrifying every nerve and muscle. With a clattering thud Zi'ib collapsed, sending his crutches flying. Tala doubled over, pressing her head into her hands. The room tilted sickeningly, Wolfie's body buckled and he fell at her feet.

Mr Forester stared down at the front row, amazed and gratified that his words were having such a profound effect.

"I think . . . now might be a good moment for a short intermission," he said, prodding the vicar with his walking stick.

The vicar stirred and got to his feet with a big smile.

"Fascinating, Mr Forester. I can't wait to hear more. Meantime, everybody, please help yourselves to refreshments. I baked the scones myself." He motioned towards a trestle table laden with urns and plates of cake.

Sarah helped Zi'ib and Wolfie back into their chairs, fetched three cups of strong sweet tea and pushed them into the children's trembling hands. She felt their brows. If anything they were abnormally cool, but their eyes burned preternaturally bright, the yellow flecks blazing against the green. A knot of anxiety tightened in her belly.

"I'd better get you home."

"No, Mum, I want to hear the rest," said Wolfie.

"Me too," murmured Tala.

Surprised, Sarah hurried to the nearest window to let in some air.

"Did it feel like you were there in that horrible dark

corridor with those coils of light coming at you?" whispered Tala, shakily.

Wolfie rubbed his eyes. "It must have been the beam of the projector and the smell of damp messing with our heads."

"Can you see my uncle anywhere?"

Wolfie shook his head. The movement made him dizzy. "I still feel funny," he groaned.

Not half as funny as I do, thought Zi'ib, rapping his forehead with his fists.

The rest of the audience finished their buns as Mr Forester climbed back onstage.

"The slides I showed you earlier were all of well-known prehistoric monuments that have survived the assaults of time. But it is my belief that many equally impressive megalithic structures have disappeared. Some have been buried beneath floods or landfalls, some destroyed by zealous clerics anxious to eradicate our 'pagan' past, others hacked to pieces by peasant farmers in need of stone to build their homes and barns.

"As part of my campaign to revive the natural technologies of our ancestors, I have made it my life's work to map the locations of these lost stone circles. I do it partly by tracking clues left on the landscape, or in place names, or fragments of folklore. But mainly by following the leys to their major crossing points." He gripped his walking stick, unable to conceal his excitement. "And so, ladies and gentlemen, I want you to prepare for a revelation, a revelation that will change the face of British prehistory.

"It is my conviction that Thornham Common was once the site of the most important stone circle in Britain. Greater than Stonehenge, older than Avebury – a megalithic site that marks the convergence of some of the most powerful leys on this planet and links us to the great secrets of the cosmos."

He paused, exultant. The astonished silence was broken by a woman sitting behind Sarah who called out, "Where's your evidence?"

"The evidence, madam, lies in the landscape – the common is a flat plain lying at the foot of a sacred hill. It lies in the place name – that sacred hill is called Dodds Hill, surely an echo of the ancient dodmen who surveyed it. It lies in the position of the church – sited on a place of pre-Christian power, it is dedicated to St Michael, whose emblematic sword pierces a serpent, a timeless symbol of the energies coursing through the earth. It lies in the folklore – Thornham's ancient rite of 'raising the giants' is, I am convinced, a re-enactment of the ritual raising of giant *stones*. And most tellingly of all, it lies in the power and pattern of the leys that converge here.

"I do not know exactly why or how or when this circle was destroyed. I can only stand on the common and wonder how many hearth-stones, whetstones, doorsteps and lintels were hewn from the great lost giants of Thornham."

A bald man with glasses raised his hand. "Rodney Beavis, secretary of the Thornham Preservation Society. So why is there no reference to this circle in the archives? St Michael's Church, the old abbey, even the dew pond were mentioned in the Domesday Book, but there's nothing about a stone circle."

"The Domesday Book was purely a catalogue of taxable assets, put together by our revenue-hungry Norman conquerors. It mentions standing stones only occasionally to describe the location of isolated farms. However, in the eighteenth century the antiquary William Stukeley did map and sketch many ancient sites, which have subsequently disappeared, and it's true that Thornham's circle does not appear in any of his works. This does not mean that it did not exist, merely that it was destroyed much earlier than the eighteenth century."

Rodney Beavis sniffed and folded his arms.

"But you are right," said Mr Forester. "We need more evidence, which is precisely why I have come to live here. Over the next few months I shall gather irrefutable proof that Thornham is indeed a plump, juicy raisin in the cosmic muesli!"

The vicar's hearty clapping roused a muted response.

"Thank you so much, Mr Forester. Most thought-provoking. I hope to see you all next week for 'Marrows of Desire', Sid Poskitt's talk on growing your own vegetables. Tickets available at the door."

Rodney Beavis accosted Mr Forester and began to harangue him loudly. Sarah, Wolfie and Tala nodded goodbye to Zi'ib and, silently immersed in their own thoughts, set off for Tala's house. She was standing on the front steps fumbling for her key when the door opened and Matthias appeared, lean and awkward in his shirtsleeves and dark glasses.

"What were you doing in the church hall?" bristled Tala.

He raised his hands in mock surrender. "Hey, I thought the talk might be interesting. Turned out not to be my kind of thing, so I left." He smiled at Sarah. "Thanks for taking Tala out. It can't be much fun stuck here with a workaholic bachelor."

She smiled back. "It was a pleasure."

Matthias widened the door. "Would you like a coffee?"

"We've got to go," cut in Wolfie. "I've got homework."

"OK, another time. Thanks again." Matthias closed the door. Tala headed for the stairs.

"Hang on," Matthias said. "We need to talk."

"Yeah?"

"I've invested some money – quite a lot of money – in a company that prospects for minerals and, well, the company is in trouble."

Tala frowned.

"You don't need to worry, but right now my finances are a bit strained. I won't be doing this place up for a while and I might have to make some trips abroad. So we need to discuss what to do with you while I'm away."

"I'll be fine by myself."

"No you won't, not overnight."

Tala shrugged. "Maybe Sarah will let me sleep on their sofa." Shakily she began to walk upstairs. "I don't feel so good. I'm going to do my homework and go to bed."

Matthias ran his hands through his hair. Winning over a difficult eleven-year-old was turning out to be a lot harder than he had imagined. He called after her. "Look, I know things are tough for you right now but it would make it a lot easier for both of us if you. . ."

Tala's door closed with a crisp click.

Wolfie opened his French book, trying to shake off the grinding throb in his brain. His homework was an essay describing a day in the life of a one-euro coin. How boring was that? He scribbled down the first thing that came into his head, but he couldn't concentrate. The throbbing was creeping down his spine and he was sure he could hear voices. He stuck his head over the side of the bed – there was nothing there except some balls of fluff and the old suitcase. The voices couldn't be drifting from Mr Forester's room because he'd gone back to the vicarage for a sherry. They couldn't be coming through the wall because the house next door didn't have an attic. Fear prickled the back of his neck. The shadows thrown by his bedside lamp seemed suddenly darker and the breeze through the broken skylight scored his cheek like the tip of an icy blade.

Steeling himself, he reached for the suitcase. The catches sprang open and a volley of chatter burst from his grandpa's radio. His relief was momentary. He may have come bottom in physics but even he knew that an old radio that didn't have a battery and wasn't plugged in shouldn't be transmitting anything. He pulled it out and spun the dial. The voices dissolved into a resonant hiss that pulsed with life, as if the vibrations flowing into his ears and fingers were disembodied feelings trying to invade his mind. Unnerved, he shifted the dial again. A blast of military music merged into a harsh male voice reading the news. Waggling the knobs didn't turn the radio off, so he searched for the screwdriver, unscrewed the back plate and poked the wiring. It made no difference. He prised out the jagged fragment of metal. The voices stopped abruptly. He held the metal to the lamplight and felt it shudder. It had to be some kind of battery. Maybe a secret prototype . . . maybe his dad had hidden it up here to stop it falling into enemy hands. He scowled. If it was that important, his dad would have stuck around to protect it.

He slipped it back into the radio and delicately turned the dial. Had he imagined that curious flurry of life among the babbling frequencies? A desperate need to find it again flooded over him, a yearning so deep it stopped his breath as his frantic fingers searched the airwaves. And then in a roaring heartbeat it was there: a rush of loneliness, hope, desperation and longing. This time there was no doubt. He really *had* tuned into someone else's emotions. Terrified, he jerked his hand back and shot a glance through the window. What if it worked both ways? What if this scrap of metal was enabling someone out there to tune into *his* mind and *his* secret fears?

PART TWO
Thornham

15

The Mastery of Tongues

Madame Dubois was in no mood for excuses. "If *I* am willing to give up my morning to mark your essays, the least *you* can do is 'and them in. I don't know what is worse: people who don't bother at all, or cheats who get somebody else to do their work for them. Wolfie Brown, 'as your family acquired a French au pair?"

A chorus of low whistles echoed round the classroom.

"No, miss."

She tossed Wolfie's exercise book on to his desk.

"Then please explain to me 'ow you 'ave produced a piece of work that can only be described as excellent, when last week you could barely string a French sentence together?"

Wolfie opened his book and found a page of flawless

French, written in his own handwriting. Blood fizzed in his brain. His thoughts spun back to the previous night. He'd been so distracted by the sounds from the radio, he'd hardly given his essay a thought.

"I dunno, miss," he mumbled. "It just sort of came to me."

"In that case, you can 'just sort of come to me' when I 'ave 'anded out these essays so I can sign your report card. If you cheat again, I shall send you to Dr 'arker." She swung round to face Tala. "And Tala Bean, you obviously learned a great deal more French at your old school than you were prepared to admit. You write with the fluency of a native."

Bewildered, Tala looked at her mark. For the first time in her life, she had got an A.

For the rest of the lesson, Wolfie stared at the board, willing the lists of irregular French verbs to turn back into their old incomprehensible fug and trying to avoid Tala's terrified face. When the bell rang she darted into the aisle and blocked his exit.

"What's happened to us?" she demanded.

He pushed past her. "I dunno. Maybe we're just remembering stuff we forgot."

"Don't be stupid. I didn't even *do* French at my last school."

Wolfie felt the urge to run, as if by getting away from Tala he could escape the fear bubbling up inside. But she stayed close, dodging and twisting to keep up. They turned the corner. A dark skinny kid was sitting outside the headmaster's office, looking scared, a pair of crutches propped against the chair beside him. Wolfie swallowed. It was Zi'ib. Dr Harker came striding down the corridor. He was tall and pale and everything about him, from his close-cropped hair to his well-polished shoes, exuded order.

"Welcome to Blackstone Comprehensive," he said, patting Zi'ib on the shoulder. He spotted Wolfie.

"Ah, Wolfie. I'm putting this new boy in your class. Make yourself useful and show him the ropes. He's called, um, Dweeb. He's from Sudan, had a tough time – you may have seen the news reports. They're sending an interpreter over this afternoon. Meantime, do what you can to make him feel at home." Nodding encouragingly, he disappeared into his office.

The three stood in silence, numbed by a shared unease. Finally Wolfie waved his key and said, "I'll show you where the lockers are."

"I don't need a locker," said Zi'ib quietly. "I haven't got anything to put in it."

Wolfie tried not to panic. "How come you speak such good English all of a sudden?"

Zi'ib looked him in the eye. "How come you speak such good Arabic all of a sudden?"

"I don't . . . I didn't. . ."

Zi'ib said very softly in his mother tongue, "Did it happen last night at that lecture? Was it like an electric shock?"

113

As he spoke, the whitewashed corridor seemed to narrow around them and a beam of winter sunlight poured through the wire-clad windows, welding their three shadows into one. They saw nothing but each other's faces, felt nothing but each other's fear and heard nothing but the pounding of each other's hearts.

"Get out of it!" came a snarling voice.

Marcus, Wayne and a gang of hangers-on came tearing round the corner. Marcus tripped over Zi'ib's crutches. He steadied himself, looked Zi'ib slowly up and down and flicked his fringe. "You're that charity kid who was on the telly." He grinned at his mates and bent down so his face was nearly touching Zi'ib's. "Dunno why they bothered. My dad says you're just another whingeing scrounger, over here to get what you can and make trouble. Why don't you just go back where you—"

Dr Harker's door burst open.

"I will not tolerate those attitudes in my school, Marcus," growled the headmaster. "Stand outside my door until I've got time to deal with you. It's fortunate that Dweeb can't understand your mindless bigotry. But I've put him down for intensive English and I shall make sure he reports any more instances of bullying directly to me."

Zi'ib grabbed his crutches and heaved himself up.

"My name's *Zi'ib*, Dr Harker, and I don't think I'll be needing English lessons *or* an interpreter," he said politely.

Dr Harker's eyes popped with surprise. "Well, I, er. . ."

he spluttered, his nostrils quivering as if sniffing for a rational explanation. "It's . . . um . . . those fools at the local authority." He nodded to himself, visibly relieved. "Yes, of course. Trust them to get it wrong. Well, any problems, just let me know. I'd better get that interpreter cancelled." He marched off to the secretary's office.

Marcus raised a gleaming designer trainer against the wall. Leaning back, he switched his gaze from Zi'ib's glittering green eyes to Wolfie's. "This another of your old man's mucky little secrets, Paper Boy?" he sneered. "He wasn't exactly picky, was he?"

Wolfie lunged, not caring that he'd never hit anyone before or that he was surrounded by a ring of hardened fighters.

Zi'ib felt Wolfie's fury fire his own. In one swift movement he jerked his crutch on to Marcus's foot and pressed down with his full weight. Marcus swore viciously and kicked the crutch away so that Zi'ib toppled into Wolfie. Tala leapt forward to grab them as Dr Harker came striding back.

"What on earth is going on?"

"My crutch slipped. I must have caught Marcus's toe by mistake," said Zi'ib. He smiled coldly at Marcus. "Sorry."

"You will be, Charity Boy," mouthed Marcus.

"All right, move along, everybody. Marcus, in my office. Now!" ordered Dr Harker.

Side by side, Wolfie, Tala and Zi'ib walked down the corridor, two dark heads and one fair, bobbing in the stream of children thronging to the canteen. They felt so confused they hardly dared look at each at other.

"Thanks for . . . back there, with Marcus," Wolfie muttered as they joined the lunch queue.

"Any time," said Zi'ib. "But . . . I . . . you . . . we. . ." The words locked in his throat.

"Shut up," hissed Wolfie, glancing round warily. "Grab a table, we'll get your food. What do you want?"

"Anything, so long as it's not steak and kidney pudding."

Wolfie and Tala piled food on to trays and pushed their way to where Zi'ib sat among the seething crush of pupils, dazed by the bewildering array of nationalities, faces and hairstyles. Zi'ib sniffed his fish pie and pushed the plate aside. He took a shuddery breath.

"Don't say *anything*," said Wolfie. "If anyone finds out, they'll think we're freaks."

"They think that anyway," said Tala grimly.

"We'll talk about it after school," said Wolfie. "Mum's got aerobics. You can come to the shop." He stopped. The words spilling from his mouth sounded so strange that for a moment he wondered if he was speaking Arabic or French. Then he realized. He wasn't speaking a foreign language; he'd just never invited anyone home before.

16

Hidden Realms

R idian Winter gazed through the window at the grey expanse of Thornham. A gang of teenagers was spraying graffiti across the bus stop bench and a pack of younger hoodlums was running riot on the common, clambering over the time-worn rockery, spearing it with sticks as if poking out the eyes of a slumbering monster. He felt sickened that a world that had once possessed the Wisdom of the Forests, Mountains and Rivers could have degenerated so far.

How easy it was to dupe these fools. For centuries the Chosen had lived among them undetected. No one at Zemogen International, the huge global conglomerate who now paid him so generously to head up their research arm, had the slightest suspicion of his contempt for their crude technologies and petty aspirations.

As dusk gathered, he prepared to send the long-awaited news. Holding his star of hammered gold to the sky, he slowly drew his thoughts away from the streets of Thornham. Focusing his will, he passed step by step through the doorway in his mind that led to the pure and perfect place where all things are known and all things are one, the place his ancestors had named the Hidden Realms of Wisdom. He waited for the surge of power to steady, and then in accordance with the custom passed down through generations, he began his transmission with the pledge of the ancient cult who called themselves the Manus Sacra.

And the Chosen shall prevail.

The star glowed with a fiery heat as his message poured across the leys, borne on the Link of Light.

The convergence is complete.

The progeny are gathered in this place and the mastery of tongues has been awoken.

It was done. But he felt moved to voice his disquiet.

They are weak, foolish specimens who show little promise.

Their ability to achieve our purpose is doubtful.

After a moment the response throbbed through his fingers.

And the Chosen shall prevail.

You have done well.

Do not underestimate the power of mingled blood.

Watch with vigilance and wait with patience.

The power of the leys is with us.

Winter laid down his star. Opening his laptop, he pulled up the latest email from his team in Anchorage and forwarded it to the Master of the Exiles. Turning to leave, he saw Wolfie, Tala and Zi'ib trailing across the common. Silently he shook his head, appalled that so great a task should lie in the hands of this trio of misfits.

17

Mystic Coathangers

Tormented by thoughts too frightening to share in any language, Wolfie, Tala and Zi'ib barely spoke until they reached the back yard of the sweet shop and heard Elvis howling and hurling himself at the door. Zi'ib hung back nervously.

"He's harmless, but he can get a bit excited," said Wolfie. He took the key from under the mat and tossed it to Tala. "When I say go, open the door." He crouched down ready to grab Elvis's collar. "Go!"

Slowly Tala opened the door. The great dog erupted through the gap, sailed over Wolfie, landed neatly at Zi'ib's feet and gently licked his hand. Wolfie and Tala looked at each other, bemused. Elvis nudged the injured boy inside the house and towards the sofa and Zi'ib sank gratefully into the cushions, moving aside a photo of a bug-eyed chihuahua in a bonnet.

"Is this some sort of rat?"

"No. It's a dog called Cynthia," said Wolfie. "Mum's painting her portrait."

"A portrait of a *dog in a hat*?" Zi'ib groaned. "I'll never get the hang of what's supposed to be normal round here."

His words hung in the silence. Would anything *ever* feel normal again?

"Look," said Wolfie. "You've got to keep this quiet, specially from my mum – she'll only get in a panic. But I think we've got caught up in some secret experiment that messes with people's minds."

His words conjured frightening visions of special agents turning up to reprogramme their brains by force.

"That would explain the thing with the languages," said Zi'ib slowly. "But not. . ." He looked away, embarrassed. This cross-looking girl and this thin pale boy might think he was mad. "Not this weird connected feeling. It . . . kind of started the minute I saw you."

It was true. They might be total strangers from three different continents, but there *was* some unfathomable connection between them. In that moment of acceptance, they felt the bond tighten.

Wolfie jumped up. "I want to test something."

He dashed to the attic. Returning with his grandfather's suitcase, he pulled out the radio, hesitated in case he tuned into those spooky emotions again, and turned the dial. He found a woman reciting Russian poetry, a sickly Italian love song and a man from Radio Mongolia bemoaning the price of pig pellets. The others nodded. They had understood every word.

"Trouble is," said Zi'ib, "I can't tell what language they're speaking, I just sort of get the meaning. Half the time I don't even know what language I'm talking myself. If we're not careful, somebody'll hear us, and even if the government or whoever don't get us, we'll still end up in some lab having our brains fried."

"All right," said Wolfie. "So let's have a code word for speaking a zillion languages. What about . . . um . . . Twizzle?"

"Sounds like a cartoon show for babies," snorted Tala.

"No, it's good," said Zi'ib. "It's like all our names mixed up."

"Then what about . . . Zolfata or Twozlib?"

"Shut up. This is serious," said Wolfie. "If one of us isn't speaking English, warn them by saying Twizzle. And from now on we'll get my mum to do our French homework so we can all get rubbish marks."

He ripped a page out of Sarah's accounts book. "Let's make a checklist of everything else we've got in common." He drew three columns with their names at the top. "OK. For a start, we've all got green eyes with yellowy bits." He made a note.

"None of our dads are around," said Tala. "And you're the only one who's still got their mom."

Zi'ib turned away and buried his face deep in Elvis's

122

fur. Wolfie winced, "I'll put 'dad – missing' for all of us," he said quickly. "Though it's not that strange. There's millions of kids without fathers."

He blinked. Meanings seemed to be slipping around the page, hidden beneath the scrawl of ink. Slowly a connection floated free.

"Hey – in our names . . . there's a meaning. Hairy beast. No . . . dog. No . . . wolf!"

Tala rolled her eyes.

"Not just mine. Yours as well." He rubbed his face in concentration. "Tala's some ancient American name for she-wolf and Zi'ib's *wolf* in, I dunno, Arabic . . . Hebrew . . . Persian?"

Tala peered at the piece of paper and looked up, shaken.

"That . . . is . . . soooo creepy."

"What is?" asked Sarah, struggling in with a bag of groceries. She beamed at Zi'ib and Tala, thrilled that Wolfie had brought friends home. Dumping the shopping on the table, she shook off her coat. Zi'ib looked away, astonished by her purple leotard, scarlet tights and thick woolly leg warmers. The others didn't seem bothered. This outfit must be "normal".

"Why did you call me Wolfie?" burst out Wolfie.

"It was your dad's idea. Why?"

"We're, um, doing a project on the origin of names," put in Tala quickly.

"I think it's old Norse or something," said Sarah. "I'll go and change, then I'll make you something to eat."

123

"Great," said Zi'ib. "The vicar's cooking is gross and the school dinners smell like old socks. I haven't had a decent meal since—"

Wolfie glared at him. Sarah gaped and Tala opened her mouth. For once nothing came out.

"Hey, guess what?" said Wolfie lamely. "Erm . . . Zi'ib's mum taught him English when he was little. And when he got injured it . . . sort of got wiped from his brain and . . . and now he's better, it's all coming back."

"Zi'ib, that's wonderful. I. . ." Sarah whirled round, deafened by the grinding bleat of a bagpipe. "What's that?"

"Just Grandpa's old radio. I managed to get it working," said Wolfie, struggling to hide the dangling plug and kick the old suitcase under the table.

"I haven't seen that for years. Where did you find it?"

"*Ach, das lag einfach so in meinem Zimmer 'rum,*" replied Wolfie, too busy trying not to fall over to realize he was speaking German.

"Zitwoz, er . . . wozzlat," hissed Tala.

"What?" shouted Sarah over the skirling Highland reel.

"I dunno, kind of lying around upstairs!" cried Wolfie, breaking into a sweat. He shoved the radio on the dresser and snatched up the *Thornham Gazette*.

"Anything good on telly?"

Sarah gazed at them, gripped by the same chill unease she had felt at Mr Forester's lecture. "I'll get changed then," she said, hurrying upstairs.

On her return she pretended not to notice them break off their whispered conversation or hurry to conceal a sheet of paper.

"It's Wolfie's birthday on Sunday," she said brightly. "Why don't we all go to the cinema and afterwards I could cook something Middle Eastern—" She stopped. What had she said? Zi'ib and Tala looked distraught.

"It's my birthday on Sunday as well," said Tala softly.

"And mine," said Zi'ib.

"Well, fancy that," said Sarah, smoothing the tablecloth. She fumbled for a comment that would have everybody laughing and agreeing that, just like the colour of their eyes, this shared birthdate was just a mildly interesting coincidence. Nothing sprang to mind.

The children turned away. Every new revelation seemed to be causing a dim, disturbing light in their minds to glow a little brighter. Tala and Wolfie stared unseeingly at the television while Zi'ib rang the vicar to tell him where he was, purposely mangling the words as he tried to explain away his sudden command of English. He need not have worried. The Reverend Peasemarsh seemed quite unperturbed and just went on speaking in the slow, disjointed staccato he always used when talking to old people and foreigners.

When the news came on there was a report by Rex Slinfold, live from Ouagadougou.

"Creep," announced Zi'ib, shifting his injured leg, which itched constantly. "He came to the hospital just once after my operation, did a quick follow-up story, and then I never heard from him again."

"Well, thank goodness for Godfrey Peasemarsh," said Sarah. "He's such a kind man."

They ate supper in subdued silence and everyone was relieved when Mr Forester came crashing through the back door, swinging his theodolite.

"I've made you stuffed apples," said Sarah.

"A treat indeed," replied Mr Forester.

"Do you want it on a tray?"

"I think I'll join you down here, if I may. I want to try a little experiment."

Pulling up a chair, he nodded at Zi'ib. "*As-salaamu alaikum*."

For one terrible moment the children thought he was speaking Twizzle, but when Zi'ib answered in startled Arabic, Mr Forester held up his hand and laughed.

"Whoa, there! Sorry old chap. *As-salaamu alaikum* is about as far as it goes for me."

Squeaky with relief, Zi'ib said, "That's OK, Mr Forester. My English is improving by the day, erm, now that my memory is coming back . . . er, after the operation."

"Good, good," said Mr Forester. "Now let me show you something."

He wrestled a couple of newly ironed shirts from the airer and, tossing them aside, used the wire-cutting attachment on his Swiss Army knife to snip the coathangers into two L-shaped rods about thirty centimetres long. Placing a beaker of water on the table, he gripped the rods by the short ends as if cocking a pair of cowboy pistols.

"Now watch this," he commanded, his eyebrows leaping like excited terriers.

Everybody stared fixedly at the rods, trying not to giggle as the seconds ticked by. Mr Forester's eyebrows drooped. "Ah, well, just one more of life's little disappointments," he sighed.

"You just need a bit more practice," said Sarah. "Wolfie's grandpa used to do conjuring tricks and it always took him ages to get them right."

"It wasn't a conjuring trick," replied Mr Forester, looking hurt.

"What was it then?" asked Wolfie, reaching for the rods.

With a loud bang the lights went out, plunging the kitchen into darkness. Elvis whimpered. The radio hissed, the water pipes shook as though they were about to explode and an eerie glow moved up the rods. When it reached the tips, they began to turn in Wolfie's hands like propeller blades, spinning faster and faster. As the noise in the pipes reached a crescendo, the rods stopped abruptly. One came to a halt pointing straight at the ceiling; the other jerked downwards, pointing to the floor. With a clatter, Wolfie shook them out of his hands. After a moment of stunned silence, the lights flickered back on.

"Heavens! What on earth was that about?" said Sarah.

"I think it was about the heavens *and* the earth, my dear," replied Mr Forester staring enviously at Wolfie. "If I'm not much mistaken, he picked up one of the energy paths that link us to the greater cosmos."

"Are you all right, Wolfie?" asked Sarah.

"I – I think so," stammered Wolfie, studying his tingling fingers.

"Your hair's all sticking up," said Tala.

Wolfie tried to flatten it with his hands but it kept springing up again.

"I've *got* to get these electrics looked at," said Sarah, hurrying to the storeroom to inspect the fuse box.

"Is that what you wanted those bits of wire to do when *you* were holding them, Mr Forester?" asked Zi'ib, wondering if this was another traditional English pastime he would have to get used to.

Mr Forester gazed at the rods in awe. "I certainly wasn't expecting anything quite so spectacular. I merely hoped they would cross when they detected the water." He thumbed through his notebook. "In fact, never in all my research have I come across anything like it – quite, quite extraordinary."

"How can old coathangers detect water?" asked Tala.

"It's called dowsing. It's a very ancient art, although seemingly it only works if, like Wolfie here, you've got the knack."

"What else can you dowse for?"

"Underground streams, minerals, metals, energy fields — if you're lucky, even lost objects, like keys. And if you dowse over a map you can search for something anywhere in the world without even leaving the house."

The itch in Zi'ib's leg was unbearable. He grabbed one of the rods and rammed it under the plaster. With a yell he yanked it out. The tip was glowing white-hot, the lights flickered and the shop door clanged.

"You too." Mr Forester gazed at him, awestruck.

"Er . . . how about a nice . . . cup of herbal tea?" said Tala quickly.

"Oh, yes. An excellent suggestion," said Mr Forester, his eyes still fixed on Zi'ib. "Perhaps we should try a calming combination of dogwort and camomile. I blended it myself only this morning."

18

The Book of Light

Mr Forester soon retired to his room to contemplate his failings as a dowser and Sarah went out to deliver a painting. Torn between curiosity and fear, the children gathered around the coathangers, wondering if Tala also "had the knack".

"Go on," urged Zi'ib.

Gingerly she prodded the metal, unsure whether the faint tingling in her fingertip was real or imagined.

"Hurry up," said Wolfie impatiently.

Taking a deep breath, she grasped both rods. The ends began to glow a deep orangey red, the metal grew hot in her hands and the kitchen lights dimmed. She felt herself being pulled through the kitchen and, moving like a dancer in a dream, she glided across the flagstones with arms outstretched, circled the table, then lurched towards the dresser. The boys watched in silence as the tips of the rods came together in a V shape, pointing towards the old radio.

"She's in a trance," breathed Zi'ib.

Wolfie snapped his fingers in Tala's eyes. She didn't blink. He shouted her name. No response. He threw the beaker of water in her face. There was a faint sizzling as the drops spattered on to the metal, but she didn't move. He reached for the rods, then froze, afraid.

"Here!" shouted Zi'ib, flinging him the oven gloves.

Shoving them on, Wolfie just managed to wrench the rods free and hurl them to the floor before the dizzying throb in his fingers grew unbearable. Immediately the lights came back on and Tala found herself staring at her outstretched hands, with water dripping from her hair.

"Something was calling to me, something glittery and spiky like . . . like a Christmas decoration," she said.

Wolfie unscrewed the back of the old radio and pulled out the jagged piece of metal. "Did it look like this?"

Tala nodded dumbly at the shiny scrap Wolfie laid on her upturned palm.

"What is it?" asked Zi'ib.

"I think it's some kind of battery. It makes the radio work," said Wolfie.

"Where's the rest of it?"

"Dunno. But this was with it." Wolfie handed him the old book.

Frowning, Zi'ib turned the brittle pages. "How old is this?"

Wolfie shrugged. "Search me."

"These notes in the front say Rivers, Mountains and Forests but the rest is weird."

Tala peered over Wolfie's shoulder. "Where d'you find all this stuff?"

"In the attic. This bright light came through the skylight and kind of led me to a hidden compartment under the window seat—" He broke off, embarrassed.

She smoothed the singed edges. "These pages have been in a fire."

"There's something under the ink," Zi'ib said. He tilted the spine so a milky mark showed through the pale parchment: a gleaming wreath of snarling beasts, their tails and muzzles interlocked in a seamless circle.

Wolfie traced the image with his finger and as they stood side by side, touching the book, a quiet fell between them. A cloud seemed to lift from the pages and the meaning of the strange script poured into their minds. Tala clamped her hand to her mouth in surprise. Instantly the meaning ebbed away.

"Put your hand back!" cried Wolfie. "Don't you get it? It only works when all three of us are touching it."

Tala slammed both hands on the book. Wide-eyed and disbelieving, they watched the mist part once more.

The Book of Light
In the dark days before the secrets of the living worlds were known, there dwelled at the foot of the Centaur a

warrior race who sought dominion over all other races. They commanded their scholar slaves to collect all the Knowledge of the earth and the seas and the skies, for the warriors believed that if they held the key to the mysteries of the past and the present they could unlock the mysteries of the future, and then they would be gods.

But the wise slaves feared the evil purpose of the warriors, and they withheld their Knowledge. Their defiance angered the warriors and the scholar slaves were persecuted and tortured until their numbers dwindled.

And so the slaves secretly planned their escape. The bravest among them was Seth, the son of Akmon, who was but a boy. In the dead of night he stole the great treasure of the warriors, placed it in a basket and led the slaves into the starless Wilderness, homeless fugitives in search of refuge. The way was harsh and treacherous, and soon even the hardiest among them grew weary and weak.

Many died on that journey and only a small band of the strong in spirit came safely to a treeless world buried beneath the ashes of a great volcano. By the light of the twin moons Dido and Elissa, they journeyed to a ridge of white mountains where the Wild Wolves roamed. And the Wolves saw the slaves were wise. They gave them meat and water and led them to a great crater in the hillside. From the centre of the crater rose a spur of black quartz whose root spread like a mantle beneath the land, and there the weary wounded travellers rested for the night, warmed by the breath of the beasts who circled them. And when the slaves awoke the next day, their eyes had become like emeralds flecked with gold, for they had drunk of the waters of the river Esh.

Three pairs of emerald eyes met for a moment and the text blurred.

"Concentrate!" hissed Wolfie.

Seth feared the slaves could not survive in the Lands of the Wolf, for the soil was scorched and barren. In answer to his doubts, the Wise Wolves told him how each living world that floats upon the Wilderness is bound by threads of force that breathe the breath of life.

They showed him how to use that force to kindle fire, to make the barren lava bloom, to heal the wounds of flesh and move great rocks to build a shelter. The slaves marvelled at these things and asked what manner of wondrous force this was. The Wise Wolves answered that it flowed from the Wisdom of the Stars, but warned that men who drew upon this force must husband and replenish it, lest it weaken and wane. The slaves hung their heads, for they knew not how to replenish such Wisdom. And the Wolves raised them up and told them that the Wisdom of the Stars is but Knowledge tempered with true understanding.

At first the slaves were doubtful and confused, but as the Wolves taught them how to read the secrets hidden in the petals of a flower, the spirals of a shell or the fallen flakes of snow, the slaves began to glimpse the eternal truths of life itself. And then the Wisdom of the Stars would appear above their heads, made manifest as sparks of force. The slaves stored these sparks in the mantle of black quartz that ran beneath the earth and they built great needles of stone to draw the precious forces through the land.

And Seth saw that the fires fuelled by these forces burned brighter than any fires fuelled by the wood of trees, and he looked upon the landscape with new eyes.

Their senses sharpened almost beyond bearing, Wolfie, Tala and Zi'ib could hear the flowing waters of the river Esh, feel the rough fur of the Wise Wolves and see the barren landscape ridged by white mountains.

"What does it mean?" whispered Tala at last.

"Who knows?" said Wolfie. "But it's like this old book's been lying up there for years, just waiting for the three of us to come together. And what I want to know is why."

The following night the exiled members of the Manus Sacra, scattered across three continents of the earth, stood clutching their stars, awaiting orders from their Leader. As the clock of St Michael's Church in Thornham struck twelve, his message shimmered across the leys, sent from a tiny planet nestling in the heart of the constellation Lupus.

And the Chosen shall prevail.
Today is the dawn of their thirteenth year.

You have done all you can and now you must stay your hands.

From this day on the progeny must walk the path in darkness.

A hundred golden stars blazed bright as the Master of the Exiles, his most trusted aide, Ridian Winter, and all the lesser exiles replied in silent, jubilant chorus.

> *So many moons have waxed and waned*
> *Since we the Chosen few were free.*
> *We watch sweet Wisdom's power profaned*
> *By worthless vassals, foul to see.*
> *Yet we a sacred oath have sworn:*
> *That pure-bred blood once more will rise.*
> *And when we greet that golden dawn*
> *The worlds shall cower before the wise.*

19

On This Day

James Bond wouldn't have any trouble tracking down mad scientists who hot-wired kids' brains together so they could decipher freaky old books. It wasn't so easy if you weren't trained as a secret agent and had no idea who you were looking for. Wolfie crammed a handful of popcorn into his mouth and took a noisy slurp of Coke, bought with Matthias Threlfall's generous contribution to the birthday celebrations. Maybe Tala's uncle wasn't a *total* creep, even if he did wear stupid shades all the time. He glanced around at the rows of eager faces staring at the cinema screen, wondering if any of them had ever been forced to wear oven gloves to stop themselves getting frazzled to death by bits of old coathanger.

They walked back through the freezing rain to the

welcoming warmth of the kitchen and had barely finished stuffing themselves with spiced Moroccan lamb when Sarah produced a huge birthday cake ablaze with thirty-six candles. After the food came presents. The vicar had sent round smart pen-and-pencil sets. Sarah gave Zi'ib and Tala hand-knitted scarves and gloves and Wolfie a wooden box of acrylic paints with his initials stamped on the lid. From Mr Forester there was a torch for Zi'ib and a delicate silver chain for Tala. He waved away their thanks, insisting they were bargains he had picked up in the second-hand shop on Dodds Hill, and handed Wolfie a large circular parcel wrapped in brown paper. Inside was the top of an old sundial. Glued upright in the centre was a magnifying glass on an adjustable stand, and taped to the number XII was a firework with the words *Deluxe Super Rocket* printed down the touch paper in bright purple letters. Wolfie did not know what to say.

"I made it myself," said Mr Forester proudly. "It's a noon-day cannon."

"A what?"

"I'll take you all out on the common when the weather is fine and we can fire it. You position it so that at midday the sun shines directly through the glass, lights the firework and . . . kabooom!"

"Great," said Wolfie politely. "Thanks very much."

Instead of birthday cards, Mr Forester gave each of them a signed copy of his seminal monograph, *Evidence for an Electric Universe.*

"Can we help with the washing up?" offered Zi'ib.

"Certainly not, it's your birthday," said Sarah. "That programme *On This Day* is on in a minute. It might be fun to see what else has happened on the fourteenth of November."

Munching third helpings of cake, Zi'ib and Tala squeezed next to Elvis on the sofa. Wolfie switched on the television and pulled out a postcard he had removed that morning from the shop window. It read: *Bargain. Laptop computer £75.*

"We've got to get the money somehow," he whispered beneath the blare of the *On This Day* title music. "We can't risk using public computers for researching weird stuff."

Rippling sand dunes filled the screen, stretching into the distance like golden waves, and with a rumble of drums a curve of pointed, red-brick pyramids shimmered into view.

"This is Meroe in northern Sudan. . ."

Zi'ib put down his cake. "That's near where I used to live," he said. The music grew eerie beneath the narration.

"Meroe remains one of the greatest mysteries of the ancient world. Its people were once the unconquerable masters of Africa and their civilization rivalled that of Egypt, but we know almost nothing of their history or culture. We have no idea where the Meroites came from or why their great cities crumbled to dust. And that's because no one has ever deciphered their language. . ."

The landscape dissolved to an inscription on a slab of stone, which to Wolfie, Tala and Zi'ib was quite obviously the story of a king snatching power from a group of evil priests.

". . .no one, that is, until a young archaeologist named Zane Bakri began work on this ancient site."

Zi'ib's mouth dropped open. The shot cut to a photograph of a handsome dark-haired man smiling down from the top of a ruin. "It's my father," he choked.

Sarah and Mr Forester rushed to the television.

"Bakri claimed he had cracked the secrets of Meroitic. Eager to share his findings with the world, he travelled to London to discuss a book deal with distinguished academic publishers Snodgrass, Beamish and Hussey, who specialize in works on ancient history."

A flat-fronted Georgian building appeared on the screen.

"Charming people," murmured Mr Forester. "They always return my manuscripts with the most courteous letters of rejection."

"But the contract was never signed, because on this day, ten years ago, Zane Bakri, his manuscript and all the notes relating to his staggering discovery disappeared. No trace of him or his work has been seen since."

The caption *Ffarley Snodgrass – Publisher* appeared beneath a man in his mid-thirties with finely chiselled features and unruly auburn hair.

"If his claims were true – as I am convinced they were – and I had been able to publish his work, Zane Bakri would

140

have been up there with Michael Ventris, who deciphered Linear B, and Jean-François Champollion, who decoded the Rosetta Stone. His discovery would have changed the whole way we think about the ancient past and possibly the whole way we think about the future."

"Blimey," said Wolfie.

Zi'ib was trembling visibly. "He vanished on my second birthday. I never knew that."

His heart was pounding so loudly he almost missed the start of the interview with Professor Yassir Salah of the University of Khartoum. The professor, who was balding and neatly bearded, spoke in almost accentless English.

"There were those who blamed Bakri's disappearance on jealous colleagues who wanted to deprive him of academic glory. There were some who claimed he had been silenced because he had discovered the clues to a priceless treasure buried beneath the ruins. And there were others who said that he fell victim to a curse that strikes all those who try to unlock the ancient secrets of Meroe." The music rose to a climax and the camera panned from the professor to the crumbling pyramids. "All we know for sure is that ten years on, nobody is any nearer to solving the mystery of Zane Bakri's disappearance or the enigma of Meroe's lost language."

The end credits rolled. Elvis jumped from the sofa and disappeared upstairs. With a tap at the back door, the vicar came in. His cheery "Hello everybody!" was greeted by a barrage of garbled accounts of the programme.

"Well, well," he said. "Did you know about your father's work, Zi'ib?"

"Not really. Mum mentioned he'd helped on some excavation but I never knew it was such a big deal." He frowned. "It's weird. It said that programme was filmed by Christie Johnson. He's the one who sent me that money." A vague picture of a kind, lived-in face scrunched against a camera drifted into his mind. "I'm going to get in touch with him, see if he knows anything more about my father. *And* I'm going to go and see that Snodgrass bloke."

"We'll come with you," said Wolfie.

"Detective work is always such fun," said the vicar, cutting himself a slice of birthday cake. "I almost wish I had time to join you."

20

The Hetherington Essay Competition

The following morning Zi'ib had a hospital appointment. He had been booked in for a series of tests but Mr Andrews was so pleased with his progress that he cancelled them and Zi'ib was back after break, just in time for a tirade from Mr Grimes about the abysmal standard of class 7G's essays on the Egyptians.

"At this rate we'll stand no chance in the Hetherington history competition," he was saying as Zi'ib pushed open the classroom door with one of his crutches.

"Who cares," muttered Marcus.

"*You* should, Marcus, because the first prize is two hundred pounds and the winner's school receives a substantial contribution to its funds."

The mention of prize money raised a flicker of interest.

"Ravenscroft Green have won three years running. We

can't let them beat us again. This year's topic is local history. Marks will awarded for original research as well as presentation."

The class groaned.

"Come on, this could be a real chance for Blackstone to shine. I'm going to divide you into groups so you can share the research, the writing, and" – he smiled wistfully – "in the event of victory – the prize money."

"So. Freddie, Jordan and Sanjay, you'll be working on the history of our local dogs' home. Jessica and Lucy – Thornham was once famous for its corset factory. I want you to research its workers, its products and its demise. Marcus and Wayne – I've got just the thing for you: the House of Juvenile Correction on Whitley Road, now an amusement arcade."

He carried on through the class until he came to Wolfie.

"Wolfie, I understand your family has been running their confectionery business for generations, so why don't you, Tala and Zi'ib find out a bit more about the history of the Browns?

"I'm giving you Friday afternoon off to do your research. The library, town hall and church all hold records which you may find useful. I want to see draft essays and photocopies of your source material by the end of next week so I can pick which ones will be worked up to go forward to the judges."

He spent the rest of the lesson showing them flickering black-and-white footage of horse-drawn carts rolling down

144

Thornham High Street, men erecting the war memorial on the old stone plinth at the crossroads, and workers leaving the corset factory. There was even a shot of the sweet shop from the 1930s with a placard outside advertising *Brown's Traditional Fudge*.

"It was in much better nick then than it is now," Wolfie said ruefully on the way to the canteen. "It even had some customers."

"I found *Snodgrass, Beamish and Hussey* in the phone book," said Zi'ib, taking long swinging steps on his crutches. "It looks like we can take the 717 bus nearly all the way there. Let's go on Friday afternoon and work on our essay over the weekend."

"If we win, we can get that computer," said Tala eagerly.

"Fat chance," said Wolfie. "Why didn't Grimes give us the dogs' home or something interesting to write about?"

Tala piled Zi'ib's food on to her tray and they looked around for somewhere they would not be overheard. Madame Dubois and Mr Pinkney were just leaving. Wolfie grabbed their table. Setting down his tray, he whispered to Zi'ib, "One thing's pretty obvious about your dad."

"What?"

"He speaks Twizzle."

Zi'ib frowned. "Maybe he cracked Meroitic by working it out."

"Come on – it's too much of a coincidence."

Zi'ib's eyes grew wide. "Do you think he got abducted by the people running the language experiment?"

"More likely by people who wanted to find out about it."

They poked at their food, their appetites gone.

"Look out," murmured Tala.

Marcus and Wayne were prowling towards their table, ready for some fun now the teachers had left.

"Let's go," said Zi'ib.

They made for the exit, almost colliding with Madame Dubois on her way back into the canteen.

"Hey, Beanpole, you forgot something," shouted Wayne, dangling the brown leather bag that had been hanging from the back of Tala's chair. The pupils at the nearby tables watched with interest as he lifted a bowl of banana custard above his head and tipped its lumpy contents into the bag.

"It's not my bag," shrugged Tala.

"No, Wayne! It is mine," shrieked Madame Dubois, her face contorted with fury. "And your wretched little life 'as just ceased to be worth living."

21

Snodgrass, Beamish
and Hussey

Icy wind whipped through a crack in the window as the 717 bus ploughed through central London. Two women got on at Vauxhall, sharing lurid secrets in Slovenian. Embarrassed, the children fiddled with their tickets and tried not to giggle. The bus swerved. One of Zi'ib's crutches fell off the seat, hitting the younger woman, who bent down to hand it back.

"Sorry about that. Thanks a lot," said Zi'ib.

"Twizzle," hissed Tala.

A blush of deepest red swept from the woman's throat to the roots of her bright blonde hair. Her companion's cackling laughter broke off. They stared at Zi'ib, aghast. This African child with strange green eyes spoke fluent Slovenian. Mortified, they got off at the next stop.

"We've really got to watch it," said Wolfie.

But living in a city as crowded and diverse as London, it was hard to ignore the constant buzz of jokes and gossip, plots and blandishments from all around the world.

They got off at the end of Great Russell Street, bought bags of roasted chestnuts from a vendor outside the British Museum, and stood warming themselves against the little metal brazier, cracking the soft, creamy flesh out of the blackened shells.

"There it is," said Tala.

She and Wolfie dodged through the traffic to a dark blue door tucked between a bookshop and a clockmaker's. Panting and nervous, Zi'ib limped after them. When he rammed his thumb against the brass doorbell, a listless voice rasped, "Yes?" over the intercom.

"We've come to see Mr Snodgrass," said Zi'ib.

"Do you have an appointment?"

"No. It's about Zane Bakri. He's my father."

After a moment's silence the door swung open. They stepped into a square hallway paved with black and white tiles. The dark-red walls were hung with framed prints of ancient ruins and posters splashed with glowing reviews of Snodgrass, Beamish and Hussey's books: *Winner of the prestigious Lorkin prize! An outstanding work of faultless scholarship!* Wolfie gazed at the selection of glossy hardbacks displayed in a glass-and-mahogany case. One lay open at a photograph of a sunlit obelisk, captioned with the words, *The Greeks saw these needles of stone as solidified celestial fire.* It was an idea which struck him as both ridiculous and strangely compelling.

They squeezed into an ancient brass lift that looked like an oversized birdcage. Zi'ib cranked the brass lever, the lift jolted upwards and they watched the scuffed brogues, rumpled trousers, threadbare linen cuffs and finally the wild auburn locks of Ffarley Snodgrass appear through the bars. He thrust aside the lift door with eyes only for Zi'ib.

"Zane Bakri's son!" he cried. "Yes, yes – the resemblance is amazing. Mopsa!" He flung his hand towards an ethereal-looking assistant with fluffy fair hair tied up with a pink satin ribbon. "Hold my calls, and could you bring us some tea?"

He led them into a book-lined office whose tall windows overlooked the columned portico of the British Museum. A log fire flickered in the marble fireplace. On the wall above it hung a portrait of an elderly man who seemed to be regarding the state-of-the-art computer on the desk with an expression of bewildered disdain. Despite his long white beard and pince-nez, he bore a distinct resemblance to Ffarley.

"Have a seat," the publisher was saying, staring hungrily at the plastic carrier bag looped over the handle of Zi'ib's crutches.

As Zi'ib lowered himself into one of the leather armchairs, Ffarley lost control. With nostrils flaring and eyes burning, he grabbed the carrier bag and pulled out a package wrapped in silver foil.

"What is it?" he breathed. "An artefact from Meroe? The keystone to the code?"

"It's some cheese and pickle sandwiches the vicar made us," replied Zi'ib.

Ffarley slung the package aside. Delving into the bag, he fished out a bundle of papers and began to rifle through them. After a minute he looked up, almost in tears.

"These are just copies of the Meroitic inscriptions. Where are the translations? Where is the manuscript?" he bellowed.

"I d-don't know," stammered Zi'ib.

Ffarley emptied the bag, kicked aside a half-eaten Aero and pounced on the framed photograph of Zi'ib's family. Zi'ib struggled to his feet.

"I'm sorry, Mr Snodgrass," he cried. "I just brought along those papers and that photo to prove I'm Zane Bakri's son."

"There's no mystery about your identity," snapped Ffarley.

To everyone's astonishment, he started to pull at the catches holding the wooden backing on to the frame.

This was too much for Zi'ib. "What are you doing?" he cried. Struggling to his feet, he lurched forward to rescue his precious photograph.

"There might be a clue hidden behind the picture," roared Ffarley, skipping nimbly out of his reach. Wolfie and Tala tried to snatch the photograph from his hands and as they wrestled, the backing came away and something fell on to the faded Persian carpet. Ffarley swooped to pick it up and held it to the light. Wolfie gasped. It was a spiky scrap of hammered metal, almost identical to the one he had found in his grandpa's radio. Ffarley carefully studied the strange web-like pattern and the series of spirals; then, certain they held no clue to Meroitic, he tossed the object on to his desk and threw himself full length across the chaise longue.

"You must forgive me. I'm sorry, I don't even know your name."

"It's Zi'ib. These are my friends, Wolfie and Tala."

"Well, apologies to all of you if my behaviour seemed a little . . . untoward, but for ten years I've been waiting for someone to turn up with a copy of Zane Bakri's manuscript. When Zi'ib said who he was, I thought that day had come. Sadly, I was wrong." He clutched his brow. "Perhaps I shall go to my grave without ever discovering what happened to Zane or his manuscript."

"No you won't, because that's exactly what we're going to find out," said Zi'ib, who had quietly retrieved the scrap of metal and slipped it into his pocket. "So we'd like you to tell us exactly what happened when you met him."

Tala took out her notebook and pen.

"All right," said Ffarley. "I'll tell you everything on condition that you contact me immediately if you find him or the manuscript."

"It's a deal," said Zi'ib.

Ffarley twisted the gold signet ring on his little finger.

"It was just after my father died and I took over the business. Things were a bit sticky. Despite my first in ancient history from Oxford and accolades for my doctoral thesis, some of the shareholders were kicking up a fuss about my ability to run the firm. Our backlist was prestigious, our authors internationally renowned, but I was under pressure to find some earth-shattering new scholarship that would prove to the world that Snodgrass, Beamish and Hussey had a dynamic future as well as a glorious past. When your father wrote to me saying he had deciphered the lost language of Meroe, naturally I suspected it was a hoax. But I knew that if he really had cracked Meroitic, it would be the making of both of us, so I agreed to meet him." He paused. "I'm not going too fast?"

Tala shook her head.

"When he turned up with his manuscript, I read a few pages and couldn't believe what I was looking at. This was it! A book whose publication would make history, and whose revelations might very well change it. I said I would read the rest of the material overnight and we arranged to meet here for breakfast the following morning.

"I took the manuscript home and I'd just finished the first chapter when I heard a crash. I rushed outside to find that some idiot had smashed into my car. He was very apologetic and took ages writing out all his details. When I got back I found the study window open and the manuscript gone. I had clearly been the victim of a cat burglar."

Mopsa entered with a tray of tea and biscuits. Ffarley bit into a chocolate digestive.

"The following morning I came into the office and waited all day, but I never heard from Zane again. And when I contacted the Department of Antiquities in Khartoum, they told me he had never returned to Sudan.

"A few days later I discovered that the car that hit mine was stolen and the driver's details were completely bogus. I had no proof, but I began to suspect it had all been a clever ruse to give his accomplice a chance to steal the manuscript."

Strange new emotions thrilled Zi'ib's nerves. Who were these people? How had they known about his dad's work? "Do you think it was stolen by someone else working on Meroitic?" he asked.

"That was my first thought, and of course I've kept a very close eye on all subsequent works on Meroitic culture, but as yet no one has plagiarized the text or claimed it for their own. It is as if Zane Bakri and his manuscript had never existed."

"And you never heard *anything* more about it?" demanded Zi'ib.

"Not a word."

"Ffarley, that's not quite true," said Mopsa. "When I reorganized your filing system, I found a letter from someone who had met Zane Bakri in Sudan, asking whether any copies of the manuscript had ever turned up."

Ffarley rubbed his chin. "Ah yes, I vaguely remember something of the sort. Could you dig it out?"

While they waited, Ffarley took down Zi'ib's address and gave him his card. Mopsa returned moments later, clutching a letter.

"Here it is," she said, tapping the signature with a crimson fingernail. "It was from a Dr Matthias Threlfall."

22

A Bolt From the Blue

"I told you Matthias was a devious creep," panted Tala. As they stumbled to the bus stop, she was still trembling with shock. "Your dad, my mum – who else does he know who just happens to have 'gone missing'?"

They slid unsteadily on to the back seat of a 717.

"Do you think Farley realized we knew Matthias?" said Wolfie.

"No. He was too busy scoffing chocolate biscuits and hurling himself on sofas. What a loony," pronounced Zi'ib. Fired by this slender lead to his father, his face had suddenly come alive.

"As soon as Matthias gets home I'm going to confront him," said Tala.

"No," said Zi'ib quickly. "He mustn't know we're on to

him. We'll search your house and see what else we can find out." He showed the pointy scrap of metal to Wolfie. "This has got to be the other half of yours."

"Put it away," hissed Wolfie, glancing round. "You never know who's watching."

The journey back to Thornham took over an hour. While Tala and Zi'ib whispered and fidgeted, impatient to begin the search, Wolfie sat very still, staring at the London streets. It wasn't *his* uncle who turned out to be connected to Zi'ib's dad, so why had the revelation severed all hope that his life would ever return to normal?

"He's never home before six," said Tala, waving them into the hallway of number 45. "We've got at least an hour. Let's start with his study. Top floor."

Zi'ib followed the others upstairs, swinging his weight between one crutch and the banister. He wanted to find out everything he could about Matthias Threlfall and he wasn't going to let a few steps get in his way.

Tala tried the handle of Matthias's study. It was locked.

"It's OK," she said. "Zi'ib, chuck me your crutch."

She ran it along the picture rail and grinned when the key fell to the floor. With a hurried glance down the stairs, she turned the lock. A sliver of light appeared. Wolfie and Zi'ib held their breath, petrified that Matthias would come storming out.

"Told you there's no one here."

"So why's the light on?" asked Wolfie. Cautiously he stepped into a stark white room laid out like a laboratory.

It contrasted sharply with the shabby disrepair of the rest of the house.

"It isn't. It's the glow from those rocks." Zi'ib nodded towards a large glass cabinet containing two pyramids of crystal bathed in a silvery-green luminescence.

"Weird," said Wolfie, pressing his nose against the glass. The crystals glowed brighter, as if responding to his presence. "Hey, look at this."

Tala and Zi'ib weren't listening. They were inspecting the tall display cases lining the wall behind the desk. Each glass-fronted drawer contained rows of rock samples laid out on beds of black velvet. Zi'ib read out the neatly printed labels. "Damascus, Carnac, Bodmin, Chichen Itza. Fancy travelling round the world just to collect bits of rock."

Wolfie dragged his gaze from the glowing crystals. "Where's his computer?"

"He always takes his laptop with him," said Tala. "Help me search the desk."

The top two drawers contained only stationery and maps. The bottom one was locked. Grabbing a thin metal paper knife, she slid it into the keyhole, turned it slowly and was amazed to hear a click. The drawer was full of papers. She skimmed through them: the deeds for the house, Matthias's copy of the custody order, a folder of letters and a sheet of faded fax paper. Tala whistled. Spreading it on the desk, she read out the message written on it in a firm hand.

. . .and so if our Link of Light is not restored soon, one of us will have to return to Lupus to get help. We can't fight this evil on our own.

If all else fails, Zan will have to publish his work on Meroe. If seekers of lost wisdom discover the truths revealed in the Meroitic inscriptions, there's a hope they might come forward to help us protect the children and guide them down the dangerous path to their destiny.

It will be risky, but we must, as always, trust in truth.

Arion

Wolfie's face was bloodless. "You know what? I've got a horrible feeling that—"

"Shhh," hissed Zi'ib. He pointed down the stairs. "Matthias." The front door slammed. "You said he wouldn't be home for ages."

Tala snatched up the fax and hastily locked the drawer with the paper knife. Tiptoeing to the landing, she locked the study and, with a leg up from Wolfie, slipped the key back on the picture rail and led them down a flight of stairs to a gloomy back bedroom. The furniture was dark and heavy and the faded pink wallpaper sprigged with damp. She flicked on the electric fire and turned to Wolfie, her eyes burning into his.

"You've got a horrible feeling that what?"

He sank on to the bed and took a deep breath. "Those kids, the ones that Arion bloke was talking about . . . I think they're . . . *us*. And I think all that stuff about *paths* and *destiny* is code for some mission we're s'posed to carry out."

Until that moment Tala and Zi'ib had been hoping he would say something different – but he hadn't. And now Wolfie was longing for them to burst out laughing and tell him he was an idiot – but they didn't. They just stood there, fighting back their terror. Wolfie jumped up, his fists flexing and clenching. "At least now we know we're not imagining all this weird stuff. And I don't care if we *are* in danger and there's no one to help us. We'll find that path and we'll make our own way down it!" He stopped, rocked by the strange feeling of purpose coursing through his body.

"Why us?" demanded Tala.

"I dunno. Maybe they picked us at random. Maybe it's because we've got green eyes or were born on the fourteenth of November."

Zi'ib said, "There was a programme the other night about these monks in Tibet who made a kid head monk just because he had a birthmark on his ear and picked the right blossom from a branch. They said that was *his* destiny."

"Forget the mumbo-jumbo," said Tala. "Let's just go down and ask Matthias straight out what's going on. He doesn't scare me—"

Footsteps thudded on the stairs. Tala rammed the fax in her pocket, hardly daring to breathe as Matthias rapped on the door.

23

Matthias's Secret

"Are you hungry?" came a smooth, deep voice. "I picked up pizzas from the deli."

Matthias opened the door. Wolfie's lips parted in surprise. It was the first time he had seen Tala's uncle without dark glasses.

"Sorry, I didn't know you had company," said Matthias. "Hi, good to see you, Wolfie." He thrust out his hand to Zi'ib. "Matthias Threlfall."

Zi'ib shook the hand and without thinking said, "Zi'ib Bakri." He bit his lip. Why had he said his whole name? Any minute now Matthias would make the connection to Zane Bakri and realize they were on to him.

"I saw your photo in the paper. You're from Sudan, aren't you?"

Zi'ib nodded nervously.

"I was there a few years ago, prospecting in the northern desert for a rare kind of mica."

"What's mica?" asked Wolfie, eager to distract Matthias's attention.

"A kind of crystal I'm using to develop new technologies – pretty amazing stuff." His eyes swivelled back to Zi'ib. "What did you say your name was?"

"Zi'ib."

"Surname?"

There was a long silence.

"Bakri."

"That's strange. I met someone called Bakri while I was there – linguist, specialized in early Meroitic. He'd found some inscriptions referring to the Meroites using what sounded like the kind of mica I was looking for, even describing the exact location of their mines. He promised me a translation, then went off to London and just disappeared. I even wrote to his publisher to see if I could get hold of the manuscript and it turned out that had disappeared too." He shrugged. "Hey, sorry, I don't know why you should be interested in my work."

Zi'ib said levelly, "I *am* interested. That man was my father."

Wolfie and Tala felt a clutch of adrenaline as Zi'ib pressed on in a small flat voice. "My father, Zane Bakri, was translating the inscriptions at Meroe. Then he disappeared." His eyes drilled into Matthias, searching for guilt, fear, remorse.

"Jeez, small world or what?" said Matthias. "Now I look at you I can see the resemblance." He smiled. "Nice guy, your old man. Did he . . . ever turn up again?"

Zi'ib shook his head.

"Oh. That's tough. I'm sorry. I liked him a lot. Look, why don't you and Wolfie stay and eat. We can easily stretch those pizzas four ways."

"Thanks, but Mum's cooking us something," said Wolfie.

"Another time then." With a nod he turned and left.

Wolfie leaned against the door and let out a long breath. "Do you believe him?" he whispered.

"I dunno," said Tala. "One minute him knowing Zi'ib's dad seems too weird for words, the next it's not."

Zi'ib glared at the worn carpet, feeling hollow and cheated. He had been so sure that Matthias was hiding something, so energized by this clue to his dad's disappearance, and now it had fizzled to nothing.

"You never said Matthias had green eyes," Wolfie said to Tala.

She shrugged. "They must run in my mom's family."

Wolfie held out his hand. "Give me the fax." He smoothed it out on the bed and they crouched over it, kneeling on the floor. "Even if he *is* telling the truth, it doesn't explain everything in this message or why it was in his drawer. Who's Arion? What's the evil he's got to fight? What's a Link of Light? And this Lupus place, it means Wolf, but where is it?"

Zi'ib carefully read it through. "Whoever Arion is, it

162

reads like he knew my father really well, so how come he's spelled his name wrong?"

"It'll be a nickname," said Tala, dismissively. She was weighing each word of the message. Suddenly, like a feral cat pouncing on a snake, she stabbed the page with her finger. "It's these 'truths' Zane discovered in the Meroitic inscriptions. *They're* the important bit."

Zi'ib looked from her to Wolfie, and something in the green of their eyes helped him to focus his thoughts. "Maybe they were so important that someone snatched Dad *and* the manuscript to keep them secret!"

Fired up with excitement, he pulled out his pointy scrap of metal and held it out to Wolfie.

"Let's see if yours really is the other half of mine."

They laid them side by side on the bed, and all at once the spiked shapes made sense.

"They make a star," Wolfie whispered. "We've both got half an eight-pointed star." He ran a careful finger along the edge. "Someone's cut them deliberately; you can see the saw marks." He tried to fit them together but it was like forcing a jigsaw piece into the wrong bit of puzzle. Irritated, he pushed harder. A zigzag of light shot into the air, hovered over the bed, then burned its way through the pillow.

"Blimey, maybe they're more than just batteries," said Zi'ib.

"That could be what this is all about," said Wolfie eagerly. "Maybe they're secret prototypes."

"So how come you've both got one and I haven't?" said Tala.

"I bet you have," Zi'ib said, gazing thoughtfully around her room.

"If I do, it's probably in the States. I hardly brought anything with me."

They rummaged through her scant possessions, pulling open drawers, hurling clothes on the floor, tipping out her rucksack. Wolfie flipped open a small cloth-covered diary.

"Don't," said Tala, snatching it from his hand.

"OK, keep your hair on."

Zi'ib tried to pull the back off her hairbrush. "Ours were hidden in something old that had been around since we were little."

"I told you. I left everything behind."

"I didn't bring *anything* with me and mine still turned up," said Zi'ib. "Have you been sent any parcels?"

"No."

"And you haven't got anything that belonged to someone in your family?"

"How many times have I—" Tala stopped. Her lip quivered. She snatched away the scorched pillow. There lay the little black box that had belonged to her mother. Their heads bent close as she turned it in her hands, searching for a hidden compartment. She shook it, tapped it, snapped the lid open and shut, and inspected the pattern of tiny gold flecks floating beneath the surface of the stone.

"Never mind," said Zi'ib. "It'll probably turn up when you least expect it."

Footsteps sounded on the landing. In panic they shoved the box and the broken stars under the duvet and dived on to the bed. Matthias threw open the door, his face taut with fury.

"Tala, I don't want to embarrass you in front of your friends, but have you been in my study?"

She swallowed hard.

"Answer me, Tala. Someone's moved the papers on my desk and left some of the specimen drawers open."

"I'm sorry. I know I shouldn't have. I was looking for. . ." she thought fast, "your copy of the custody papers. I wanted to check what they said."

Matthias's expression darkened. His muscled bulk blocked their escape. The room seemed to shrink. Wolfie stood up.

"Sit down," growled Matthias, his jaw barely moving.

Wolfie sat down.

"I want the truth. Were all three of you rooting around up there?"

"Yes," said Zi'ib quietly. "We wanted to help Tala."

Matthias regarded Tala with cold, angry eyes. "I thought we had an agreement to respect each other's privacy."

Stubbornly she stared at the floor. A charged silence filled the room. Matthias seemed to come to a decision.

"It's probably safer to tell you the truth than have you blurting things out to other people."

Afraid, wary, excited, they shifted on the bed.

"As you know, I'm a geologist, an academic, but I also do a bit of . . . let's call it freelance consultancy for the government. I experiment with minerals to develop new technologies, specifically the generation of new forms of energy and the storage and communication of complex data. There are millions of dollars invested in this field and a lot of foreign governments, not to mention private companies, who'd go to almost any lengths to get hold of my research. Which is why I don't want anybody knowing about the samples I've collected or the experiments I'm conducting. Do you understand?"

They replied with solemn nods.

Matthias relaxed. "I suppose it's my fault. I'm not very good at this cloak-and-dagger stuff. In future I'll do a better job of hiding the key. OK, guys. No harm done. But in future I don't want *any* of you going near my study." He left, shutting the door behind him. They listened to his fading footsteps.

Zi'ib blew out his cheeks. "That was close."

"I *knew* there was some secret government stuff going on," said Wolfie. "No wonder he was so angry."

"Yeah, well, he'll go ballistic if he finds this fax missing," said Tala grimly. "How am I going to put it back, now he's moved the key?"

"If you can't sneak in when the door's open, we'll help you pick the lock."

"Thanks, Houdini. That makes me feel loads better."

Zi'ib threw back the duvet. "Do you think he saw the stars?"

"No," said Wolfie, shunting the chest of drawers across the door. "But there's no point taking chances."

"They've got a hole in and they're broken – why?" Zi'ib smacked them together in frustration. The stars flew from his hands and a second bolt of light shot towards Tala's box. They watched in wonder as an answering strip of light appeared around the lid. Tala forced a nail into the glowing crack. The lid split apart. Tucked inside a hidden cavity lay a third broken star.

"I knew it!" cried Zi'ib.

The star throbbed in Tala's hand as she laid it on top of the other two.

It was a solemn moment, a coming-together heavy with portent – yet of what they had no clue. The quality of air changed and the dingy little room grew still and expectant. Out of nothing, a ring of cold, white flame flared up around the three broken stars. It seemed to tear at the children's heartstrings, pulling and twining as if to weave one great rope of all their innermost dreams and torments. The flame died away.

Slowly Wolfie reached out and shifted the three shining shapes this way, that way, trying once more to match them together. The edges scraped and jarred, refusing to fit. It didn't make sense. They had three halves of three separate stars and no idea what they were for or who had the other halves.

24

Wolfie's Chart

Early next morning an emergency locksmith came round to put a high-security lock on the door of Matthias's study. When Wolfie arrived with the papers the van was blocking the drive. Tala came running out in her pyjamas, flushed and breathless.

"Did you sneak the fax back?" asked Wolfie.

"Only just. I had to creep down and give that van and Matthias's Alfa Romeo a good kicking to set off the alarms. You should have heard the racket. This fat guy in overalls and Matthias went tearing round the garden looking for car thieves. It would have been funny if I hadn't been so scared they'd find out it was me."

Wolfie was impressed.

"I stuffed the fax back, quick as I could, and I found something else in that drawer." Her eyes flicked nervously to the upstairs windows. "I'll show you later. I'll be round as soon as I've finished my chores."

They had planned to spend that Saturday afternoon working on their essay for the Hetherington prize, but when Tala burst through Wolfie's back door, the history of the Brown family was the last thing on her mind.

"I just put my star on that chain Mr Forester gave me. It was amazing. The minute it was round my neck, the jumble of languages in my head sorted itself out and I could tell which one was which. There's this fuzzy background interference all the time, like on your grandpa's radio, but those weird pulses got really strong and clear and I knew, don't ask me how, that they were coming from you and Zi'ib. I can feel them now . . . something's making Zi'ib really happy."

She was rummaging for string in the dresser drawers so Wolfie could wear his too when the vicar's rusty Mini pulled up outside. Zi'ib rushed in, and with a shout of "Ta daa!" did an unsteady twirl. His plaster and crutches were gone. Sarah looked in from the storeroom and with a whoop of joy caught him in a hug.

The vicar stood in the doorway, smiling his gappy smile. "The hospital couldn't believe the bone had healed so quickly. Of course, he'll need a long course of physiotherapy, but it's a little miracle."

Zi'ib pulled up his jeans and displayed the ragged purple scarring on his shin. "You've no idea how good it felt when they cut off the plaster! Come on, Wolfie. Let's see this famous attic."

Sarah looked on fondly as Zi'ib made a lopsided dash for the stairs. "He deserves some good news for once. Not many boys his age could have coped with all he's been through."

"Indeed," nodded Reverend Peasemarsh, his slack lips tightening. "He's a very special child. Very special indeed."

Zi'ib climbed through the trapdoor. Elvis regarded him for a moment with adoring amber eyes, before knocking him flying. In a flailing mass of flesh and fur they rolled around the floor, play fighting like excited puppies, until Zi'ib finally wriggled free.

He sat up, staring at the fantastical drawings stuck round the walls. His gaze settled on the portrait on the mantelpiece. "Who's that?"

"My dad. Mum painted it."

"What happened to him? You never said."

"He ran off when I was a baby."

"Oh."

Tala handed both boys a length of string, telling them bossily to hang their stars round their necks.

Rolling their eyes, they did as she asked. Tala gave a tight little nod of approval at the sudden play of wonder on their faces.

"It's like I can feel your heartbeats . . . no . . . more than that. It's your. . ." Zi'ib searched for words to describe the strum of Wolfie and Tala's emotions shaking his core like the throb from distant engines.

"Life forces," said Wolfie simply.

They glanced nervously at each other, feeling vulnerable and exposed, yet somehow safer.

Tala pulled out a letter. "Listen to this. I found it when I was putting the fax back. Turns out Matthias *has* been lying about being my uncle, but only 'cos Mom told him to."

Dear Matt,

Congratulations! I never dreamt you'd find crystals of that quantity or quality. But be careful. I'm sure we are still being watched, although when I look around, I see only shadows.

I'm enclosing a copy of the custody papers. Let's hope you never need to use them, but if you do, you must pretend to be Tala's uncle – the authorities here would never understand the true nature of the bond between us. Come and see us as soon as you get back.

Keep safe and trust in truth,
Kara

Tala's voice grew stiff and small. "Mom was being watched. She was in danger. Dad always said she didn't run out on us, whatever the neighbours and the cops thought."

Wolfie glanced at the portrait of his dad, wondering for

one wild moment if he had misjudged him. "Did she just kind of vanish? You know, like one minute she was in the room and the next she wasn't?"

Tala gave him a scathing look. "Course not. She told Dad she had to go away for about a week and she'd explain everything when she got back. She organized a babysitter and everything."

"Just like my dad," sighed Zi'ib. "He went on a trip and never came back."

Wolfie felt a spark of hope sputter and die.

"What does she mean, 'the true nature of the bond between us'?" said Zi'ib.

"She can't mean a bond like . . ." Tala touched her star. ". . . like ours. Not with a creep like Matthias."

"*She* must've liked him or she wouldn't have made him your guardian," Zi'ib pointed out.

Wolfie shut the trapdoor. "There's some bit of this puzzle we're just not seeing."

He tore a large sheet of paper from his sketchpad, tacked it to the wall and with a few deft pen strokes drew three figures in the middle, rough outlines, yet easily recognizable as the three of them.

"What are you doing?" said Tala.

"It helps if I draw things," said Wolfie, colouring the figure's eyes in green. "OK. Let's put in all the similarities between us we've found so far. Eye colour; our names all mean wolf." He added three wolfish silhouettes. "And same birthday." He wrote in the date.

"We can all do dowsing," said Zi'ib.

Wolfie drew rods in their hands.

"Put our parents in," said Tala.

Wolfie added three stick-figure family trees and began to fill in the names. "These are my mum and dad, Sarah and Ron. Your mum and dad, Kara and Jack. Zi'ib's dad, Zane, and his mum. . .?"

"Shadia," said Zi'ib.

His mental flash of her frightened face, her arms reaching out to protect him, struck raw pain through Wolfie and Tala's stars. Appalled, they stood motionless until the sharpness of his anguish had receded.

Wolfie wrote in Shadia's name. Then slowly he scored red crosses through the figures of their missing parents.

"I'm not sure my dad disappearing counts," he said. "He just did a runner while mum was making Grandpa's cocoa." He pressed his lips together. "Right. Who did you get your eyes from? Mine are from my dad."

"My dad," said Zi'ib.

"My mum," said Tala.

Wolfie coloured the relevant parents' eyes green. He added two more figures and labelled them Matthias and Arion. "Matthias has also got green eyes. What else do we know?" He began to draw in connecting lines and to dot them with chunks of information.

"Kara suspected she was in danger, went on a trip and disappeared. She was *really* good friends with Matthias, who knew Zane. But we don't know if she and Zane ever

173

met." He linked Zane and Kara with a broken line and a question mark.

"Arion's fax mentions a place called Lupus, which means wolf." He put LUPUS and a wolf next to Arion's name. "And we're pretty sure we're the kids he talked about who had to follow a dangerous path to their destiny, which is probably code for carrying out some mission. That's all we know about him, but from his fax, it looks like he was the one in charge; the one making plans." He glowered at the portrait of his father. Arion wasn't some lying loser who dumped his girlfriend with a kid, then ran off. "Zane found something important in the Meroitic inscriptions. When he came to London to see about publishing his book, he *and* his manuscript disappeared. Ten years later, within days of each other, Shadia got abducted and Jack disappeared."

Zi'ib came and stood by the chart. "We've all got a broken star that may be some kind of battery *and* transmitter. We don't know how they work, but they could be the reason we can speak Twizzle. Like those internet translation programmes, only this one plugs straight into your brain."

Wolfie looked at him, surprised, then drew little half stars by their names with a speech bubble by each one.

"They might be secret prototypes," added Zi'ib. "We know Matthias is involved in developing secret technology. That's got to be a link."

"And put in *The Book of Light*," said Tala. "It needs all

three of us to read it *and* it goes on about wolves and people with green eyes flecked with gold."

Wolfie did as they asked. Elvis, who was taking up most of the bed, raised his head and followed the children's gaze as they took in the colourful labyrinth of criss-crossing lines studded with stars and wolves and people.

Tala blinked. "Why have you written the notes in Aramaic?"

"So Mum can't read it – if she asks I'll tell her it's a school art project."

Tala leaned against the great dog and sighed. "We'll never find out about new technologies and brain experiments without a computer and internet access."

Zi'ib grinned, unzipped his rucksack and pulled out a laptop.

"I went round last night and got it with the money Christie Johnson sent me."

Wolfie crowed with delight. "But. . ." He looked worried. "I thought that was for your ticket back to Sudan."

Zi'ib flipped up the screen. "If this helps find my dad, *he* can buy my ticket home."

He plugged it in and pressed the power button. Nothing. He fiddled with the cable and pressed more keys, with no result.

"Cheek!" he fumed. "I'm going round right now to get my money back."

"Hang on," said Wolfie. The others looked on, mystified, as he untied his broken star. "It made the radio work." He fitted the sliver of metal into the disk drive. A whiplash of light flickered across the room.

"These stars are amazing," said Zi'ib. "It's like they're alive." He clicked the mouse button. A swirling mist filled the screen, thinning to reveal an image of an ancient city spread beneath a vast purple sky. The towers of a tall marble building glistened on a starlit hill, framed by a pair of sickle moons. Beyond the towers a glassy dome stared up from the slope like the lens of an all-seeing eye. In a flash the image was gone.

"What was that?" Tala exclaimed.

Wolfie shrugged. "Some kind of screensaver."

"This is great," said Zi'ib, nudging the others out of the way. "It's picked up someone's wireless connection."

Puzzled, Wolfie watched Zi'ib's fingers fly across the keys. "Did you learn about computers in Sudan?"

"Nope," said Zi'ib, intent on the screen. "It's like speaking Twizzle. I had a go on Godfrey's the other night and it just kind of clicked." He glanced up, sensing their unease. "Maybe I'm just a natural genius."

No one laughed.

"Look up that Lupus place," said Tala.

Zi'ib typed "Lupus" into the search engine. "It's an illness, a group of stars located between the constellations Centaurus and Scorpius, and there's a Lupus Street in Pimlico. It can't be any of them."

"Maybe L-U-P-U-S stands for a company or a secret organization like the CIA or the KGB," said Tala.

A loud banging made them jump.

"Are you ready?" called Mr Forester, rapping on the trapdoor with his walking stick. "It's nearly twelve o'clock."

"Rats!" muttered Wolfie. "He wants to show us how that noon-day cannon thing works. We'd better go or Mum'll moan at me. Coming!" he called.

"Take that stinky dog with you so I can give the place a good airing," said Sarah grumpily as they filed into the kitchen, pulling on their coats. "I wish his real owners would hurry up and claim him."

"I couldn't bear it if someone took him away," Tala said fiercely. She threw her arm round Elvis's neck and kept it there as they ran to catch up with Mr Forester.

Wolfie and Zi'ib followed behind, taking turns to carry the cannon.

Mr Forester halted beside the ruined foundations of Thornham Hall and instructed the boys to rest the cannon on the tallest stone. He watched a flock of birds flying overhead, their bodies forming a perfect arrow. Lifting his arms to the sky, he exclaimed, "Can you sense it? Doesn't it send a quiver through your marrow?"

"What?" grinned Wolfie. "The pong from Sid Poskitt's compost heap?"

"No, Wolfie. The earth energy. Those birds are using it to navigate the skies and our megalithic ancestors were once equally in tune with its ebb and flow. Of course, back then, before we polluted and corrupted the current, the force was much stronger. But this month's *Earth Mysterian* magazine reported a steep rise in the energies linking certain cardinal power points, which might explain why you three picked up such strong vibrations with the dowsing rods."

"Is Thornham a cardinal power point, then?" said Zi'ib.

"Of course. That's why there was a stone circle here. I've been plotting its exact layout and I'm sure that this foundation stone is the megalithic marker that pinpointed both the centre of the circle *and* the crossing point of the most powerful ley lines in southern England. What I've yet to establish is whether Sir Guy de Monteneuf built his house around it out of knowledge or ignorance."

"If you can't see these ley lines, how do you find them?" frowned Zi'ib.

Mr Forester smiled. "Dowsers like you can sense them using rods or twigs, but even if you can't dowse it's still very easy. You just take an Ordnance Survey map of any area and a pencil and ruler and join up the dolmens, megaliths, sacred pools, hill forts, crossroads and churches. You'll discover time after time that they're built on straight lines that can stretch for hundreds of miles."

"How come?"

"Because our ancestors built all sorts of structures on these energy lines in order to harness their power."

He pointed back down the common. "For example,

there's one extremely powerful ley that passes directly north–south through the sweet shop, this foundation stone, the church and the vicarage and carries straight on all the way up Dodds Hill." He nodded at Zi'ib. "That's probably why your leg healed so quickly; all that positive earth energy flowing through your bones every night."

Zi'ib wiggled his foot suspiciously.

Mr Forester grew thoughtful. "You know, it's rather interesting that both you boys are living in houses built exactly where a key ley line cuts the lost circle. Some might be foolish enough to call it a coincidence."

Their stars tingled with alarm.

"Personally I never use that word," continued Mr Forester. "It implies that such links are accidental when in fact they are usually part of a great pattern that could never be caused by happenstance. I've invented my own word to describe them, based on the concept of a nexus of kinship. Just as ties of kin can stretch across continents and generations, so everything tied by the power in the leys is 'kinnected' in a way that transcends time and space."

"I don't get it," said Zi'ib bluntly.

"Imagine vibrations rippling through a great, multidimensional spider's web, causing every thread and every insect trapped on those threads to resonate at the same frequency. Well, that's how the energies in the leys kinnect certain people, places and events that appear otherwise to have no link at all."

Seemingly random people, places and events strangely and suddenly connected by an invisible force? A month ago Wolfie, Tala and Zi'ib would have snorted with laughter at the very idea. Right now it didn't seem so funny.

"So where are the other leys round here?" murmured Tala. She kept her eyes fixed on the ground, while Wolfie and Zi'ib stared at the sky, willing Mr Forester to go on, yet dreading what he would say.

"There are many, but the other key line goes directly east–west, passing though the pub, the bus stop, the old dew pond, this stone and that ivy-covered house halfway down the crescent."

The blood thudded in Tala's heart.

"You mean the one on the corner of Rag Tree Road?"

"That's right," said Mr Forester.

He was pointing to her home.

It was one more unfathomable puzzle piece to add to Wolfie's chart.

25

Costantino Bruno

"To us this is a just bit of amusement," said Mr Forester, adjusting the position of the noon-day cannon and wondering why his companions looked so troubled. "But to the ancients, harnessing the power of light and shadow was a mystical art. Just as this sundial uses the sun to measure the hours of the day, so the great stone circles used the movements of the celestial bodies to measure the seasons and the years and to indicate points of power."

He checked his watch and tilted the magnifying glass until a beam of sunlight pierced the lens and cast a bright dot on to the dial. As the dot crept slowly towards the firework, Wolfie couldn't help thinking about the fiery shaft that had spilled through the attic skylight and led him to the window seat. The church clock chimed midday, the dot reached the rocket and a trail of smoke rose from the touchpaper, bursting into flame as the vicar came striding across the grass.

"Watch out!" shouted Mr Forester.

The fizzing firework screeched past the vicar, through the lychgate, into the churchyard and exploded in a cascade of purple sparks.

"This is an outrage!" yelled Godfrey Peasemarsh. "I'm surprised at you, Remus. I didn't have you down as a hooligan."

"I'm so sorry, Godfrey," apologized Mr Forester. "I was giving our young friends a practical lesson in sciatherics and I'm afraid I got a little carried away."

Tutting angrily, the vicar strode away.

"Oh dear," said Mr Forester.

They spread out across the churchyard in search of the fallen firework, Elvis trotting ahead, snuffling among the neglected, ivy-covered monuments. He stopped, suddenly tense. Wolfie ran over to find the great dog pawing the undergrowth near his grandparents' grave. Almost all the surrounding stones bore the name of Brown. Most of them were Stanleys, but there were a couple of ancient Sarahs, a William, three Georges and an Agnes. Wolfie scowled. An essay on his boring ancestors was never going to win any prizes – all they'd ever done was sell sweets. They'd probably picked these burial plots overlooking the shop so they could keep an eye on business from the grave. With a yelp Elvis leapt into a tangle of nettles and snatched up the scorched remains of the firework.

"Got it!" called Wolfie. "Good boy! Come on, let's go."

Elvis blinked his amber eyes and refused to move. As Wolfie stooped down to grab his collar, he saw a mossy, weather-worn stone poking through the undergrowth. The carved inscription, barely legible, read *Costantino Bruno 1460*.

"Hey, look at this!" he shouted.

The others came running.

"This headstone is over five hundred years old."

"Bruno . . . that's . . . Italian for Brown," said Zi'ib. "Is he one of your relations?"

"Maybe," said Wolfie thoughtfully. "And if he is and I can trace my family back to the Middle Ages, we might just be in with a chance of winning that two hundred quid." He scrambled to his feet and ran to the lychgate. "See you later."

"Where are you going?" shouted Zi'ib.

"Library!"

Thornham library was a sombre red-brick building on the high street decorated with busts of gloomy worthies, glaring down from little niches encrusted with pigeon droppings. Picking muddy paw marks off his parka, Wolfie headed to the enquiry desk. A thickset woman with sleek dark hair wound in tight coils above her ears watched him coming. Wolfie hesitated. Her hairstyle, the expression in her eyes and the curl of her lips reminded him of Sarah's portrait of Mr B, the slavering Rottweiler from number 52.

"You're that nasty paper boy who's always upsetting my Mr Booboo," said the woman accusingly.

"Sorry. Next time I'll let him gnaw my leg off," replied Wolfie.

The librarian flashed him a look of contempt. Wolfie squinted at her badge. It read Leonora Grindle.

"But . . . Miss, er, Grindle, I'm trying to find out about someone who lived in Thornham in about 1460."

"Who?"

"One of my ancestors."

She sniffed. "In the Middle Ages, only the lives of the great and the noble were recorded for posterity. *Tradesmen* and *peasants* lived and died in obscurity, unless of course they were notorious criminals."

Wolfie ignored this. "Haven't you got *anything* on medieval Thornham?"

A pleasant-faced man whose badge read *Edward Leadbetter, Chief Librarian*, came past carrying a pile of thrillers.

"You could have a look through the Preservation Society papers. We're storing them till they find a new archivist. They're sure to have something on early Thornham." He dropped his books on to a trolley. "They're in the storeroom down the corridor, last door on the left. But they're for reference only, I'm afraid –

184

you'll have to photocopy anything you want to take home."

Wolfie thanked him and dashed away.

"The copier is broken," Leonora Grindle called after him. "The engineer can't come till next week."

The small, windowless storeroom smelled of dust and floor polish. At the far end, next to an assortment of mops and buckets, stood a cupboard filled with stationery, packets of biscuits and tins of instant coffee. The other walls were lined with metal shelves crammed with boxes. Wishing he had had some lunch, Wolfie picked one at random, blew off the dust and opened it. The top file read: *Minutes of the Thornham Preservation Society AGM 1969–1972.*

The next box was full of yellowing invitations to a "Stop the Bypass" rally. It was going to be a long afternoon.

After wading through forty years of meeting agendas, endless correspondence about the foundations of Thornham Hall and a tedious pamphlet about the buttressing of St Michael's Church, Wolfie was starving. He rummaged around in the cupboard, searching for a small packet of biscuits that wouldn't be missed. The slim package he pulled out was wrapped not in colourful cellophane but drab oilskin. Intrigued, he undid the knotted string and found a cracked, leather-bound book.

It was in Latin. As he turned to the title page, he felt a rush of elation as the words of the long-dead language offered up their meaning: *The Chronicle of Thornham*. Leafing quickly through the thick, ivory-coloured pages, he came to the last chapter. The heading read: *The coming of the stranger, Costantino Bruno.*

"Yes!" he whispered, and grabbing a pencil, a notepad and a packet of ginger nuts, he settled down to read.

26

The Chronicle of Thornham

Tala thrust her head through the trapdoor. "What's up?"

"I found a book called *The Chronicle of Thornham* written by this monk Adam from Thornham Abbey. It's got a whole chapter about Costantino Bruno and he's *definitely* my ancestor," said Wolfie proudly.

"Is that all?" Tala scowled. "When Matthias said you'd phoned I thought you'd found out something important, like what's happened to our parents or what's behind that freaky thing with our houses all standing on ley lines."

"That's just it, it's all linked. I can't explain; it's all jumbled up in my brain."

"How can your ancestors have anything to do with us?" asked Zi'ib, coming up the steps behind her.

"Just listen. It's complicated but it's really amazing."

"Let's see the book."

"They wouldn't let me borrow it, but I took lots of notes."

Zi'ib slipped his star into his laptop. "All right, you read them out. I'll type them up."

The image of the moonlit city flickered across the screen. He clicked the mouse button. "This stupid screensaver. I've tried everything. I can't delete it." He opened a new document. "OK. Ready."

Wolfie smoothed his notes. "In medieval times, Thornham was a village called Thornham Magna, surrounded by dense thorn forests. It lay in the fiefdom of the de Monteneuf family, who lived in Thornham Hall. They had a servant called Agnes Lovell and the villagers kept away from her because she was always drawing weird pictures."

"Just like you," said Tala.

Wolfie ignored her. "And they were scared of this big dog she had, claiming it was the reincarnation of some legendary devil dog that had the power to call up all the dogs in the area and" – he skimmed his notes – "'*stir them to such madness that even the most docile would turn against its master*.' There was also a rumour that the Lovell family were descended from a tribe of ancient Druids. But that didn't stop everyone running to Agnes when they got ill, because she knew how to make medicines from herbs and flowers and stuff.

"Anyway, one day this Italian bloke called Costantino

Bruno turns up in the village saying he'd followed an ancient line of power that led to Thornham's stone circle and he wanted to investigate its mysteries."

Zi'ib looked up. "So Mr Forester isn't bonkers. There really was a stone circle here."

Wolfie nodded. "It had an outer ring of huge upright stones and an inner ring of smaller ones. And the line of power Costantino followed has got to be some kind of ley line."

"Go on," Tala said.

"The villagers thought Costantino was a sorcerer, especially when he started courting Agnes. The only person who stuck up for him was Adam, the monk who wrote the *Chronicle*. But their friendship was frowned on by the abbot of Thornham Abbey, who was called Godfrei. It's pretty clear Adam hated Abbot Godfrei. He described him as having '*a bloated face, a distended belly and gat teeth*'."

"Sounds like the vicar," grinned Zi'ib.

"After about a year, Costantino married Agnes. They had a baby boy and called him Stanley." He paused. "Guess why."

Tala shrugged.

"Because *stan-ley* means stony meadow or *ley*," said Wolfie, relishing the thrill of her astonishment shooting through his star.

"Costantino spent ages drawing maps of the area and measuring the stone circle, but the Abbot said it was a . . .

um . . . *'heathen abomination'*, and so a villager called Thobias Harrison decided to smash it up and sell off the rubble. He started digging fire pits under the stones and when they got really hot he doused them with cold water so they cracked in pieces, and he got the nickname 'Stone-Killer Harrison'. The villagers used to come out to watch him at work, because when the slabs cracked open the sparks of some *'fiery element'* would light up the sky.

"Costantino was always trying to stop Harrison destroying the stones, so they had this big feud going. Then one day Sir Edgar de Monteneuf fell ill and was dying. Agnes cured him with one of her potions and as a reward he offered her a piece of land. She picked a plot right where the entrance to the stone circle used to stand because she said it had an ancient connection to her family. Costantino managed to salvage some of the broken stone from the circle and he used it to build a house." An overwhelming sense of awe swept over him. "This house."

Elvis raised his head and his eyes gleamed liquid amber, as if lit by an inner light.

"How do you know that?" demanded Tala.

"Because Adam says it stood at the outer edge of the common, directly in line with the manor house and the church. And this house is really old *and* built of stone *and* it's been in my family for years and years."

Tala gazed around the scruffy little attic. "If Costantino died in 1460, your ancestors were living here before Columbus discovered America!"

"I know," Wolfie said, feeling guilty that he'd been so eager for his mother to sell up.

Zi'ib was dubious. "How come nobody else goes on about how old this place is, or how long your family's lived here?"

"Maybe there's no other record of it. If you weren't rich or powerful or a criminal, people didn't write about you," said Wolfie. "So why would anyone bother about a family like ours or a measly little building like this?" He scanned his notes.

"Costantino and Agnes lived up here on the top floors. The ground floor was an apothecary shop selling Agnes's potions, and out the back they built a workshop and a walled garden where she grew her secret herbs. Then when Harrison started demolishing the inner circle of stones, he and Costantino had a huge fight."

"You know what?" said Tala. "I bet Stone-Killer Harrison is Marcus Harrison's ancestor."

"Maybe. Adam describes him as '*slow of wit but quick of ire*'."

"That settles it," grinned Zi'ib. "What happened next?"

"Harrison accused Costantino of sorcery and the abbot had him arrested. But just before his trial Costantino fell ill and died."

"That's terrible," said Tala. "Why didn't Agnes cure him?"

"She told Adam that someone had used dark skill to create a poison more powerful than all her medicines.

191

Then Abbot Godfrei had a fit when Adam gave the *'heathen foreigner'* Costantino a Christian burial in the churchyard.

"After that, Abbot Godfrei started harassing Agnes, accusing her of being a witch. He said her dog was a devil in disguise who helped with her spells and he confiscated all her drawings and threatened to burn her *and* the dog at the stake unless she confessed her secrets and surrendered all her *'heretical tools and artefacts'*. She begged Sir Edgar de Monteneuf for help but even he was scared of the abbot's inquisitors. He advised her to change her name from Bruno to Brown and to stop selling potions and start making sweetmeats. That helped for a while, but then she was suddenly struck down by the same weird illness that had killed Costantino. Instead of staying in bed, she used up all her strength painting a picture on a panel of wood. And listen to this. The painting was full of strange symbols – including a man and a wolf standing in a labyrinth of paths."

Zi'ib stopped typing.

"That's not all. When the picture was finished, she sent for Adam and asked him to write a message on the back of the panel and keep it safe for her son until he came of age. She told him that only those of her bloodline *'steeped in the Wisdom of the Forests'* would be able to decipher its meaning. But before they could walk the ancient path and find the secret they would have to *'open their hearts to the Wisdom of the Stars'*."

"Sounds a bit deep for a kitchen maid," said Zi'ib. "No wonder they thought she was a witch."

Tala's face was scrunched in concentration. "The Wisdom of the Stars was in *The Book of Light*," she breathed. "It was the source of the energies flowing through the Lands of the Wolf. But I don't get the rest of it."

"I wrote it out word for word. It's really spooky – like she's talking directly to me. Listen:

"'*To those of my bloodline who shall come hereafter, it is of a great secret that I propose to make you guardians; but I conjure you, by the name of all that is good, to lock it up in the cabinet of your hearts, under the seal of silence. If the time should come to unlock the secret, then open your hearts to the Wisdom of the Stars and follow the labyrinth to where the phoenix rises from the rose. For there, cradled in the earth, lies a treasure beyond price, which doth, with equal counterparts conjoined, keep fast a twofold power. A power which used aright can save the worlds from wrack, but used amiss will smite the worlds with boundless woe. As you walk the ancient path, beware the hand that offers help and succour. Those steeped in wicked arts oft mask their lust and greed with gentle deeds*'."

The dying Agnes had dictated those words in this very room, perhaps with her last breath. The silence seemed suddenly thick with her fear and desperation.

"Maybe she was delirious," said Zi'ib.

"No," said Tala. "Just determined to make sure this

secret didn't die with her. But she must have meant 'save the *world* from wrack' and 'smite the *world* with boundless woe' – you've put *worlds*."

"No, I double-checked. It's definitely worlds," said Wolfie.

"Who cares? What happened next?" said Zi'ib.

"When Agnes died, Sir Edgar took baby Stan to be brought up at the Hall until he was old enough to take over the shop."

"What happened to her dog?" asked Tala, scratching Elvis's ear.

"Sir Edgar took him in too and said he was the most faithful hound he had ever possessed."

"And the painting?"

"Doesn't say."

Zi'ib scrolled to the top of the document. "I s'pose you realize that Lovell is old French for *little wolf*?"

"I know!" cried Wolfie. "It's *got* to be linked to all the other wolf stuff. And when I was reading the *Chronicle* it was like, I don't know, looking into a shattered mirror where your reflection is all broken into little bits but you still know you're looking at yourself."

The others nodded.

Tala struggled to steady her voice. "So Agnes's secret might be the key to *all* this weird stuff."

"It's got to be," said Wolfie. "Which is why we've *got* to find her painting."

"But if it *is* all linked, shouldn't we keep quiet about

Agnes and use some other angle for our essay?" said Zi'ib.

Wolfie shook his head. "No. I want to win that money. We don't have to mention her secret; we'll just say she left her son a picture she'd painted."

He added Costantino, Agnes and baby Stanley to the chart, linking Agnes and *The Book of Light* with a line labelled *The Wisdom of the Stars*.

"OK," said Zi'ib, typing fast. "It's such an amazing story, that prize money is as good as yours."

"Ours," said Wolfie.

"You've done all the work."

"Course we'll share it," insisted Wolfie. "Though it's not just the money. The best bit will be seeing the shock on Grimes's face when we win."

There was no room in Wolfie's mind for doubt. He was determined to win that prize and whatever it took, he would find Agnes's painting. Not just to solve all this mystery, but for the sake of his brave, persecuted ancestor who had died to save her secret.

27

Dark Riders

Wolfie, Tala and Zi'ib were among the first to hand in their competition essay, and in the days that followed they couldn't stop thinking about the prize money. When Friday came, Wolfie spent his whole paper round imagining Mr Grimes praising their work, and the words *excellent, astounding* and *first class* were still echoing through his brain when he hurried into the classroom.

"Quiet, please," said Mr Grimes, selecting three essays from the pile on his desk. "On the whole I was more than pleasantly surprised by the standard of your efforts. I think a couple of these stand a very good chance of taking third, second or even" – he struggled to form the unfamiliar words – "first prize."

Tala caught Wolfie's eye and held up her crossed fingers.

"It's amazing what the thought of two hundred pounds can do. Marcus and Wayne, I was particularly pleased with your work on the House of Juvenile Correction. The quotes from Marcus's grandfather about his experiences as an inmate are exactly the sort of primary research the judges will be looking for. Well done!" He surveyed the rows of unusually eager faces. "And Lucy and Jessica, your study of corsetry was a fine piece of work. Illustrating it with advertisements from early copies of the *Thornham Gazette* was an excellent idea."

As Hector Grimes walked slowly down the aisle towards Wolfie's desk, he could see the boy grinning at him expectantly. He'd been concerned about Wolfie for a couple of weeks now. Madame Dubois had caught him cheating in French and he'd obviously cribbed his maths homework off the internet, because the last set of equations he'd handed in would have made Einstein's eyes water. And now this business with the history essay. He wasn't a bad kid; he'd never shown any devious tendencies before, but he'd always been a loner. Maybe this sudden outburst of deceit was an attempt to impress his new friends. For his own sake it had to be stamped out before he went the slippery way of Marcus and Wayne. He dropped Wolfie's essay on to his desk. "Wolfie, did you really think that anyone was going to believe the mishmash of piffle you concocted? Stone circles, witchcraft, Druids. It read like the plot of a third-rate horror film."

Wolfie was speechless. A deep flush crept over his face.

"But, Mr Grimes, it's true, honestly. I found the whole story in an old book in the library called *The Chronicle of Thornham*."

"All right, let me see this book."

"They wouldn't let me borrow it."

"I assume you made a photocopy of the relevant passages."

"No . . . the copier was broken."

"Hands up anyone who used the Thornham Library photocopier on Friday afternoon."

A scatter of hands shot up.

"I wasn't there on Friday," mumbled Wolfie.

"I see, so you bunked off during the study period and thought you'd make up this fairy story instead of doing some proper research. Come on, lad, at least have the decency to own up."

Tala pushed back her chair and declared hotly, "He's telling the truth. We can go to the library right now and. . ." She met Wolfie's frown and remembered – the book was in Latin. How would they explain that away?

"And what, Tala?"

"Nothing." She sat down.

Mr Grimes sighed. "Your essay will not be going through to the judges and your decision to cheat has earned the three of you a detention."

"Losers," muttered Marcus Harrison.

The class sniggered and Wolfie, Tala and Zi'ib spent the rest of the lesson hunched in sullen silence.

The cold air cut into their lungs as they trailed home.

"It's so not fair," wailed Tala. "We deserve every penny of that prize money."

They turned off the main road and took their usual short cut through the maze of industrial units clustered around the shell of the old corset factory. The alleyways between the massive metal sheds were deserted, lit only by weak spot lamps high on the walls and thin strips of light seeping from beneath the shuttered doorways. A white delivery van swung out of a darkened warehouse, the driver talking animatedly into his mobile.

"Watch it!" yelled Zi'ib, dodging the arc of muddy water spraying from its wheels. "What makes *me* puke is Marcus Harrison smarming up to Grimes and strutting round like he was Brain of Britain."

"It'll shut them *all* up when we find Agnes's treasure," said Wolfie. "I bet it's worth loads more than that stupid Hetherington prize, and when this is all over and they interview us on telly we'll tell them how our so-called history teacher mocked our research and was forced to eat his words."

"You sound like Mr Forester," giggled Tala. "You should get yourself a tweed hoodie."

Wolfie waggled his eyebrows and did a passable imitation of Mr Forester's breathy enthusiasm: "My dear, you really must read my latest monograph. It's called *Evidence for an Electric Kettle*. I know mine exists because I've just used it to make a delicious cup of newt-fungus tea."

A roar of engines drowned their laughter.

"Look out!" yelled Zi'ib.

Four black motorbikes sped towards them, the riders' faces obscured by darkened visors. Wolfie and Tala spun round – only to see the white van swerve to block their exit. Three of the riders leapt from their machines, closing in like eyeless insects. Wolfie dropped his bike. The three children backed towards the wall, desperately casting up and down for help. A leather-clad hand wrenched Wolfie's arm behind his back, jolting agony through his shoulder.

"We haven't got phones . . . or money. . ." he stuttered.

"Shut up," growled a faceless voice.

Zi'ib was thrown against the wall. He saw his mother's face, smelled the sweat of the gunman in Sudan and felt the wretched sickness of relived terror. Tala erupted in a wild frenzy, screaming, twisting, volleying kicks. An enormous gloved hand smothered her face; another held her arms. She rocked and jerked, jabbing her elbow into the man's stomach. Through her panic she smelled the taint of something truly vicious and malign. The fourth rider had dismounted, and was probing her pockets with narrow, powerful fingers, tossing pens, bus tickets and sweet wrappers to the ground.

"I haven't . . . got . . . anything," choked Tala as hands pressed her throat. "No, please no!" She thought of her father: she'd never see him again, she'd never find her mother. Gasping, half-blinded, she felt her chain being jerked out of her shirt. She waited for the broken star to be wrenched away. Instead came a moment of stillness and a soft thud as the star fell back against her chest. The hand on her face shifted, and through the slits between the gloved fingers she saw the fourth rider move on to Wolfie and Zi'ib, searching their blazers, thrusting beneath their collars to pull at the knotted strings around their necks. Suddenly it was over. The white van was drawing away, the bikers leaping on to their machines and disappearing in a cloud of grey exhaust.

They stood gasping and shaking in the alleyway.

"You OK?" said Wolfie.

"That guy . . . in the van. . . He was waiting for us," Tala said, dazed. "He phoned the bikers when he saw us coming."

Wolfie rubbed the bruises on his wrists, trying to make sense of the horrifying encounter.

"Yeah, well, he messed up," he said hoarsely. "They'll have been after some other kids who've been nicking things."

Zi'ib fumbled with his shirt buttons. "So why did they go for our stars?"

"If they'd wanted them, they'd have taken them. They

were after something else and when they realized they'd got the wrong kids, they drove off," insisted Wolfie. What other explanation could there be?

Tala could still feel those callous fingers clawing at her throat. "Shouldn't we tell the police?"

Wolfie shook his head. "They'd tell Mum. She'd only get upset."

"Yeah, and Godfrey would stop me going out on my own," said Zi'ib.

Tala frowned. There had been something odd about the fourth rider: the movements, the touch.

"The one who did the searching – it was a woman," she said suddenly.

Wolfie shrugged, ashamed that Tala had put up such a fearless fight while he and Zi'ib had been too stunned to resist. He picked up his bike. They fled the industrial estate, starting nervously at the echo of their own footsteps.

They took the long way home, eager to reach the cheerful familiarity of Thornham's brightly lit shops and burger bars. As they turned into the high street, they met chaos. The engineers investigating the recent spate of burst water mains and strange fluctuations in the electricity supply were digging a line of trenches all down the road and fencing them off with metal barriers; mounds of turned tarmac had been banked up around the war memorial and the cars were crawling past, hindered by slow-moving diggers, a series of temporary traffic lights and two men in a council cherry-picker stringing Christmas decorations from the street lamps.

The boys kicked a can down the pavement, trying to act as if being roughed up in an alley was no big deal. As they left Tala at her door, Wolfie said grimly, "Meet round mine tomorrow morning. We're going to find Agnes's painting."

Minutes later Ridian Winter's name flashed up on the Master's mobile. He answered quickly. "What news?"

"The riders have confirmed that the children bear the broken stars."

The Master smiled. "The power of the leys is with us, Ridian, and every day it flows a little faster."

28

The Sidereal Pendulum

Zi'ib hurled a stick high across the windswept playground. With a graceful, twisting leap Elvis snapped it in his jaws and landed lightly on the frosty tarmac.

"So where do we start?" said Tala, rotating slowly on the metal roundabout.

Wolfie jumped from the swing, letting the seat jerk wildly on its chains. "Since we've got zilch to go on, I thought we could . . . dowse for it," he suggested hesitantly.

"What? Wander round Thornham waving bent coathangers and fusing the street lamps?"

"There's no need to leave the house. Mr Forester said you could dowse for things using a map."

Zi'ib shrugged. "OK. Just don't forget what Agnes said about keeping her secret locked up. We can't trust *anyone*.

And don't let on we've *all* got extra-strong dowsing powers; he'll get suspicious."

They ran across the common to the shop and pounded up the stairs. With a cursory tap Wolfie threw open Mr Forester's door to find him sitting by a roaring fire, stretching what looked like one of Mrs Poskitt's beaded hairnets over a large melon.

"Oh . . . sorry," said Wolfie, embarrassed.

Mr Forester beckoned them in. "It's quite all right. I'm just preparing a prop for a talk I'm giving this afternoon at the SILK symposium."

"What's SILK?"

"The Society for the Investigation of Lost Knowledge."

He tightened the hairnet and held the melon up for them to see. "I've removed some of the beads to make their dispersal more random and to allow for oceans and suchlike."

"OK," said Wolfie dubiously.

"But if you imagine the remaining beads to be ancient edifices erected on the crossing points of the leys, you get a fair idea of how our world would look if we could actually see the lattice of energy currents girding its crust."

He nodded towards a bowl containing an assortment of neatly netted fruits, a ball of wool he'd borrowed from Sarah and some large crystal beads. "I'd be very grateful if you could give me a hand. Measure off some lengths of wool, would you, Wolfie? About nine inches should do it.

And Tala, if you could bundle them up and thread them through the beads, perhaps Zi'ib could attach one end of each length to the smaller fruits and the other to the melon. That way we can begin to build up a model of the way I see the ley system connecting all the planets that support life."

It took a lot of sucking on the wool to thread it through the beads and some heated debate about the right way to attach it to the hairnets, but in the end Mr Forester seemed satisfied.

"If you get peckish during the demonstration you can always knock up a fruit salad," said Wolfie.

Tala kicked him.

"What are these crystal things?" said Zi'ib, flicking the wool so the beads wobbled.

"Spheres," said Mr Forester. "'*A sphere which is as many thousand spheres. . . Ten thousand orbs involving and involved.*'"

"Pardon?"

"A quotation from the poet Shelley. I see the Spheres as fragments of cosmic debris, remnants of a long-exploded star that act like junction boxes at the crossing points of the leys, able to accelerate or weaken the flow of energy to and from the inhabited worlds and change the fates of all humanity. In fact, the mystery of the Spheres is going to be the subject of my next monograph. I'm calling it *A Switch in Time – Controlling the Cosmos*. Now, what can I do for you?"

"Could you show us how to find something using dowsing?" said Wolfie.

"What sort of thing?"

"A painting by one of my ancestors. It's . . . for our history homework."

"Interesting." Mr Forester switched on the kettle. "Tell me more."

Over steaming mugs of hibiscus and nettle tea they told him the story in the *Chronicle*, carefully avoiding any mention of Agnes's secret. Mr Forester's eyebrows twitched uncontrollably. Finally he leapt to his feet. "At last!" he cried. "This book is exactly what I need to prove the existence of Thornham's stone circle. I shall visit the library and make a copy of it."

Zi'ib glanced nervously at Wolfie. Hopefully he'd never think of looking for it under a stash of biscuits.

Mr Forester delved in his wardrobe. "We'll start by looking locally. If we get no result, we'll move on to a wider area."

He unrolled the parchment map of Thornham dated 1457, holding it down with a tartan Thermos, an ammonite, a teapot shaped like a cabbage, and a statuette of a man wearing only a fig leaf and a winged hat.

"Who's he?" said Zi'ib.

"Mercury," said Mr Forester. "The god associated with ley lines, whose symbol is an upright stone. Now, for this sort of job we need what is called a sidereal pendulum. Tala, pass me that pyramid-shaped crystal on the silver chain."

Tala lifted the crystal from the mantelpiece. A buzz of power shot up her arm, causing her to shake violently. Zi'ib's reactions were the fastest. He barrelled across the room, knocked the pendulum out of her hand and, scooping it up with a copy of *The Earth Mysterian*, flicked it on to the table. "Oops," he said, trying to look as if nothing strange had happened.

Tala thumped her head with her hand and jiggled up and down to stop the tingling.

"So," Mr Forester said quietly. "All three of you are gifted dowsers."

Zi'ib scowled into the magazine and felt the stifling threads of coincidence tighten. Spread across the page was a photo of a document written in the language of *The Book of Light*.

"C-can I borrow this?"

Mr Forester waved his hand distractedly. "Of course." He slipped a thick leather glove on to Wolfie's hand and showed him how to hold the pendulum between thumb and forefinger above the map.

"I don't get how this is going to work," Tala said. "I can just about see how you can pick up a signal from something that's actually there – but a map's just a bit of paper!"

"I can't give you a definitive explanation," said Mr Forester. "The mysteries of dowsing have baffled minds far cleverer than mine for thousands of years. But I rather favour the theory that dowsers step out of their rational minds and access a higher realm of wisdom, which already knows the answers to everything. But I might be wrong. All right, everyone, concentrate hard."

The coals shifted in the grate. Beams of sunlight danced over the crystal, flushing its glistening facets from white to purple as the pendulum swung in a wide circle. Three pairs of green firelit eyes watched the swirling motion ease to a narrow, mesmeric swaying. Time held its breath. With a frisson of wonder they watched the crystal lurch suddenly forward at a sharp angle, pulling the silver chain rigid.

"Is it a trick?" murmured Tala, feeling the air for hidden wires.

"I assure you it is no more of a trick than a compass finding north or a homing pigeon returning to its loft," Mr Forester said. "What's more, I think we've found your painting." He marked the spot on the map where the tip of the crystal was pointing. "In the Middle Ages I'm pretty sure this was the site of the abbey refectory. If I'm not mistaken, the building there now is the church hall."

"The vicar'll never let us dig up the floor," groaned Zi'ib. "He's just had the parquet revarnished."

"That may not be necessary," said Mr Forester, poking among his papers. "Somewhere I've got a print of a woodcut of Thornham Abbey."

Wolfie studied the map, his eye caught by two curly ink smudges above the drawing of the compass. Beneath the bevelled lens of Mr Forester's magnifying glass, the letters C and B loomed into view.

"Hey! I think this map belonged to Costantino Bruno," he cried. "These are his initials, and the date 1457 fits because the *Chronicle* said he'd lived in Thornham for three summers before he died in 1460."

"I suppose it's possible," said Mr Forester. "From what you say it sounds as if Bruno arrived here by following the ley lines, just as I did. And this map was definitely used by someone who knew about the leys. You can see where they've marked some of them in."

He ran a finger reflectively across the criss-cross of lines sketched on the paper. "But if this *is* Bruno's map, it's quite breathtaking that I found it in a junk shop miles away in Bodmin and ended up lodging with his descendants in the very house he built. But then Bodmin Moor *is* on another major ley crossing and this does have all the hallmarks of one of those *kinnections* I was telling you about. I don't know why people are so resistant to my theory – history and folk memory are full of such curiously linked incidents, but usually they bring some ancient quest full circle."

"What do you mean?" said Tala quickly.

"Oh, some stranger is thrown from his horse outside an isolated farmhouse. The owners nurse him back to health and he falls in love with their ward and whisks her off to a foreign town where they just *happen* to bump into her long-lost relatives and she's wearing a locket that holds the key to some long-kept family secret that enables her to right an ancient wrong . . . you know the sort of thing."

"Kind of," said Tala, mentally retracing the series of strange coincidences that had brought her and Zi'ib to Thornham. "But s'posing something gets in the way – I dunno – the locket gets stolen, or the stranger gets killed when he falls off his horse or the girl loves someone else?"

Mr Forester smiled an odd little smile. "The power in the leys works like water flowing to the sea. Whatever halts and detours it's forced to make, it will always reach its goal in the end."

"How?"

"Sometimes by rousing the other elemental forces of nature, sometimes by interacting with human consciousness. But no interference, whether human, demonic or accidental, can stop it reaching that goal. And all those who have ever believed they were manipulating the power of the leys for their own ends, eventually discovered that all along, the power of the leys was manipulating them. Are you all right, my dear?"

Tala was examining Mr Forester's lined, ruddy face, his eyes so bright and intelligent, and feeling an overpowering urge to unburden the weight of dark mystery surrounding their lives.

"It's just that all these weird things keep happ—"

Zi'ib shot out a hand, knocking his tea over her trainers. "Oh, sorry," he said, glowering at her, furious. She glared back. He turned quickly to their host. "Were you saying the power of the leys might have brought *you* here, Mr Forester?"

Delight spread across Remus Forester's face. "It would be wonderful to think so," he said, handing Tala his handkerchief. "Although I'm not sure what the ancient powers would want with a retired civil servant who can't even dowse or find the stellar alignment he's been seeking for over a decade. Anyway, I digress." He upended a box of papers and rummaged for the print of Thornham Abbey. "Hah! Here it is." He laid the picture on the table. "Right. Let's have a go at narrowing down exactly where this painting is hidden."

This time the pendulum hovered for a moment before swinging in sharp zigzags that seemed to tug the thoughts from Wolfie, Tala and Zi'ib's minds, quivering to a halt over a point where the refectory was obscured by the branches of a yew tree.

"Hmm," said Mr Forester, marking the spot. "No need to worry about digging up the floor. It's pointing halfway up the wall."

He slipped the print into a plastic folder. "Here, take it with you."

"Thanks," said Wolfie, heading for the door.

"I wish I could come with you," said Mr Forester, hurriedly packing his model of the cosmos into a carrier bag. "But I'm off to Covent Garden for lunch with the editor of the *Earth Mysterian* before the symposium."

Once out of the house, Zi'ib seized Tala's wrist. "You idiot, you were going to tell him."

She twisted free. "It's hard sometimes—"

"It's hard for all of us, but we can't trust *anyone*."

Tala tossed her hair and ran ahead, Elvis bounding at her side.

The boys ran after her, desperately trying to grab on to something familiar and safe in the swirling tide of emotions roused by their conversation with Mr Forester.

They found Tala stroking the wizened trunk of the great yew tree that towered over the graveyard, draping the surrounding grass in dense, leafy shadow and scraping the wall of the church hall.

"It's got to be the tree in the woodcut!" she cried. "My dad knows all about trees. He says yews can live for hundreds, even thousands of years."

Wolfie pushed aside the branches. Holding up the print, he ran his fingers over the spot on the wall indicated by the pendulum. "There's stone here, set into the brick," he exclaimed. "Maybe it's a bit of the ruined refectory."

Through the grimy windows they could see Leonora Grindle the librarian and Mrs Baxter from number 29 playing an ungainly game of badminton.

"Never mind them," said Zi'ib, shouldering open the swing doors. "If they complain, I'll say the vicar sent us on urgent jumble-sale business."

29

Backstage Clutter

Ignoring Leonora Grindle's imperious stare, they leapt on to the stage and into the wings. They found themselves in a painted cardboard forest left over from last year's production of *Little Red Riding Hood*. Every nerve in Wolfie's body was focused on his goal as they scrambled over a pyramid of folded trestle tables and ducked beneath a stepladder. He pushed past a tower of costume hampers and there, set into the wall, stood a small door painted a curious shade of purple. This must be how mountaineers felt as they emerged through ice and mist to see the summit just ahead, he thought, jerking up the latch.

He pushed aside a dusty straw-filled manger, some papier mâché shepherds' crooks, three foil crowns bejewelled with fruit gums and a metre-high panel of night sky made from navy blue crêpe-paper emblazoned with an enormous golden star, trimmed with moth-eaten tinsel. That was it. Nothing else.

"It's not here!" Wolfie howled. Crushed with disappointment, he tried to convince himself that he did not care; that Agnes's painting meant nothing. Who was he kidding? He cared. He cared so much it was as if finding that painting was the only thing in the world that could give his life meaning and like everything else he'd ever attempted he'd failed.

"It's *got* to be here," insisted Zi'ib.

"Maybe there's a hidden compartment," suggested Tala. She fetched the ladder and pushed at the stones in the upper wall while Zi'ib tapped along the skirting, sounding for cavities.

Wolfie poked disconsolately at the props from the nativity play, familiar from his nursery years, when he had played various camels and sheep before finally landing a speaking role as the innkeeper. He remembered standing at the front of the church, pointing to that same crêpe-paper sky propped on top of a crudely camouflaged stepladder. As he proudly uttered the words, "Behold, there is a brand new star in the heavens", the heavens had fallen, scattered the sheep, missed the camel by a whisker and hit the floor with an echoey thud. A thud that, now he thought about it, could never have been made by a prop made solely of paper and cardboard.

Tipping the panel forward, he fingered the wrinkled

crêpe-paper. Brittle with age, it split beneath his touch. He plucked at the puckered edges and, easing the rip wider, exposed brown paper scarred with yellowed Sellotape. Emboldened, he tore down to a page of newsprint dated May 1914. Beneath the headline "Suffragette Outrage at Thornham Town Hall", a woman in flowing skirts brandished a hammer at two policemen with twirling moustaches. Tala jumped from the ladder to see what he was doing.

Pulling away layers of newspaper, Wolfie came to a covering of sacking. The rotting fibres crumbled beneath his fingers, exposing folds of soft, pale linen patterned with markings. He thrilled to its touch, sensing that this finely woven cloth had lain hidden for centuries. It was wrapped in bandage-like strips around something square and flat. Gently he unwound the fabric, letting it coil on the floor like the thin, shed skin of a snake. The first inches of revealed wood were bare, but, little by little, faint spidery markings appeared, growing slowly into lines of handwriting:

"To those of my bloodline who shall come hereafter, it is of a great secret that I propose to make you guardians. . ."

Wolfie stopped, seized by a pang of fear. Was he ready to take possession of an ancient secret that could "wrack the worlds with boundless woe"?

"Go on," urged Tala, her fierce attention never wavering from the panel.

Barely breathing, he turned it around to reveal the

painting: a central grid filled with curious symbols encircled by a labyrinth of branching paths. At the entrance to the paths stood a man with his hand on the thick pale ruff of a wolf. Around the edges, bright against a strip of purple sky, gleamed a pattern of stars and planets. They stared at the intricate imagery, reaching through the shadows for meaning that floated far beyond their grasp.

"What are you up to?" barked a grating voice.

Tala dropped her mac over the panel and Wolfie shoved the shredded paper into a fire bucket.

"Sorting jumble," called Zi'ib, stuffing the strip of linen into his pocket.

Leonora Grindle's pasty, suspicious face craned around the door. "I shall check with the vicar that you have permission to be in here." She glared at them with flinty contempt before stalking away.

As they waited for the outer doors to slam, Wolfie wrapped Tala's mac tightly around the panel. Then, sending the others ahead to make sure the way was clear, he carried Agnes's picture back to the house where it had been painted over half a millennium before.

They sneaked the painting upstairs while Sarah was serving in the shop and, heady with success, threw themselves on to Wolfie's bed.

"Shame we can't shove it under Grimes's nose and make him apologise," said Zi'ib.

Wolfie clasped his hands to his chest and put on a pained expression. "Pleeease, Mr Grimes, get up off your knees and stop grovelling. It's sooooo embarrassing."

They were still laughing as he unwrapped the panel and stood it against the fireplace.

"Nooo. . .!" breathed Tala as her eyes travelled up from Agnes's finely wrought images to the symbols and criss-crossing connections on Wolfie's hastily drawn diagram. In the bright daylight the similarity was uncanny, as if Wolfie had drawn his chart after seeing Agnes's painting in a half-remembered dream. "Look! Agnes even painted three broken stars!"

Three tiny golden stars, riven by a gash of purple sky, seemed to leap across the centuries, shaking the pieces of the puzzle enveloping their lives into daunting new shapes. Astounded, they crouched down to examine the other images.

The outer circle of sky, dotted with stars and planets, was divided into fifteen equal sections. The labyrinth of paths entwining the central grid had three exits, each one marked by a miniature landscape set in a circlet of gold: a snow-capped mountain, a branching river and a grove of trees. The grid itself consisted of nine squares, each containing an image: some still vibrant with colour, others so damaged it was impossible to make them out. The top row of squares contained four outstretched hands, nine stars and two crescent moons. On the next row only the middle square, showing five oak leaves, had survived, and in the bottom squares there was a purple flower with eight petals, a fragment of a hook-beaked bird on what looked like a nest of crimson flame, and the faded outline of a building with six towers.

Somehow, from that crazed profusion of motifs, shapes and colours they were supposed to work out the whereabouts of Agnes's treasure and unlock the mysteries overshadowing their lives. How on earth were they going to do it?

Zi'ib and Tala spent the next two hours browsing websites about medieval imagery, myths, government plots and ley lines. One video on YouTube, filmed at a place called Chichen Itza at the spring equinox, held them spellbound for many minutes. It showed a strange play of light and shadow rippling across the steps of the Kukulkan pyramid to form the body of a massive serpent slithering down to a carved stone snake's head. But the rest of the sites were either boring or crazy or just plain creepy, and none offered any explanation of the symbols in Agnes's painting or any means of decoding them.

All the while they read bits out to Wolfie, who was hurriedly painting a replacement night sky on a piece of wood salvaged from the remains of the window seat. He was using his new acrylic paints, experimenting with blobs of shiny colour that felt stiff and unwieldy compared to the watercolours he usually used. They dripped and splattered, swirling myriad dots on to a sky of purple haze. In the centre gleamed a globe that looked more like a world than a star, flanked by two pale moons.

"It doesn't look much like the old one," said Zi'ib.

Tala cocked her head to one side and said tartly, "That's 'cos he's painted the Lands of the Wolf."

"What do you mean?" snapped Wolfie, unused to his work being criticized.

"*The Lands of the Wolf* have got two moons – Dido and Elissa – it said so in *The Book of Light*."

"So what?" Wolfie said sulkily. "I'll just shove it in the prop cupboard and hope that that old bag Grindle doesn't let on she caught us backstage."

Starving and disheartened, they went downstairs to make lunch and sprawled on the sofa, munching toasted cheese sandwiches.

"My brain's turned to mush," moaned Tala. "It's like I've crammed it so full of clues and symbols and creepy old documents, it's stopped working."

Zi'ib pulled out the crumpled copy of the *Earth Mysterian* he had borrowed that morning from Mr Forester. "Yeah? Well, you're just going to have to ram in a bit more."

"What do you mean?"

"Listen to this."

"'*Lost Language Mystery – We Need Your Help!*

"'*Arthur Sedgwick of Baldock discovered the ancient document reproduced below in a local junk shop. Curious to* know what it said, he sent it to us. Incredibly, none of the linguists, historians or cryptographers we contacted was able to identify the script, so we're throwing open the challenge to our readers. A copy of UFO or Spoofo? by Lesley G Pinkney goes to anyone who can identify the language, and a boxed set of My Travels in Atlantis by Dame Esmé Hiram-Glottis is yours if you send us a translation.'"

"So?" said Tala.

"It's a page from the *The Book of Light*."

Zi'ib dropped the magazine to the rug and, thrusting their hands on to the centrefold, they felt themselves drawn once more into the story of Seth.

Over many months the scholar slaves cultivated the barren plains and built a city of stone. And when Seth saw that his people were settled, he went alone into the White Mountains. For many days and many nights he lived among the Wolves and drank deeply of their lore. When he returned he sent men to quarry a great crystal from a cave in the mountains and carve it into a dome, and raise it above the crater in the hillside to make a chamber filled with light. And from the spur of black quartz that rose through the centre of the crater he bade them fashion a great black seat that was called the Judgement Seat. All about it he laid a floor of pure white marble, circled with a mosaic of Wise Wolves entwined in a seamless wreath.

Then he gathered the scholar slaves into the chamber and released the great treasure he had stolen from the race of warriors. It was a glowing Sphere as pale and delicate as a bubble of spun glass and nestling within it, like life within a seed, lay a droplet of the pure and perfect essence of all things.

As the Sphere rose from the basket, and floated up towards the crystal dome, its inner fires flickered and brightened until it shone like an infant moon. And Seth stood before the scholar slaves and told them all he had learned of its mysteries. How before the living worlds were born, a great star had floated on the void. And when it reached the number of its days, its fiery core erupted in a mighty burst of power, shattering the star into more pieces than there are raindrops in a storm. Like ripples on windless water, the power spread out across the void, wave upon wave, scattering the shattered pieces in its wake. And from those far-flung shards the living worlds were born. Some were great enough to harbour men and beasts and seas and forests and some, of which the glowing Sphere was one, were small and smooth as rounded seeds. And when, with time, those ripples of power grew still, they stayed like fiery threads that circled and enmeshed the living worlds. And through them flowed the very force that gives and nurtures life.

A description of the creation of ley lines! The story seemed both strange and familiar, as if once, like a forgotten song from babyhood, they had known it well.

"It's a myth," said Wolfie, snapping back into the moment. "Vikings, Egyptians, Greeks, they all had them to explain stuff they didn't understand."

"So why does it take all three of us to read it? And why do the leys link every blimmin' thing that's happening to us?" said Zi'ib.

Silently they dropped their hands back on to the magazine.

Yet all between those threads and shards there was a nothing-place, a dark and dismal wilderness. And still beyond that nothing-place there lay a nether void that neither man nor beast could look upon and live.

Wolfie's fingers trembled. Was this "nothing-place" Mr Forester's Wilderness Between the Worlds, the sinister emptiness he had glimpsed in the attic starlight? How could it be? The story of Seth was just a myth.

And though the glowing Spheres were small and frail, they held a rare and precious power. For they could twine and twist the flows of force, and shape and turn the shifting tides of fate. So living world was linked to living world, and all were governed by the glowing Spheres.

A vision of Mr Forester's woolly web of leys, strung with plum planets, melon worlds and crystal beads, rose before their eyes.

And Seth was troubled in his heart, for he knew such power could tempt the minds of men. But he put aside his fears and bade the scholar slaves to trust in truth. And he built a gate upon the dome that opened to the web of fiery threads and through that gate he sent explorers to other living worlds in search of Knowledge. And from the Wolves they learned the ways of the beasts, the birds and the fishes who hold an inner compass in their hearts to guide and help them home.

And the explorers returned with fossils and rock specimens, stardust, rune stones, books of magic and alchemy, vials of strange dark matter, maps and weapons, skeletons and seeds, fragments of long-forgotten languages, songs and sagas, drums and pan pipes and arrowheads from civilizations barely emerging from darkness.

Seth stored this Knowledge in the towers of a great library of marble that stood upon the hill above the city. But every journey the explorers made drank deep of the precious forces stored within the mantle of quartz, and the scholars laboured hard to turn that Knowledge into Wisdom to replenish their supplies.

With time, there came new fugitives from other worlds, who braved the wilderness or travelled the web of fiery threads to seek refuge in the Lands of the Wolf. And Seth welcomed the war-torn and the weary, the hungry and the sick at heart, and bade them share the Wisdom of the Stars and gaze upon the beauty of the Sphere.

And there rose up a band of the first slaves who had sought refuge in the Lands of the Wolf, and they called themselves the Manus Sacra. They were the greatest of the scholars and they travelled deep into the hidden realms of wisdom. They studied the mysteries of the Wilderness, and though they held the keys to many doors that were locked to lesser men, they yearned to know the secret of the Spheres. And they declared that they alone were noble enough in blood to wield the Wisdom of the Stars and strong enough in mind to control the flows of force that turn the tides of fate. For they believed that they alone had been chosen to use these sacred gifts to wield dominion over all the living worlds.

Tala said, "If these Spheres really could control the 'tides of fate', you can see why those Manus Sacra scholars were so desperate to have one."

They lapsed into silence, imagining what might happen to the world if that sort of power ever fell into the wrong hands.

30

The Phoenix and the Rose

Tala and Zi'ib went home that night exhausted and dreamt fretful dreams about a pack of wolves deciphering the clues in Agnes's painting. Grumpy with lack of sleep, they returned the following morning to find the attic floor littered with Wolfie's drawings of hands, moons, stars and leaves copied from the panel.

Tala yawned irritably. "Maybe the clue isn't even *in* the pictures; maybe it's in the numbers."

Wolfie whipped round. "What numbers?"

"You know – four hands, nine stars, two moons. . ."

Wolfie gazed at her, narrow-eyed. "Of course! I'm an idiot."

He drew a hurried grid on his chart, three rows, three columns, and wrote in the numbers "4-9-2" on the top row. He counted the images in the painting again. Muttering "Five oak leaves . . . eight petals . . . six towers", he wrote "?-5-?" on the middle row and 8-?-6 on the bottom row.

"What about the blanks?" said Tala.

Wolfie focused on the missing images, feeling a number buzz around his brain like a wasp in a jar. A number he had seen recently. A number that had stayed imprinted on his mind. The number 317. He quickly wrote 3 in the blank in the first column, 1 in the blank in the second and 7 in the third.

4	9	2
3	5	7
8	1	6

"OK," said Zi'ib. "You've filled in all the numbers up to nine, but how do you know you've put them in the right place?"

Wolfie searched for an answer, dizzied by the infinity of associations tumbling around his mind. They stilled abruptly, frozen in breathtaking formation.

"Because," he grinned, "the rows add up to fifteen whichever way you look at them! Across, down – even diagonally. And there's fifteen signs around the edge of the picture. And together the numbers all add up to forty-five. That's three lots of fifteen."

Zi'ib's eyes flicked across the chart, following Wolfie's

calculations. "Pretty weird," he agreed. "But how does it help us?"

Wolfie's excitement vanished like air from a punctured tyre. "I'm not sure."

Tala eyed him suspiciously. "Yeah, and since when could you do math?"

Wolfie said quietly, "Since that night at the lecture."

Sarah's voice drifted up the stairs, calling them to eat.

"Remember, not a word to Mum about the painting."

The kitchen table was set with plates piled high with roast chicken, roast potatoes, carrots, stuffing and buttery peas.

"There's gravy in the jug." Sarah turned up the stove and shook a pan.

Mr Forester looked up from his newspaper. "Find your painting?" he asked as the children, suddenly ravenous, piled into their lunch.

"Er . . . no," mumbled Wolfie, "'cos . . . um—"

"We had a look," cut in Tala. "Nothing doing."

"How odd," frowned Mr Forester. "The sidereal pendulum never lies."

"Don't worry, we'll find another topic for our project," Zi'ib said quickly. "Did the, er, thing with the fruit go all right?"

"So-so. There's always resistance to new ideas, even in the most enlightened circles. But my thesis that the leys are withering through neglect caused a lot of contention. I'm meeting some colleagues this afternoon

228

who are also convinced that human consciousness must play its role in nurturing the energies in the cosmic web. I just wish we could find more evidence to back up our theory. Even an old myth or a bit of folklore would help."

Zi'ib stole a glance at Wolfie, wondering what the members of SILK would make of the story of Seth and the scholar slaves, taught to replenish cosmic energies by turning knowledge into wisdom.

"Sorry, Mr Forester, your caramelized peaches aren't quite ready," said Sarah, sitting down to eat.

"No matter, it'll give me a chance to finish this Sudoku."

Sarah laughed. "I wouldn't know where to start with one of those."

"It's simple. You just have to get all the numbers from one to nine appearing once in each of these grids. Fun, but compared to the tricks the ancients played with magic squares, terribly unimaginative."

The blood had fled from Wolfie's face. He stared wildly at Tala and Zi'ib. They had stopped eating.

"W-what's a magic square?" he asked in a strangled voice.

"It's where all the numbers in a grid add up to the same thing horizontally, vertically and diagonally. They're fascinating. Since numbers are the secret language of the universe, the early sages often used magic squares to encrypt sacred knowledge."

The old man's words hovered tantalizingly in the air. Could Agnes have hidden her secret in a magic square?

"I don't understand," said Zi'ib with forced calm.

"Well, for example, you can express a magic square as a geometric shape with a particular significance and then incorporate that shape into a temple, or even a landscape," explained Mr Forester.

Wolfie, Tala and Zi'ib were desperately trying to work out how they could pump Mr Forester for more information without arousing suspicion. They had hardly noticed the treacle tart Sarah had laid on the table, decorated with a crisp lattice of golden pastry. Mr Forester drew it towards him, inspecting it closely.

"Would you like some?" asked Sarah, surprised.

"Oh, no, thank you. This is exactly the kind of thing some people would be foolish enough to call a coincidence but I call a *kinnection*. Just as we're talking about magic squares, as if by magic one appears!" He smiled at Sarah. "Who knows what mystic force guided you to make a lattice of precisely four vertical and four horizontal strips."

"The mystic force of necessity," she replied, handing him his peaches. "I ran out of pastry."

Mr Forester laughed heartily. Wolfie, Tala and Zi'ib barely smiled.

"It's just that a three-by-three square like this, where the numbers in all the rows add up to fifteen, has been on my mind rather a lot recently." He sighed. "Still, you shouldn't listen to the ramblings of an old earth mysterian.

These days I seem to see mystical significance wherever I look."

"N-no, it's really interesting," urged Wolfie. "How *do* you turn a magic square like that into a shape?"

"Easy. You just write out the numbers one to nine in order along three rows and join them up in the order they appear in the magic square."

Within minutes they were back upstairs. Wolfie grabbed a pencil and ruler and, as Tala read out the three rows of numbers, he followed Mr Forester's instructions. Line by line, two V shapes emerged. They overlapped to form a diamond with extended arms, bisected by a single vertical line.

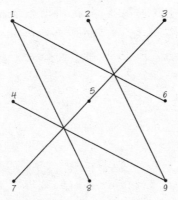

"Oh," said Zi'ib, dully, "I thought it was going to be something amazing."

Wolfie twisted his head from side to side. "It's quite cool that it's symmetrical."

Tala said, "Now what? Do we find an old building with

something shaped like that in it? What about a church? One of those points could be the steeple."

"No," frowned Wolfie. He prowled the room reaching for a single image trapped in a frozen stream of memories. "I've seen that exact pattern somewhere, I *know* I have." He glanced at his chart. A little hammer shattered the ice.

"I've got it!" he cried. "It's the pattern of the leys on Costantino's map."

31

Across Land and Sea

They ran downstairs to ask if they could borrow Costantino Bruno's map, but Mr Forester had already left.

"He won't mind if we take it," said Tala. Diving into his room, she flung open the wardrobe.

"Hurry," urged Wolfie from the landing. "Mum'll have a fit if she catches us."

"It's not here."

"Look on the table," Zi'ib hissed.

"Look yourself," retorted Tala. "Why should I be the only one to get in trouble?"

Zi'ib tiptoed across the room.

"It's here, he's been using it."

On the table, lit by the ragged firelight, lay Costantino's map of Thornham Magna, a ruler, some pens and a large modern map showing the sacred sites of the ancient world.

"Look at this," he breathed.

From a spot on the world map that Mr Forester had labelled "Thornham Henge", he had drawn a web of radiating ley lines. Some ended at the British coast, a few continued across Europe before petering out in France or Italy, but it was the two highlighted in thick red ink, stretching for thousands of miles across land and sea, which held them mesmerized. One line joined Thornham to Meroe in northern Sudan. The other joined Thornham to Mount Shasta in California. They shrank back as if the lines had lashed out like whipcords to bind them tight.

Tala slumped into Mr Forester's armchair, her shoulders heaving as all the confusion of the last few weeks poured out.

"I hate it," she sobbed. "I never wanted to believe all this stuff about ley lines messing with people's lives, yanking them round the world. But it's true." Her head dropped helplessly into her hands. "I want to go home. I want my dad."

She rocked back and forth, keening for her father. Where was he? Where was Jack Bean, the kind, funny, scruffy father who always made her feel safe? He'd know how to stop all these horrible "*kinnections*" from choking the joy out of her life. She suddenly grew rigid. "It took him, didn't it? That's why he disappeared. The power in the leys took my dad . . . so I'd end up here." She was whimpering, bleats of distress breaking through her words. Then she looked straight at Zi'ib. "*And* it sent those men to take your mom."

He flinched as if she had struck him.

"I'm sorry. I didn't mean to upset you. I'm scared. These spooky coincidences, jerking us around like we're puppets. . . I've had enough . . . I can't take it . . . I want—"

"Stop it!" cried Zi'ib, wild-eyed and breathing fast. "I don't care if it's the power of the leys or Martians, zombies or headless chickens that took our parents. All that matters is getting them back. At least this way there's some clues to follow, something to fill your head with – instead of a great big empty nothing gnawing at you every minute of every day till you go mad!"

He snatched Costantino's map and ran upstairs.

"Anyone want a Coke and some treacle tart?" said Wolfie, ten minutes later. He dumped down a tray and a roll of greaseproof paper.

The sweet fizzing drink and the sticky pudding helped to calm Tala and Zi'ib down. But, as Wolfie unrolled the greaseproof paper and began to trace a copy of Costantino's map, unstoppable thoughts about his own father made his hands cold and sweaty.

St Michael's Church, the common, Dodds Hill, even the pond, the crossroads and the pub were clearly marked on the yellowing parchment – stubborn landmarks unfazed by time. The old tithe barn and a scattering of single stones dotted randomly about the village had vanished completely, but as Wolfie traced the rest of medieval Thornham Magna, he felt as though he were filleting the plump flesh from the modern suburb he knew, to expose its ancient skeleton beneath. The old straight track, which had become the high street; the double row of standing stones that had once circled the common; the outer ditch of the "henge" defining the curve of Greyfriars Crescent; the two monoliths flanking the entrance to the stone circle (now the site of the sweet shop) and the abbey refectory whose remains still clung to the walls of the church hall. At the centre of it all stood Thornham Hall, now just a ghostly outline in the grass.

Taking a purple highlighter, he carefully traced in the ley lines marked by Costantino, whose pattern had been encrypted in the horizontal rows of the magic square. Although the two overlapping V shapes fitted neatly around the outer circle of stones, the figure looked unfinished; expectant, as if yearning for completion.

Zi'ib and Tala were watching quietly now, willing him on.

The tips and midpoint of the lines made three perfect rows of three. He numbered them one to nine, as Mr Forester had instructed, and, tilting the ruler to the left and right, carefully joined up the numbers as they appeared in the *vertical* and *diagonal* lines of the magic square, muttering "4-3-8, 9-5-1, 2-7-6, 4-5-6, 8-5-2" like a frenzied bingo caller. Slowly another shape emerged.

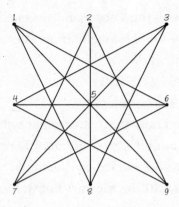

A perfect eight-point star. It outlined the ley lines wrought from the meandering patchwork of the Thornham landscape, its four long and four short points creating a vast and intact version of the broken fragments hanging from their necks.

In that shocked moment of first-seeing, the leys stood out like glowing wires, as seemingly random details of building, road and grassland revealed their hidden role in the elegant symmetry of the star. It was crazy and frightening and they laughed aloud with nervous wonder.

Two major ley lines running down from the tips of the long points met at the heart of Thornham Hall. The tapering lines making up the short points hit this central cross at the exact position of the shop, the vicarage, Tala's house and, oddly, the Wish Hound pub. But what did it mean? Wolfie touched the tracing as if his fingers could cross the bridge between the pattern and its secrets.

"Now we know the Thornham leys match the shape of our stars, maybe we *should* tell Mr Forester everything and get his help," he said.

"No way," said Zi'ib flatly.

"Why not? He's harmless."

"How do we know that? Remember what Agnes said? *'Those steeped in wicked arts oft mask their lust and greed with gentle deeds.'*"

Tala nodded. "Zi'ib's right. I know *I* was tempted to tell him, but we mustn't let on to anyone, not even Mr Forester."

"I s'pose it *is* a bit strange him turning up just when all this started *and* being into weird stuff," conceded Wolfie. "But if he really *was* up to something, wouldn't he pretend to be a trainspotter or a birdwatcher instead of a ley hunter?"

"We can't risk it," said Zi'ib. "We've got to do this on our own." He lifted the greaseproof paper and played his torch across the original map.

Wolfie rammed his fist into his palm. "Then we need a *proper* clue like on old pirate maps. You know: 'Go to the third rock on the beach and walk ten paces west.'"

"West," murmured Zi'ib. "West . . . east . . . north. . ." He pounded the parchment with his fist. "That's it! The star shape of the leys is identical to this diagram of the compass on the map. The markers for north, south, east and west are the long points of the star and the ones for the halfway points are the short ones."

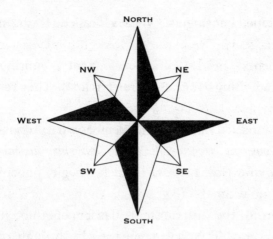

"Freeeaky," said Wolfie. "The map is a compass. Or maybe the compass is a map. . ."

Tala tucked her hair behind her ears, concentrating hard. "So, if Agnes's treasure was buried at the tip of one of the compass points, the only clue we'd need to find it . . . is a direction."

"Brilliant!" said Wolfie.

"I know."

Like an angry interrogator, Zi'ib shone the torch at Agnes's painting. "Come on," he shouted. "Give us another clue."

Illuminated by the bright circle of light, the colours grew richer and the ghostly markings on the damaged squares seemed to thicken until the fragments of the hook-beaked bird on the bottom row revealed its shape.

"That's one of those birds that sets fire to itself every few hundred years, then rises from the flames," said Tala.

She snapped her fingers. "What's it called? It was in *Harry Potter*. . ."

"Phoenix," said Wolfie, excitement mounting. "But those red things round it aren't flames. They're flower petals!"

"It's a rose!" cried Tala. "Remember what Agnes wrote? '*To unlock the secret, follow the labyrinth to where the phoenix rises from the rose*'? Quick, google 'phoenix' and 'rose' and 'compass'."

Ignoring the intermittent flashes of the cityscape screensaver, Zi'ib spooled impatiently through pages of websites offering ringtones and car insurance. He clicked the mouse. "Come on," he urged as a diagram of an eight-point compass star slowly filled the screen.

"This must have something to do with it. It says this compass shape was also called a 'wind rose' because it showed the paths of the eight winds."

"So where's the bird?" said Tala.

Zi'ib moved the cursor over the points. The Latin names for the wind directions popped up: ". . .Aquilo . . . Wuturus . . . Argestes . . . Phoenix! It's the Latin name for the south-east wind." He sat back, his eyes glittering. "South-east! That's where the phoenix rises from the compass rose."

"And there," cried Tala, "'*cradled in the earth, lies a treasure beyond price*'!"

With shaking hands Wolfie repositioned the tracing of the star of leys over Costantino's map. At the tip of the south-east point, his ancestor had drawn the faded symbol of small domed stone. It was in direct alignment with the centre of the star and the stone cross, which in medieval times had marked the centre of the crossroads.

"Where is it. . .?" demanded Tala.

"Halfway down the high street . . . bang opposite the crossroads."

"What? Where the war memorial is?"

"Yeah."

"So what's there now?"

Wolfie closed his eyes, picturing the street. "I think it's . . . the dry cleaner's!"

"That's absurd!"

"No . . . no, it's not. You remember when I knew those missing numbers in Agnes's grid were 3,1 and 7? It's because I saw 317 on a dry-cleaning ticket pinned to my grandpa's old suit."

"But how. . .?"

"Never mind that, what do we do now?" cut in Zi'ib.

"There's roadworks all down the high street," said Wolfie, his eyes bright with excitement, "so we sneak out tonight, get into that trench and start digging."

32

The Trench

The town hall clock struck midnight. Strings of neon snowflakes dangled above the high street, scattering silvery webs across the line of parked diggers and barricaded roadworks snaking down the high street. The pavement was deserted save for a few minicab drivers in Puffa jackets sipping tea from plastic cups and a man in a reindeer party hat clasping the postbox in a loving embrace. He politely wished the children a very merry Christmas before transferring his affections to an abandoned supermarket trolley.

Wolfie grasped Sarah's cake slice, wishing his mum kept sensible things round the house like shovels and torches. Tala lugged Matthias's spade, carefully camouflaged in Christmas paper.

Wolfie handed her the cake slice.

"Here, let's swap."

Zi'ib's torch poked from his pocket and he carried an old trowel with a wobbly handle, plundered from the vicar's shed.

Cold and shivering, they pulled their scarves a little tighter as they crept past skips and darkened alleyways. A rat scuttled from beneath the metal barriers. The thought of climbing into a deep, slimy ditch to look for a treasure that probably didn't even exist grew less enticing with every step. They reached the dry cleaner's. In the window stood a chipped plaster mannequin, tipping its top hat to the empty street. This was madness! It *couldn't* be the right place. Wolfie was on the verge of turning back when he saw two dots of light glinting in the gloom. Elvis was sitting in the doorway. As if he had been waiting for them, he stood up, slowly swishing his tail and, for a moment, Wolfie experienced the strange tingling in his fingers he had felt when dowsing.

"Look! Down there," cried Tala.

Wedged against the wall of the shop, partially obscured by a row of wheelie bins, Wolfie saw a small domed milestone. His brain did a fast rewind. He had passed that stone a thousand times before without ever noticing its existence.

He unwrapped the spade and hissed, "Quick, chuck me the torch."

Squeezing through a narrow gap in the barrier, he shone the beam into the deep trench, picking out islands

243

of grey froth floating on the stagnant water. With the torch clenched between his teeth, he plunged the spade into the mud, gripped the shaft and swung himself down, his feet bumping over oozing layers of clay and gravel before hitting a large pipe submerged beneath the slime.

"It's OK, there's a pipe at the bottom," he called, his voice muffled by the torch.

Elvis lay his head on his paws and watched Zi'ib and Tala scramble after him. Pressing their hands against the clammy walls, they edged along the pipe. After a few steps it dog-legged sharply to the left. Wolfie slipped and lost his footing, smashing his shoulder against the mud. He scrabbled to stay upright, catching at the empty air. With a squelch the wall gave way, the torch slipped from his mouth and he was engulfed by raw, dank darkness.

"Wolfie!" called Zi'ib, trailing his hand through the icy sludge in a frantic search for the torch. It bobbed into reach. He wiped it against his trousers, gasping with relief as a thin trickle of light filtered through the slime-smeared glass.

"Hang on, I'm coming." He swung the torch into the gaping emptiness of an underground cavern. A gush of brown water swirled over his feet.

"What happened?" called Tala, wading after him.

"I dunno. I saw Wolfie fall and now . . . he's gone."

Gripping the edge of the opening, Tala peered inside.

"Wolfie!" she called, panic rising in her voice. There

was no reply. She touched her star. His pulse had grown so faint she could barely feel it. Zi'ib flashed the torch around the cavern walls.

"There's a gap, come on."

The tunnel beyond narrowed sharply. They blundered down it, frantically calling Wolfie's name. Zi'ib shook the torch, squinting anxiously into the bulb. "I don't know how long these batteries are going to last," he said.

Tala pointed to a greenish glimmer up ahead. "Don't worry, we'll use Wolfie's to get back."

"He didn't bring one," whispered Zi'ib.

Raising a finger to his lips, he switched off the beam and crept forward. After a few feet the passage twisted to the left. They halted, shocked by the sight of Wolfie spreadeagled on the floor of a little round chamber whose eerie beauty stilled their breath. Its curving walls were covered with prints of splay-fingered hands etched in earthy shades of yellow, ochre and brown overlapping at every angle, as if a great throng of people were trying to push their way through a thinly stretched veil. Tala bent to pull Wolfie up.

"Don't," Zi'ib hissed. "I think he's in a trance. Maybe he's sensing Agnes's treasure. Like when you were dowsing and sensed his broken star."

Lit by the unearthly green glow, Tala sank down at Wolfie's head and Zi'ib at his feet. They stared at the handprints, waiting silently for him wake up. Slowly, a deep tranquillity descended on the little chamber, and out of a stillness that hovered between past and present, time and place, Wolfie's thoughts came gliding towards them. Like swallows on a summer evening, their minds moved as one, rising and plummeting in the light and the darkness; reaching out across soil and stone through sweet strange sounds to push at the veil; thumb against finger, palm against thumb, until the veil parted to reveal a sweep of glistening threads flung from a spinning sphere of pulsing light; clear as crystal, bright as liquid fire. A scrap of stardust floating on the void, just like the one described in *The Book of Light*. And they knew, as Seth had known, that nestling within it, like life within a seed, lay a droplet of *the pure and perfect essence of all things*. In a rumble of shifting earth the glimpse was gone and they drifted back into the silence of the chamber, where their bodies lay like shoes discarded by a back door that had opened on to bliss.

Wolfie eyes blinked open. He stared into the darkness. "I lost the torch," he murmured.

"I've got it," called Zi'ib, flicking it on. "What happened?"

"Dunno. One minute I was walking along the pipe, the next I was being pulled in all directions like a lump of pizza dough and then . . ." He faltered, embarrassed. ". . . then I kicked off my body and we all went skydiving and there was this weird music and a spinning sphere."

"Like one of the crystal beads on Mr Forester's model of

the cosmos," said Tala. "And the Sphere in *The Book of Light*."

"Listening to all that stuff has turned our brains," said Zi'ib. "That green light that was in here when we found you, where was it coming from?"

"I don't think it was coming from anywhere. I think it just *was*," said Tala, rubbing her neck. "But *that* definitely wasn't there before."

A niche had opened in the wall and inside it, lit by the fading torchlight, stood a pillar of pinkish granite.

"What is it?" said Zi'ib.

"An obelisk," said Wolfie.

"'*A treasure beyond price that can save or destroy worlds*'," breathed Tala.

With unsteady fingers Wolfie touched the cool polished surface. The stone was the height of his arm from fingertip to elbow. Each of its four faces was the width of his palm, planed at the top to form a pyramid. The column was unadorned except for a dark patch that felt rough beneath his fingertips and a line of hair's breadth grooves winding diagonally around the central section. They could not know that this obelisk had been wrought thousands of years before by craftsmen-priests who had bequeathed their skills to the Druids, but they were awed by the powerful simplicity of its shape and proportion. A night bus rattled down the high street, shaking the chamber.

"I don't see how this is going to solve any mysteries *or*

get our parents back," sighed Zi'ib. "But let's get it out of here before someone comes."

The stone was astonishingly heavy, so they wrapped it in Wolfie's parka and took turns to drag it back down the passage towards the opening.

Zi'ib gazed at the steep walls of the trench. "How do we get it up there?"

"Haul it with our scarves," said Wolfie, unwinding his from his neck.

"Will they hold?" asked Zi'ib.

"'Spect so. Mum's knitting is pretty indestructible."

Tying one end of the knotted scarves around the obelisk and the other around his ankle, he heaved himself on to Zi'ib's meshed fingers. Sticking the trowel and cake slice into the mud, he scrambled up to where Elvis was waiting patiently by the barrier. Something moved. Wolfie twisted round. It was only the drunk in the reindeer hat slumped in a doorway.

"It's all right, but be quick," he called, securing the scarf to a fire hydrant.

Clinging to the stretched scarves, Tala and Zi'ib clambered to the top and with all three pulling hard, they slowly hauled up the obelisk.

"So how do we get it home?" said Zi'ib.

"Wait here." Tala disappeared behind the diggers. She ran back pushing the abandoned supermarket trolley.

"Good thinking," whispered Wolfie. "Come on."

They heaved the obelisk into the trolley and careened

down the high street with Elvis leading the way, his head held high in the moonlight.

As they trundled the trolley into the outhouse, the drunk slipped behind the wheelie bins, pulled off his party hat and reached for his star of hammered gold. Moments later a message darted across the leys, seeking out all the members of the Manus Sacra waiting anxiously on two different worlds.

> *And the Chosen shall prevail.*
> *They have found the first stone.*

The reply from the Leader came quickly.

> *And the Chosen shall prevail.*
> *The mingled blood proves strong.*

33

Messages from Meroe

Woken at 2.00 a.m. by the sound of running water, Sarah emerged sleepily on to the landing and caught Wolfie and Elvis leaving the bathroom looking suspiciously scrubbed and clean. She gasped at the muddy scum clinging to the bath.

"Sorry, Mum. Elvis got out . . . and . . . jumped down a hole in the road. I had to pull him out and we both got a bit muddy." Wolfie glared at Elvis. "Bad dog."

Elvis dropped his head and pawed the lino.

"That animal is a menace. No wonder no one's claimed him," grumbled Sarah, shuffling back to bed, but she didn't mean it. Over the past weeks she had grown as fond of Elvis as Wolfie had.

*

The next day Wolfie, Tala and Zi'ib sat through their lessons, silently reliving their midnight encounter with the extraordinary. As the bright Sphere danced before their eyes, the same question gnawed away at each of their minds – what on earth were they supposed to do with the obelisk hidden in the outhouse?

Zi'ib walked home to the vicarage in the gathering dusk, trying to make sense of everything that had happened to him since he had arrived in England. He spoke a different language – well, three or four thousand different languages, actually – wore different clothes, ate different food and had even begun to get used to the murky weather. For the first time in his life he had even found true friendship, but he missed his mother and his longing for her grew deeper every day.

It was less painful when he thought about his father because he couldn't remember him at all. He always imagined him in black and white, wearing the suit he wore in the photograph now propped beside his bed. But strangely, all the clues and *kinnections* they were chasing seemed to be bringing Zane Bakri alive, turning him from a monochrome image into a full-colour, three-dimensional being.

A pair of crows rose, cawing, from the ancient yew as he entered the churchyard. He shone his torch over the graves of Costantino and Agnes, wondering how the tragic story of these two medieval Europeans could have opened so many doors in his brain that refused to close.

251

A thought fluttered through the misty layers of confusion in his mind, just out of reach. He had missed something vital. The thought nagged him as he hurried indoors, distracted him while he did his homework and didn't stop when he tried to force down the vicar's gristly rissoles.

"I'm off to the over-sixties whist drive," said the vicar, clearing the plates. "Would you like to join me?"

"Er – no thanks, Godfrey," said Zi'ib, scrabbling for an excuse. "I've got some . . . reading to do."

The vital connection burst free.

Arion's fax had talked about publishing the truths revealed in the Meroitic inscriptions. Ffarley Snodgrass had said those rescued papers of his dad's were copies of those inscriptions. So somewhere in that bundle of scrappy transcripts was the information that his dad had wanted seekers of lost wisdom to know – and that the people who snatched him and the manuscript had wanted kept secret.

His scalp tingled. Apart from his dad, the only people in the world able to translate that long-forgotten language were him and Wolfie and Tala.

"It's reading for a project I'm doing with Wolfie and Tala," he said, barely able to conceal his excitement. "Can they come round?"

"Of course," said the Reverend Peasemarsh. "I'll be back around eight-thirty."

*

Within half an hour Wolfie, Tala and Zi'ib were digging feverishly through the bag of papers. They skimmed the pages, tossing them aside, then snatching them back again in case this proclamation about the building of a new temple or that eulogy to a dead king, carved by ancient unknown masons, contained some crucial scrap of information they had missed.

The text was written in two different scripts. The one recording prayers and stories was pictorial, using hieroglyphs similar to those of ancient Egypt. The other, made up of gently curving lines, loops and zigzags, recorded everyday administrative matters.

"This one's some garbage about taxing goats," groaned Wolfie.

"These are all about the power of the priests," said Zi'ib. "Sounds like they were a right load of. . ."

A bolt of terror shook their stars.

"I think I've found something," said Tala in a hoarse whisper.

"Read it out," said Zi'ib.

"I – can't, you do it." She handed him the crumpled pages.

Thunder rumbled across the common and a tongue of white flame shot up the chimney, sending puffs of ash fluttering on to the hearthrug.

"'*In the time of our ancestors there came a rush of wind and light, and a band of green-eyed wanderers appeared on the steps of the temple. Some had skin the colour of honey and*

253

hair as black as night and some had skin as white as milk and hair the colour of sand and others were as dark as the men of Meroe."'

Zi'ib did not have to look at their reflections in the mirror over the mantelpiece to know that those shades of sand and honey, milk and night were flickering in the firelight. Struggling for calm, he read on.

"'The priests were angry and demanded to know how these strangers had entered this sacred place. The wanderers replied that they had come from the Lands of the Wolf in search of Knowledge.'"

"The Lands of the Wolf," said Tala unsteadily. "It's picking up the story in *The Book of Light*."

Wolfie's green eyes glimmered. "So if these Lands of the Wolf *aren't* some mythical place, where are they?" He had a flash of insight, like a break in the clouds, but it was gone before he could grasp it, leaving him more confused than ever.

"'And the wanderers showed our ancestors how to melt the rose-red ore to make a wondrous metal, how to knit the threads of number into patterns that revealed the secrets of the skies and how to summon the forces of the earth to move great blocks of stone. The priests marvelled at these things and fell down and worshipped the green-eyed wanderers, but the wanderers refused their homage and said, "We are not gods; we merely bring you the Wisdom of the Stars."'"

"That's the third mention of the Wisdom of the Stars,"

cried Tala. "First Agnes, then *The Book of Light*, now here. It's everywhere we look."

"'*And in return our ancestors taught the wanderers the Wisdom of the Nile. They shared the mystic skills of their fakis, gave them music sweeter than any they had heard before and told them of the powers of the pyramid.*

"'*For many centuries the wanderers from the Lands of the Wolf returned to trade Knowledge with our people. Then one night when the waters of the great river were in full flood, a band of weary wanderers arrived on the steps of the temple. Burdened with fear and sadness, they begged the priests for help. They told how their wise men had discovered a piece of Knowledge that no mortal man should know. It was the secret of the sacred Spheres that rule the celestial fires and turn the tides of fate on all the living worlds. And the wanderers told how this had caused a mighty schism between their people, dividing the proud and lofty who craved dominion over all humanity from those who were humble and feared the evil such Knowledge could do. The proud and lofty were scholars of ancient blood who named themselves the Manus Sacra. And many of them were overthrown and exiled from the Lands of the Wolf. But it was feared there were some who kept silent like snakes in the shadows, and waited to take the secret to themselves. And so the wise men divided the secret into three parts and placed each part in a sacred stone.*'"

Their stars dinned a wild, jangling note that seemed to glitter in the silence.

"'Only three tribes of earthly men were deemed worthy to share the guardianship of these stones, and our people were of that number. When the priests heard this they were sorely troubled. They debated for three moons and consulted the oracles, and when the fourth moon approached, they agreed to shoulder this terrible burden.

"'And together the wanderers and the priests locked away one of the sacred stones, and combined the Wisdom of the Stars and the Wisdom of the Nile to make keys to the hiding place. When the deed was done, the wanderers went in search of the Wisdom of the Forests and the Mountains to lock away the other stones. And so the burden was shared among the guardians.'"

Tears blurred Tala's eyes, but her mind was sharp with understanding.

"Nile, forests, mountains – the Nile flows through Sudan, Thornham used to be surrounded by ancient forests and I was born on Mount Shasta. It says there were three worthy tribes. Think about it. We're each from one of their homelands. *The Chronicle of Thornham* said Wolfie's ancestors were descended from Druids. They'll be the ones with the Wisdom of the Forests. Zi'ib's must have been the Meroites, who knew the Wisdom of the Nile, and I must be descended from the ancient Native-Americans who knew the Wisdom of the Mountains." Her voice wobbled. "And the obelisk in the outhouse . . . must be one of the sacred stones."

Wolfie's chest was bursting. "That's what Agnes meant

about *equal counterparts conjoined*. She was talking about the other two stones they hid using the Wisdom of the Nile and the Mountains. Go on – read the rest of it."

"'*The guardians vowed never to unite the stones unless to destroy an evil greater than the greed of men. But fearing the fickleness of mortal minds, they issued the following decree – if that evil should threaten when the sands of ignorance have buried the Wisdom of the Nile and the Forests and the Mountains, then those who trust in truth should seek out children born of love, whose blood mingles. . .*'"

Zi'ib stopped.

Wolfie gripped his chair. "Whose blood mingles what?"

"I dunno, someone's torn off the bottom of the page," choked Zi'ib. "But it doesn't matter what the rest of it says. We *know* it's talking about us . . . and now we know that my dad and his manuscript vanished because someone wanted the story of the stones kept quiet."

A flash of lightning lit the room. The door creaked open. "Brrr, it's chilly out there," said the vicar, poking his head round the door. "It's awfully late, you know. Why don't I make us all a nice hot cup of cocoa before I run Wolfie and Tala home?"

34

The Wilderness

The following afternoon, Rex Slinfold set off for the Wish Hound in the hope that a pint of beer might soothe his concerns about his career. Three times in the last few weeks his bosses had pulled him off a story and sent someone younger and less experienced. He studied his reflection in a darkened window, wondering if the fine lines around his eyes or his thinning hair could be the problem. A blob of yellow shimmered in the glass. He swung round to see a figure in a yellow sou'wester waving at him from across the common. By the time he had recognized it as that old nutter from the sweet shop it was too late to escape.

"I say, Mr Slinfold!" hallooed Mr Forester.

Rex pulled up his collar and tried to look moody and unapproachable.

"How fortuitous. I've been wanting to pick your brain for some time," effused Mr Forester. "I've had an idea for a documentary about ancient Thornham. You see, I've discovered it was the centre of a powerful web of—"

Rex quickened his pace. "I don't do domestic. Foreign news only, I'm afraid."

"Oh yes, your report on young Zi'ib Bakri was marvellous. He's become firm friends with my landlady's son, so I see quite a lot of him. Charming boy."

Anxious to avoid a lecture about his responsibilities to Zi'ib, Rex broke into a trot. To his annoyance, the old man had no problem keeping up.

"Of course," went on Mr Forester, "it was quite a surprise when we saw that programme about his father, but it all links in with what I was saying about these ancient lines of power connecting Thornham, Meroe and—"

Rex stopped abruptly. "What programme about his father?"

"The one in the *On This Day* series. His father, Zane, was working on the decipherment of the language of ancient Meroe when he mysteriously vanished some ten years ago."

"*That* was Zi'ib's father?" Rex was incredulous. He'd been furious they hadn't asked him to stay on in Sudan to cover the Zane Bakri story. His boss had spun him some rubbish about the piece being more "thought-provoking" without a presenter.

"Oh yes," continued Mr Forester. "It turns out that *both* the poor boy's parents disappeared in tragic and mysterious circumstances."

"The boy whose parents disappeared," said Rex, an idea forming in his mind. What if he took Zi'ib back to Sudan and filmed him searching for his mum *and* his dad? That'd get the viewers blubbing into their Christmas puddings, and show his boss a thing or two about "thought-provoking". He nodded sympathetically. "Yes, poor kid – terrible, terrible. I haven't seen as much of him as I'd have liked. I've been on location." He pulled out his mobile. "He's not round your place now, is he?"

"He'll probably be along later. He and Wolfie often do their homework together."

"I'll just make a call, then I'll pop in and say hello."

"I'm sure he'll be delighted. . ."

Leaving Rex talking eagerly to his boss, Mr Forester walked back to the common, where Elvis was keeping loyal guard over his theodolite.

The obelisk lay in the shopping trolley, inert, beautiful, incomprehensible. The children had rushed to the outhouse after school, unwrapped the mysterious column of granite from Wolfie's mud-crusted parka, and now were staring down at it, hoping for a blinding moment of insight. None came.

Tala turned away, despondent. Dully illuminated by the dusty light bulb, it was clear that this low, stone-built shed had once been used as a kitchen. There was a rusty hot plate, a chipped china sink, and a wooden bench lined with earthenware jars full of blackened utensils. Beneath the bench stood a big wooden cask with "sugar" stencilled on it in thick black letters, and from the ceiling hung a row of corroded copper pans as big as buckets, whose curved handles threw strange arced shadows across the walls.

"What are these for?" she asked, tapping one of the pans so it swung creakily on its hook.

"My gran used them for making fudge – the Browns were famous for it. They had some old recipe they'd been using for years," said Wolfie. He pulled the trolley towards him and together they lifted the obelisk on to the bench.

"How can you hide Knowledge in a lump of rock?" frowned Tala, letting her hands linger on the column.

"You can put a whole encyclopaedia on a CD and that's just a slice of plastic," said Wolfie. "And even the tiniest drop of blood holds all your DNA."

Tala ran her fingers over the patch of darkened ridges in the granite. "This mark feels like the imprint of a plant. It's got leaves and a stem – a cluster of little flowers at the top and a knobbly seed at the bottom."

Zi'ib squinted at the mark. "It's a fossil. That's weird. Why pick a piece of stone that isn't perfect for something so important?"

Wolfie was exhausted and irritable. "There's loads about all this that doesn't make sense," he said. "And we won't

261

get to the bottom of it till we find the rest of that inscription. All we do know is that *one*, we probably *are* the children it was talking about; *two*, we're supposed to find two more of these blimmin' stones; and *three*, somehow our" – he frowned – "your parents were mixed up in all this."

Zi'ib shook his head and kept on shaking it, unable to stop. "So what you're saying . . . is that finding the other stones is my only hope of finding my mother?" He sounded close to tears. "How can we? It's impossible!"

"We've found one stone, haven't we?" said Wolfie. "And we'd better hide it somewhere really safe. I stashed Agnes's painting behind my chest of drawers, but there's no room up there for a ruddy great obelisk."

Tala kicked the wooden cask. "What about in here?"

"Fine. No one's looked in there for years."

The cask was empty except for a sheet of stained paper stuck to a greying crust of sugar crystals, which Wolfie stuffed into his pocket. Zi'ib helped him to lower the stone into the cask.

"What about the trolley?" asked Tala.

"Hide it under those sacks," said Wolfie. "It'll come in useful if. . ." he caught Zi'ib's eye, "*when* we find the other stones."

In the kitchen they found Rex Slinfold sitting at the table with a mug of coffee and a large slice of banana cake, regaling Sarah and Mr Forester with tales of the front line.

Zi'ib hovered awkwardly by the door, but Rex jumped up to clap him cheerily on the shoulder.

"How're you doing?" he asked.

"Fine, thanks."

Rex eyed him curiously. "Sounds like you've made some headway with the language."

"I get by."

"I've been telling Sarah and my friend Mr Foster here about my idea. I want to take you back to Sudan for a week and film you searching for your parents. My boss thinks it'll make a great subject for the *My Story* slot. It's a half-hour fast-turnaround show – human stories with a topical twist."

Zi'ib frowned. "What could I find out in a week?"

"There'd be researchers to do the donkey work, follow up any leads and so on." Rex framed his outstretched thumbs and forefingers around Zi'ib's face, making the shape of a television screen. "But the focus would be very much on you – your experiences, your thoughts." He dropped his voice. "Your pain."

Zi'ib said coldly, "I'll think about it."

"It's a great opportunity," said Rex, bemused by his lack of enthusiasm. He tossed down his card. "Call me!" he shouted as Zi'ib stomped upstairs.

"That creep's all over me now he thinks he's on to another story," said Zi'ib as the others followed him into the attic. "When I came out of hospital, I could have slept in a skip for all he cared."

"But if you did the filming, *you'd* be you using *him*," said Tala. "It's a great chance to find out what happened to your mum and dad."

"We know what happened to them," wailed Zi'ib. "They got snatched by some ancient force, so I'd end up here looking for a load of old stones."

Wolfie said quietly, "If you went to Meroe, you might find the rest of the inscription, or even some clues to the second stone."

Zi'ib sat up. His face pinched and determined, he pulled his school atlas out of his rucksack and wrenched his star from his neck.

"What are you doing?"

"I'm sick of clues and inscriptions. I'm going to get this whole thing over with and dowse for the other stones. I don't know why we didn't think of it before." Holding his star by the string, he dangled it over a map of the world. "All right, where's the second stone?" he demanded, as if confronting a classmate who'd made off with his dinner money.

The star circled slowly over Europe, Russia and Africa, picking up speed as its sweep widened to touch Asia, Australia and the Americas. Soon the makeshift pendulum was horizontal, spinning so fast it was a blur. A curl of flame suddenly flared from the star, swirling tiny trails of smoke before shooting up the string to scorch Zi'ib's fingers.

"Ow!" He dropped the string and sucked the burn.

He had the oddest feeling that he had just been punished.

"Looks like we'll have to do it the hard way," Tala said.

"Which means *I'll* have to go filming with Rex Slinfold," Zi'ib said bitterly. "But it won't help. Everything we've found out so far has needed all three of us working together, and even then it's been tough. We're the last people on earth *anyone* would pick to carry out some ancient quest."

"Speak for yourself," said Tala.

"Come on. There'll be thousands of people descended from those old tribes, and I bet they all know loads more about ancient wisdom than we do. I just don't get it."

"Could I trouble you to join me for a cup of tea?" called Mr Forester through the trapdoor. "There's something I'd like to discuss with you."

They trooped down to his room and sat down amidst the muddle of books, magazines and orange peel.

"I popped into the library today and had a look through the TPS archive, but I couldn't find *The Chronicle of Thornham*."

"Oh, er ... it was definitely there last week," said Wolfie.

"This happens so often," Mr Forester sighed. "A vital piece of evidence appears for one tantalizing moment, then slips through my fingers." His face brightened. "No matter. Thankfully my other avenues of research have borne fruit and I am delighted to say that I now stand on the threshold of a breakthrough in mystical science that will rock the world. By tracing the ancient monuments for miles around, I have completed a map of the ley lines converging on Thornham Henge." With a flourish he held up a map of Thornham. Overlaid on it was an eight-point star of leys, identical to the one Wolfie had drawn.

"It was no surprise that the lines at such a potent place should form this shape, for it represents not only the cardinal points and the direction of the winds but also the turning wheel of the solstices, the inner mechanism that sustains the very life of our planet. In fact, this pattern is so powerful that I believe the stone circle at Thornham was built for a very special purpose."

"What purpose?" asked Zi'ib.

Mr Forester took off his glasses. "I am convinced that Thornham Henge was one of a series of gateways used for entering and exiting the earth without the aid of any sort of spacecraft."

The trouble with Mr Forester, thought Wolfie, was that just as you got your head around one of his weird theories, he'd come up with something so random it made you feel as bonkers as he was. If only they could filter the facts from his fantasies. There was obviously something in all this ley line stuff – but gateways to other worlds?

"Don't tell me," he scoffed. "You want one of us to jump out of the attic and launch ourselves into outer space."

"Don't be ridiculous," said Mr Forester.

The grin wilted from Wolfie's face. The absurd mental image he had just described was melting into the desolate landscape he had glimpsed through the eyelet in the star-shine, and there, clinging to the darkness, was the ragged figure he had doodled on the paper bags. His thoughts zoomed in on that lone traveller, and he recognized the emaciated face he had drawn in his sketchbook. A manic part of his brain began to buzz. He held his head, barely listening as Mr Forester held up his map of the world and pointed to the thick red lines joining Thornham, Meroe and Shasta.

"There are probably many such gateways scattered across the world, but there are two with a particularly potent link to Thornham." He looked from Zi'ib to Tala. "One is in Meroe. The other on Mount Shasta." He leaned a little closer. "Which could well explain *how* you two have been drawn here, although I am still at a loss to work out *why*."

Tala and Zi'ib stared fixedly at the map, hoping Mr Forester would think them speechless with surprise.

"To prove my theory, I must demonstrate that the leys in at least one of these other locations form the distinctive star shape. I can't use maps, because there are none that chart the ancient power points in enough detail, so the only alternative is to dowse for them." He smiled nervously. "That's where you come in. Not only are you extraordinarily sensitive dowsers but I have noted that each of you responds to a different frequency of the energy pulse, so between you, you could chart the whole force field.

"If you prove my theory," continued Mr Forester, his eyes shining, "we will share the honour of rescuing the study of earth mysteries from the barren wasteland of heresy and restoring it to the verdant pastures of orthodoxy."

He plopped four grubby tea bags into four even grubbier mugs and added boiling water.

"I don't see how we can help you, Mr Forester," said Tala.

"I'll explain. I've been planning to pursue my research in Sudan for a while now, and when Rex Slinfold mentioned that he needed a chaperone to accompany Zi'ib during the filming, I thought I might offer my services." He glanced hesitantly from Wolfie to Tala. "If I took you two with me, we could give Zi'ib some moral support and the three of you could dowse for the leys at Meroe."

In the silence that followed, Zi'ib gave Tala a sharp nod, urging her to say yes, but she was studying Mr Forester's eager smiling face, harried by doubts and questions.

Did this all-too-timely offer of "*help and succour*" mask some darker purpose? Had he been eavesdropping on their conversation? Was he after the stones? On the other hand, could they afford to throw away this chance of finding the rest of the inscription and the second stone?

Wolfie was no help. He seemed barely to have registered

what Mr Forester had said. She touched her broken star through her jumper and made a decision.

"Yes, Mr Forester. Of course we'll come, won't we, Wolfie?"'

"What? Oh yeah, great," Wolfie muttered.

"I'm so grateful," said Mr Forester. "All I have to do now is convince your respective guardians to let you take the time off school, and apply for our visas."

"I'll go and check out some cheap flights. . ." Zi'ib's mouth shaped the word "home", but the sound died in his throat. He wasn't sure where home was any more.

When he and Tala had left the room, Wolfie lingered behind, trying to find the courage to ask the question burning in his brain.

"Mr Forester," he began nervously, "there's something I've wanted to ask you for ages."

"Yes, Wolfie?"

"What exactly *is* the Wilderness Between the Worlds?"

Mr Forester gazed at him steadily. He sat back, quietly touching his fingertips together. "Take this as you will – and I know you find some of my theories a little far-fetched – there is a great deal of evidence to indicate that between the known and navigable ley paths through the cosmos lies an uncharted wilderness of time and space."

"But. . ." Wolfie frowned. "None of the space shuttles get lost in this wilderness, and you're not telling me *they* follow the ley paths."

Mr Forester smiled wistfully. "If only our space

scientists had the intelligence to seek out the ancient paths. As it is, our astronauts merely paddle in the shallows of the cosmic ocean, oblivious to the great currents of truth swirling beyond their reach. The paths *I'm* talking about lead far beyond the imagination of even the cleverest scientist at NASA. You see, it is only the worlds capable of sustaining life that float in the Wilderness and are connected by the ley paths. Which is why no space craft will ever reach them." He saw the doubt clouding Wolfie's face. "Perhaps one day you will be lucky enough to see the proof with your own eyes. Then you will understand."

"Proof?"

"Very occasionally, perhaps once in a decade, a particular alignment of stars will cast a beam of light through which the Wilderness can be glimpsed. In fact, I came to this house because I had calculated that just such an alignment would converge on this very room and I'd hoped to be one of the fortunate few to glimpse the Wilderness for myself. Sadly, my calculations failed me."

Wolfie shuddered, feeling anything but fortunate to have seen the terrible image seared into his memory.

Mr Forester sighed. "I'm an old man. Who knows how much longer I have left? If I had been very brave or very foolish I could have snatched the moment, thrown caution to the stars and climbed through the opening."

The image of a frail figure clinging to bleak crags of

desolation flared in Wolfie's brain. Was that how his dad had disappeared a decade ago from the locked shop? Had he been sitting in the attic on the night of the alignment and climbed through the opening into the Wilderness? If so, had he been very brave or very foolish?

He asked in a small voice, "If you go through the opening, is it easy to find your way back?"

Mr Forester shook his head. "No, Wolfie. The Wilderness is a terrible place from which few return."

"How can you know that?" demanded Wolfie passionately. "You said yourself you've never even seen it."

"That is true, and I'm still searching for evidence to back up my theories, but I believe it is mental rather than physical stamina that is needed to cross the Wilderness. Mind over matter, if you will."

For the next few nights Wolfie sat up staring at the stars, trying to decide if his father really could have climbed into the Wilderness to get to another world. Half of him longed to get to Meroe to see if the missing inscription would shed any light on the mystery. The other half feared that what he discovered there would destroy the spark of hope that now burned in his secret dreams.

The Master of the Exiles crossed Chelsea Bridge, feeling the energies of the Thames quicken beneath his feet. He stared down at the muddy building site surrounding Battersea Power Station. A gargantuan crane swayed above the derelict turbine halls and men in yellow hard hats swarmed up and down the scaffolding-clad walls.

In its heyday the sight of streams of vapour pouring from the station's four great fluted chimneys must have stirred onlookers with awe akin to that felt by their ancestors when they beheld megaliths rising from the ancient landscape. He smiled thinly, amused that the electricity once generated here had been such a pale shadow of the energies those ancestors had known how to harvest and control. Yet, he mused, some residual recognition of those neglected forces must have lingered on in the minds of these modern degenerates. Why else would they have built this and so many other power stations on a nexus of major leys?

Now the global energy company Zemogen International had chosen to convert this crumbling building into its new headquarters. Surely proof of the enduring influence of this potent site.

Although the renovation would take another two years to complete, the enormous glass eco-dome designed to cover the gaping roof space was due to be lowered into place over the next few days. One wing of the building was already finished. The directors of Zemogen had just moved into their new suite of offices overlooking the river, offices that the Leader and the Master himself would soon occupy. For it was from this building, in the glorious culmination of a thousand years of meticulous planning, that they would orchestrate the rise of the Manus Sacra.

This edifice might lack the age and history of the Chamber of Lupus, but it had a raw, inspiring majesty of its own. How beautiful the Sphere would look, floating beneath the dome in the central turbine hall, how perfect the chimneys would be for storing Knowledge, but, most importantly, how matchless a location this was for controlling the leys of this and every other inhabited world.

Like a cuckoo entering a nest of unsuspecting sparrows, Ridian Winter had already infiltrated Zemogen's senior development team: overseeing its research projects; contracting out its excavations; diverting its funding; preparing the way. The Master's eyes darkened. It was a bitter irony that the success of this scheme lay in the ability of those three misbegotten brats to find the sacred stones. Despite millennia of study, the power of the leys could still move in ways unfathomable even to the Chosen. When the Manus Sacra secured the secret of the Spheres, however, all that would change.

The Master turned and walked back over the bridge, glad that in the days of waiting it was Ridian and not he who had to suffer the self-important imbeciles on Zemogen's board, with their meaningless meetings and flow charts, projections and agendas.

35

A Secret Recipe

"**N**ot Marcus Harrison, Mum!"

"Someone's got to do the papers while you're away," said Sarah, stirring a pot of something thick and gooey. "He was very polite when he came in, said he was reliable, hard-working and had even won third prize in some county-wide history competition."

Wolfie scowled. Sarah took in his hollow eyes and sunken cheeks. "What's wrong? Are you worried about the trip? Rex assured me it's safe and you'll have a local driver and interpreter with you all the time."

"I'm fine; it'll be those jabs I had," said Wolfie, slumping on the sofa. He *was* worried, but not about his safety, and he didn't want to talk about it. When Zi'ib and Tala arrived, he pretended to be watching an old disaster movie and they pretended not to notice the anxiety pounding from his star. They were curled in front of the television watching Bruce Willis save the world from destruction when the telephone rang. Sarah answered it, signalling to Wolfie to lower the volume.

"Bad news, I'm afraid," she said, putting down the receiver. "That was Rex's boss. Rex can't go filming. He's been rushed to hospital with appendicitis."

Desperate tears welled in Zi'ib's eyes, Tala buried her head in Elvis's fur and Wolfie punched a cushion so hard a flurry of feathers shot across his knees. Sarah was taken aback. A week ago they'd been calling Rex a creep. She laid a comforting hand on Zi'ib's shoulder. "Having your appendix out is pretty routine these days. He'll be fine. They're sending that Christie Johnson who made the programme about your father instead. He's going to call you."

They looked at her open-mouthed before jumping joyously up and down on the sofa, shouting, laughing and hitting each other with cushions. Elvis joined in, barking at the whirling feathers. Sarah retreated to the stove. Maybe this was what the magazines meant by "pre-adolescent mood swings".

"Calm down and try some of this. I need you to taste test it for me." She brought over a plate of little brown cubes.

Wolfie took a bite. A smoky sweetness exploded on his tongue. "What is it?"

275

"Fudge. I found that old recipe of your gran's in the laundry basket. I've no idea how it got there."

Tala sucked the stickiness from her teeth. "It's amazing."

"Good. I thought I'd make some to sell in the shop. People used to queue right round the block for it when I was a child."

Zi'ib bit into a square and inspected the crimp of tooth marks. "It's got some herb in it. Is that what gives it that unusual taste?"

Sarah laughed. "That would be telling. The ingredients have been a family secret for generations. According to the recipe it's supposed to *'delight the palette and cure all manner of ills'*."

Tala nudged Wolfie. "I bet it's some witchy concoction of Agnes's."

PART THREE
Meroe

36

The Waters of the Nile

Christie Johnson had been amazed to discover that the injured child he had filmed in Dr Margani's hospital was the son of Zane Bakri, the man whose disappearance he had covered for the *On This Day* series. To be offered the chance to film Zi'ib's search for his missing parents had struck him as an oddly poignant twist of fate. Although he knew from Zi'ib's emails that he had made a remarkable recovery, he barely recognized the fit, smiling boy who ran to greet him at Heathrow Airport.

On the plane, Christie sat next to Mr Forester. As he listened to his proposal for a documentary about ley lines, he fell asleep and dreamed he was in a strange country where everyone's eyes were as green and startling as Zi'ib, Wolfie and Tala's.

Wolfie sat hunched by the window, thinking about his father. Zi'ib tried to concentrate on the in-flight movie but his thoughts kept drifting – from rosy daydreams of running into his parents' arms to scenes of horror in which he discovered they were both dead. Then he would flinch and Tala would look up from her book and squeeze his arm, for she too struggled to keep her darkest fears at bay. There had been no response to her advertisements, in fact no news of her father at all, and whenever she tried to imagine where he might be, she saw nothing but a withered void.

It was mid-afternoon when they landed at Khartoum Airport. Zi'ib was very quiet as they waited for their baggage. He had hoped that the smells and sounds of his birthplace would ease his sadness, but they just made it worse. Every clink of a gold bangle, every swish of a *tobe* and every glimpse of a smiling, dark-eyed woman reminded him of his mother.

They were met by Musa the driver, who greeted them like long-lost friends. Mr Forester, who had expected to step out of the plane into a land of ancient and exotic mystery, was a little disappointed to find that the road into Khartoum was a wide expanse of tarmac, jammed with lorries belching diesel fumes.

At the Hotel Saladin they unpacked and showered before meeting up amidst the wilting potted palms in the lobby. Everybody was in jeans and T-shirts except for Mr Forester, who was kitted out in calf-length khaki shorts, a baggy cotton shirt covered in pockets and a pith helmet. Stifling a smile, Musa suggested a short sightseeing trip before supper.

The calls of the muezzin summoning the people to prayer drifted through the hot dry air as he drove them through the bustling streets towards the old city of Omdurman, ploughing through fleeting gaps in the traffic with a nonchalant flick of the steering wheel. They passed mosques and markets washed by the late-afternoon sunlight, mud-brick houses cowering beside half-built skyscrapers, sleek saloon cars jostling donkey carts laden with sugar cane, and puttering rickshaws spilling over with people and parcels. Musa parked beside a woman selling tea from a charcoal stove, her cups and boxes piled neatly around her, and led them on to a wide metal bridge to watch the muddy waters of the Blue Nile join the pale frothy flow of the White Nile.

They stood amidst the beeping traffic staring into the seething water. Was it their imagination or the effects of the long flight which made the forces within the rivers seem to rise up to meet them? As if two immense currents of power were colliding beneath the foam, surging up and over the walkway to swirl and whisper at their feet? The sensation was so strong they had to clutch the rail to keep from falling.

"This is one of the most important confluences of energy in the world," observed Mr Forester, squinting down at the junction of the rivers. "From here onwards the twin forces flow as one, scything through the deserts of the north to Al Khem, where alchemy was born. It's the place we now call Egypt. Historians claim it was the waters of the Nile fertilizing the *land* that enabled the ancient Egyptians to flourish. In truth it was the energies within these waters fertilizing the *minds* of the people of the Nile Valley that made their civilizations so extraordinary."

Christie Johnson gazed down at the converging rivers as if seeing them for the first time. Forester was a funny old bloke, but he certainly made you think.

Back at the hotel they rang home to say they had arrived safely. Wolfie dialled Sarah and put her on speakerphone. It was weird hearing her voice from so far away and annoying to learn that Matthias had just been round for coffee.

"What did he want?" Wolfie said grumpily.

"He asked if we could have Tala to stay for a week or two when you get back. He's got to go to Alaska of all places. Of course I said yes. Are you OK with that, Tala?"

"Sure," said Tala. "He said he might have to go away."

"He's going to contact the sheriff's office and give them this number in case there's any news."

On the cool, lamplit hotel terrace, they ate grilled lamb and rice and soft ripe mangoes while Christie and Zi'ib went over the filming schedule.

"There's nothing in Rex's notes about meeting the rest of your family," said Christie. "Have you been in touch with them since you've been away?"

Zi'ib shrugged. "Mum's parents died years ago and her uncles and cousins stopped talking to her when she married Dad. They didn't approve of him because he didn't come from round here."

"Where were his people from?"

"Not sure. Mum always said he was a wanderer and that we were all the family he needed."

Wolfie crumbled a piece of bread. That was just the sort of thing Sarah used to say.

"OK," Christie said, trying to imagine what it must be like to be twelve and to have no one and nothing.

Zi'ib cheered up when he heard that the following day they would be filming with the archaeologist Professor Yassir Salah, who had worked with his father.

"He wants to meet at the site of Meroe's pyramids," said Christie.

Mr Forester tapped his map excitedly. "According to my calculations, that's the bit of the ancient city where all the leys converge."

"Really? The atmosphere there is extraordinary. It feels as if you're entering another world."

Mr Forester's eyebrows twitched. As he launched into his theory of interplanetary ley travel, the children said goodnight and slipped away to bed.

Wolfie and Tala had both brought *Teach Yourself Arabic* books with them, which they made a great play of consulting whenever anyone was looking. This ploy had seemed to satisfy Mr Forester's curiosity about their fluency in Arabic, but Christie was bewildered. He knew children picked up languages more quickly than adults, but there was something uncanny about the ease with which they had spoken to the customs officials and the waiters. As for Zi'ib's English, that was another mystery. Even if his mum *had* given him lessons when he was little, his accent and vocabulary were extraordinary. He sat up late into the night puffing on a thin cigar and watching the stars, wondering why he felt so uneasy.

They set off for Meroe immediately after breakfast, driving through dusty suburbs, past factories and huge refineries ringed by barbed metal fences fluttering with tattered plastic bags. Gradually the traffic thinned and the buildings grew smaller and sparser, until by midday the jeep was following the flow of the Nile through endless plains of flattened, sun-baked mud. Mr Forester sat next to Musa, periodically consulting his compass and squinting at the flawless blue sky, Christie stretched out on the middle bench cradling his camera, and Wolfie, Tala and Zi'ib shared the back seat.

They stopped for lunch in the busy market town of Shendi and followed Musa through narrow, noisy streets rich with the smells of dried spices, roasting coffee and sizzling oil, past women in brightly coloured *tobes* piling pyramids of tomatoes and mangoes on to squares of cloth. They came to a café crowded with men gossiping over hubble-bubble pipes, where they chose a table outside in the shade. Mr Forester ordered a bowl of little pink and green guavas while the others ate peppery stew, scooping up the juices with lumps of gritty bread. Afterwards, while the adults relaxed with cups of sweet black tea, Wolfie, Tala and Zi'ib wandered away to explore.

"Don't go too far," called Musa. "We need to leave soon."

The townspeople were shutting up their shops for the afternoon. A love song drifted from a distant radio and an air of lazy contentment settled over the street. They strolled into a tapering alleyway where two goats and a scrawny dog lay drowsing in the hot dust. A woman sat beneath an umbrella, rearranging a display of pots, beads and baskets. With a fluid sweep of her wrist she beckoned them over to inspect her goods.

"Let's get something for Sarah," said Tala. They chose a copper coffee pot, a string of shiny green beads and a soft oval basket with plaited handles. Turning back towards the café, they were surprised when a shaven-headed, barefoot boy ran up and pulled Wolfie's T-shirt.

"Come, he wants you," he whispered.

"Who does?"

The boy pointed to a low doorway in a whitewashed mud wall. Warily they followed him into a cool, shaded courtyard. Beneath the overhanging canopy of purple bougainvillea sat a very, very old man whose gnarled fingers rested on a tall knobbled stick. His long, stooping body was swathed in a pure white *jelabiya* gown and on his hairless head he wore a small round cap. He had the largest ears that Wolfie had ever seen. They clung in undulating folds against the sides of his scalp, their pendulous lobes curving beneath the hollowed line of his cheeks. Deep furrows wrinkled his forehead and his thick, arched brows frowned above steely eyes. From a wooden beam above his head hung a dried yellow gourd as large as a football, suspended from ropes of plaited twine. In the stillness of the hot afternoon it began to swing as if blown by a gentle breeze.

The boy scuttled away and the children greeted the old man politely.

"I have been watching you," he replied.

"Why?" asked Tala.

"The old Wisdom flows in your veins," said the old man, as if this were explanation enough. After a long silence, he spoke again. "I see the dark shadow standing at your shoulders, watching and waiting as it has done for centuries, hiding its accursed hands beneath a cloak of trust. For evil is reborn in every age and shifts and shapes its form to fit the times."

His words invoked the memory of the dark riders so vividly that Tala smelled once more that acrid taint of malice.

"The djinn in the gourd grants each of you an answer."

Wolfie gazed at the swaying gourd. "We haven't asked a question," he said.

286

"The djinn answers the questions in your heart, not on your tongue."

Motioning to the others to do the same, Zi'ib sat down at the old man's feet. "He's a wiseman, a *faki*," he whispered.

The old man rocked back and forth, his soft crooning drowning the sounds from the street in a low dark hum that turned to liquid in their ears. Unbidden, the children gave up the fight against their fears and allowed the questions hidden in their hearts to break free. The old man lifted his right hand. On his thumb he wore a curious ring of beaten metal that flared towards his wrist in the shape of a little cuff and caught the sunlight as he leaned to touch Zi'ib's head. Zi'ib held his eyes tight shut. There was only one question in his heart.

"They live," said the old man.

Tears stung Zi'ib's eyelids. His parents were alive. And now he yearned to know if he would ever see them again and where he could find them, but the old man had removed his hand to Tala's tousled hair and was turning his head as if listening to an otherworldly whisper.

"He is trapped in the Wilderness Between the Worlds," he said.

Tala looked up, mystified. Wolfie stiffened and stared into the dust. The few seconds before the faki's hand descended on his head were unbearable. He felt as if his heart would burst with longing.

"He is your father," murmured the old man.

Joy. Sheer, agonizing, unbearable joy gave way to pride

287

and hope, then sadness and regret, until Wolfie felt as if he had lived a lifetime in that moment.

"Please answer just one more question," he begged.

The old man shook his head. "I know nothing of your questions, neither do I understand the answers. I am merely the blank paper on which the djinn writes his message. For the rest, I can only tell you what I see."

He moved his stick, stirring the dust. "You walk an ancient path in darkness, but the Fires of Understanding will light your way."

Silently they stared at the lines and craters carved by the stick. The old man lifted his head towards the house. "*Ya*, Anwar!"

The boy came out carrying an earthenware dish covered with a piece of muslin and set it on the ground, carefully removing the cloth.

"Look into the water," said the faki. "It was drawn from the Nile on the night of the summer solstice."

They gazed at their reflections, ridged by the inner surface of the hand-thrown clay: shades of sand and honey, milk and night rippling beneath their breath. Little by little the water grew as calm as glass, the sides of the bowl turned pale and smooth and in its white marble depths they saw a broad-shouldered man whose piercing green eyes stared out from a hawkish face. His head was thrown back and all about him rose a shower of golden sparks.

*

Suddenly it was just a plain brown earthenware bowl again and the little boy was rushing to help the faki to his feet. He took him by the hand and together they entered the house, the old man tap-tapping his stick on the floor with the precision of one who has been blind for a long time.

As if waking from a drugged sleep, the children stumbled into the street, deserted now save for a flea-bitten dog nosing in the dirt. They sank down against a wall, hoping the warm mud-brick on their backs and the sun on their faces would chase the ice from their bones.

"Scary or what?" shivered Tala. "That stuff with the water! Who was the guy with the sparks?"

"Dunno. But I've seen him before," said Wolfie.

"Where?"

Wolfie screwed up his eyes. "Not sure."

"Do you think he could see us?" asked Zi'ib. "It felt like he was looking straight into my mind."

Tala closed her eyes, trying to erase that startling image from her memory, but she knew it would never leave her.

"That old faki said exactly the same as Agnes, warning us against the people we trust. It's horrible."

Zi'ib slid a glance at Wolfie. "What question did you ask?"

"Who Arion was."

"And he told you he was your dad?"

"Yep," said Wolfie, feeling a deep warmth in his stomach.

"I thought your dad was called Ron."

"That's what Mum called him. It must be short for Arion."

Tala leaned her chin in her hands. "At least you both learnt something you wanted to know. The answer I got was useless. What did the djinn mean about my dad being trapped in the Wilderness Between the Worlds?"

Wolfie had thought about this moment for so long, planned what he'd say and how he'd say it, never imagining that something so momentous would come tumbling out as they cowered in a dusty backstreet with a yellow-eyed dog sniffing at their feet. He drew a long breath. "Mr Forester told me the Wilderness Between the Worlds is the infinite uncharted emptiness between the inhabited planets. Which exactly matches that bit in *The Book of Light* about the 'nothing-place', the 'dark and dismal emptiness' that surrounds the living worlds."

Tala's eyes held his, unflinching. "So being in the Wilderness is the same as being dead."

"It's not like that. I'm pretty sure that Arion –" he flushed, "– my dad, entered the Wilderness of his own free will."

"How?"

"The night I found *The Book of Light* and Grandpa's radio – the light pouring through the skylight kind of – well, this hole opened in it, and I saw the Wilderness. Miles of never-ending nothing."

"How do you know it was the Wilderness?"

"Mr Forester told me that every ten years there's an

alignment of stars that converges on the shop and opens on to the Wilderness, and if you dared, you could climb through it."

The whole world grew still as he said, "I think that's how my dad disappeared."

Tala's head jerked up. "Even if it was possible, why would he *do* that?"

"In his fax, Arion – Dad – said someone had to go back to Lupus to get help."

"Yeah."

"I've been going over and over it in my mind and all the evidence points to the same thing – Lupus and the Lands of the Wolf are different names for the same place. And that's where my dad was trying to reach."

Tala shrank back against the wall. "*The Book of Light* says the Lands of the Wolf are on another world."

Wolfie nodded. "I started wondering about it when Mr Forester was going on about gateways and space travel." He looked from Zi'ib to Tala, hardly able to believe that he – Wolfie Brown of Brown's Sweet Shop, Greyfriars Crescent, Thornham, London, SE 29 – was even thinking, let alone saying, any of this.

"I think our dads and your mum were a team of explorers from a world they called Lupus and the ancients called the Lands of the Wolf. I think they travelled across the leys and came here looking for the stones. It's the only solution that makes sense."

"It doesn't make *any* sense. . ." Tala's voice faltered.

"Because that would make us . . . aliens . . . or at least half-alien. It's ridiculous."

Zi'ib felt a confusion of tiny doubts and suspicions settle into place, flooding his mental image of his father with life. "Maybe it's not ridiculous," he said slowly. "But if it's true, why didn't Arion go through one of the gateways and use the leys to get back to Lupus?"

"Maybe he couldn't. Maybe the gateways were locked; maybe the leys ran out of power . . . I don't know!" cried Wolfie.

"And what's *my* dad doing in this Wilderness?" Tala demanded. "He's not an explorer from Lupus, he's a woodsman from Weaverville, California."

Wolfie clasped his hands to his head. It was as if he were adrift in a deep, dark ocean, and every time he thought he saw land, a great wave would rise up and knock him off course.

"We'd better get back," he said.

They returned through the narrow streets, dizzied by the conflicting emotions flying through their stars.

"Everything all right?" Christie asked. Something had happened, he could see it in their eyes, sense it in the way they moved.

"Fine," lied Tala. "We stopped to do some shopping."

They climbed into the jeep, unable to look at Mr Forester or Christie or even Musa without wondering what might lie hidden beneath the cloak of trust woven from their warm smiles and friendly concern.

37

Secrets in the Sand

Wolfie, Tala and Zi'ib did not talk on the way to Meroe, letting the silence between them grow heavy with all that was unsaid. They didn't even look up until Mr Forester called excitedly, "Look at that!"

In the distance, the ruins of the royal cemetery shimmered into view. Steeply pointed pyramids of rust-red stone peeped over the horizon, smaller and narrower than pictures they had seen of the pyramids of Egypt. Some had been damaged, their tops lopped off to leave rough-edged ridges pointing to the sky. The children's eyes narrowed in the sunlight when they saw that the surviving tips were of the exact same shape and proportion as the top of the obelisk stashed in Wolfie's outhouse.

With a cheerful warning, Musa hit the accelerator and swerved off the road, racing over the shifting sand to stop the wheels from sinking. Out of the dust a pack of wiry dogs bounded towards them, their pelts crusted with sand. Eyes slitted, ears flattened, they flanked the speeding jeep like presidential outriders.

"I'll get out first," said Christie as Musa pulled up at the entrance to the ruins. "These feral dogs can be a real nuisance."

Stepping warily from the jeep, he looked round in surprise. The dogs had disappeared, melting back into the desert as swiftly and silently as they had come.

Professor Salah was waiting by his car, dapper in a crisp white shirt and beige chinos. He shook everybody's hand and clasped Zi'ib by the shoulder, telling him how much he looked like his father and how saddened he had been when Zane Bakri had disappeared. He unlocked a gate in the security fence and led the way up the sweep of wrinkled dunes circling the ruins. Christie carried the camera bag; the others floundered behind, the soft sand sucking at their feet. At the top they flopped against a wall of baked bricks to wipe the trickling sweat from their faces.

Before them spread a wide, shallow valley of caked mud, fringed with the ghostly remains of a city of sandstone pyramids. Like spectres conjured from antiquity, a herd of camels wove their way among the sharp black shadows, dipping and bobbing beneath the endless swathe of sky. Mr Forester was so moved he could barely breathe.

"Noble, noble beasts of Nubia. Imagine the rituals witnessed by their ancestors and the mysteries they hold in their hearts." He took off his pith helmet and wiped his brow. "Musa, old chap, I wonder if you would be so kind as to help me fetch my equipment?"

"Don't worry, it's on its way," smiled Musa.

Christie pinned radio mikes to Zi'ib's T-shirt and the professor's collar and slipped little battery packs into their pockets. "We'll keep it simple. I'll just follow you round as you chat about Zane and his work. I won't interrupt unless I have to."

"Can we start by looking at the inscriptions?" asked Zi'ib.

"Of course," smiled Professor Salah, "although there are rather a lot of them."

Wolfie looked pleadingly at Christie. "Can me and Tala tag along?"

"Sorry, it'll be too cramped." Christie pulled out his mobile. "But you can use this to pick up the remote feed from the camera." He flicked through the menus, showing Wolfie which icon to select. "Don't drop it, and whatever you do, don't get sand in it."

"Thanks, Christie."

Wolfie and Tala found a shadowy passageway where they crouched over the little screen. The professor led Zi'ib and Christie through a low wooden door into the cool entrance of the first pyramid. The square of sunlight thrown on to the back wall illuminated an inscription written in Meroitic hieroglyphs. The professor watched Zi'ib study the pictograms, impressed by the boy's quiet concentration. How differently he might have reacted if he had known that this solemn-faced twelve-year-old was actually reading the words and contemplating the achievements of the priest buried in the chamber beneath.

Zi'ib ran his fingers over the dips and hollows of the lost language, imagining the ancient mason chiselling the words. This was not the inscription he longed to find. But had it been carved by the same hands who had shaped the crucial key to the mysteries buffeting his life?

"Your father hoped his work on the script would help to fill the huge gaps in our knowledge of Meroitic culture," the professor was explaining. "As it is, we've had to piece together what we can from reports made by visiting Greeks and Egyptians and the stories told by the wall carvings. We do know the Meroites worshipped many of the Egyptian gods, although they did have one of their own – Apedemek, the lion-god. There are images of him on many of the temples and, according to your father, a lot of the inscriptions are prayers invoking his blessing."

They spent a few moments drinking in the peaceful symmetry of the little chamber and marvelling at the precision of the interlocking blocks of stone from which it had been constructed. Leaving Christie to take some close-ups of the interior, they stepped back into the bright sunlight.

"How come my dad was working with you?" said Zi'ib.

"He just turned up one day and volunteered to help out," said the professor. "It was quite obvious that he really had deciphered the hieroglyphs, because he led us to some extraordinary new finds. But for a long time he seemed loath to publish his work. Then, just before he disappeared, he announced that he was off to meet Snodgrass, Beamish and Hussey in London. I never understood his sudden change of heart, and sadly I never got to read the manuscript."

"*Ya*, Hassan, *yallah*!" called Musa.

A boy of about twelve, who had thick-lashed almond eyes and wore a grubby white *jelabiya* and flip-flops, appeared over the sandbank, leading a pack camel. Strapped to its back were Mr Forester's theodolite, his battered leather suitcase and a plastic cooler box full of drinks. At its side, on spindly legs, trotted a pure white camel calf. Wolfie and Tala came running over to stroke its soft, bobbly coat.

"This is where I need Elvis," said Mr Forester, unpacking his equipment. "He has an uncanny knack of sniffing out exactly where I need to put the next marker." He began to scurry about, taking measurements and hammering staves into the cracked mud.

Professor Salah watched him curiously for a few

minutes before asking politely what was going on. The children eyed each other nervously as Mr Forester plunged into an explanation of his theory of ley lines and cosmic gateways, but to their surprise, instead of laughing or looking bewildered, the professor nodded.

"I have heard of such lines before – oddly enough, from Zane Bakri. He was also convinced that these pyramids stood at the hub of an ancient grid of power." Seeing Zi'ib's excitement, he went on. "A few weeks before he disappeared, he told me he was sure that the natural pattern of energies at this site had been disturbed. He contacted others with an interest in these matters and learned that the same thing had happened at similar sites across the world. For many days he sat out here waiting for the energies to resume their former pathways. But then he seemed to despair and turned all his attention to Naqa, the site we'll visit tomorrow."

When pressed for more details, the professor insisted he had told them all he knew and, in answer to a summons from Christie, he hurried Zi'ib away across the dunes, leaving Wolfie and Tala to brood on this new twist in the tale.

"Come, we've got work to do as well," said Mr Forester. He handed Wolfie and Tala thick pairs of gauntlets and led them to a spot at the edge of the valley marked with a wooden stake.

Hassan tethered his camels to a tree and sat down to watch. He was used to funny foreign tourists but had never seen anyone quite like this red-faced old man in a tin hat and these children with strange green eyes. What were they doing?

"Be careful," warned Mr Forester. "The forces here have been less exposed to the so-called 'advances of modernity'. They'll be extremely potent."

Tala and Zi'ib approached the marker cautiously. A tense silence fell over the sands. Even the scuttling lizards stood still.

"Ready?" asked Mr Forester, holding out two pairs of dowsing rods.

They nodded gravely. Bracing themselves, they grasped the rods. Nothing happened.

"Ah," said Mr Forester. He ran to consult his notes, leaving Wolfie and Tala feeling hot and foolish. After a hasty recalculation he waved them to a new position. They took two steps and at once the earth began to tremble. A murmur of sound swelled to a raucous clamour in their skulls as a blinding flash of understanding thrust their bodies down the slope, hurling the dowsing rods into the air. It felt as if a layer of debris had been burned from their brains. Tala lay there winded and retching. Wolfie squeezed his temples violently, feeling the current sweep through his mind, fuse with his thoughts and pour back into the parched yellow earth.

Mr Forester hurried over to dab their foreheads with a dampened handkerchief. "Are you all right? Do you want to stop?"

"No, we've got to go on," insisted Tala breathlessly. She laid her head against a pillar of warm stone, entranced by the strange harmonies captured by the ancient architects.

"At least let me give you some protection." Mr Forester carefully wound some strips of insulating tape around the handles of the dowsing rods. "Take things gently. Let the forces guide you but try to stay in control."

They took up the rods again. Stopping every few feet to steady their focus, they moved methodically across the valley, following the paths of power. Using signs and gestures, Mr Forester enlisted Hassan's help, and together they followed behind, trailing sticks in the sand to join up the spaces between the dowsers' footprints.

When Wolfie and Tala had finished, the four of them collapsed in the shade, staring at the meaningless criss-cross of lines.

Tala pulled a face. "I'm sorry, Mr Forester. We did our best."

Mr Forester seemed unconcerned. "Don't worry, my dear. Have a rest." He reached for his tartan Thermos and filled some paper cups with tea. Musa joined them, carrying a tin of buttery biscuits coated with icing sugar that his wife had baked especially for the trip.

Astonished, Hassan listened to these foreign kids praise her cooking in fluent, easy Arabic. He nibbled a biscuit before finding the courage to ask shyly, "There are stories of an ancient secret buried here. Is that what you and the old man are looking for?"

Wolfie sat up.

"W-what stories?" said Tala.

"My brothers say they're nothing – all rubbish."

"Go on. We – like stories."

Hassan dug his bare toes into the sand. "Well, they say that many years ago some local wise men hid a great secret in the desert, vowing that they and their descendants would guard it until the righteous seekers came to find it."

Breathing slowly, Tala reached for her notebook and pen. "What was this secret?"

"Some sort of knowledge that gives power over all men." Hassan's eyes flashed. "But cursed strangers steeped in dark wisdom claimed this knowledge was rightly theirs. They knew how to disguise themselves as princes, shepherds, priests, anything they wanted, and they swore that they and *their* descendants would go on searching for the secret until the ends of time."

"Where did these strangers come from?" Tala asked, scribbling fast.

Hassan waved his hand in a wild arc. "Egypt, America, the moon, somewhere far away. And the storytellers always end with the words, '*May you live to aid the righteous seekers and smite the cursed hands that call themselves blessed.*'"

Tala carefully underlined the words *cursed* and *blessed*. She didn't trust herself to speak.

Hassan lowered his thick lashes. "I know it's just a dumb story, but I used to pretend that one day the

301

righteous seekers would turn up and it'd be me who helped them find the secret. When I saw you, for a minute I thought. . ."

"It's all right for some," called Zi'ib, leaping down the dunes towards them. He grabbed a biscuit and gulped down the last of Tala's tea.

Mr Forester sprang to his feet. "We were waiting for you. As I suspected, I need all three of you to complete the pattern."

Zi'ib glanced at the footprints in the dust, and without a word, put on a pair of gauntlets and reached for the rods. A hot breeze tugged his hair. Wolfie and Tala felt a soaring in their stars as the music of the pyramids roared through his body. He seemed to master the rush of energies more quickly than they had done, and within minutes he was moving purposefully across the sand, borne along by the powers of the earth. With a jolt the music struck a shrill, discordant note, jarring their stars. They saw him stumble, thrown off course. He struggled to right himself and regain the path. Four times it happened.

When he laid down the rods he had joined up the jumbled lines and an enormous eight-point star lay etched in the dust. Although smaller, it was almost identical to the star of leys they had plotted on the map of Thornham. There was one disquieting difference. The four lines at the central axis were broken, twisted back on themselves like snapped wires. There was something unnatural, almost repulsive about this distortion of the star's perfection. With a sickly feeling inside, Zi'ib said, "What does it mean?"

"It's a disturbance of the energy flow," said Mr Forester, raising his binoculars. "It's obviously the problem that Zane picked up on."

"What's caused it?"

"If it had only happened here I would attribute it to some localized trauma – an earth tremor or a battle, but if Zane was right and this was happening to the gateways worldwide, it would indicate that some person or persons with a breathtaking understanding of cosmic forces had done it on purpose."

"What for?"

"At a guess, to shut the gateways and prevent anyone from entering on to the web of ley paths and travelling to another world."

A fragment of their story seemed to float before them, like a feather caught on the desert breeze.

Zi'ib was the only one who managed to speak.

"So, if you were desperate to get from here to another planet, you'd have to risk crossing the Wilderness Between the Worlds?" he asked.

The intensity of his question made Mr Forester hesitate. "Yes . . . but it would be like plunging into a desolate wasteland without trackways or landmarks. You'd have no way of knowing how long it would take or if indeed you had the mental capacity to survive such a journey."

The pulses quickened in their stars, dissolving all

remaining doubt. Denied access to the ley paths, Wolfie's father had been so desperate to get to Lupus he had risked everything to get there across the Wilderness. Whether he had ever reached his destination, they had no way of knowing.

Tala seized Mr Forester's arm. "If you'd already left before the gateways were blocked, could you still get back?"

"Oh no, my dear," said Mr Forester, gazing into the fiery sadness of her eyes. "All entry as well as all exits would have been barred."

Amazed by the size and symmetry of the star in the sand, Christie was taking sweeping shots of the site. These kids clearly *had* been mapping some kind of force field. Perhaps a film about ley lines wasn't such a ludicrous idea after all. The professor was equally impressed, and busied himself questioning Mr Forester and taking notes.

Tala quickly told Zi'ib the camel boy's story, quoting the final words carefully from her notes.

Zi'ib shrugged. "The Sudanese love stories. Some garbled stuff about the stones was sure to have trickled down over the years."

"Sure – but those bits about *'cursed strangers'* from far away, steeped in dark wisdom who were after the secret? And the *'cursed hands that call themselves blessed'*?" She looked expectantly from Zi'ib to Wolfie. "Hello?"

They stared at her blankly.

"Honestly! In *The Book of Light*, the proud and lofty Lupans who coveted the secret and got banished from Lupus called themselves the Manus Sacra!"

The boys nodded.

"In Latin, *manus* means hand and *sacra* means cursed *and* blessed."

They nodded again.

"You two can be so dumb sometimes! These strangers wandering about steeped in dark wisdom – they've *got* to be the exiled Manus Sacra. And if they swore they'd go on looking for the stones till the end of time, their descendants will still be hanging round looking for them."

A piece of puzzle clicked into place. Wolfie paled. "So that's who Agnes and the faki were warning us about."

"Yeah – it's got to be. And the dark shadows my mum kept seeing, I bet that was them too." She looked scared. "*The Book of Light* said they were the smartest of all the scholars and knew stuff no one else did. They'd know how to block the gateways."

"If they're so blimmin' clever, why didn't they track the stones down years ago?" said Wolfie.

Zi'ib stiffened. "Shh." He swung round and saw dark shapes gathering on a distant ridge. He grunted with relief. "It's just those desert dogs."

A soft howling floated across the dunes. He turned back to see the baby camel tottering across the sand, stalked by a great grey dog with a thick pale ruff.

"Hey!" he yelled, scrambling to his feet.

Hassan ran after him, waving his whip. Everybody gave chase. Zi'ib sprinted the fastest, his trainers skimming the sand. As he drew level with the calf, the dog swerved and locked its attention on to him. He backed towards the rising ground, sensing the rest of the pack closing in. Massive and menacing, the grey dog bared its teeth. A low rumble poured from its throat and its eyes flashed molten gold. Hassan cracked his whip. As Musa, Christie and Wolfie edged towards it, rocks gripped in their hands, a sharp breeze scudded across the sand, enfolding them all in a whirlwind of grit. The dog pounced. Blurry figures shouted, blundering blindly in the dense brown haze. Heavy paws pinned Zi'ib down. He fumbled for a weapon, discarding little stones and clumps of dry weed until his fingers closed over a hard, heavy lump. He swung it high. The wind stood still, as if time itself had stopped. The shouts and yowls died away. Slowly the dust settled and sunlight filtered through the confusion. Watching them calmly from a little way off stood the baby camel, its jet-black eyes unblinking. The dogs had gone.

Tala came racing over, shaking with relief. "What happened? Where did they go?"

Dazed, Zi'ib shook the sand from his hair. "Dunno."

Christie searched the dunes for a hidden tunnel that might explain the sudden disappearance of the dogs. He found nothing.

Hassan ran to recapture the calf. Leading it over to Zi'ib, he held out the frayed tether. "It's weird. Somehow that dog must have crept up and chewed right through the rope." His puzzled gaze returned to the mother camel, who was resting placidly beneath a thorn tree. "I can't believe it; she's usually so protective. One good kick should have sent that dog flying."

The professor came up, panting. "Zi'ib, that was very brave, but you could have been badly hurt." His face puckered. "What is that in your hand?"

Zi'ib looked down at a black metal object, studded with lumps of dirt. It consisted of two flat discs set at right angles to each other.

"I don't know. I just picked it up to protect myself."

The professor's breath grew shallow. He laid a starched handkerchief on the sand and pulled on a pair of white cotton gloves. "Please, put it here. Gently; don't drop it. I don't understand how years of excavation and countless fortune hunters could have missed a relic like this." With reverential awe he began to brush away the caked sand and inspect the finely wrought detail. Each disc was about two centimetres thick and the size of a side plate. From the top of the upper disc jutted a carved handle, shaped like the head of a shaggy, long-snouted animal. From the centre of the lower one rose a short, narrow cylinder.

"Hang on!" shouted Christie, hurrying to where he had left the camera running on the tripod. Zi'ib following in his father's footsteps and making a major archaeological discovery would make a great sequence for the documentary.

307

"Please step back," commanded the professor. "There may be other treasures lying just below the surface. I must cordon off the area as soon as possible and get this straight back to my lab for analysis."

"All right, Professor, tell us why this find is so significant," said Christie, hoisting the camera on to his shoulder.

The professor cleared his throat. "This object is made of iron. Not only that, the work is of a delicacy I have rarely encountered. Meroe was one of the earliest civilizations to use iron in the making of tools and weapons. It is a complex process that gave the Meroites an extraordinary military and economic advantage over their neighbours. Unfortunately we have no idea how they learned their skills, but their subtle knowledge of what we now call chemistry was truly magical." He smiled. "It was not their priests but their metal-workers who were the real wise men. I always tell my students that they must have smelted their ore in the Fires of Understanding."

The words of the faki seemed to echo across the sands. "*You walk an ancient path in darkness, but the Fires of Understanding will light your way.*"

Did this strange metal object hold a clue to the second stone?

Zi'ib stepped forward. "What exactly is it?"

"Stay back," ordered the professor. "This area must not be trampled." He crouched protectively over the relic.

"Please," begged Zi'ib, his voice cracking with frustration. "I really need to see. . ."

"It's OK," said Wolfie. "Come here." He tugged off his T-shirt and held it over Christie's mobile, flicking through the menu to find the camera feed. Zi'ib and Tala crowded close, peering at the image on the little screen.

"It is clearly a lamp, but of a type I have never seen before," continued Professor Salah. He pointed to the upper disc, which was inset with bronze and engraved with a dirt-encrusted wreath. "This appears to be a flame guard, which would have been polished to reflect the light. Oddly, it seems to have a holder for a wick, yet no receptacle for fuel.

"The handle is in the shape of a dog's head. It could be a Nubian interpretation of the Egyptian dog-headed god Anubis. But. . ." He peered intently through his glasses. "Anubis is usually depicted with a sleek head. This animal is rough-coated and thick-maned."

Zi'ib blinked at the tiny image. The carved beast was remarkably similar to the wolfish dog who, not half an hour before, had led him to that mound and then disappeared.

The professor turned the lamp over, his excitement mounting.

"On the back, there is an inscription in a script I do not recognize."

"Hold it steady," called Christie. "I'm going to focus in tighter."

The image on the mobile grew blurry and then suddenly sharp. Tala let out a cry. The mysterious script was the language of *The Book of Light*.

Zi'ib's chest was bursting. "We've got to touch the lamp."

"Put your hands on the phone," ordered Wolfie.

"What?"

"Do it!"

"Quiet!" called Christie.

Adrenaline pumping, Zi'ib and Tala wedged their fingers around Wolfie's on the handset, marvelling as the meaning grew clear.

Seek where the great sword wounds the heart of the lion born of the serpent, born of the flower.

Tala looked round for her notebook.

"It's OK," whispered Wolfie. He punched the clue into the phone memory and pressed save. "All we've got to do now is find a carving with a sword, a lion, a serpent and a flower."

Tala glanced over at the camel boy, who was soothing the spindly calf. "It's a real shame," she whispered.

"What is?"

"Hassan will never know that he *did* live to help the righteous seekers after all."

38

Scattered Jewels

Professor Salah had arranged for everyone to spend the night at the on-site rest house owned by the Department of Antiquities. They arrived at the rambling mud-brick building to find one of his students waiting in her car to whisk the lamp back to the safety of Khartoum University. Zi'ib and Wolfie watched her drive away, thinking about the faki's words. They might be walking an ancient path in darkness, but the message on that old lamp, forged in the Fires of Understanding, had cast a glimmer of light into the shadow.

Tala had just finished copying the clue into her notebook when Christie came in with his camera gear.

"Thanks," she said as he took back his phone. "It was great being able to see what you were filming."

"No problem. I'd better charge it up for tomorrow."

Christie glanced at the screen, bemused. "Was this a text for me?"

"No, sorry. It's, er, some riddle . . . to do with Mr Forester's ley line thingy."

"OK if I delete it?"

"Sure."

Christie frowned. These kids were an odd bunch, with their interest in ley lines and old ruins. After a day in the desert their faces looked strained and their green eyes were rimmed with red.

"Why don't you rest before supper?" he suggested.

When the professor showed them up to a small whitewashed bedroom, they collapsed, exhausted, on the camp beds. So much had happened in the last ten hours it felt as if they had set out from Khartoum in another lifetime.

"My star's going mad," said Zi'ib.

"Mine feels like it's going to burst," said Wolfie, "and all the time there's that constant crackle of interference."

"Yeah, like a blocked signal trying to break through. But I'm kind of getting used to it now."

Wolfie lay back. His fingers ached to scratch out the name "Ron" on his chart back home and write in the name "Arion". In his mind he saw those five letters, ink-black against the crisp white paper, and felt them shift the dynamic of the puzzle, filling an emptiness he had lived with all his life. Deep in the moment, he mentally added a picture of a planet and labelled it Lupus.

Tala sat up, her eyes darting wildly in her sunburned face. "Arion said someone had to go back to Lupus to get help to fight the Manus Sacra, right?"

Startled, Wolfie opened his eyes and nodded.

"And we know my mom was the first to disappear. So what if this mystery trip she planned was to Lupus? She manages to get there across the leys, thinks she'll be back in a week, but while she's away, the Manus Sacra close the gateway." In her head she heard an iron door clang shut and saw her mother trapped on the other side, trying to claw it open.

Zi'ib caught the story like a hastily thrown ball. "That leaves my dad and Arion. They can't get help from Lupus, so my dad rushes off to London to get his book published, hoping seekers of lost Knowledge will join the fight against the Manus Sacra. But the Manus Sacra snatch him *and* his manuscript."

"Now there's just my dad left and he's panicking," said Wolfie. "So when he sees the opening into the Wilderness, he goes for it."

He rubbed the sand from his eyes, refusing to face the possibility that his father had died in that "nothing place".

Tala said suddenly, "Do you think my dad knows about Lupus?"

"I'm sure my mum doesn't," said Wolfie. "Though maybe deep down she knows there was something weird going on with my dad. She never lost faith in him, not even when everyone told her she was crazy."

"I don't think my mum knows either," said Zi'ib. "But she was always frightened, always making us move house, like she thought the people who got Dad would come back for us." His face crumpled. "And they did."

They ate a supper of bread, cheese, fried eggs and cold chickpea patties, while Professor Salah, still fired up with excitement about the lamp, smiled and nodded at his new friends. Afterwards he led them into the sitting room overlooking the starlit desert to drink tea. A warm light spilled from a table lamp, throwing soft shadows on to the cuttings and photographs crowding the whitewashed walls.

"This will interest you," he said, handing Mr Forester a photocopy. "It's a fragment of papyrus discovered by Dornford Blaker, a colleague of mine at Oxford. It refers to a group of astronomers who lived in pre-dynastic Egypt and describes the way they saw the cosmos."

"Oh, do let me see," said Mr Forester, dropping his glasses from his forehead to his nose.

"Preliminary analysis indicates it may have been written by the Greek geographer Strabo. Possibly a scrap of his lost *Histories*. He spent a lot of time in this part of the world, you know."

Mr Forester examined the text. "Do you have a translation? My ancient Greek is rather of the schoolboy variety, I'm afraid."

"On the back. Dornford had a stab at the poetry, but his translation's a bit flowery for my taste."

Mr Forester read out the words. ". . .'*These wandering astronomers recorded their findings in poetry and song. Typical is this verse, still sung in various forms along the Nile valley. . .'* My goodness! Listen to this:

> "'*Like scattered jewels the living worlds are cast,*
> *Across a darkling void, deep, wild and vast,*
> *Where flesh and blood grow weak and strong men*
>   *quail,*
> *For only mind and will can there prevail.*

> "'*And there is naught to soothe the traveller's*
>   *breast,*
> *No sight, no sound, no hope, no East, no West,*
> *No guiding light, no marking of the way,*
> *No breaking dawn to kindle night to day.*'

"At last! A description of the Wilderness Between the Worlds," he said, tremulous with excitement. "Imagine the strength of spirit necessary to withstand such conditions. No wonder there are no first-hand accounts of it."

Wolfie caught Tala's eye and saw her body sag with misery. Could either of their fathers have survived such a place?

"May I quote this in my book?" Mr Forester was asking the professor.

"You'll have to check with Dornford," came the reply. "I'll give you his address."

315

Mr Forester leaned back in his chair, clutching the photocopy contentedly, certain that years of rejection by the academic establishment were soon to be replaced by glory and recognition. He closed his eyes, mentally compiling a letter to Snodgrass, Beamish and Hussey, offering them the first refusal of his manuscript.

Tala was staring blankly at a photo of a figure from one of the temple friezes labelled King Arnekhamani when her attention snapped towards a tiny detail. On his thumb the king wore a curious flared ring, just like the one worn by the faki.

"What does this ring mean, professor?"

"A good question. There's been a lot of debate about that. Some archaeologists believe these rings were worn by archers to help them draw their bows." He pointed to a larger photograph showing the whole frieze. "However, you can see here that the lion-god Apedemek is also wearing one, which makes me think they were a sign of sacred power, perhaps worn by initiates of a secret sect."

That night the children lay anxious and overwrought beneath the jerky ceiling fan. Thoughts of other worlds, blind soothsayers, the dark designs of the Manus Sacra and the horrors of the Wilderness made sleep impossible. Wolfie found himself wishing Mr Grimes would appear out of the desert to dismiss it all as twaddle and give them a few hundred lines for letting their imaginations run wild.

He switched on the lamp and leafed through his sketchbook, searching for the haggard figure he had drawn the night he moved into the attic. He was now convinced that he had sketched his father, ravaged by his nightmare journey back to Lupus, and he hated himself for ever having doubted him. His glance fell on the second image he had drawn that night. With a cry he dropped the sketchbook.

"What's the matter?" Tala bent to pick it up. In astonishment, she recognized the man they had seen in the Faki's bowl.

"When did you draw this?" Zi'ib demanded.

"Weeks ago, before you two even got to Thornham! I knew I'd seen him before," said Wolfie.

They gazed at the drawing for a long time. Any distinctions they might once have made between the possible and the impossible, reality and imagination, had become meaningless. Even their sense of who they were had melted away. They were stranded in a strange new world of overlapping connections, without barriers between past and present, mind and matter; a world which offered no comfort and no certainties.

Five thousand kilometres away in Thornham, the Master of the Exiles grasped his star, sensing the web of power draw tighter. But would those base-born brats succeed? Or would they freeze and cower before the rolling tides of Knowledge?

39

Written in Stone

O n the way to the ruined town of Naqa, the speeding jeep slowed only to avoid flocks of bony flap-eared sheep wandering across the tarmac. Zi'ib pressed his nose against the window, watching two old women and a little boy at the roadside. The boy waved, jogging memories of pain, thirst, the village women frantic to flag down a vehicle. He blinked and saw the gunman, blinked and saw his mother reach out in horror, blinked again and she was gone. The agonizing loop of images never dimmed. He focused on solving the second clue and finding the rest of the inscription. That was all that mattered now; nothing else could bring his parents back. Yet when they arrived at Naqa and saw the ruined dreamscape of temples, homes and markets, half-buried by the desert, he felt a kind of dread.

"Naqa was an important staging post, lying about a day's camel ride from the river," the professor explained as they began the day's filming. He picked his way up a slope of tumbled stones. "This is where Zane was working before he disappeared. He was concentrating on the inscriptions on the wall just up here."

Zi'ib felt a rush in his star. "Did he say why?"

"I assume they contained a key passage of text that he hoped would clarify some aspect of Meroitic."

Passing through a colonnade of fractured columns, they came to the remains of a temple half-hidden behind a screen of scorched weeds. Zi'ib swept aside the foliage. His heart lurched. Carved into the stone was the inscription he had crossed a continent to find.

. . . if that evil should threaten when the sands of ignorance have buried the Wisdom of the Nile and the Forests and the Mountains, then those who trust in truth should seek out children born of love, whose blood mingles . . .

He read on, his world emptied of everything but the words of the guardians.

. . . the wisdom of the wanderers with the wisdom of the worthy tribes. For just as the waters of the Nile combine the power of two rivers, so the hearts of each child will beat with the wisdom of two worlds and the power of two peoples.

It was true! It had been one thing to stumble towards the belief that they were half Lupan, quite another to see it written starkly in stone.

Keep the children apart and in ignorance until the dawn of their thirteenth year, when their minds will be ripened yet unsullied. Then call upon the righteous to guide them on the path, for truth must seal the circle when the stones unite.

The next portion of text was badly weathered but still legible.

If accursed hands should creep from the shadows to guide their way or snatch the sacred stones, those stones shall turn to dust and their secret shall be lost for ever.

His breath caught in his throat.

But let the worlds be warned. If those of mingled blood should walk the path in darkness. . .

The final section had been hacked away.

"Where's the rest of it?" he cried.

"I don't know," said the professor. "And neither did Zane. But these modern chisel marks suggest that the missing portion was removed relatively recently, probably stolen to order for some private collector." He gazed across the ruined city. "Zane knew it was a lost cause, but he spent days sifting this rubble looking for it."

A lump rose in Zi'ib's throat. "Can we take a break?" he asked.

"Sure," said Christie.

Zi'ib wandered away and slumped on to a wooden day bed left in the shade by the site watchman. He watched Wolfie and Tala crouch before the ancient text and felt their wonder and excitement soar and crash just as his own had done.

320

"I wanted it to tell us how to get our parents back," said Wolfie, flopping down beside him. "Who needs more warnings about *'walking the path in darkness'*? I'm scared enough already."

Tala scuffed her foot in the dust. "I s'pose it did tell us one new thing. That bit about *'accursed hands'* creeping from the shadows. It's *got* to be talking about the Manus Sacra. And if they've been searching for the stones for generations, I bet they found that inscription ages before we did."

Wolfie almost smiled. "Which means – they know there's no point in them trying to snatch the stones! Pretty smart, those guardians."

Zi'ib looked doubtful. "Maybe they weren't smart enough. Maybe there's something really important in the missing bit."

"Whatever it was, we've got no hope of finding it now," said Tala.

"Cup of tea, anyone?" called Mr Forester, heading towards them with a tower of paper cups and a Thermos.

Christie, sensing the children's need to be alone, called out, "Hey, Mr Forester, leave the tea, I've got something to show you."

He led the old man away to a gentle dip where the ruins of two squat buildings faced each other across the sand. He pointed to the less ornate one, which was roofless, square and badly weathered.

"Ah, the Lion Temple," said Mr Forester, inspecting a

relief of a plump woman smiting her enemies. "That must be Queen Amanitare. Charming."

"But come round here," said Christie.

"Mmm, the lion-god."

"The lion-god with the body of a serpent emerging from a flower."

"Indeed. I'll lend you my guidebook if you want to read up about it."

"Isn't it the answer to that riddle you need to solve for your research?"

Mr Forester stared at him blankly.

"You know . . . *the sword piercing the heart of the lion born of the serpent, born of the flower* – this must be it."

"Sorry, old chap. I have absolutely no idea what you are talking about."

Mr Forester rejoined the children and sipped his tea. "I think the sun is getting to our friend Christie. He just dragged me over to look at a relief of the lion-god with a snake's body. He doesn't understand that it's not the decoration but the *positioning* of sacred edifices that—"

He was talking to himself. Wolfie, Tala and Zi'ib were already racing across the ruins towards the Lion Temple.

There were two carvings of a lion-headed serpent emerging from a lotus flower, one at each corner of the temple. Both were quite badly damaged, the soft sandstone pitted and notched by the gritty desert winds, but some of the intricate detail of the petals and the tiny scales chiselled into the serpents' coils had survived. Laughing and breathless, they dashed from one carving to the other looking for a sword. There wasn't one. They circled the temple. The figures on the other panels were unarmed and the weapon wielded by Queen Amanitare pointed to the sky, not the serpents.

Zi'ib called to the professor, who was coming over to find them. "Are there any more carvings of swords round here?"

The professor shook his head. "What is most interesting about this temple is the depiction of the lion-god with many arms, possibly indicating an Indian influence."

Zi'ib didn't care about arms and influences; he wanted a sword that would point them to the second stone. "Any other lion-headed serpents?"

Professor Salah tutted. "No. These are as unique as they are remarkable."

For the rest of that hot, dreary day, Tala and Wolfie trailed around scrutinizing the wall carvings, while Christie, Zi'ib and Professor Salah continued filming.

"If I see one more pot-bellied priest with a palm frond fan I'll throw up," moaned Wolfie.

It was a relief when the sun set and they pitched camp on a patch of desert overlooking the ruins. Musa lined a dip in the sand with smooth rocks and lit a fire to cook supper. Mr Forester had bananas baked in the embers and the others sat in the firelight, dipping bread into a communal dish of bean stew. Zi'ib, who had said very little all evening, suddenly asked, "Professor, did you ever meet a man called Matthias Threlfall? He met my dad out here years ago."

Professor Salah stroked his beard, picturing a man he hadn't seen for over a decade. "Threlfall. Hmm. Geologist, shortish, with red hair and green eyes?"

Zi'ib kept his voice steady.

"He's got green eyes, but he's really tall with brown hair."

"How odd. With an unusual name like that, there can't be two of them." The professor stabbed the fire irritably. "I used to pride myself on my memory for names and faces. I must be getting old."

40

The Great Sword

"Maybe Matthias came back from Sudan, went on a crash diet and dyed his hair," whispered Zi'ib, squashing into the stuffy gloom of their tent.

"And had his legs stretched? Don't be stupid," snapped Tala.

"So is the bloke we know the *real* Matthias? If not, who is he?"

"Green eyes, gives us the creeps, thinks he's cool. I bet he's one of the Manus Sacra, '*watching and waiting from beneath a cloak of trust*'."

Tala spoke with bravado, but inside she quailed. Across the darkness they heard the desert dogs howl and their stars seemed to cry out in reply.

"But what's he waiting *for*?" said Wolfie.

"For us to find the stones, of course," said Tala.

"What's the point, if they're going to disintegrate the minute any of their *cursed hands* touch them?"

"There's got to be some loophole in that missing bit of the inscription," said Zi'ib. "Something they think they can use to weasel round the rest of it. Shh. Someone's coming." They heard footsteps, muffled voices and then the sound of a tent being unzipped.

Wolfie waited until there was silence. In a low voice he said, "What do you think they've done with the real Matthias?"

Tala sat up. "Who knows? But . . . he had green eyes *and* he knew Zane *and* had some special bond with my mom *and* he disappeared. I bet he was another explorer from Lupus. There must have been four of them. Arion, Kara, Zane and Matthias."

"And now there are none," said Zi'ib.

"So what do we do?" said Tala. "Turn over the fake Matthias to the police?"

"Oh, good idea," said Wolfie, putting on a whiny American accent. "'Scuse me, constable, I think my uncle's been abducted by aliens."

Tala gave a little snort of laughter, but punched him all the same and said crossly, "It's OK for you, you haven't got to live with him."

Eventually she and Wolfie fell into a troubled sleep. Zi'ib lay in the darkness picking through the words of the clue: lion, serpent, flower, sword. The message on the lamp *had* to refer to the carving on the Lion Temple; they just weren't looking properly. He pulled on his shoes and unzipped the tent. Outside, the full moon blazed bright, slashing the pale sand with shadow. He walked through the ruins and huddled against a jut of rock overlooking the temple. A breeze brushed his skin, wafting woodsmoke from a faraway village, stirring memories of life with his mother. Just as he had always done, he sought comfort in the patterns of the stars, tracing his favourite shape glimmering in the arc of the sky. For a moment he found peace. Suddenly he jumped up. Cursing his own stupidity, he stumbled back to the tent and prodded the others.

"Get up, I've found the sword!"

Tala sat up, blinking.

Wolfie rolled over. "Great, show us in the morning."

Zi'ib shone the torch in his eyes. "No, now! Quick!"

"OK, OK," grumbled Wolfie, pulling on his shoes.

They followed Zi'ib through the shadows, unnerved by the ragged shapes of the ruins rising through the gloom.

"Where is it?" demanded Wolfie blearily.

Zi'ib pointed to the sky. "The sword in the stars. I used to think up stories about it when I was a kid."

They followed his finger and there, glowing brightly, as if relishing the contact with their willing minds, gleamed the star-studded outline of a sword with a rounded hilt and a long narrow blade. But how and where did it pierce the heart of a lion?

Wolfie and Tala started to duck and weave, searching for

327

a point where the glowing shaft appeared to pierce one of the carved lion-headed snakes, but whichever way they looked, the sword just disappeared behind the temple wall.

Zi'ib watched them for a while, perplexed by a pull of energy drawing him *away* from the temple. He followed it, step by step, until his foot struck a piece of smooth black granite glistening beneath a dusting of sand. Fixed immovably in the ground, the stone had two curved indentations carved down one edge. He set his heels against them and returned his gaze to the sky. Something odd happened. Although the tip of the sword was still obscured, from where he stood a series of shadowed pits in the wind-worn stone continued its exact shape. It was as if the blade had plunged deep into the temple wall, piercing the heart of the lion-headed snake and pointing to a spot between two stone blocks. To a casual observer by day, there would be nothing to mark it out. To a righteous seeker by moonlight, it was as clear as a flashing neon sign.

"It's there!" he called, pointing up at the stonework.

Wolfie and Tala dragged the wooden day bed across the sand, propped it against the temple and held it steady while Zi'ib clambered up the webbing and squeezed his fingertips into the join, testing for any hint of movement. He stepped back, teetering on the edge of the bed frame, and as he reached to steady himself, the pads of his splayed fingers slipped into five of the tiny scales carved into the serpent's body. With a gentle click the stone swung open on a hidden midpin. He pushed his hand deep into the cavity and with a sharp tug pulled out a cylindrical metal box. He leapt down, sending a judder of pain through his injured bone. He hardly noticed.

The box was about fifteen centimetres high and ten centimetres in diameter, fastened with a clasp of hammered bronze. There was almost no corrosion, just a thin greenish crust that scraped away easily beneath Zi'ib's fingernail. Wolfie and Tala were deaf to the sounds of the desert and blind to everything but the small steady movements of Zi'ib's thumb easing open the clasp. The lid fell back on a spiral hinge, revealing its underside, which was embossed with a pattern of rising and setting suns surrounding a circular plain at the foot of a hill. Around the plain, with a blade in its belly, slithered a lion-headed snake.

Zi'ib flashed his torch into the box. His howl of frustration rang across the desert.

It was empty.

He felt as if he had rushed to take a long-awaited phone call just as the line had gone dead.

Baffled, Tala grabbed the box from his hands.

"We can't give up," said Wolfie in a small voice. "So far the power of the leys has found a way round most problems."

"Yeah," said Tala, struggling to hide her despair. "Maybe this picture's another clue. Maybe the professor'll know what it means."

*

Next morning Musa set out breakfast on a fold-up table. Wolfie and Tala held their breath as Zi'ib laid the little box next to Professor Salah's plate, wrapped in a clean T-shirt.

"What's this?" asked the professor, laying down his cup and opening the folds of material. He gazed at the box. "I don't understand."

"We found it near the Lion Temple last night when we went for a walk," said Zi'ib. "Over by those fallen bricks."

The professor fumbled for his white gloves. "Can everyone stay clear of the area until I've had it sealed off?"

Carefully he inspected the box. "It's a beautiful piece, quite exquisite. Probably made for storing spices or unguents."

"What about the picture in the lid?" said Zi'ib.

The professor frowned. "The craftsmanship is of the highest quality, but I have no idea what it means."

Mr Forester peered over his shoulder.

"How interesting," he said. "This is a message map designed to pass on secret knowledge between ancient astronomers. It's using the position of the planets to pinpoint an expanse of flatland beneath a sacred mound at the winter solstice. May I?" He picked up the little box in its T-shirt wrapping and examined it intently. "In this instance it looks as if the light and shadow will strike certain targets on the plain to create a calendrical marker in the form of a snake coiling towards the hill."

He looked up to see three pairs of green eyes staring at him with rapt attention.

"Hills and high points are always steeped in power, for they are where the earth touches the sky," he went on. "But to be recorded for posterity in this way, this particular hill and plain must have had exceptional significance."

Zi'ib scanned the surrounding desert with its many rocky knolls and dunes.

"So, where is it?" he said, excitedly.

"Unfortunately our understanding of ancient astronomy is so rudimentary, it could be located almost anywhere on the planet."

Mr Forester's words left them stunned.

They had come so far and now the trail of clues had gone cold. What good was it to know that somewhere, in a place they could never find, the second stone lay buried on a sacred plain, beneath a sacred hill?

Zi'ib hardly knew how he managed to get through the next few days. He talked to policemen, aid workers and local journalists and was even granted an audience with a pompous government official. They told him nothing new about his father's disappearance and could only confirm that his mother had been abducted by unknown gunmen who seemed to have staged their raid purely to take her. He felt so numb that even the return to his old home failed to move him.

331

On the evening before they left Sudan, the children barely spoke, preferring to nurse their own private grief. No rosy daydreams played in Zi'ib's head on the long journey home, and although he now knew that his parents were alive, all hope of ever finding them had died.

41

The View Over Thornham

Listless and irritable, Wolfie and Zi'ib lay slouched on the sofa, playing a half-hearted game of *Doom* on Zi'ib's laptop. Tala leafed aimlessly through a magazine. The frustration that had been welling up inside them since leaving Sudan had grown unbearable when the presenter on the morning news announced that this was the shortest day of the year – the winter solstice. That meant that at sunset, in some secret, sacred location, an ancient calendrical marker would be pinpointing the hiding place of the second stone. And they would not be there to see it. On top of that, they were getting increasingly anxious about Matthias's imminent return.

Sarah had been trying her hardest to cheer them up all day. Using the profits from the sales of Brown's Traditional

Fudge, she had gone out and bought an enormous Christmas tree, strung fairy lights from every corner of the shop and cooked a delicious lunch, which no one had eaten.

Zi'ib's misery was understandable and her heart went out to him, but she could not understand why Wolfie and Tala were so moody and withdrawn. They had practically ignored poor Elvis since they'd got back and now he was moping about with his tail between his legs. She handed him a square of fudge. He licked it gloomily. She piled the rest on a tray, arranging them into a steep pyramid ready for display in the shop window.

The grandfather clock struck three. Elvis scratched at the back door, whining, and thrashing his tail against the wall.

"For heaven's sake, take that dog for a walk. Some fresh air will do you all good," she said.

"Later," said Wolfie, flicking on the television.

"No, now," said Sarah, losing patience. "You can't moon around inside for the rest of the holidays."

Grunting and huffing, they pulled on their coats and trooped into the yard. Without warning, Elvis barged through their legs and, like a porpoise rising through water, leapt over the wall into the street.

"Heel!" yelled Wolfie. Elvis scooted in front of a taxi. Brakes screeched. The driver swore and shouted. The dog didn't turn a whisker. He ran straight across the common, bounding past the bus stop, over the rockery, round the church and up towards Dodds Hill. The road was steep. Zi'ib streaked ahead, his long, thin legs moving effortlessly. Wolfie and Tala panted behind. Outside the garden centre they bumped into Leonora Grindle and her barbarous Rottweiler Mr B, his bared teeth swinging spittle as he turned to give chase.

"There! You've upset Mr Booboo again," she shouted.

Wolfie ran on up the hill, his lungs on fire. As he tore around the corner, he saw Zi'ib grab Elvis by the collar. Wolfie staggered up the last few feet of the incline and threw himself down on the square of cold, damp concrete, described on local maps as the "Dodds Hill observation point". On a clear day if you stood at the edge and squinted, you were supposed to be able to make out Battersea Power Station, the Millennium Wheel and Windsor Castle, although Wolfie had never bothered trying.

"Elvis . . . you . . . bad, bad dog. What's got into you?" he gasped.

Elvis slunk towards him, raising his head just enough to let him clip on the lead. Tala collapsed next to him, gazing down over Thornham.

The setting sun had turned the sky a rich pink-gold slashed with purple, swathing the common in a light so unearthly it was easy to imagine the great megaliths that had once towered from this ancient grassland.

Zi'ib screwed up his eyes and pointed. "Look. From up here you can see a circle of marks in the grass, like scars in the landscape. I bet it's where the inner circle of stones used to be."

Elvis stopped panting and sat up, looking strangely noble, his ears stiff and straight and his long limbs tucked neatly against his body, as if he were carved from stone. The sunset was a too-painful reminder of Tala's last night at home in the cabin. She turned away, and watched two old ladies shuffle to the bus stop and sit down to share a bag of fudge. A number 717 swung into the lay-by. They climbed aboard and the bus swept up the hill, revealing the empty bench. Tala had sat on that bench countless times since arriving in Thornham without realizing what an odd-looking thing it was, jutting at a strange angle with its jumble of legs, some fat and wide, some pointed and spindly, supporting a thick, flat slab of rock. She closed her eyes, trying to think what it reminded her of. After a few seconds she pulled Wolfie's arm.

"The bench – it's just like one of those dolmen things we saw at Mr Forester's lecture."

Wolfie merely nodded, his eyes riveted on the common. As the light and shadow cast by the setting sun fell across the tumps and ridges in the grass, something odd was happening. A narrow coiling line, like the rippling body of a great serpent, seemed to be weaving its way from the wizened foliage of the municipal flower beds and tracing the path of the vanished inner circle of stones. From there it wrapped a loop around the bus stop and snaked around the edge of the grass to the rockery. Was it his imagination or did those huge craggy boulders, dotted with wilting ferns and old crisp packets, seem to rise from the grass like the head of a great stone lion?

He stood up, craning to see better, and let out a deep cry.

In a subtle alchemy of earth, light, shade and stone, the blade of the bench's thin central support seemed to plunge through the curving shadow as if piercing the heart of a lion with the body of a serpent.

Seek where the great sword pierces the heart of the lion, born of the serpent, born of the flower.

This was the hill and the sacred plain depicted in the message map of Meroe!

They raced back down the hill. Yelping with excitement, Elvis ran ahead, his lead trailing in the gutter. The shadows were fading, but it didn't matter; nothing could erase that image from their minds. They reached the bench and Wolfie hurled himself on to the mud, wrapped both hands around the support and tugged hard.

"It won't budge," he groaned. "We'll have to dig round it."

Zi'ib stood grave-faced and immobile.

"Don't just stand there," cried Tala. "Go get Matthias's spade."

In a strange gruff voice, Zi'ib replied in the tongue of his Meroite ancestors, "There is no cause to disturb the earth, for *this* is the stone that awaits the righteous seekers."

Wolfie's eyes met Tala's. How could he tell and why was he talking in that spooky way? Dropping to his knees, Zi'ib began to scrape the support with his penknife. Cleaned of lichen, the stone gleamed pale and smooth in the dying light. Reaching behind it, he rubbed the hidden face with his cuff, his solemnity dissolving to a wide grin when the material snagged on a patch of roughness. "Told you," he said in a voice once more his own. "It's got the fossil imprint!"

Days of festering misery exploded in a frenzy of triumph. They had found the second stone.

"It's been here for a few thousand years, so I s'pose it's safe to leave it till we find the third one," said Zi'ib, snapping his penknife shut.

Tala frowned. "You went all weird."

Zi'ib shrugged. "Come on, I'm starving."

Hungry for the first time in days, they ran back to the shop, where they met Mr Forester standing on the step, looking unusually dejected.

"Are you all right?" asked Wolfie.

"It's the winter solstice. According to my calculations, there should have been a particularly interesting alignment of light over the common at sunset." He sighed. "I must have been standing in the wrong place. You didn't see anything unusual, did you?"

Wolfie blushed and shook his head. "Sorry." He

followed the others inside, wishing he could have told Mr Forester the truth.

In his sunlit office at the University of Khartoum, Professor Salah turned the little black box in his white-gloved hand, studying the etching inside the lid, saddened that he would never know the meaning of its message. An assistant entered carrying the lamp Zi'ib had found and laid it in front of him.

The dirt had been cleaned away, revealing the exquisite detail of the decoration circling the flame guard. The professor was mystified. It was an image he had never seen before: a wreath of snarling beasts, their muzzles and tails interlocked with perfect, mathematical precision.

42

Christmas

It had been arranged for ages that Zi'ib would spend Christmas day at the shop. Sarah invited the vicar to join them for lunch, but to everyone's secret relief, he explained that he always nipped out between services to eat Christmas dinner at the old people's home.

"Mrs Poskitt told me he's got a soft spot for the matron," giggled Sarah, putting the phone down. The children rolled on the sofa, making retching noises at the thought of Godfrey Peasemarsh getting a girlfriend.

On Christmas morning, Sarah dragged everybody to church and grew tearful during the performance of the nativity play. Someone had tacked a border of fairy lights around Wolfie's sky-scape in an attempt to make it look more festive, and as the three wise men in their foil and cardboard finery led their sackcloth camels down the aisle, she whispered, "It's a shame about the new star. That tatty old one had been around since I was a kid. Do you remember when it fell down and nearly knocked you out?"

The boom of the organ echoed through the ancient church as the congregation rose for the final carol. Wolfie looked about him, through swathes of holly and the smoky glitter of candles, wondering what other events in his childhood had been shaped by the power of the leys. The stained-glass image of St Michael spearing the serpent held his gaze for a long time; the frond-headed gargoyles gurning from the rafters seemed to whisper their ancient secrets, and the marble tombs of the de Monteneuf family gleamed in the shadowy niche beneath their coat of arms. He looked up at their crest. A feeling like icy water dripped down his spine. It was a golden eight-point star riven in two, encircled by a ring of thorns above the motto *Trust in Truth*.

Before the final notes of "Good King Wenceslas" had faded away, he was pulling Zi'ib and Tala down the side aisle to look more closely at the de Monteneuf tombs.

Sir Edgar's booted feet rested on the back of an enormous hound. It had rough bristled hair and huge ears that hung over its eyes. Was this the animal described in the *Chronicle of Thornham*? Agnes's faithful "devil dog", taken in by Sir Edgar after her death? Or had the flimsy barrier between past and present been snatched away to reveal an effigy of Elvis? Wordlessly they touched the cold marble muzzle, sensing the power of the leys resonating around them, weaving its ghostly web across time and place and imagination.

They arrived home to find that Elvis had nosed open the larder and eaten a whole ham and all the mince pies. He grovelled at Sarah's feet, looking so pathetic that any thought of him being some kind of canine time-traveller seemed absurd. The de Monteneuf crest was real enough, however. They rushed upstairs to add it to the crowded chart of *kinnections* on Wolfie's wall.

For the rest of the day they tried to forget the forces of destiny and to immerse themselves in the joys of roast turkey, silly games and brightly wrapped presents. Sarah loved the coffee pot, beads and basket they had bought for her in Shendi and Tala was thrilled with her present from Sarah: a beautiful black coat with a purple lining. She tried it on and for a moment she looked like a stranger. Mr Forester gave Sarah a silver locket from the second-hand shop in Dodds Hill, and each of the children a crystal dowsing pendulum wrapped in a ten-pound note. Wolfie made everyone laugh by picking his up with the fire tongs.

Mr Forester's eyes grew moist when he unwrapped his present from the children. Zi'ib and Tala had framed one of Wolfie's paintings: a view of Thornham Common, not as it was today but as he imagined it might have looked when Thornham Henge was still standing. Dodds Hill towered in the distance and the double ring of dark stones, haunting and beautiful, rose from the foreground like great black giants. Sarah watched the old man and the three green-eyed children staring captivated at the image. A shadow passed over her face. Beckoning hurriedly to the boys, she said, "Your presents from me are outside."

Propped against the outhouse stood two mountain bikes. Although they weren't new, the paintwork was barely scratched and the man at the shop had had them completely reconditioned. As they ran across the yard whooping their thanks, Wolfie tripped on a bag of compost.

"What's that doing there?"

Sarah dragged it out of the way. "I've been potting up seedlings."

"In the middle of winter?"

"They're in the airing cupboard. Come on, let's give those bikes a try."

Zi'ib's edition of *My Story* was scheduled for the day before New Year's Eve. He had spent the previous morning at the television studios being fussed over by people with headphones and clipboards, while he recorded the voiceover. There were photographs of him in a couple of the national papers and a full-page article in the *Thornham Gazette*. Sarah sat clipping them out. "Look, they interviewed Mr Andrews. He says your recovery is so remarkable he's going to write about it for some medical journal."

343

"It's really weird," said Zi'ib. "My leg still hurts sometimes, but I can run much faster now than before I was shot."

"I told you," said Mr Forester. "It's the healing power of the leys. I shall write to the *Gazette* and explain. Unfortunately it doesn't seem to be having the same effect on my arthritis. It's really flared up over the last few days."

At six o'clock they settled in front of the television with a large bowl of fudge. Christie had woven Zi'ib's search into a gripping tale of frustrating dead ends, insoluble mysteries and personal loss without making it sensational or sentimental. Everyone agreed that Zi'ib came across really well, particularly when he talked about wanting to follow in his father's footsteps and become an archaeologist. The final shot was of him walking alone through the desert. Slowly it mixed through to the photograph of him as a toddler with his mum and dad. His voice rose through the music, explaining that he would never stop searching until his family was united once more. Sarah blew her nose and put on the kettle. "You were so good, Zi'ib. It was one of the best programmes I've ever seen." She looked over at Tala and saw silent tears sliding down her face.

An hour later a message from the Master of the Exiles flew across the leys to the Leader, who waited alone in the Lupan Chamber.

And the Chosen shall prevail.
All is ready.
Release Jack Bean.

PART FOUR
Shasta

43

Jack Bean

Something has changed. Jack Bean can sense light on the other side of the darkness and voices beyond the silence.

Memories shuffle through his mind. A call about a fallen tree near Klamath Falls. Tala waving from the step. Driving over the mountain roads. Pines rising from the slopes. Leaves fluttering in the windless sunlight. Deer in the undergrowth, nervy and jumpy. Birds dipping and darting as if pulled by unseen threads. His flesh tingles. The landscape is uneasy. He is uneasy. Clouds swallow the sun. A rock crashes down the hillside, hits the truck. He gets out and stands above the jutting crags, fearful that an earthquake or a flash flood is on its way. He worries about Tala alone in the cabin. He must get home. An enormous black juggernaut roars past, sucking the air. He jumps back and rolls down and down the hillside, buffeted by rocks, sure he can hear the rattle of his truck being driven away. He strikes his head. Blood blinds him. Are those branches or fingers clawing at his clothes, pulling him into a dark chasm that has no beginning and no end? A lost, shadowy place from which everything he understands has disappeared. He cries out, but the void pulls him deeper, leaving him alone and afraid for a long, long time.

And now he can hear voices and feel crisp sheets beneath his skin and he is not afraid any more.

"Tala, can you answer that?" called Sarah, stuffing copies of the *Thornham Gazette* into Wolfie's delivery bag. "It'll be someone complaining their papers are late. Wolfie, hurry up, it's nearly quarter past."

Tala dropped the knife she was using to cut up Elvis's breakfast and reached for the telephone. Her stomach swooped as a clipped American voice said, "This is Lorraine Sylvester at the New Sion Hospital in Trinity County. May I speak with Sarah Brown?"

Tala fell back against the wall. She wanted to vomit. Wolfie stopped spooning cornflakes into his mouth, alarm surging through his star.

"Have you found Jack Bean? Is he all right?" cried Tala. "I'm his daughter."

"I'm sorry, dear," said the voice. "I know you're the next of kin, but I need to speak to an adult. The sheriff's office gave me the name of Sarah Brown."

Tala thrust the receiver at Sarah.

"This is Sarah Brown." Sarah's expression was unreadable as she listened for a few minutes, replying in monosyllables. She jotted down a number.

"Thank you, Mrs Sylvester. I'll call you back." She put down the phone and grasped Tala's shoulders.

"They've found a man in the hills who had your dad's wallet on him."

"Why wouldn't she talk to me?"

Sarah struggled to soften the impact of Mrs Sylvester's words. "They tried to identify him from photographs, but . . . he looks so poorly it's difficult to tell whether he is Jack Bean or not. He's in intensive care."

Tala shoved her hands into her armpits and shut her eyes. A muscle trembled at the corner of her mouth.

"They want you to see if you can identify him," went on Sarah. "If you aren't sure, they can do a blood test to find out."

"Course I'll know if it's him."

Sarah nodded. "I'm sure you will, and if it *is* your father, the sound of your voice may help to bring him round. Maybe you can stay with those neighbours again – what were they called?"

"The Holts."

Sarah flicked through her address book. "OK. Let's give Matthias a call about getting you a ticket."

Tala shot her a look of panic.

"He's got money problems. He'll say no – then what'll I do?"

"Don't worry. I'll talk to him," said Sarah. "And I'll see if he's got a number for the Holts."

She dialled Matthias's mobile, got his voicemail and left a message.

"If you can't face school today, you can stay here with me."

Tala shook her head. "I'd rather go in. It'll keep my mind occupied."

She regretted her decision. It was one of the longest days she had ever lived through, worse in some ways than the day her father had disappeared. At least then she hadn't been forced to sit, nauseous and trembling, through geography and double maths or worry that Jessica Albright would taunt her for snivelling in the washrooms. Wolfie had given her his old bike and as soon as the bell went, she raced back to the shop.

"Do you think it is her dad?" asked Wolfie, pulling his own bike out of the rack.

"Dunno. I mean, I want it to be, for her sake," said Zi'ib. "But I was sure we wouldn't find any of our parents till we'd discovered all the stones. Still, you never know; while she's there, she might find the clues to the third one."

"Maybe. But it'll be tough on her own, and if this bloke *is* her dad, she'll stay in America and we'll never get to the bottom of any of this."

They cycled slowly down the street, feeling selfish and confused.

*

Tala burst into the shop and jiggled from foot to foot while Mrs Baxter paid her paper bill and complained about the sudden influx of demanding guests who had descended on her B&B and sat around all day cluttering up her lounge.

"What did he say?" Tala demanded as soon as Mrs Baxter had gone.

"Let's go in the kitchen."

Tala sat down at the table. Sarah put on the kettle.

"You were right about Matthias's money problems. In fact, he's going to be away longer than he thought, sorting out that big excavation in Alaska. But he promised that if the man they've found comes out of the coma and turns out to be your dad, he'll get you a ticket home."

"But I've got to go *now*," wailed Tala, burying her head on her hands.

"It's tough, I know, but just listen. A couple of hours after I spoke to Matthias, a Dr Walker rang from the States. She said the hospital was anxious to identify this man as soon as possible, and that if there was any problem paying for your trip, there was a fund that could help."

Tala looked up in disbelief. Sarah stretched across the table and took her hand. "I explained the situation and she's going to book you a ticket for the day after tomorrow. I hope I did the right thing."

"Course you did, but don't you think it's weird? Why would a hospital do that?"

"I don't know. From what I've heard about American

healthcare, they don't give you anything for free, so I rang the hospital and checked this Dr Walker out. She specializes in coma and trauma, lectures part-time at the university, and she's published of lot of highly regarded papers. I'm sure it's all fine."

Tala nodded, but she still felt uneasy, and deep down, so did Sarah.

44

Green-Eyed Wanderers

The vicar took a swig of coffee, bit hurriedly into his toast and flicked through the post. "Gas bill, electricity bill . . . donation for Dr Margani . . . and a package for you."

Zi'ib looked up from his porridge and took the thick brown envelope.

"That'll be fan mail," teased the vicar, "now that you're a celebrity." Zi'ib grimaced. He was fed up with being stared at by strangers and kids at school who had seen him on television. Godfrey Peasemarsh pushed back his chair. "I've got to go. Can you leave your washing out for Mrs Poskitt? Your lunch money is on the hall table. See you later."

Zi'ib ripped open the package. It was full of letters forwarded by the corporation, mostly from viewers saying how much they had enjoyed his programme, one from a couple in Wales offering to adopt him and another from a theatrical agency wanting to represent him. He shook two charred sheets of pale parchment from the last envelope. The room seemed suddenly to grow very cold. They were two more pages of *The Book of Light*. The accompanying letter was from a Major Cridling-Stubbs (retired) of The Nook, Bagshott, Surrey.

Dear Zi'ib,

My wife and I were very impressed by your film the other night. The world could do with a few more youngsters with the kind of grit you have shown in the face of rotten luck.

I was stationed in the Soudan after the war and found the enclosed documents in an old chest I picked up in the souk at Omdurman. I recognized the script as being similar to the writing on the lamp you found in the desert, so I thought you might like to have them. If you ever manage to find out what they say, I would be most interested to see the translation, and if you ever find yourself down our way, do pop in and tell us how you are getting on.

May I wish you every success in your future endeavours.

With kindest regards,
Henry Cridling-Stubbs

Zi'ib slipped the pages into his rucksack. At least they would have a chance to read them before Tala left next day for the States.

"Pleeeease let it be the clue to the third stone," begged Wolfie later that evening as they laid their hands on the paper and watched the meaning unfold.

Among the most trusted of Seth's advisers was a man called Nessus, who studied the mystery of metals. He saw that in the mantle of quartz wherein they stored the Wisdom of the Stars there hung droplets of gold. He smelted those droplets in the Fires of Understanding, lit from the celestial flame that burned in the Sacred Sphere. And he wrought that gold into stars shaped as the ways of the winds and the cycles of the seasons, and gave them to the scholar slaves. The stars cleaved to their bearers and no stranger could take them for his own. And with those stars they shared the mastery of numbers, music and tongues and spoke to one another with their minds. Seth named this bond of minds the Link of Light, and though the scholars laboured hard to fathom its subtle workings, they learned only that it was driven by the action of the Sphere.

Wolfie crept a hand to his throat, feeling for the sliver of metal wrought in the forges of another world. "Droplets of Lupan gold that store the Wisdom of the Stars, shaped as the ways of the winds," he murmured, astounded that so extraordinary an explanation could feel so reassuring. "So it *is* our stars making us speak languages and do maths and stuff."

He dropped his hand back on to the page.

And Seth knew that the distant worlds that floated in the Wilderness were fraught with danger and he vowed that no man should journey through their depths to die alone. He commanded each wandering band of explorers to lay their stars one upon the other in the Fires of Understanding, and from that time until the days of their deaths those stars would pulse as one.

With renewed wonder they felt the pull of the bond between them.

Zi'ib said quietly, "The only Lupan explorers who'd want to share their stars with us are our parents." He gave a soft exclamation. "Do you think if their Link of Light was working we could speak to them?"

Tala frowned. "I'm always talking to Mom in my mind, but I don't know what I'd do if she started talking back."

"Maybe that's what that constant interference is," exclaimed Wolfie. "Maybe it's them!"

They squeezed their eyes tight shut, trying to isolate the whispered under-note beneath their pounding heartbeats, willing it to be the pulsing stars of Arion, Kara and Zane. As if strengthened by their passionate concentration, the signal grew clearer.

It was a single, solitary life force.

"None of them are dead," said Wolfie quickly. "The faki would have said. Two must be somewhere the signal doesn't carry."

But which two? Wolfie left the question unspoken,

knowing it would lie in wait to ambush them in the night. He turned briskly to the chart and snatched a pen.

"OK. Recap. We've all got one parent who we're pretty sure is an explorer from this other world called Lupus." He wondered, not for the first time, if he had gone mad, like those people who thought they were Napoleon or Attila the Hun. Zi'ib and Tala were gazing at him expectantly. Maybe they were bonkers too. He tried to concentrate. "They've got golden stars that link their minds." He drew yellow half-stars next to the figures of Arion, Kara and Zane. " Years ago they came to Earth with a fourth explorer called Matthias, looking for three stones that the ancient Lupans had hidden with the help of three earthly tribes. To find them they not only needed their own Wisdom of the Stars but also the Wisdom of the Forests, Mountains and Nile, which had all been lost. But the inscriptions at Meroe said children descended from both the Lupan and the earthly guardians could still find the stones because they'd have both lots of Wisdom flowing in their veins."

"Right now it doesn't feel like I've got anybody's wisdom flowing in mine," said Zi'ib grimly.

"We don't know what happened to the real Matthias, but somehow the other three explorers found descendants of these earthly tribes and had us. Pretty soon they lost contact with Lupus 'cos their Link of Light broke down and they suspected the Manus Sacra were trying to wreck their mission."

"That's why they broke their stars in half!" cried Tala.

"In case something happened to them before we were old enough to start the search."

Zi'ib and Wolfie considered this. It fitted the rest of the crazy story they were piecing together, but as far as finding a way to get their parents back, they were scoring a big fat zero.

"So my mom returned to Lupus to get help and while she was there the Manus Sacra closed all the gateways so she couldn't get back to earth. Then they snatched Zane *and* his manuscript and Arion was so desperate he tried to make it back to Lupus through the Wilderness."

Zi'ib joined Wolfie by the chart. "Ten years later my mum and Tala's dad disappeared as well and we ended up in Thornham. And now we're stuck here with no parents and no idea how to find them *or* the third stone," he added savagely.

"Yep, that's about it," said Tala. "And we don't even know why they wanted the stones in the first place. So all we can do is go on looking for them and see what happens when we bring them together."

"OK. So what do we know about this third stone?" said Wolfie.

"Not much. Only that it was hidden with the help of my ancestors using the Wisdom of the Mountains."

Wolfie gave Zi'ib a faint nod. Zi'ib stood for a moment, shifting from one foot to the other. "Look, we got Mr Forester to do a map of the place where the ley lines converge at Mount Shasta." He handed her a piece of paper. "It's called Crystal River. So just in case you find yourself anywhere near there. . ."

Tala stuffed the paper into her coat pocket, feeling suddenly afraid. Afraid of what awaited her at the New Sion Hospital in Trinity County and afraid that she would fail the other bearers of the broken stars, who were now relying on her and her alone to find the clues to the third stone.

45

Dr Dulcie Walker

Every surface in the reception area of the New Sion Hospital glinted with efficiency. Brightly lit corridors branched from a marble-floored waiting area where rows of stainless steel chairs curved round a circular desk of pale wood. The air smelled of flowers and warm plastic and thrummed with the insistent purr of computers, lights and whispered conversation. Staff in starched uniforms glided up and down. Tala felt invisible. As she walked up to the reception desk, a tall man in a business suit brushed her aside.

"Where can I find Cardio?" he barked.

For nearly ten minutes, Tala stood unnoticed while a stream of people came and went. Suddenly she felt very tired.

"I need to see Jack Bean," she said in a raw, jagged voice that was much too loud.

Heads turned. The receptionist took a moment to focus on her. She didn't see many grubby, tousle-haired kids in her job.

"I need to see Jack Bean."

"Jack Bean." The woman tapped her keyboard. "Oh, yes." She read a note on the screen and flicked a curious glance at Tala. "You must be Tala. . . One moment, please. Take a seat."

Tala sat down and glared at each of the turned heads until they looked away. This place was nothing like the public assistance clinic she had been to when she fell out of a tree and broke her arm. It was more like a luxury hotel.

A tall, slim young woman in a white coat walked purposefully towards her. Tala sat a little straighter. The woman had smooth golden skin, shiny black hair and tranquil brown eyes edged with a neat smudge of darkness. Her pink lipstick shimmered when she smiled. She held out a slender hand that smelled of scented soap.

Tala had a fleeting feeling she knew this face.

"Tala? I'm Dr Dulcie Walker." The doctor glanced around. "Is anyone with you?"

"No."

"Why don't we go through to my office?"

She led Tala through a series of glass doors into a smart room furnished in wood and chrome with a view of the hospital grounds on one side and a wall of framed photographs on the other.

"Would you like a drink? Cup of coffee, soda or something?"

"No thanks."

Dr Walker motioned Tala to a chair and sat down next to her.

"This is going to be difficult for you either way, Tala. If the man we're treating is your father, it will be a shock to see someone you love looking so ill. If it isn't him, I know it will be a dreadful disappointment."

Tala nodded, unable to speak.

They took a lift to the fifth floor and walked through a maze of gleaming corridors to a room marked "No Unauthorized Entry". Dr Walker tapped a code into a brushed metal keypad and gently pushed open the door.

"You mustn't be frightened. Just remember, this man has been through something terrible."

Tala stepped into a darkened room lit only by a greenish glow from a bank of screens. A narrow hump lay motionless on the bed, beneath a web of tubes and wires. Tala clenched her fists. She looked down at the skeletal face and let out a sob.

"It's my dad," she whispered.

"Are you sure?"

Ever since she'd been a baby, Tala and her father had been so close she would have recognized his voice, his smell, his walk, his shadow anywhere. Something had wrung all the life from the creature before her, but still she knew him. She knew because the grinding emptiness inside her had filled the minute she had looked down at that pale, sunken face, and for the first time in weeks she had begun to feel real again.

"He has a scar. It's at the bottom of his left thumb. He did it chopping wood."

Dr Walker lifted the bony hand and turned it over. A long, curved scar puckered the papery skin. Tala remembered how her father had hopped around the yard cursing and shouting while she'd tried to staunch the wound with a towel and how the towel had turned bright red. It was difficult to believe that the frail being lying on that bed had ever sworn or bled, or would ever do either again.

"Will he get better?"

"I don't know. We're doing everything we can, but it may take a long time. Months, maybe longer."

Tala had managed to hold back the ravages of jet lag, the shock and relief of seeing her father in a coma and the turmoil of the last few weeks, but her frustration at being a child – helpless, penniless, powerless – was suddenly too much to bear.

"How can he stay in a place like this?" she demanded angrily. "We don't have any money or any medical insurance."

"There will be no charge for his treatment."

Tala shook her head. "This is weird. First you pay for

me to come here, next you're offering to treat him for free in this swanky hospital. There's something going on and you'd better tell me what it is."

Dr Walker handed her a tissue, her exquisite face impassive. "I promise you there it is nothing sinister about any of this. When he was found, your father was admitted to the public hospital. He was seen by a colleague of mine who does volunteer work there. She thought I should take a look at him because his symptoms were so extraordinary. When I told the people sponsoring my research, they arranged to admit him here so I could study his condition."

"Why? He's in a bad way, anyone can see that. But I read about it on the internet. There's nothing special about being in a coma."

"It's more than that, Tala. It's as if his body has been stopped like a clock and suddenly it's started working again after a long time without water, nourishment, stimulus – perhaps even air."

"You mean like he's been frozen?"

Dr Walker nodded. "Yes, a bit like that. But it's strange. Even though he was found in the snow, all the tests I've done show that he hadn't been subjected to cold temperatures for very long. Something *else* slowed his life processes to almost nothing, which is why my colleague contacted me. You see, I'm doing research into states of suspended animation."

"And that's why you're treating him for free?"

"Yes."

"But it must be costing thousands of dollars."

"It's kind of an investment. There's big money to be made if we can find a safe way of replicating this kind of altered state. It would be useful for all sorts of things – preserving the sick until we find a cure for their illnesses; making it possible to travel into deep space."

Tala closed her eyes. The Wilderness. The infinite emptiness between the living worlds. The faki had been right. That's where her father had been and that's why he had ended up like this.

"Where was he?"

"A hiker found him up by Black Creek Canyon."

"Are there any strange old rocks up there?"

Dr Walker's eyes widened. "What do you mean?"

Tala could have kicked herself, but it was too late now.

"I want to go there. I want to see where they found him."

"Why?"

Tala fiddled with her soggy tissue.

"Tala, is there anything you know about your father's disappearance that might help us work out what happened to him?"

Tala shook her head. "Can I stay with him for a while, on my own?"

"Of course. If you note any changes, don't worry, there's a nurse down the hall checking his monitors. Come and find me when you're done. I'll be in my office."

Dr Walker left the room. Tala pulled a chair next to the bed and clasped her father's hand between her own.

"Dad, it's me," she murmured. "If you can hear me, move your fingers even just the tiniest bit."

She sat talking in a soothing whisper, straining every nerve to feel the faintest twitch, but he lay cold and still like a slab of stone. An hour later she felt completely drained. With a promise to return the next day, she kissed his lifeless cheek and left.

Dr Walker was working at a slim silver laptop when Tala tapped on the door of her office. She glanced up. "You look tired."

"I'm fine. Can I use your phone? I need to call Mrs Holt to get a ride."

Dr Walker pushed the phone towards her. "I've been thinking about what you said."

"About what?"

"About wanting to see where your father was found."

Tala kept her eyes on the handset as Dr Walker stood up and shut the door. "I have a day off tomorrow. I thought perhaps I could take you there myself."

A warning sounded in Tala's mind: *Those steeped in wicked arts oft mask their lust and greed with gentle deeds. . . The shadow watches and waits . . . hiding beneath a cloak of trust. . .* "I don't understand," she said quietly. "Why do you want to do all this for me?"

The doctor took a step forward. "Tala. I promise you can trust me."

She tried to look Tala in the eye, but Tala was staring over her shoulder at the framed photographs on the wall. They were shots of moonlit megaliths.

The Holts looked on suspiciously as Dr Walker swung her jeep into their yard the next morning. She hopped out, wearing jeans and a pink jumper under a black padded jacket, her hair swaying loose and shiny as she shook their hands. Tala could see them struggling to equate the word "doctor" with this young, attractive Native American woman and she hurried outside, embarrassed. As soon as they were on the highway, Dr Walker winked at her.

"I'm used to it, don't worry." She handed Tala a bar of chocolate. "Tell me about your dad."

Tala peeled back the foil wrapper. Bright winter sunshine poured through the windows, stirring the comforting smells of perfume and warm leather. Fearing she might relax and let slip her secrets, she sat up very stiff and straight and told Dr Walker what a great cook her dad was, how they had spent most of their time fishing and roaming the woods together and how they laughed about their busybody neighbours who grumbled that he let her run wild.

"What happened to your mom?"

"She left when I was a baby."

"Are you OK living in England?"

"It's fine."

"Can you stay there indefinitely?"

"S'pose."

"It's just, as I explained yesterday, your father's recovery may take a very long time."

The sky was clear blue, save for a disc of dense white cloud looming above the volcanic peaks of Mount Shasta. As they drove into the foothills, the cloud darkened to a leaden grey and the landscape grew steadily more bleak and rugged. Tala wished that Zi'ib and Wolfie were there. She bit into a piece of chocolate. The sugar gave her a little rush of courage.

"Those photos in your office. Did you take them?"

She sensed a quiver of tension, but Dr Walker's voice was matter-of-fact.

"Yes. Photography is one of my hobbies."

"Where were they taken?"

"In these mountains. Not far from where they found your father."

Tala felt as if she were crossing a fragile crust of ice that had formed over a dark and dangerous sea. She took another step.

"There's this old guy I met in England. He's really interested in megaliths and stuff. He thinks the people who built them were trying to harness cosmic energies or something." She laughed as casually as she could.

Dr Walker didn't laugh. She kept her eyes on the road and ran the tip of her tongue across her lips.

"Modern science has a lot to learn from ancient wisdom. In my work it would be foolish to dismiss it all as mumbo-jumbo. There are countless stories of ancient peoples harnessing natural energies to enable their mind, soul, spirit – call it what you will – to fly away from their bodies." She paused. "And there are some that hint at negative forces being used to steal a person's spirit from them."

Tala stilled the little sound that rose in her throat.

"These old folk tales often hide clues to ancient truths, and one of those truths may hold the key to my work on suspended animation." Dr Walker smiled. "Luckily my sponsors are cool about me spending half my time researching ancient energies."

The jeep left the main road and headed down a rutted track. Snow-dusted pines towered on either side, their twisted roots jutting through the frozen soil. Dr Walker parked near a small creek of dark water where mist floated above the reeds and overhanging branches trailed in the ripples. She laid her hands on the wheel and turned to Tala.

"One of the things my research has taught me is that there is no such thing as coincidence. I am not surprised that you know about ancient energies. I think we both suspect they are the key to what happened to your dad. Am I right? Tell me what you know, Tala. It may help me to treat him."

The temptation to confide in this woman with her pretty face and gentle voice was almost too much to bear. Tala dug her nails into her palms, refusing to look up.

"I-I don't know anything. I just want to see where they found him."

Dr Walker reached into the back seat and handed Tala a pair of sturdy leather boots. "They might be a bit big, but we've got to walk from here."

Tala put the boots on and followed the doctor across the snow-covered boulders. Twigs snatched her hair, spattering her face with icy slush. Slipping and sliding, they moved deeper into the forest, until the canopy of trees blotted out the winter sunshine. Bracken quivered, but she couldn't see any deer or rabbits. No birds fluttered from the ground or called from the branches. Sensing danger, Tala stopped to pick up a thick branch and dropped it again, feeling foolish. As she hurried to catch up, she felt the pulses in her star drum a warning. She scanned the ancient woodland. Ridges of lava broke through the earth, scarring it with clefts and gashes that hinted at dark hollows beneath. The energies here were the strongest she had ever felt, but they were cloying and heavy and throbbed with malice. It was as if weights were pulling at her limbs and sapping her spirit. The little creek no longer gurgled and splashed: its sound was an eerie moan.

"I don't like it here; it's creepy," said Tala.

"Local folklore says it's a bad place," said Dulcie Walker, stepping over a fallen tree trunk blackened with fungus. "I don't believe in magic, but I do believe there are powerful forces coursing through the earth – positive and negative. Just as with animals, our senses tell us to keep away from the negative ones. These 'creepy' feelings are primeval warnings of real danger."

"What danger?"

The doctor took a shivery breath. "Every legend about this place says it's a kind of opening."

"Into what?"

"A place outside our world."

"You mean space?" said Tala, feigning confusion.

"No – a place beyond what we know as space; a negation of everything we can see or understand or possibly even imagine."

"The Wilderness Between the Worlds," murmured Tala.

The doctor raised an eyebrow. "There are some who call it that. Local stories imply that the opening here is permanent, but usually such apertures appear for just a few seconds when the alignment of the earth and stars is right, then close over again."

"How do you know?"

"I read, I talk to people and, as I said, I study folklore." She pointed down the gully. "It's not much further now."

They emerged into a clearing edged with sickly, stunted saplings. In the centre was an outcrop of rock split by a dark slash like a grimacing mouth.

"That's where they found him – at the entrance to that cave."

Tala ran forward, her feet smashing the ice-crusted mud, her star pulsing against her chest. The gloom of the gully closed in on her, crawling over her flesh. Repulsed yet fascinated, she seized the lip of the opening and forced herself into the darkness. Her star went dead, as if someone had thrown a switch. Without it she felt bereft, terrified and abandoned, lonelier than she had ever felt.

Dimly aware of Dr Walker calling her name, she stared into the depths of the cave, her breath ragged with fear. This dank fissure was nothing like the chamber where they had found the first stone. It had no beauty, no purpose, no secrets, only clawing emptiness. A flux of negative energy bore down on her. With a scream of defiance she lunged forward, pitting her will against the powerful current forcing her back. The doctor was wrong. This was not an entrance to the Wilderness. It was an exit; a gap through which the Wilderness could disgorge its unwanted jetsam. The current spat her backwards; hands grasped her shoulders. Crushed and gasping, she lost her footing and collapsed into Dulcie Walker's arms.

"It's OK, it's OK," soothed the doctor. "I shouldn't have brought you here."

"No, I'm glad I came. I needed to know."

She stumbled away through the gully, clutching the broken star beneath her coat. Slowly, as the tiny pulse reawakened beneath her fingers, her breathing steadied.

Dr Walker found her shivering in the jeep. "Get this down you," she said, pouring a beaker of hot coffee from a flask. "Please, Tala, tell me what happened back there. What did you feel in that cave?"

"I don't know. I don't know anything. It was . . . horrible."

Dr Walker revved the engine.

"We need to find some positive energies to stop you feeling so unsettled."

She drove back to the main road. With each spin of the wheels they drew further from the loathsome chasm and nearer to the sunshine. Tala closed her eyes, trying to shake off her nausea. Even the scalding coffee and the warm air billowing from the heater did nothing to ease the chill in her bones.

Dr Walker glanced at her sideways. "You know, some people would have felt nothing in that gully. They've lost the ability." She took a breath. "Then there are those like you, who are hypersensitive to natural energies both positive *and* negative."

They drove in silence over the crest of a hill to where the land fell away into a gentle valley drenched in winter sunlight. Snow glistened gold and pink against the soft darkness of the towering trees that sloped down towards a narrow thread of river. The silvery waters wound their way around a wide pillar of boulders, piled haphazardly one above the other, as if placed there by the unsteady hand of a giant toddler.

"No one knows the age of that cairn," said Dr Walker, pulling up. "But analysis has shown that the stones were quarried hundreds of miles from here."

Tala stepped out, feeling the sharp breeze chase the

ghostly touch of the Wilderness from her skin. She gazed down at the cairn. Even without her dowsing rods she sensed lines of energy coursing around her, and knew that something within her had grown strong enough to control her reactions to their power.

"What is this place?" she asked.

"They call it Crystal River."

Tala put her hand into her pocket and crushed Mr Forester's map beneath a jumble of tissues and sweet wrappers, as if afraid that Dr Walker's bright brown eyes might pierce the fabric of her coat and read her secret.

"Pretty name."

Dr Walker nodded. "Some say it's because the waters of the river are crystal clear, others that it's because the river often freezes like crystal in the winter, but there is another legend. . ."

Tala looked up nervously.

"It says that if you look into the river at the right time, you can see another place."

"What kind of place?"

"Another world that's linked to this one by lines of energy. A world where the people can look up into a giant dome of crystal and see you looking down into the water. They say many sacred pools and rivers have this power."

Tala thought about the dome of crystal arching over the Chamber of Lupus and she thought about the fierce, proud face they had seen in the bowl of Nile water at the house of the faki. Had those piercing green eyes been staring up at them through that same Lupan crystal?

Something flared in her star. She felt Zi'ib and Wolfie's low, steady pulses quicken in response. They'd be asleep now and she knew she was disturbing their dreams. The faint fourth pulse tugged at her heartstrings, telling her that the bearer of that other star was restless and awake. Guiltily, she prayed it was her mother.

"There's another legend," Dr Walker was saying, "probably from Palaeolithic times, that wolves disguised as men arrived here from the sky-world and taught the human race how to hunt and grow seeds and so saved them from starvation."

Tala was barely able to mask her excitement. Was this a distorted account of Lupan explorers coming here to trade knowledge? Every nerve in her body was telling her that this was the place where her ancestors had hidden the clue to the third stone. Whatever Dulcie Walker's motivation might be, she was sure that the power of the leys had used the doctor to bring her here.

She focused on the valley, visualizing the eight-pointed star pattern of the leys. She heard the cairn call to her, softly humming the songs the pyramids had sung. She longed to touch the stones, longed to drink in their message, but she needed to do it alone.

"Feeling better?" asked the doctor, refilling Tala's beaker.

Tala nodded. "This is a good place. And you're right about me being sensitive to atmospheres and stuff."

A nerve flickered in the doctor's eyelid.

"I think I need to go down to those rocks to get rid of the bad feelings from the cave."

"OK, let's go," said Dr Walker.

"No. I'll go on my own," said Tala. She pushed her cup into the doctor's hand and ran.

The throb of the leys was pure and powerful. She approached the stones feeling awkward, suddenly aware that there must be customs she should follow in such a place. She reddened, ashamed that she and Zi'ib and Wolfie had blundered around the temples of Meroe without giving their sacred significance a thought. Brushing snow and withered moss from the edges of the stones, she walked slowly around the cairn until she was shielded from the watchful eyes of Dr Walker. She pulled out her star, seeking its comfort and guidance. She felt an urge to embrace the rocks that was as strong as the longing she had felt all her life to reach out and touch her mother.

The upper boulders were carved with wispy spirals and clusters of circles. Some, she knew at once, were symbols of circling sounds and energies; others were clearly star maps. The larger rocks at the base were zigzagged with rows of dots and lines, age-worn and weathered. Tala traced them with a fingertip, sensing heads, hands, bodies forming a human chain encircling the pillar, receiving the solace she craved. This must be the ritual method of communing with the stones, but she had no one to form a chain with. She was alone: just a kid with short, skinny arms. She searched higher up the cairn for images of lone worshippers and found a gap where some of the stones had fallen away. Did the clue lie hidden inside? Warily she clasped the boulders and poked her face into the hole. A slow vibration shook her body and a wonderful symphony of shapes and sounds poured through her ears and eyes and skin, easing her pain and loneliness. Tears slid down her face. Her head tipped forward. With a gentle clink her broken star slipped smoothly into a cleft carved into the rock and a message melted into her mind.

Listen to the voice of the dead.

Horrified, she jerked her head back. What did it mean? This couldn't be a clue to the third stone. How could she talk to the dead? Her impulse was to run from these rocks with their ghostly, soundless voices; to race screaming across the valley and throw herself into the soft, perfumed arms of Dr Walker. She broke out in a sickly sweat. There had to be another meaning to those chilling words. Squeezing her eyes shut, she thrust her face back into the hole. Her broken star found the crevice but the stones refused to speak again. Shivering with cold and terror, she staggered back to the jeep.

The doctor saw the fear in her eyes. "Let's go back to my house and get something to eat." She started the engine and switched on the radio. A blast of Elvis Presley's "Hound Dog" burst from the speakers, and the thought of the great grizzled mongrel waiting for her at the sweet shop made Tala feel strong.

Dr Walker drove to a newly built estate nestled at the edge of the woods. She parked in the driveway of a trim, single-storey house and led Tala into an airy sitting room that was as ordered and attractive as the doctor herself. A pair of white sofas faced each other across a low wooden table on which a single stem of pale fleshy flowers stood in a narrow vase. Carefully arranged photographs dotted the wall above the fireplace: some were of seers and shamans performing rituals; others were of ancient sites. The alcoves on either side held bookshelves. The opposite wall was covered by glass cabinets. As Tala went over to look at them, the doctor flicked a switch, flooding them with light. Laid out in neat compartments were feathers, bowls and talismans, carvings, lumps of rock, a skull and some strips of plaited hide.

"What is this stuff?" asked Tala.

"Ritual objects I've collected over the years. I call it my library. Sometimes objects can contain more knowledge than any book or parchment."

Tala stiffened. Her eyes slid over the cabinets. Had the doctor found the third stone? Was she testing her, watching to see if she could identify it? Faking interest in some scraps of weaving, she studied the rock specimens. Some were flecked with crystals, others were nuggets of sandstone and granite. None bore the fossil imprint.

"Chicken or tomato?"

"What?"

"Soup."

"Oh. Tomato, please."

Dr Walker pushed open the kitchen door. A fretful voice let out a cry. Tala looked round, surprised. It was the voice of a very old woman. Minutes later the doctor came back with a tray of microwaved soup and crusty rolls.

"Help yourself."

"What about the old lady?" asked Tala. "Isn't she going to eat with us?"

Dr Walker threw back her head and laughed. "I never let her in here. That's why she's always so angry. Come in the kitchen, I'll introduce you."

Tala followed her into a perfect white kitchen. She was met by a screech of fury from an enormous grey and purple parrot who was chained to a wooden perch. The bird puffed up its mangy feathers and spat a mouthful of nutshells across the spotless floor.

"She's called Tikaani."

Tala shivered. *Tikaani* meant wolf.

"I sort of inherited her from an old lady who agreed to help me with my research if I promised to give this bad-tempered bird a home. Careful!"

Tala leapt back as the parrot screeched and flew angrily at the doctor. Only the short metal chain attached to its foot prevented it from damaging her flawless face.

"At the time I thought it was fair exchange. Now I'm not so sure."

"How was the old lady helping your research?"

"She was a shaman, and well over a hundred when she

died. Her English was perfect but she was also the last speaker of her people's ancient language. I spent weeks talking to her, recording as much information as I could." She sighed. "Of course, all the chants and incantations meant nothing to me. It was really frustrating knowing that so many mysteries were going to die with her."

The parrot opened its great curved beak, wobbled a fat grey tongue and spoke in a querulous voice. To the doctor it was a jumble of sounds; to Tala the meaning was clear.

"The wounding tree that aids the old man's tread,
Bounds the seat of giants, threshold to the skies. . ."

She gripped the marble worktop, powerful pulses pummelling her star.

The doctor swept up the nutshells. "It's uncanny; she sounds exactly like the shaman." She turned back to the sitting room. "Come on, our soup's getting cold."

"Can I get a glass of water?" called Tala.

"Sure, the glasses are in the cupboard next to the sink."

Tala snatched a pen and paper from a little magnetized container on the fridge. The parrot's bulbous black eyes stared at her. The vicious beak parted and a message poured forth in the voice of the dead shaman.

"The wounding tree that aids the old man's tread,
Bounds the seat of giants, threshold to the skies,

Step softly as you enter, seek with dread,
For there, entrenched, the fearsome burden lies."

For five thousand years, the guardians of the Wisdom of the Mountains had handed down the clue to the hiding place of the third stone. Now at last it had reached the ears of a righteous seeker.

Tala spent a week sitting beside her father in the dim silence of his hospital room, running Tikaani's chant over and over in her mind. She was sure that *the seat of giants, threshold to the skies* referred to giant stones marking one of the gateways to other worlds. If the *fearsome burden* was the third stone, then *the wounding tree that aids the old man's tread* had to be a clue to the gateway's location. But she had absolutely no idea where it could be.

She emailed Wolfie and Zi'ib a couple of times from the public computers in the hospital, telling them the news about Jack and adding messages for Sarah, telling her when she would be back. But she kept silent about the clue, refusing to trust her secrets to cyberspace.

She saw Dr Walker every day, and every day she fought the temptation to tell her everything and ask her advice. Sometimes she thought she saw a flicker of life in Jack Bean's skeletal face; other times she fancied she felt his fingers press against hers in response to a whispered question, but she could never be sure. On her last morning, Dr Walker gave Tala her card.

"Of course, my sponsors will pay for you to come back if there is any change in your father's condition. I've got Sarah Brown's phone number. Is that the best way to keep in touch?" Her voice and manner seemed more brusque than usual. Tala nodded, glancing at the card. Beneath the doctor's details gleamed a golden Z shaped from tongues of flame.

The doctor opened her desk drawer. "Before you go I'd like you to take a blood test. It won't hurt."

Tala's eyes darkened. "Don't you believe he's my dad after all?"

"Of course, but I want to know if there's anything in your family's genetic make-up that might have contributed to his – condition."

"OK," said Tala uneasily.

Dr Walker sat her down and wrapped a rubber strap around her arm. She removed a little vial of blood using a syringe and quickly covered the nick in her skin with a plaster.

"All done." She pulled down Tala's sleeve and looked into her eyes. "I'm sorry you never felt you could trust me. You have my card. If you ever feel there is anything you want to share with me, just get in touch."

She held out her hand. Tala shook it. "Thanks for everything, Dr Walker," she said. She *was* grateful, but as she walked through the lobby, she slipped into the washroom and rinsed the lingering smell of the doctor's scented soap from her fingers.

46

Tala Returns

For days, Wolfie and Zi'ib's stars had been alive with Tala's excitement. On the afternoon of her return they sped back from school, desperate to hear what she had discovered. They ran inside, snatched her away from Sarah and practically dragged her up to the attic. Wolfie slammed the trapdoor. "Tell us, before I explode," he cried.

Tala waved the copy of Tikaani's chant and spoke the words she had once feared she would never say. "I found the clue to the third stone!"

Wolfie and Zi'ib leapt in the air, palms slapping together, their yells shaking the rafters. Wolfie snatched the paper from her hand.

"How did you do it?"

They listened eagerly as she outlined her story, then made her go over it again and again, hungry for detail.

"Did the cairn stones say anything about Lupus?" demanded Zi'ib.

"No. But Dr Walker mentioned this old legend about the waters of certain pools and rivers letting you see into another world where the people can see you through a dome of crystal – like the one Seth built over the chamber."

"So that bloke in the bowl *was* looking at us," said Wolfie. "Tell us more about this Dr Walker."

"She was Native American, brown eyes, dark hair, and all smooth and neat, like someone in a shampoo advert. I was really surprised she knew about earth energies. She wasn't anything like Mr Forester."

"You didn't tell her anything, did you?"

"Course not."

"What's her first name?" asked Zi'ib.

"Dulcie."

He tapped Dr Walker's details into his computer and a whole page of entries appeared. "There's a group photo here from some earth sciences conference she was at – which one's she?"

Tala leaned across, searching for the delicate features of Dulcie Walker. Her finger froze above a tall figure staring from the centre of the shot. In a voice as hollow as the feeling in her stomach, she said, "It's the fake Matthias!"

It was definitely him, only without his dark glasses. Tala checked the date. "This was taken at the conference he was at when Dad went missing. It was in the folder of stuff he showed me. I *knew* I'd seen her before."

Wolfie was completely dazed. "Maybe when the kinnections get going they spill over and link up stuff that doesn't matter, like when you're painting and the colours run, or you hit the ketchup bottle and it splurts everywhere."

"What are you going on about?" said Tala.

"Maybe it's not that suspicious they were at the same conference. They're both scientists, both into old rocks and stuff."

"Course it's suspicious!" fumed Tala. She ran the cursor over the image. A name tag popped up: Dr Ridian Winter.

They had known since the night Professor Salah had described the real Matthias that this man who claimed to be Tala's uncle was an imposter. Now they knew his name.

"Ridian Winter," breathed Tala, tapping the keyboard. A dozen published papers appeared, several mentions in Zemogen International press releases and a list of conferences he had spoken at going back over the last fifteen years with a couple more photographs.

"If this isn't proof he's not Matthias Threlfall, I don't know what is," Tala said. "I'm going to the police."

"If they arrest him, you'll get sent straight back to the States," said Zi'ib. "Besides, it won't stop the rest of them."

Three pairs of frightened green eyes slid to Wolfie's chart. A lamplit jar of brushes cast a finger of shadow at a group of figures he had added on return from Khartoum. It was labelled "Exiled Manus Sacra".

Wolfie snatched up Tikaani's clue. "So let's crack this and bring the stones together before he gets back from Alaska. OK. We're looking for a place that means *wounding tree* . . . tree that wounds . . . any ideas?"

Zi'ib tried googling the words, and brought up endless pages about conserving damaged woodland. "Maybe it means a wooden weapon," he suggested without conviction.

"Try *aids the old man's tread*," suggested Tala.

"Nothing," said Zi'ib, scrolling through entries. Angrily he pushed the laptop away. "This is ridiculous. We've got to be smarter than some mangy old parrot."

47

The Wounding Tree

Wolfie and Zi'ib spent the next day brooding over the clue and sneaking into the school library between lessons to pore over atlases and books on rare trees. Tala stayed at home sleeping and wandering about being grouchy. It was only later that evening, when she had finally shaken off her jet lag and had a long hot bath, that she had a flash of inspiration. "Instead of finding a place meaning wounding tree that might be a gateway, let's find all the gateways and see if any of them mean wounding tree."

It was worth a try. They found Mr Forester in his room, his leg propped on a pile of books, gazing at a photograph in an oval frame and sharing a bag of fudge with Elvis. He wiped a frosting of sugar from his lips. "Purely medicinal," he said guiltily. "I can't understand why my arthritis has flared up like this. The Thornham leys should have eased my old bones, not made them worse."

As he handed round the fudge, Tala could not resist craning forward to look at the smiling, pretty face in the photo.

"That's my Hetty before we married," sighed Mr Forester. "I miss her a great deal."

Tala's dark brows drew into a frown. She had never thought about Mr Forester's life before he came to Thornham, never imagined that he too might have lost someone he loved. "Do you have any children?" she asked.

"Just one. A daughter – Stella." He pointed to a snapshot beside the bed. "She's a good girl and keeps in touch, but she's an interpreter, does a lot of travelling, so I don't see her as much as I'd like. Still, I've got plenty to keep me busy. Now, what can I help my favourite dowsers with today?"

"We need a list of all the possible cosmic gateways in the world," said Zi'ib.

"We, er, fancied doing a bit of our own research," chipped in Wolfie. "Seeing if we can find any other links between them."

Mr Forester cheered up a little. "You really have got the bug, haven't you? Once you start investigating earth mysteries, it's impossible to stop. I'm sure I've got a list somewhere." He reached for his walking stick.

"I'll get it, just tell me where it is," said Wolfie.

"You overestimate the efficiency of my filing system," smiled Mr Forester. "Anyway, it does me good to move around."

Remembering the frustrations of his own crutches, Zi'ib watched the elderly earth mysterian hobble to the desk, rocking his weight against the support of his stick.

"I see it as my life's work to trace the leys entering all these sites to see if they form the distinctive eight-point star formation," Mr Forester was saying as he fished a typed sheet from the chaos and handed it to Zi'ib.

Zi'ib barely glanced at the names before passing the list to Wolfie, who groaned loudly. There were nearly a hundred sites on the list: Carnac, Chichen Itza, Machu Picchu, Easter Island and loads he had never even heard of. It would take weeks to check if any of them had links to some kind of "wounding tree".

"Mr Forester, what wood is your walking stick made of?" burst out Zi'ib.

Tala and Wolfie looked at him as if he had gone mad.

"Blackthorn."

"Why not oak or pine?"

"They've been making sticks and staffs out of thorn wood for thousands of years because it's so strong and the knobbly roots make such natural handles. This whole area was probably covered in Blackthorn trees at one time – hence the name *Thorn*-ham."

"Yes!" whispered Zi'ib, clenching his fist.

"'The wounding tree that aids the old man's tread'," said Tala.

"Very poetic," smiled Mr Forester, "but less of the 'old man', if you don't mind."

48

Step Softly As You Enter

"**W**e're idiots!" Wolfie dropped the trapdoor shut. "The *wounding tree* bounding *the seat of giants* was obviously Thornham, where the thorn trees circle the giant stones."

"'*Step softly as you enter . . .*'," muttered Tala, taking slow, deliberate steps across the attic, "'*. . . seek with dread, for there, entrenched, the fearsome burden lies*.' The sweet shop stands at the *entran*ce to Thornham Henge, so the third stone must be '*entrenched*' right here where this building stands."

"Then it probably got carted off when Marcus Harrison's ancestor broke up the stone circle," Zi'ib said glumly.

Tala picked at the flaking plaster. "Maybe not. If Costantino salvaged what he could to build this house, there's a chance it's somewhere in these walls, right under our noses."

Wolfie grimaced. "I'm not sure I fancy something that can smite the worlds with evil propping up my bedroom."

In the days that followed, they scoured every inch of Wolfie's home. Claiming they had to make a scale drawing of the building, they even borrowed a ladder from Mr Baxter and inspected the exterior walls, stone by stone. It was hopeless. Any one of the rough dark slabs could have had a fossil imprint hidden out of sight.

They were gathered in the outhouse one cold, foggy evening, staring dejectedly at the obelisk, when Tala began to run her fingers over the furrows of the fossil. "I wonder if there was something special about this *particular* plant," she said thoughtfully.

Suddenly animated, Zi'ib fitted his star into the disk drive and fired up his laptop, searching for a website that identified fossils. He tapped in the details of the long thin leaves, the spindly stem and the fan of roots sprouting from a fat, round seed. The flowers were too squashed up to make out with the naked eye, so Wolfie ran to fetch Mr Forester's magnifying glass.

"I need the shape, size and number of the petals," Zi'ib told him when he came back.

Wolfie tilted the lens over the dark outline of the fossil. Slowly, the shape of the petals came clear.

"The petals are all pointed," he said at last, his voice

catching in his throat. "There's eight on each flower, four large and four small. Just like the wind-rose . . . and the stars round our necks . . . and the pattern of the Thornham leys . . . and the turning wheel of the solstices."

Like the scholars of Lupus who tempered Knowledge with understanding to create the Wisdom of the Stars, he grasped a fragment of eternal truth. He glimpsed a pure and never-ending chain of interconnecting patterns, more beautiful than any music or painting created by human hands. The Fires of Understanding flared in his mind, electrifying his senses, rocking him back against the workbench. The cooking pans shifted on their hooks, their dulled copper curves lit by the golden rush of sparks fizzing around Wolfie's head, kindling the fiery flecks in his eyes. As the whirl of flame poured into the reservoir of energy that had been collecting for weeks beneath the site of the lost stone circle, the force exploded into life and surged towards the town centre, sweeping down the high street, shaking the pipes and rattling the billboards. The plaster mannequin in the window of the dry cleaner's swayed on its pedestal, smashing to the floor as the pavement over the hidden chamber caved in. A parked digger slid slowly forward and crashed through the hole, its metal scoop scything through an electricity cable and plunging the whole of Thornham and most of Dodds Hill into darkness.

Elvis raised his muzzle and let out a deep, wild howl, thrilling and resonant as a call to arms. In answer came a barking and baying from all around the common. He burst out of the outhouse, over the fence and down the crescent towards the pub, just as an enormous articulated lorry came thundering past on its way to the garden centre. Disoriented by the sudden blackout and the low mist swirling across the tarmac, the driver mistook the curve of the bus lay-by for the path of the road and swerved violently to avoid the bench. A huge beast dashed into the headlights, its eyes a flash of amber. The driver hit the brakes. The lorry slewed on to the common, its massive trailers jackknifed and overturned, hurling their cargo of trees and shrubs across the grass. The mist rolled on.

Terrified by the grinding screech of brakes and the brutal crash of metal, Wolfie, Tala and Zi'ib tore, panic-stricken, out of the yard. In the distance cars were slowing and stopping, their headlights glinting on the twisted trailers. The lorry driver had leapt, shaken but unhurt, from his cab and was being escorted into the Wish Hound by someone who was waving a torch and shouting instructions. To the children, the shadowy scene seemed to unfold in silence and, as if moving through jelly, they neared the crashed lorry, sickened by what they might find.

"Elvis. . ." called Tala, her voice growing smaller and hoarser. "Elvis. . ."

Far across the common, two specks of amber glinted like tiny flames, widening into bright lamps of liquid gold as the great dog bounded through the gloom. Sirens wailed. The children's wild panic slipped away. They saw the dim outline of Sarah running out of the candlelit shop to peer across the darkness at the crash site and the dark silhouette of Elvis slinking back down Stoneygate Street.

Still trembling, they rushed after him and found him sitting in the doorway of the outhouse, lit by the pale glow from Zi'ib's laptop. He responded to their frantic scolding and tearful nuzzling by swishing his tail and batting them with a paw, then turned away, his ears pricked to catch a distant sound.

On the screen behind him, the towered cityscape with its glassy dome seemed to float in the darkness, the reflection of its glimmering crescent moons dancing in their eyes.

Zi'ib brushed the image with his hand. A thrill of revelation tingled through his fingertips. "It's not a screensaver," he said. "The twin moons, the marble city with its crystal-roofed chamber. . . It's Lupus! It must be coming from the memory banks of my star. No wonder I couldn't erase it."

Wolfie and Tala gazed spellbound at the screen. The air around them crackled and the pulse of their stars beat faster.

Bathed in the watery light from the laptop, they saw Mr Forester's magnifying glass, stuck halfway up the obelisk.

"The stone's been magnetized," said Wolfie, straining to free the metal handle. "It won't come off."

The pull was so strong it took all three of them to prise it away.

Sarah was in the shop making lanterns out of night lights and empty sweet jars. "This drift fog *and* a power cut. Thank goodness that lorry didn't hit the pub. Can you put the rest of these outside? We don't want any cars crashing into the shop."

They ranged the jars beneath the shop window, watching far-off beams of light slice the darkness as the police cordoned off each end of the crescent and barricaded the overturned lorry lying curled around the bus stop like a huge broken-backed beast.

Wolfie stared up at the shop's facade. It was taller and narrower than the surrounding houses, its outline a gaunt reminder of the great monoliths that had once towered on this spot. Something shivered in his star. A feeble pulsing he had never felt before. The heartbeat of another of their parents had just awoken. He saw Zi'ib and Tala lift nervous fingers to their throats, counting and recounting the pulses fluttering beneath their own. There were two. Only two. They dared not look at each other. One Lupan parent was still stranded somewhere where their life force was deadened to nothing.

The church clock struck six. A beam of light zigzagged in the darkness, footsteps echoed on the pavement and a group of shadowy figures loomed closer, following a flashlight held aloft by the plump kid-gloved hand of

Leonora Grindle. She trotted towards the shop, her fleshy feet crammed into a pair of red high heels, and glared at Wolfie. He smiled sweetly. She plucked an evening paper from the rack, jerked Mr B's lead, and dragged him inside. Zi'ib placed a sweet-jar lantern beside the door and kicked the step. "*Step softly as you enter*," he muttered under his breath. "Why softly? You can't squash a bit of stone."

"Don't move!" cried Tala. Diving to her knees, she pushed his trainer aside. From a crack between the doorstep and the pavement peeped a cluster of purple flowers attached to a long, thin stem. Each flower had eight pointy petals. Cupping her hands around the little plant, Tala tugged it free. She shook a dusting of ancient mortar from a tangle of roots that sprouted from a seed as round and hard as a cherry stone. An explosion of understanding, terror and excitement erupted through their stars. They had found the third stone, but the plant attached to it was not a fossil – yet.

Mr B tugged on his lead and came snarling towards them. Leonora Grindle teetered down the step behind her dog. Her hips swaying, her red shoes crunching the crumbled mortar, she hastened towards the common.

Moments later a flashlight and a pair of kid gloves dropped to the ground. Two pudgy hands held high a star of hammered gold and a ring of dark figures clustered close as the Link of Light flared bright.

And the Chosen shall prevail.
It is time.

The reply was prompt.

Let the Chosen assemble.

49

A Window on Water

Flurries of activity stirred the fringes of the common. Candlelight flickered in the windows of the church hall, framing anxious silhouettes that hovered and regrouped like bees on a honeycomb. The sign outside the Wish Hound pub, with its painted devil dog calling up the hounds of Thornham, swung in the breeze as a noisy crush of customers burst out of the firelit warmth of the bar and melted into the darkness.

Gently, Tala wrapped the little plant in a dampened tea towel while the boys ran to the outhouse to collect the obelisk. Sick with nerves, they heaved the precious relic into the supermarket trolley. What would happen when they brought the stones together? Would their parents suddenly materialize? Would their lives be scrambled and upended yet again?

"If any of the Manus Sacra turn up, just keep cool," said Wolfie, trying and failing to sound confident. "They won't dare touch the stones."

They slipped through the back gate, glad of the darkness. Elvis crept behind them, weaving between the legs of the passers-by. A sliver of moon peered through the clouds, dappling light on to the crowd of guests leaving Mrs Baxter's B&B. A pack of stray dogs fighting over a discarded burger paused to watch them go by, their eyes glinting gold.

Tala led the way across the common, swinging Zi'ib's torch with one hand and helping to pull the trolley with the other. Soft winds brushed the trees and dark shapes milled around the gasworks, merging with the throng now leaving the church hall. Heaving and pushing, the children negotiated the soggy turf, their reflections rippling over the greasy surface of the pond.

Eerie moans drifted from the play area. The seesaw creaked. Paws padded across the tarmac, bristled bodies slunk beneath the swings. Struggling to keep the trolley from foundering in the mud, Wolfie, Tala and Zi'ib darted around collecting plants scattered by the jackknifed lorry to shore up the wheels. Wolfie tripped. Something jagged his ankle, leaving a bloodied gash. He kicked the offending branch away. It twanged back, dangling its label in the torchlight: "Prunus Spinosa – Blackthorn".

"The wounding trees are back, just for one night," he

said, unaware that he spoke in the lost tongue of his Druid forebears.

The mist rolled back across the ancient common, carrying gusts of malevolence that dimmed the pulse of their stars. They looked up. All around them the commuters, the pub-goers, the guests from the Baxter's B&B and the crowd from the church hall, eighty, ninety people, maybe more, were converging from the gloom. In a moment of pure, primal fear, Wolfie, Tala and Zi'ib saw the hunger and hatred in their gold-flecked emerald eyes and knew them for who they were: the exiled Manus Sacra, gathering to claim the secret they had coveted for millennia.

A shout rang through the darkness. "Seize them!"

The voice was as familiar as the clang of the sweet-shop door. Scraps of warning hurtled through Wolfie's mind: *Those steeped in wicked arts oft mask their lust and greed with gentle deeds . . . hide beneath a cloak of trust . . . disguise themselves as princes, shepherds . . . priests.* No! With a hollow, kicked-in-the-stomach feeling, he watched Godfrey Peasemarsh step from the shadows.

"You!" gasped Wolfie.

Peasemarsh's flabby gap-toothed smile tightened to a thin sneer. Without his tinted contact lenses, his eyes glittered piercing green and flashed with a cold, calculating intelligence. From his neck dangled an eight-point star of gold. Zi'ib pitched forward, his insides curling with shock. Strong hands reached for the bearers of the broken stars, holding them fast.

"Get off me!" screamed Tala. She swore viciously at Peasemarsh, bucking like a colt.

Leonora Grindle stepped from the crowd, grabbed Tala's hair and jerked her head back. "Show respect for the Master," she snarled.

"You'll never get the stones," spat Tala, twisting and struggling. "The guardians made sure of that. *We're* the ones who were born to find them."

Peasemarsh twisted his bloodless lips. "And *we* are the ones who were born to wield their power. For the secret they contain embodies wisdom so vibrant, so numinous its release will unleash more energy than your unworthy minds could ever comprehend."

"You can't even touch them," cried Wolfie. "They'll crumble to nothing; their secret will be lost for ever."

"You foolish innocents," hissed Peasemarsh. "Did you really believe that by hiding the stones in this pitiful backwater and swaddling them in mystery, the 'guardians' could keep the Chosen from what is rightfully theirs?"

"Yes," choked Zi'ib, "because they put their trust in truth."

"Truth is a trickster, my dear Zi'ib. To the guardians your birth was a mingling of the great wisdoms of the ancients. To us it was a necessary evil that brought shame upon the wise. But your misbegotten blood proved strong, and thanks to you, the Chosen shall soon control the fates of all the living worlds."

"W-what do you mean?" Wolfie gasped, doubt

spreading like poison through his veins.

"Your friend Remus Forester is no fool. The inhabitants of this and a host of other arrogant and regressive planets have been neglecting and abusing the cosmic energies for so long that the whole ley system has been corrupted. The grid is withering. Without a massive injection of power, the leys will die, and one by one the living worlds will drop into the Wilderness like rotten apples from a blighted tree."

Wolfie's thoughts raced. *So that was the "evil greater than the greed of men" that had brought their parents in search of the stones.* He heard Tala cry out, "So why wreck our parents' mission? You're insane!"

Leonora Grindle slapped her hard.

"Wreck? I prefer the word *adapt*," said Peasemarsh calmly. "This way we save the leys but also right the ancient wrong done to the Chosen. For when the stones unite, we shall gain possession not only of the secret of the Spheres but also of the Sphere of Lupus. The very outcome that the 'guardians' strove so ineptly to prevent."

"The gateway . . . will you open the gateway to get the Sphere?" demanded Tala, all resistance broken by the thought of freeing her mother.

The Master gave a snort of contempt. "And let the Lupan rabble come flooding in to interfere with our plans? No. Our crystals – from deposits that Matthias Threlfall so helpfully discovered just before his 'accident' – will channel just enough energy for us to create a temporary pathway to Lupus. Our people there will use it to bring the Sphere to earth."

"You might have killed Matthias, but you can't make *us* unite the stones," said Wolfie, frantically weighing the choice of evils before him. "And *you* can't touch them."

Peasemarsh eyed him with amused contempt. A low vibration shook the ground, mounting slowly to a harmony deeper than the song of the pyramids, more haunting than the music of the cairn at Crystal River; an echo of the melody now rippling from their broken stars. Their captors twisted them roughly around. With helpless horror, Wolfie, Tala and Zi'ib saw the shopping cart rise from the mire and, bathed in a greenish glow, begin to move slowly forward of its own accord, drawn irresistibly by the attraction of the magnetized stones: the battered mesh glittering, the wheels spinning soundlessly over the grass.

Eight figures stepped forward, holding up great shards of white crystal like votive offerings, while those behind clasped hands to form a sealed ring with their bodies. In Wolfie's head he heard voices, screaming out the warning of the guardians. *"Truth must seal the circle when the stones unite!"* If they could circle the stones at the final moment, might there just be a chance of wrecking the Manus Sacra's plan? He grabbed Zi'ib's hand, then reached frantically for Tala's fingers.

Peasemarsh saw what he was doing. He snapped his fingers and, without emotion, said, "Cast these base-born brats from the circle."

Powerful hands wrenched the children apart and flung them across the grass. Winded and dizzy, they slithered through the mud beside the pond. Booted feet pressed them down. For a moment they saw their own dazed reflections in the greasy water; then the slick of darkness grew pale, and in its chalk-lined depths appeared a starlit chamber, familiar not from dream or memory but from the story of Seth, described in *The Book of Light*. A great black seat, hewn from a spur of gold-flecked quartz rose through a white marble floor, circled by a mosaic wreath of snarling beasts, their tails and muzzles seamlessly intertwined. High above the seat floated a Sphere of pulsing light, pale and delicate as a bubble of spun glass. A crowd was gathering; some stared up at the faces of Wolfie, Tala and Zi'ib, floating on the limpid surface of the dome. Others were setting out a ring of glowing crystals. A hooded man had ascended the steps leading to the seat. Raising his arms, he addressed the crowd.

The strange harmony vibrating through the common grew louder. Peering through the legs of the Manus Sacra, the children watched the little plant slip through the folds of the tea towel and rise with the swelling sound. Swaying slowly in the darkness, its stem, stone and leaves glowed silver beneath the purple flowers and in its wake glided the obelisk, steady and upright as if carried by sure-footed bearers. With a soft thrumming the ancient dolmen began to glow and the capstone lifted a little to allow the blade-like central support to pull free from the ground. Inch by inch, unaided by human hand, the sacred stones were drawing together, ready to encase the living flower in the folds of the fossils.

The image in the water flickered. Two figures burst from the shadows of the Lupan Chamber, a man and a woman. Tala tore her eyes from the stones to stare down at the woman and saw an older version of herself. Her mother, Kara, stared back, drinking in the face of the daughter she had not seen for a decade. Wolfie could not take his eyes from the fair-haired man. It was the thin, haggard figure he had drawn in his sketchbook: his father, Arion, emerged from the Wilderness. Zi'ib scanned face after face in the crowd, searching wildly for his own father, but Zane was not among them.

The man on the seat dropped his hood to reveal the proud, hawkish face they had seen in the faki's bowl. Arion and Kara were shouting at him, angry, gesticulating, desperate. Raising a hand, the hooded man roared a command. Wolfie and Tala watched in torment as dark, determined figures closed in on their parents. Arion stepped forward to shield Kara, one frail, emaciated man against a strong, unyielding throng. Powerless, he looked up at the crystal dome, locked eyes with his son and mouthed, "Wolfie!"

A blur of silver glistened behind him: a weapon raised to silence Arion for ever.

"Dad!" cried Wolfie. Instinctively he slammed down his fist to stave off the blow, smashing the surface of the water into a myriad spray of flying droplets. In that moment the dome above the Lupan Chamber shattered, and a million shards of crystal exploded into the night, mirrored by the swirl of glistening splashes falling back into the pond. As if watching through a shaken kaleidoscope, Wolfie, Tala and Zi'ib saw fractured images dancing on the water, reflected through the splinters of crystal skittering across the chamber floor. They saw Arion and Kara leap back as wave after wave of grey, rough-pelted beasts sprang down through the broken dome to attack the Manus Sacra. Eyes burning with molten force, fangs bared, these wolves were not the mythic beasts of legend but the living keepers of the Wisdom of the Stars, returned from the White Mountains of Lupus to wreak vengeance upon those who had betrayed their trust.

An unearthly baying echoed across Thornham Common. Out of the darkness bounded Elvis, his head thrown back, a soul-wrenching howl rising from his throat, flanked on one side by Mrs Poskitt's Monty and on the other by Leonora Grindle's Rottweiler, Mr B. Behind them streamed hounds of every sort and species. Cosseted pugs, lean whippets and glossy Labradors familiar from Sarah's portraits ran shoulder to shoulder with flea-bitten strays and abandoned mongrels escaped from Thornham Dogs' Home. At the back, panting to keep up, ran a tiny Chihuahua with bulbous eyes, and a pink-eyed, arthritic Dalmatian. Lips peeled back in snarls of rage, teeth flashing white and sharp, the hounds of Thornham swarmed across the common, knocking aside the men holding the children, breaking the circle and rounding the exiled Manus Sacra towards the foundations of Thornham Hall.

The ground rumbled, the moon slipped behind the clouds, and a vaporous wave of dark energy poured from the ground, enfolding the time-worn brick and stone in mist as the ancient vault, built by Sir Guy de Monteneuf, wrenched itself open to suck the Manus Sacra down into the nether void beyond the Wilderness Between the Worlds.

The children flung themselves into a terrified heap, covering their faces. Sodden, frightened, exhausted, they huddled together in the shadows. Had the earth really opened its jaws to swallow the Manus Sacra like an angry, hungry beast?

The ghostly howls died away. The moon peered out from the clouds. The dogs were running back, bounding across the grass to form a whirl of flesh and fur around the stones. Slowly they sank on to the mud, their bodies forming a seamless wreath of intertwining tails and muzzles.

The circle was sealed, but not by human forms.

The unearthly music grew urgent, rising to a pitch of unimaginable sweetness as, swathed in wisps of mist, the three hovering stones finally came together as one.

The seed of the little plant nestled into the casing of its own fossil, bending time and space into a perfect circle of birth, life, death and rebirth.

The three sacred stones were reunited.

At the moment of fusion, the secret of the Spheres – the terrifying knowledge of how to turn the tides of fate – poured forth in an explosion of pure, untrammelled energy. To many it was invisible. To some it was a cascade of blazing sparks dancing in the darkness. But scattered across the face of the earth, a handful of people looked skyward and, like Wolfie, Tala and Zi'ib, saw flaming tongues of force leap across the firmament, illuminating a gossamer web of fading leys that stretched beyond time and imagination. And, with a gasp of awe, the favoured few watched the celestial fires flow through those withered channels, suffusing their secret centres, cleansing, restoring, revitalizing the life-giving arteries of the cosmic grid. In a heartbeat the vision was gone, leaving a fretwork of purple scars on the darkness that slowly faded to black.

The secret of the Spheres, once the troubling burden of the wise and worthy guardians, sped onward into oblivion, seeking its rightful place beyond the meddling reach of men.

On the high street a team of emergency engineers completed a temporary repair of the severed cable. Slowly the street lamps around the common flickered back into life. Dogs ran in all directions, scampering back to their firesides, their scavenging or the meagre comforts of the dogs' home.

411

Wolfie, Tala and Zi'ib stumbled to their feet, dizzied by the powerful energies now coursing through the earth and the sudden, jittery flutterings in their stars. By the bus stop, the support-stone of the dolmen had returned to its place beneath the capstone, the little plant lay limp on the ground and the obelisk was back in the trolley. There was nothing left of the Manus Sacra except a ring of muddy footprints and a splinter of white crystal. Wolfie glanced into the pond and saw only his own frightened face. Tala put the crystal in her pocket and picked up the plant, her eyes shiny with grief. They had revived the leys and saved the living worlds from the sinister control of the Manus Sacra, but all they had ever wanted was to bring their parents home.

"At least she's alive," she sobbed.

"He said my name," whispered Wolfie.

Denied even a glimpse of his father, Zi'ib said nothing.

They trundled the trolley back across the common, warily skirting the foundations of Thornham Hall. There was nothing to see. The grass and brickwork had already settled back into place, re-sealing the secret vault built by Sir Guy de Monteneuf nearly a thousand years before.

"Agnes . . . the faki . . . they warned us about people we trusted," Tala said bitterly, "but I never suspected *him*."

Zi'ib stared at the ground, wishing the hate-filled leader of the exiled Manus Sacra had been an imposter and that the real Godfrey Peasemarsh was even now performing some errand of mercy in the parish.

Tala stopped, struck by a hideous thought. "Ridian Winter – he's still in Alaska."

"What harm can he do us now?" said Wolfie wearily.

All around them the bewildered inhabitants of Thornham were stumbling over the grass, some clutching babies, others gabbling into their mobiles. Beneath the wail of police cars and fire engines there were shouts about freak lightning, terrorist bombs, black magic rites and exploding lorries. Police walkie-talkies crackled. A group of inmates from the old people's home huddled beneath the trees, reminiscing about the Blitz. No one paid any attention to a trio of kids with a stolen supermarket trolley. Microphone in hand, a harassed reporter from the *Thornham Gazette* grabbed Wolfie's arm.

"You see anything?"

Wolfie fixed him with a dazed stare. What if he told him the truth? What if he climbed on the trolley and shouted out the whole weird, wild, agonizing story? Who would believe him? He had trouble enough believing it himself. He shook his head. The reporter rushed on.

At the back gate, Elvis came trotting towards them. Wolfie touched his muzzle.

"Who are you, Elvis?" he whispered.

Elvis licked his hand and looked up at him with clear amber eyes.

They wheeled the trolley into the outhouse, covered the obelisk with their mud-caked coats and rinsed their hands and faces in the chipped sink.

Sarah called from the back door. "Did you see what happened? I caught a flash of something, but by the time I'd rushed outside it was all over."

"We were mending our bikes," Wolfie said. "It was probably a bit of lightning."

As they followed her into the kitchen, a sprightly step sounded on the stairs and Mr Forester appeared carrying a large, glossy book.

"Marvellous! I was lucky enough to be looking through my telescope when it happened. I've read a lot about anomalous lights appearing over ley crossings but I'd never witnessed any before. What's more, the energy they released seems to have done wonders for my arthritis." Flexing his leg, he eagerly pulled up a chair. "All in all it's been a very satisfying day. You know I've been corresponding with Dornford Blaker?"

Silence from the children.

"You remember, the Oxford archaeologist working on that fragment of Strabo's *Histories*? He's letting me quote the verse about the Wilderness in my work, and this morning he sent me a copy of his latest book – a pictorial history of the excavations of Upper and Lower Egypt. It's got some wonderful photographs of a dig at Meroe from the early 1900s." He slid the book, open at a sepia spread of the ruins at Naqa, across the table.

The image of the ancient city lay before them untouched. Only when it began to sing out a silent song, drawing their eyes to its detail, did they see with bitter wonder that the photograph had been taken when the inscription telling the story of the stones was still intact. There, too late, lay the longed-for lost passage. They felt no elation as they pulled the book closer and held Mr Forester's magnifying glass over the words of the guardians.

"But let the worlds be warned. If those of mingled blood should walk the path in darkness, the secret unshackled when the stones unite will brook no check or hindrance by our righteous will. For we the guardians are but mortal men, and all our arts and wisdom here conjoined have sought to bind and tame immortal power."

There it was: the fatal flaw. If the children of mingled blood fulfilled the seemingly impossible task of finding the stones without knowing what they were looking for or why they were looking for it, there was nothing to stop the Manus Sacra from snatching the secret of the Spheres.

It was as if someone had shone a bright light on the dark confusion of the past few weeks. That was why the Manus Sacra had wanted their Lupan parents out of the way. But all the while Godfrey Peasemarsh and Ridian Winter must have been eaten up with frustration at having to stand passively by and watch three "misbegotten brats" stumble blindly from clue to clue.

Tala let the wilting stem of purple flowers fall from her fingers. Sarah lifted it tenderly.

"Where did you find this?"

Tala barely summoned the strength to say, "Outside."

Sarah dropped the plant in her glass of water. "Don't tell anyone. It's the secret herb I use in the fudge. When I was young it used to grow out of all the chinks in the stonework of this house. I only managed to find a couple of bits of it, but I've been cultivating the cuttings in the airing cupboard."

Mr Forester examined the little plant with interest. "I like to think I'm quite an expert on flora, but I've never come across this before. I think it may be an extremely rare species, perhaps as yet unnamed." He sniffed the smoky fragrance. "I think we should call it . . . 'Saravita'. A combination of you, my dear, and the very essence of life itself."

"Saravita," repeated Sarah. "I like it."

Elvis's ears swivelled to catch a faint banging. He barked loudly.

Sarah sighed. "There's someone at the shop door. Honestly, can't they see we're closed?"

"I'll go," offered Mr Forester. Hurrying after the dog, who had bounded into the shop and was whimpering at the dim figures standing outside the door, he mouthed, "Sorry, we're closed. Try the garage shop."

"We're not here to make a purchase!" cried a deep, plummy voice.

Peering through the glass, Mr Forester recognized the distinctive chiselled profile of Ffarley Snodgrass.

"My goodness, hang on." He struggled to loosen the bolt.

Snodgrass, Beamish and Hussey must have realized the explosive nature of his manuscript and sent Ffarley round in person with the book contract. He threw open the door. To his surprise, the publisher had his arm around a dark, long-haired man in a crumpled suit whose bloodshot eyes stared from a harrowed face swathed in a tangled, grey-streaked beard. The man gripped the door jamb, breathing in sharp, pain-wracked gasps. If this was Mr Beamish or Mr Hussey come to help finalize the deal, he appeared to have risen from his deathbed to do so.

"Do come through. . ."

"Thank you," said Ffarley, heaving his companion up the step. Elvis turned and wedged his firm, high back beneath the man's other hand.

"This way." Mr Forester led them into the kitchen. "Sarah, this is—"

"Ffarley Snodgrass!" exclaimed Wolfie.

Zi'ib shrank back. Ffarley's companion was staggering towards him, his arms flailing, his mouth opening and shutting in an agony of emotion.

Sarah planted herself protectively in front of Zi'ib. "Who are you? What do you want?"

"I am . . . Zane Bakri," rasped the man, and collapsed on to the sofa.

There was shocked silence until Sarah snapped into action. "Quick, Wolfie, fetch the cooking brandy; Tala, bring a blanket; Mr Forester, put the kettle on."

"Zi'ib," moaned Zane. Zi'ib stumbled forward and took his father's hand, afraid his touch might cause this apparition to disappear. He saw the outline of the broken star through Zane's threadbare shirt and stiffened. Wolfie saw it too and could hardly drag his eyes away as he poured a glass of brandy.

"I think I'll have one of those as well," said Ffarley, sinking on to a chair.

"Me too," said Mr Forester.

"Could somebody please tell me what's going on?" Sarah demanded, tilting the glass into Zane's mouth. He spluttered and turned away.

"I hardly know myself," said Ffarley. "The police called a couple of hours ago saying the guards at the British Museum had found a very sick man wandering in the basement, carrying some ID in the name of Zane Bakri and my business card. Of course, I rushed straight there. He refused to see a doctor and just kept repeating Zi'ib's name, so I drove him to the vicarage. It was empty, but we met a Mrs Poskitt in the churchyard, searching for her dog, and she told us Zi'ib spent most evenings here with Wolfie."

Zane's breath rattled in his throat.

"Shall I call an ambulance?" asked Sarah.

"No. I'll be all right," he wheezed.

His eyelids fluttered open and he gazed, spellbound, at his son, raising his arms to reach out across the weary years of separation. Zi'ib bent awkwardly against his father's body, wary of this unfamiliar masculine affection.

Slowly the strangeness ebbed away and he stopped being an outsider, alone and afraid, and gave himself up to the deep, precious pleasure of being a child who had come home. Wolfie and Tala gazed at the reunion, wracked by longing.

Zane lifted his head. "Wolfie . . . Tala. . ."

A shadow darkened Sarah's face as Wolfie and Tala approached the haggard, green-eyed stranger from a faraway world, whose frail life force was pulsing through their broken stars.

"Milk and sand and night," rasped Zane.

"Delirious," said Ffarley.

Sarah made tea, her tears splashing into the pot.

Zane pulled his son closer. "Where is your mother?"

"Our village got attacked. She was abducted."

Zane closed his eyes. "I swear to you I'll find her."

"Where were you, *Baba*?" Zi'ib whispered.

"Trapped . . . in the Wilderness. Where is Arion?"

"On Lupus."

"I don't understand. The leys have been rekindled, I can feel it. Who has been guiding you on the path?"

"No one," said Zi'ib, with a sudden swell of pride. "We walked the path in darkness."

On the top floor of the New Sion Hospital in Trinity County, a thin hand lifted slowly from the bed sheet and a puckered, crescent-shaped scar caught the dim gleam of the monitors. Puzzled, Dr Walker rechecked the feeds.

Something was firing Jack Bean's spirit, re-energizing his wasted will, slowly easing his body back from the dark, debilitating effects of the Wilderness.

Back in her office, she emailed an update on his sudden improvement to Ridian Winter, her sponsor at Zemogen International, who had taken such a close interest in the baffling case of Jack Bean.

50

The Link of Light

Unable to get hold of the vicar, Sarah made up a bed of cushions for Zi'ib in the attic and shooed everyone out of the kitchen so Zane could sleep in peace. As soon as the house was quiet, the children tiptoed back to stare in wonder at the gaunt figure slumped in the firelight with Elvis at his side. As if guided by unseen hands, Zi'ib slipped off his broken star and laid it beside the half-star nestling at his father's throat. With a fresh stab of longing, Wolfie and Tala saw the star made whole and felt its healing power-flow quickening Zane's life force.

After a moment his eyes blinked open, fierce and alert in his derelict face.

"Tell me everything," he said.

Wolfie stoked up the fire and they took turns in the

telling, struggling to make sense of the many twists and *kinnections* that had led them to the stones. By the time they had finished, the fire had burned low and their voices were scratchy with tiredness.

"All this heartache and horror so you would walk the path in darkness," said Zane quietly. "And Shadia and Jack tossed aside like old rags so the Manus Sacra could monitor your every move." He rubbed a wasted hand across his face. "Your story confirms what we suspected all along: their cleverest scholars were still on Lupus, tampering with the gateways and the Link of Light, casting people in and out of the Wilderness and attempting to manipulate what was left of the energies in the earthly leys. I'd give anything to know who it was you saw in the Chamber."

"Their leader – I did a sketch of him ages ago," said Wolfie. Fetching his pad, he showed Zane the picture. Saddened, Zane looked away.

"Who is he?" asked Wolfie.

"Therion, the Keeper of Wisdom," said Zane. "The most revered elder on Lupus. He'd been monitoring the erosion of the leys for a thousand years."

"What?" Zi'ib started back, incredulous.

Zane held his son's bewildered gaze. "Time ceases to touch those who travel deep into the hidden realms of wisdom. In fact, I suspect that this Abbot Godfrei, who tried to get Agnes to confess her secrets, was the same man you knew as the Reverend Godfrey Peasemarsh."

"So are you, Mom and Arion . . . really old as well?" asked Tala.

"Perhaps a little older than you imagine, but only scholars like Therion and Peasemarsh, who devote their whole lives to the pursuit of wisdom, survive for centuries."

Frightened and enthralled, they huddled closer on the rug, grateful for the comforting rise and fall of Elvis's ribs against their backs as they listened to the threads of their lives being rewoven into a new and alien fabric.

"For years our scholars had been pumping energy back into the cosmic grid, trying to compensate for the damage being done by the regressing worlds, but it was a losing battle. The situation became critical. Despite the risks inherent in freeing the secret of the Spheres, there was no other way to save the leys, so Therion sent us to find the stones. But as you discovered, the wisdom of the earthly guardians who helped to hide it had been lost long ago. All we had to go on was a list of their homelands and the remnants of *The Book of Light*, snatched from the burning ruins of the ancient library of Alexandria. The trouble was, no one could decipher it."

"How come *we* can?" cut in Tala.

"Because it's written literally in 'words of wisdom' devised by the guardians. Only minds that combine the Wisdom of the Stars, Rivers, Mountains and Forests could decode it. The book was reputed to tell the story of their four civilizations, to set the righteous seekers on the path.

"Although the leys were dangerously depleted, I

managed to get to Meroe, Arion came to Thornham, and Kara and Matt entered through the gateway at Shasta. From there Matt went on to Alaska, looking for a rare form of crystal that could channel and control the vast flood of energy we hoped to release.

"We adapted our names from Arion, Zannor and Amathon to Ron, Zane and Matthias and took local surnames."

"What's Mom's real name, then?" demanded Tala.

"Akara, but she hates it. She's always been known as Kara."

Tala turned this morsel in her mind as he went on. "For months we got nowhere, and then I discovered the inscriptions at Naqa. It seemed that if all the old earth wisdoms were lost, all we had to do was produce children with the descendants of the guardians. But how could we identify such people?

"It was Kara who realized the key phrase was 'children born of love'. Love would draw *us* to the true descendants, just as love would prevent the *Manus Sacra* from producing offspring of mingled blood purely to find the stones."

"How come?" frowned Zi'ib.

"Well, even if they did tarnish their 'noble' blood by mingling it, any offspring they had with one of the 'unworthy' would certainly not have been born of love.

"But we told nobody about our mission, not even our partners, because Therion had sworn us to secrecy. He said the truth would cause mayhem on a planet as degenerate as this, and we'd probably all be incarcerated before we could find the stones. But after our Link of Light went dead and Matthias was killed in a suspicious mining accident, we realized that the real threat came from the twisted brilliance of the Manus Sacra. We needed help, and we needed to warn the Lupan Council that some of the Manus Sacra were still on Lupus, helping and directing the exiles. So Kara went back."

"Why her?" demanded Tala.

"As the strongest in spirit, she would put the least strain on the depleted leys. Unfortunately, she would have gone straight to Therion. He must have instructed his people to shut the gateways."

"When we realized what must have happened, Arion and I decided to break our silence and publish my book. We hoped that righteous seekers of lost wisdom would read the story of the stones and come forward to help us. Some enlightened ley hunter might even know a way to reopen the gateways or repair the Link of Light.

"So I came to London to see Ffarley Snodgrass. As I left his office, a passer-by greeted me by name, claiming he was from the British Museum and he'd met me on a study trip to Meroe. I didn't recognize him, but I agreed to have a look at some artefacts they were having trouble identifying. He took me down to the museum basement and showed me eight columns of stone set in a circle, inscribed with strange markings. Intrigued, I stepped into the circle to examine them. It was a trap. The Manus Sacra had managed not only to create an artificial opening into the Wilderness but also to destroy my inner compass. I was sucked into that vast nothingness with nothing to guide me through the void." Zane closed his eyes. "To be lost in the Wilderness is a living death. I travelled for days, months, years and arrived nowhere. And then – it must have been when the power of the Manus Sacra was destroyed, a rip appeared in the darkness. I found myself back in the British Museum and the leys brought me here."

"I still don't get how they work," said Zi'ib.

"Countless scholars have spent lifetimes studying their mysteries. Yet no one has ever reached a true understanding of how the life force they channel interacts with the other forces of nature or even with the conscious mind. All I can tell you is that the energies flowing through the cosmic grid derive from perfect wisdom. They create a fathomless self-regulating harmony that we must nurture and replenish by seeking to understand."

Wolfie, Tala and Zi'ib exchanged looks of utter bewilderment.

Zane smiled slowly. "And it seems we have much to thank your Mr Forester for. It is people like him, with their dogged determination to seek out and retread the forgotten ley paths and infuse them with the power of their conscious minds that have kept the earthly leys from withering to nothing."

"So can we tell him the truth now?" asked Wolfie, imagining the old man's wonder.

"No. He must continue his own journey to understanding. The leys clearly utilized his thirst for knowledge in order to help *you*, just as they once used Costantino's curiosity to help Agnes. They may have need of him again."

"What about Elvis?" demanded Tala. "How does he fit into all this?"

Zane touched the great dog's head. "While the life force in the leys flows through everything in the living worlds, its purest form can take many shapes: animal, vegetable, aetheric and mineral. But these manifestations are no less 'real' than the flawed versions we encounter every day."

Wolfie opened his mouth but found no words to express the numberless questions smouldering in his mind.

Zane had not told them how worried he was that Ridian Winter was still at large or shared his fear that the leys had not finished with them yet. Instead, pulling the blanket around his shoulders, he stood up shakily and asked to see the obelisk. They helped him across the frosty yard to the outhouse, and as they lifted the column of granite on to the bench, he gave an involuntary shudder.

"What's wrong?" said Zi'ib.

Zane ran a ragged nail down the edge of the stone, catching the hairline notches scored across the granite. "This was designed to hold a message," he said quietly. "A message marked on a strip of leather or cloth that only gives up its meaning when wound around *this* obelisk following the angle of *these* lines."

He looked at each child in turn, and weak though he was, his eyes seemed to pierce their innermost being. "Have you come across such a thing? Think. Think hard."

Wolfie and Tala slowly shook their heads, but with a little cry, Zi'ib stuffed his hand into the pocket of his parka and fished out the strip of ancient linen that had been wrapped around Agnes's painting. Wordlessly Wolfie and Tala helped him to wind the fragile fabric around the obelisk. Inch by inch the meaningless scatter of markings reformed to shape a message. A message in the language of *The Book of Light*.

"Wolfie, read it out," commanded Zane. And Wolfie did.

> *When wasted lie the pathways of the wise,*
> *Two bloods will bond to fight a common foe,*
> *As righteous heart with evil intrigue vies,*
> *A greater deed from this dark quest will flow.*
>
> *Accursèd hands, which from the shadows creep,*
> *To thwart the noble aims of beast and man,*
> *Shall find a purpose ancient, proud and deep,*
> *Has lain within the leys since time began.*
>
> *For evil is reborn in every age,*
> *And fits the times by shifting shape and guise,*

Forever tempting shaman, seer and sage,
To use for ill the power of the wise.

And so the force of light must weave and twine
The sacred threads that bind the worlds of men,
And set new champions 'gainst that dark design,
Until the scales are balanced once again.

His voice slowed as he read the last stanza.

Three born to wage that battle, side by side,
Bearing broken stars of hammered gold,
Must face the dark with sorrow as their guide,
Their blood's own truth, but to itself untold.

"It's about us, isn't it?" he said, glaring angrily at Zane. "After all this, we're s'posed to do other stuff as well."

Zane's voice faltered. "I told you the power of the leys was fathomless. It would seem that everything, from the hiding of the stones to our hasty mission to find them, was all part of a greater purpose to bring you into this world at this time." He turned his eyes from their frightened faces. "It is a great honour to have been born with the power to fight the dark."

"Forget it," choked Tala. "I'm not fighting anything, ever again." She stood there stubborn and defiant.

"Yeah, we found the stones *and* defeated the Manus Sacra. What more do they want?" said Wolfie bitterly.

429

Zane looked at his son.

"I just want Mum back," said Zi'ib.

Profound sadness clouded Zane's eyes. How could he tell them that wherever they went, whatever they did, they would never escape their destiny? He shuffled unsteadily back to the kitchen. When he spoke again, his voice was firm.

"Lay your stars on the table. Zi'ib, switch off the lights. Now that the hold of the Manus Sacra has been weakened, we may at least be able to restore our Link of Light."

Wolfie and Tala felt their anger dissolve and excitement rush in to take its place: how did this strange communication work? Would they hear their parents' voices – or just their thoughts? Would their parents hear them? They watched eagerly as Zane added his own broken star to the heap on the table.

"Erase everything from your minds and concentrate on making the connection," he said. "Call to them as if you were standing on a distant shore separated by howling winds and a storm-tossed sea."

They called silently to Arion and Kara through the aether, dizzied by the passionate roar of hope in their hearts and the blood in their ears. Their stars glinted and flashed, flinging gossamer strands into a rope of light that rose through the air. They held their breath. The light slowly melted away.

"Place your hands on mine," ordered Zane, splaying his fingers over the stars.

They obeyed. The glistening threads rose a little higher, then fizzled and faded.

"We need to boost it," said Zane.

Wolfie glanced wildly around the kitchen. He saw his grandpa's radio on the dresser, and a picture of Arion sitting in the attic turning the dial flitted through his mind. Suddenly, he knew exactly what his father had been doing.

"Hang on!" He grabbed the radio and slipped the two halves of Zane's star inside it. Zane extended the aerial and propped the other broken stars against the dial. They clamped their hands around the speaker and felt the forces grow stronger, crackling and buzzing through the air. Zane closed his eyes. "I can sense them; they're trying from their end. We need just one more spark of power to make the connection."

The kitchen door swung open and Sarah appeared in her dressing gown. She yawned. "I took a sleeping pill but I still can't drop off. Anyone fancy a cup of tea?"

"Come here, Sarah," said Zane. "Lay your hands on the stars."

She slid her fingers on to the metal. A spark of wisdom forged by her Druid ancestors pulsed from deep within her and a trail of radiance burst from the radio, cutting through the air to clutch at a glowing filament that trickled down from the darkness. The two beams hovered in the gloom, separated only by a narrow strip of emptiness. Tensing every nerve and muscle, six bearers of the broken stars on two different worlds willed the straining threads to touch. Elvis laid his paw softly on Wolfie's knee. With a jolt, the beams fused together. The hazy outline of Arion and Kara wavered beside the fireplace, their stars gripped in their hands.

A lifetime of longing caught in Wolfie's throat. "Dad. . ." He could barely whisper the word. "Dad. . ."

Tala just stared, struck dumb by the proximity of her mother. The images flickered in the firelight as Arion and Kara cried out across the aether.

"There's no time . . . the Sphere is floating through the shattered dome. . . Without it we can't sustain the Link of Light or repair the gateways . . . never forget us . . . never forget. . ."

Their voices faded, the images dimmed to nothing. Tala sank her head on the table, a tide of despair washing through her star.

". . . that we love you. . ." Their words stilled to a whisper as Arion and Kara watched the glimmering Sphere spiral into the night.

Wolfie choked back harsh, angry sobs and snatched up his broken star, feeling it throb with a pain beyond his own anguish – the pain of generations of lives torn apart by the secret in the stones. Sarah stroked his hair in the way she used to when he was small and frightened. "You are your father's son," she murmured.

He felt the pain ebb a little, quelled by a dizzying

strength: the blood of a born explorer roaring through his veins. He pushed her hand away.

"I'll bring them back," he said. "Whatever it takes, I swear I'll bring them back."

Sarah blinked and stretched. "Sorry," she murmured, "I must have dropped off. I've just had the weirdest dream."

Wolfie closed his eyes. He saw once more the blurred vision of Arion hovering in the firelight and realized how far he had reached out across time and space to unearth the truth about his father. That truth had proved to be more heroic than anything he had ever dared to dream or draw. And yet it was a part of him, a strange, shocking and barely explored part that would link him for ever to the bearers of the broken stars, and the vast unfathomed mysteries that lay within the leys.

ACKNOWLEDGEMENTS

A huge thank you to Sarah Curtis and Joe Softley for reading an early draft and encouraging me to go on, Anwar who took me to see a Faki when I was young and many years later took me to Meroe, Faried Osman and Sowsan for help with the Sudanese Arabic, Alice Swan, Jessica White, Andrew Biscomb and the team at Scholastic, Chris Tennant and Selina Macnair for testing out the maths and Lynne Wilson, Vanessa Armitage, Bev Hathaway, Jo Mills and Louise Woodall for their kindness to me and my family while I was writing this book. My first agent Janice Swanson, who I hope is enjoying her retirement and my new agent Stephanie Thwaites, my publisher Marion Lloyd for having faith and for her unfailing enthusiasm, my children Charlotte, Murdo and Lily for sharing their lives with Wolfie, Tala and Zi'ib for so long and my husband James for everything.

No matter where you live archaeology is all around you and if you want to get involved in digs and events in your area go to the Young Archaeologists' Club website www.britarch.ac.uk. If you want to find out more about megaliths, the megalithic portal www.megalithic.co.uk is a wonderful treasure house of information and photographs. For theories about megaliths, ley lines and earth energies have a look at the books of John Michell – particularly *Megalithomania* and *The New View Over Atlantis*, *Quicksilver Heritage* by Paul Screeton, *The Sun and the Serpent* by Hamish Miller and Paul Broadhurst. And of course *The Old Straight Track* by Alfred Watkins, the groundbreaking book about ancient trackways that has inspired generations of ley hunters.

I would love to hear from you so if you want to share your thoughts about *Quicksilver*, tell me about an ancient site near you or find out about Book Two, my website is www.samosmanbooks.com.